TALISMAN

TAM DERUDDER JACKSON

Editor: Nikki Busch Editing
Copy Editor: Rhiannon Root
Cover Design: Steamy Designs
Formatting: Damonza.com

For Grady
I love you.

and

*For Dr. Michael Sexson, Professor Emeritus of English,
Montana State University. A long time ago, you believed
in me when I didn't believe in myself. Thank you.*

PROLOGUE

Scotland, Tenth Century

BLOOD DRIPPED FROM Findlay Sheridan's sword, drops of gore trailing him as he stumbled across the battlefield, too weary for elation at the outcome of the day. Once again, his warriors had taken on the Morrigan's minions and won, but at great cost. The earth and sky converged in one horizonless hue of red—grass, shields, swords, bodies, sky, sun—all red. Blood red. Ailsa foresaw the victory. And the blood. She'd told him as much. He knew she worried for him while he worried for his sons and his friends.

He remembered seeing his eldest, Graeme, struggling with the Morrigan's champion while she kept Findlay occupied with two lesser warriors. Findlay fought them remorselessly until they succumbed to his superior strength and skill. Still, more came, always more. Through the din of battle, he could hear the banshees screaming, shrieking the names of the dead.

Urgently, he traversed the field, trying to remember where he'd seen the Morrigan setting her champion on Graeme. The wounded and dying called to him, but in his singular mission, he blocked them out, desperate to know about his sons. He'd lost sight of Riordan and Owen, the twins, early in the battle, but he counted on them to take care of each other as they always did. All should be waiting at the rendezvous point at the standing stone near the loch. The burning need to reach his sons goaded him as his legs ate up ground on his way to meet up with his family.

His journey to the meeting place took a roundabout route through the fallen and the dying. Halfway across the field, the mists rose around him, and he struggled to find his way. All at once, a form materialized from among the dead, the Morrigan's champion. The distant wails of the banshees told him the dying wasn't over.

Automatically, Findlay put away thoughts of his family as he readied himself for one last battle. The Morrigan's champion stood at least a head taller than Findlay's six feet, his torso streaming blood. In the recesses of his mind, Findlay thought Graeme had damaged this warrior. Then there was no time for thinking—only acting and reacting as the combatants danced their deadly dance.

The eeriness of their lone battle echoed in the single clanging of one sword on the other, one sword bashing one shield, one man grunting and screaming as he lunged again and again at the injured warrior, knocking him back toward the stream feeding the loch. At last, Findlay saw an opening and plunged his sword to the hilt in the Viking's chest. The man blinked, stunned, before tumbling backward in an ungainly heap of weaponry, flesh, and blood.

Without ceremony, Findlay put one foot on the warrior's chest and retrieved his sword, which is when he saw the other wound in the man's chest, equally deep, equally fatal. How did the man rise up? How did he fight again? Recognizing magic at work, Findlay spun around searching for the goddess, knowing she taunted him, baited him. The Morrigan, the Washer at the Ford, stood beside the little stream running thick with the day's blood. By her side stood a beautiful woman, her black hair cascading in waves down her straight back. Findlay's heart dropped into his stomach as he recognized the woman, his own dear Ailsa. Why did she stand with the Morrigan? Why did she stand in blood?

He blinked and shook his head, trying to clear his vision. Still, he saw the same picture. The Morrigan turned slowly toward him, her red eyes glowing evilly.

"So, Findlay Sheridan, you thought you won today, and indeed the field is littered with my warriors." She flicked her hand nonchalantly. "They were expendable, merely a distraction for the real prize I coveted." Her evil expression nearly stopped his heart. "Ailsa. Without her, you can no longer win. You can no longer fight. Your failure to pay homage to my sister Maeve has brought you to this point. Think on that during the long nights to come in your lonely bed in your great hall." The venom in her smile turned the blood in his veins to ice as he watched her lead Ailsa across the stream.

"Noooo!" Findlay screamed. "Ye cannae take her! She isnae a warrior. Ye're only allowed tae take warriors across yer river of blood. Ye defy the Dagda! Ye defy Danu!" Findlay lunged toward the stream, yet he could not cross it. An invisible barrier, a wall he could not see, prevented his progress.

"The gods make alliances with whom we will for our own purposes. The times are changing. The rules are changing. Man must adjust." The Morrigan stepped across the river, leading Ailsa who looked back one last time, her eyes filled with sorrow, before she disappeared into the mists. Findlay fell to his knees, his glorious golden hair turning snow white in an instant as his life force died within him.

For a man to be a warrior, he needed three things: his name, his weapon, and his talisman. A man could fight for a while with only his name and his weapon, but he would taste defeat early. If he wished to be mighty, if he wished to be victorious in battle, a warrior must have his talisman, the one woman the fates chose to complete him, or he was nothing but an ordinary man with ordinary skill—a foot soldier easily bested in combat. Without Ailsa, Findlay was nothing. The Morrigan had won. He sat on the bank of the stream and wept.

&

When Findlay's sons found him at last, relief and shock shone on their faces. In the morning when they'd all set out to battle, Findlay was a man in his prime—tall, straight, massive, his hair flowing in golden waves over his broad shoulders—a warrior leader his men revered and followed without question. Now an old gray-haired man sat on the banks of the stream, defeated. His battle gear marked him as Findlay Sheridan; otherwise, his sons would not have recognized their own father, so changed was he.

In a reedy voice, Findlay gave his sons the news. "The Morrigan has taken yer mother. She made sure I made it tae the ford in time tae watch but tae late tae stop her. 'Twas her plan all along, tae start a battle tae distract us from her real purpose—taking yer mother, my talisman, my wife." He stared blindly into the distance, all his tears spent. "My one true love."

"But Father, the Morrigan cannae take a talisman. She can only take warriors in the heat o' battle. Mother was never a warrior," Graeme protested.

"The rules have changed. The gods have formed new alliances among themselves. Not only can she take an unprotected talisman during battle, but she can also limit the time fer a warrior tae find his talisman. From now on, a warrior cannae begin the search fer his talisman until he reaches his twenty-first year, and he must find her by midnight o' his twenty-eighth year or he becomes subject tae the Morrigan. He can join her as one o' her champions fighting against his fellow warriors, or he can become a fugitive whose only allies are fugitive warriors like himself."

"How soon until this second condition begins?" asked Riordan.

"It has already begun. Graeme, ye have three days tae find yer talisman or submit tae the Morrigan or become a fugitive yer brothers and I cannae aid," Findlay said. The tears resumed. No longer had he the strength to control or hide his fears. Graeme paid the price. Within a month of the battle, he crossed the ford with the Morrigan while his brothers watched helplessly. At least he died fighting her and her minions rather than turning against his family. The supreme war goddess's bloodlust and her sexually voracious sister Maeve's unrequited desire for Findlay Sheridan led to a blood feud with the most powerful warrior family in Scotland. The war would last for centuries.

CHAPTER ONE

Montana, Twenty-First Century

HE DREAMS KEPT coming, more frequent, more urgent. What started as one or two a month after Gram Afton died at the summer solstice had escalated to one or two a week. Alyssa Macaulay's sleep loss meant she couldn't concentrate on her thesis writing. Even more disturbing, she heard strange noises around her house when she awoke from those dreams. Shadow was edgy as well, insisting on sleeping on the floor at the foot of her bed rather than in his usual spot on a rug in the laundry room.

At first, she thought the dreams came from her research, but the battles were modern, the warriors dressed in jeans, leather jackets, and boots rather than chain mail, wool, and leather leggings. The battles, however, were as bloody as any medieval combat she'd read about. She could hear men screaming and feel the disturbance in the air as they wielded their mighty swords. None of it made sense, yet all of it was vivid and so, so real. As were the tracks of someone's boots in the thin layer of snow outside her cabin this morning, a circumstance that sent her online investigating local security firms.

When she arrived at the offices of Security Consultants Unlimited, the understated sign beside the door on the second floor of one of the converted hotels in town reassured her. Inside, she observed modern chrome-and-leather furniture in the reception area, which exuded an atmosphere of competence and efficiency. The muted colors of a watercolor landscape of a mountain meadow at sunset softened the starkness of the décor. The receptionist, a woman with graying hair cut in a close spike and wearing a chic charcoal suit over a magenta silk blouse, addressed her. "How may we help you, miss?"

The woman's desk plate bore the name Isla, a Celtic name, which gave Alyssa an odd sense of comfort. "I need to speak to someone about a home security system, please."

"Of course. One moment." The woman pressed a button on her phone alerting someone in one of the two offices adjoining the reception area.

During the few minutes Alyssa waited, the receptionist remained busy at the two computers on her desk. Alyssa hoped the business would have time to help her as soon as she needed it.

"Mr. Sheridan will see you now, miss," Isla said, her tone business-like, her expression kindly.

According to the internet and the front door of the office, Rowan Sheridan was the branch manager for Security Consultants Unlimited. She'd formed an idea he'd be a fatherly type who would assure her that his company could be of service in the very near future—like today. When she opened the door to his office, she stared at the man sitting behind the huge oak desk on which sat three computer monitors and some files. She consulted the name on the door again to be sure she'd entered the right room.

This man was no father figure who would gently assuage her fears. Dressed in a brick-red Henley, he looked more like an outfitter for a hunting camp than a security professional. The man was all shoulders and chest. As he arose gracefully from his chair, she saw he stood at least a foot taller than her own five feet two. His size overwhelmed her when he came around the desk to greet her. At least that's what she told herself to account for the butterflies taking flight in her belly.

"Hello, I'm Rowan Sheridan." His large hand swallowed her much smaller one in a firm handshake. When he touched her, a tingling ran up her arm and lasted for several seconds after he let her go. He looked at her with a curious expression, and she realized she hadn't introduced herself.

"My name is Alyssa Macaulay. I-I'm interested in a home security system."

The man's intense aquamarine eyes bored into her, and she wondered what he tried to see.

"Do you have certain items or rooms you'd like secured, or do you need a system for your entire residence?" He leaned casually against his desk and crossed his big arms over his massive chest.

His baritone voice called to her on a visceral level, and she had to drag her attention from the sound into the conversation. Giving herself a mental shake, she responded, "My residence. I'm not looking to protect treasures." She shrugged. "I don't have any. But I live alone in a somewhat remote area, and lately I've been hearing weird noises around my house at night."

With a flick of his hand, he indicated the leather chair behind her. "Please. Have a seat."

She sat.

"Do you want motion sensors outside and inside your home? Or what were you thinking?"

He didn't seem to notice her nerves, or maybe he was being polite to make a sale.

"I hadn't thought that far. Perhaps I need someone to come out to my house and determine the best course of action. Would any of your employees be free in the next day or two?" Alyssa was hoping that as the manager, Rowan Sheridan only consulted and sent out the other employees on installations. The office looked small, but he was obviously monitoring systems, so that must mean someone else did the legwork, which would suit her just fine. So unexpectedly handsome and intense a man made her nervous.

His buzzing phone interrupted them, and he excused himself to take the call. Following a few noncommittal comments, he ended the conversation.

"I'm sorry, Miss Macaulay. I have a service call, but my secretary will be able to schedule an appointment for you."

"Oh, I thought as the manager, you worked from your office." Alyssa wanted to take it back as soon as she said it, especially in the accusatory tone in which it slipped out.

"Actually, I spend as much time in the field as I do in the office. I'll be taking your case personally." He gave her a pointed look. "Isla will figure out a time that works for both of us. Nice to meet you." He stepped around his desk again and took her hand. This time he held it a fraction of a second too long, and the tingling was even more intense than the first time. Alyssa couldn't figure out what happened between them as he ushered her back into the reception area.

He closed the door to his office, and Isla looked up at Alyssa expectantly.

"Apparently, Mr. Sheridan is being called away. To be honest, I'd hoped someone could look at my home soon, like maybe today."

"I'm afraid Mr. Sheridan is booked until the end of the week, but I can put you on his calendar for Monday morning. Will that work?"

She checked her calendar and realized Monday morning would be the soonest she was available too although she gladly would have rearranged her schedule if she could have had someone out earlier. She took the date, but as she left the office, she wondered if Monday was too long to wait.

⁓

Alyssa snapped awake, her heart pounding a wild rhythm in her chest. It took several seconds to ascertain she'd fallen asleep on top of her research notes. Sitting up at her desk in the cubbyhole masquerading as her office in the university graduate school, she sucked in several deep breaths to calm herself down. The dreams were coming during the *day*? And the warrior she'd been dreaming of now had a face. He looked exactly like Rowan Sheridan. What was up with that?

The vividness of her dream unnerved her like nothing in her previous experience. In perfect detail, she recalled the events she'd dreamed. Like sitting in the front row of a movie theater, she'd watched as the Rowan Sheridan look-alike took on an even larger man than he in hand-to-hand combat using the claymores of ancient warriors. Rowan wore a heavy leather jacket over his red shirt as a kind of armor against the blows of the combatants battling him.

The size and fierceness of the warrior he faced didn't faze him, but to Alyssa's horror, the other man didn't fight fair. Three of his buddies took turns aiming slicing blows at Rowan's back, cutting his jacket to ribbons.

He fought on, apparently oblivious to the blows he sustained, focused on his singular mission to best his opponent. At last the huge man made a fatal mistake when he reacted to Rowan's feint, and Rowan ran his sword through the man's chest. The big man blinked several times in surprise before his eyes rolled back, and he slumped to the pavement.

The Rowan look-alike rested on his sword, his breath coming in rapid pants before his eyelids fluttered closed, and he slid, boneless, to the ground. Out of nowhere, another warrior who looked a lot like Rowan raced to his side and shouted at him. As she watched the two men together, she thought Rowan should be taken to a hospital immediately, but he didn't want that. At the very least he should be taken to his own bed, she'd decided.

That's when she'd awakened. The ability to recall so many details of her dream afterwards rattled her almost as much as the dream itself. If she didn't know better, she would have thought it wasn't a dream. Obviously, she needed to go home, regroup, maybe leave behind her studies for the evening. Perhaps these Celtic warriors would let her be if she put them aside for a little while.

⸙

"I left you a note to let me be. What are you doing in my room shouting about calling a healer?" Rowan growled.

"Your bloody clothes on the bathroom floor made me think you had a bit of trouble this time, so I thought I'd better check on you. Your back's a mess, Mr. Universe, in case you didn't know, so I was *thinking* about calling a healer. Jesus."

"I know my back isn't pretty anymore. Six long wounds that will leave scars. It's a message, Seamus, and I got it loud and clear. Now let me rest." Rowan said the last bit into his pillow.

His roommate, Seamus Lochlann, grumbled something obscene under his breath, but he paid no attention. The wounds on his back were on fire. But if he concentrated on the silver-gray eyes of a certain beautiful pixie he'd met in his office that afternoon, he could ignore the pain. If only he could ignore the message.

CHAPTER TWO

RIDAY NIGHT, ALYSSA sat in the lounge area of the bar alone, nearly swallowed up in the cushions of a low couch. Instead of a drink on the table in front of her, she'd fanned out her research notes. She only had her thesis on Celtic mythology left to complete her master's degree, yet she couldn't concentrate. The battle dreams from her catnap in her office the day before haunted her. When the man she watched went down, her desperation to save him overwhelmed her. It still did.

At home the night before, she'd had trouble falling asleep. Sensing her unease, Shadow whined at the foot of her bed. Her whole body prickled as awareness of something evil lurking outside her cabin washed over her. When Shadow jumped up onto her bed, a habit she'd broken him of while he was still a puppy, she didn't discipline him or push him off. Instead, she took comfort in his enormous size and his loyalty, petting him and trying to sort out her thoughts. This morning when she'd stepped outside for wood for the stove, she'd noticed a concentration of footprints outside her bedroom window. Well and truly spooked, she decided to lodge a report with the police and wished again that she'd been able to acquire a security system yesterday—or even last week.

The tracks outside her house reminded her of when she'd lost her parents in a home invasion. She couldn't remember any details other than she'd been visiting her Grandma Afton on that fateful night and had lived with Gram until it was time to go off to college. Though it had been nine months since her grandmother died, Alyssa hadn't adjusted to being orphaned. Current events weren't making things any easier for her. Truly alone in the world for the first time, she was afraid.

Ceri Ross's exuberant entrance interrupted her morose thoughts. "Hey, girl! What are you doing here with all those notes scattered everywhere and not a drink in sight? You couldn't say 'back off' better to all the cute guys in this place if you put up a neon sign." The tinkling bells of Ceri's laughter accompanied her words as she unzipped her shearling jacket and dropped it on the couch opposite Alyssa.

"If I looked like you, I couldn't pile notes high enough to scare guys away. Me, I'm more the invisible type, drink or no drink. Besides, I didn't want to get too far ahead, even if you're driving."

"You wouldn't be invisible, you know, if you decided to dress in color. Your monochromatic black from head to foot makes you look like a professional mourner." Ceri rolled her eyes as she unwound her rainbow-colored cashmere scarf from her neck and dropped it on her coat.

"You know, not all of us have your sunshiny coloring that lends itself so well to a rainbow palette," Alyssa said with a sniff.

"What are your plans for tomorrow? Because we should go shopping. How Bill ever found you in all your black, I'll never know."

Alyssa gasped, and Ceri amended her tone promptly. "I'm sorry. I shouldn't have brought him up. He was a first-class creep, but at least he had good taste in women." She winked. "Even if you are especially hard to find in a dimly lit room."

"Good thing I had all my notes spread on the table since the one person with whom I want to share a drink on a Friday evening had no trouble finding me." Sarcasm dripped all over her words.

"Sorry, hon. That was rude of me." Ceri glanced around the room. "I'm restless. There's a big storm coming in, and the change in pressure or something has me on edge."

"It couldn't be that you're between boyfriends, could it?" Alyssa's eyes sparkled with mischief.

"That too. White wine as usual? I'll buy the first round."

Ceri's generous offer didn't fool Alyssa who knew her friend wanted to scope out the available prospects in the Under-Cover Lounge. She thought the name of the bar unfortunate, but she liked the relaxed atmosphere and the décor of low tables, deep couches, and rich pine paneling. The place exuded an ambience more like a library or a den than bar. The clientele tended to business types and grad students rather than the rowdy undergrads populating the sports bars and dance clubs in town, which suited her. She'd met Bill Forbes in a sports bar, and the whole competition thing there should have warned her that theirs would not be a long and happy relationship. Still, it hurt she hadn't measured up, especially in bed as he'd so graphically described to her the night he walked out.

"Wow, do you look down. Does an afternoon of shopping weird you out that much?" Ceri asked, as she set a glass of wine in front of Alyssa.

"Sorry. Thinking about my thesis. I'm having writer's block. I'm not sure what I want to say, so I keep going back to my research notes, hoping something will magically jump out at me."

"I know it's March Alys, but give it a rest. What you need is a mini-break, maybe a trip to Chico to soak in the hot pools and have a massage. Or we could book a flight to Denver, do some power shopping, take in a hockey game or a concert. I could use a change of scenery for a few days too."

"You're not going to let up on the shopping thing, are you? Would it help to know I went online last night and ordered a sapphire-blue vest?"

"You went shopping online? Hello, you went shopping at all?

I can hardly believe it." She cast her eyes heavenward. "Maybe my little girl is finally becoming a woman."

"There are times, Ceri, when you can be supremely annoying."

"Alyssa, you need to drink rather than sip your wine because I'm in need of a story," she said, changing the subject. "See the guy at the end of the bar, the one in the tweed jacket and Wranglers? Probably just in off the ranch and looking for a little love."

"He's not wearing boots. Those loafers peg him as a professor, probably visiting from somewhere. The perfectly styled hair doesn't say rancher either. He must use half a bottle of mousse on that mane after he gets out of the shower."

"At least we have the same target. So, he's a visiting professor. Now what?"

"Let's see." Alyssa sipped her wine. "He's here on loan from MIT to teach engineering to the hickabillies. He left his girlfriend at home because she has a great job as a manager at Nordstrom's, and they're gearing up for the St. Patrick's Day sale."

"Wait a minute. How do you, Miss Please-don't-make-me-shop-ever, know about major department store sales? I'm having trouble wrapping my head around you being anywhere near a store like Nordstrom's voluntarily. Give me a minute with this." Ceri grinned and slugged back a gulp of wine.

Irritated colored her voice. "Are we still playing the game or what?"

"Sure." Ceri looked anything but chastised.

Alyssa glared at her friend from beneath her brows before she continued. "He's left behind his girlfriend, and he's already hooked up with an aerobics instructor on loan to the P.E. department. She's from California and will sashay in wearing an oversized puffy coat and skinny jeans stuffed into knee-high leather boots with four-inch heels."

Enjoying her story, Alyssa leaned back against the cushions and smirked. "She's going to order some fruity drink that comes in a tall fancy glass and needs at least two garnishes—a couple of citrus slices or an umbrella or both."

"Why a fruity drink? Why not wine—or a beer?"

"She wants to see if the guy is cheap or not. It's early days in their relationship. The fruity drinks cost a mint, so she's feeling him out. If he buys her one and then suggests a switch—or worse—he expects her to go dutch—she knows whether she's going to dinner with him or catching a movie on her own."

Ceri scooted to the edge of her couch and stretched up to watch. "Check it out. He looks expectant."

Alyssa craned her neck to see around other patrons in her line of sight of the door. "I don't see her, do you?"

"Oh hey, we were way off. She's definitely a stylish lady, but she looks old enough to be his mom."

As the woman walked up to the professor, he held out his hands and greeted her warmly, kissing her cheek and saying "Hi, Mom" in her ear, his lips easy for Alyssa and Ceri to read. Both women burst out laughing.

"I bet you the next round she still orders an expensive drink," Alyssa said.

"You're on."

CHAPTER THREE

HE SCARRED ME this time, deep and permanent. She's serious, and I'm running out of time," Rowan said.

"If you'd taken the help I offered when you returned from this latest fight instead of holing up in your room, maybe you wouldn't have scars, Superman."

"Seamus, I think there are harpies out there who nag a whole lot less than you do, and they're probably prettier and better cooks."

Seamus shook his head and changed the subject. "I dreamed of a long-legged, honey blonde, built to your exact specs. Maybe today is the day we meet her."

"Long-legged, honey blondes are your dream girls, not mine," Rowan reminded him.

"Yeah, I keep forgetting you aren't particular." Seamus laughed.

Snow swirled around them as the men walked along the street. Rowan and Seamus were similarly dressed in insulated denim jackets, jeans, and gloves. Still, the men hunched their shoulders against the wind making an insidious assault on their body heat. Installing a security system in the unheated confines of a new house made them even more susceptible to the nastiness of the weather, so when they passed a bar popular with the professional set and Seamus suggested stopping, Rowan didn't argue.

"Looks like we're a bit late for a table."

"We can still grab a beer and stand near the bar. That would go a long way toward helping me face Taranis's latest tantrums out there." Seamus gestured outside at the snow and wind.

Rowan nodded and stepped up to the bar to place his order. While Rowan ordered beers, Seamus scanned the scene. When he didn't waste time arguing about who was paying, Rowan blinked in surprise.

"I found us a place to sit. Follow me."

He paid for the drinks before following Seamus to a table where two women sat deeply engaged in conversation. The women were so engrossed they didn't even look up when the two men approached.

"Your honey blonde is gorgeous—easily one of the most beautiful women I've ever seen," Rowan communicated telepathically to Seamus. The long layers of her hair curled slightly as they cascaded over her shoulders and down to the middle of her back. The soft turtleneck she wore accentuated her ample curves. Then she glanced up at them with meadow-green eyes the color of her sweater. Her full lips curved into a half smile as she gazed at the two of them.

Only when she turned to her friend for an opinion did either man acknowledge the other woman seated across from the blonde. The woman lifted one delicate raven wing of an eyebrow above her silver-gray eyes, and Rowan felt sucker-punched.

"Would you gentlemen like to join us?" the blonde asked with a smile.

Seamus nearly spilled both of their drinks taking the seat nearest the blonde, and Rowan grinned at his friend's obvious interest. The arrangement suited him fine since it meant he would be seated right next to the woman whose eyes had given him something else to focus on rather than his pain.

❧

Alyssa's breath lodged in her throat as she took in the athletic beauty of Rowan Sheridan. Seeing him in the ordinary confines of a bar was far better than watching a facsimile of him battling a nasty warrior who didn't play fair. At least she'd only dreamed of him since he obviously didn't bear any wounds from a sword fight as he gracefully lowered himself onto the couch beside her.

"Thanks for sharing your table, ladies," his blond friend began smoothly. "What's the bet, and can we get in on it?" He pointed back and forth at himself and Rowan. "I'm Seamus. And this brooding beast is Rowan. Nice to meet you."

Seamus smiled in a way that included everyone. Ceri smiled back and subtly moved closer to him. However, if someone had asked Alyssa later about this first encounter with these men, she wouldn't have been able to describe Seamus beyond his hair and his smile. Her gaze clung to Rowan.

Rowan Sheridan was about the sexiest man she'd ever seen. Logically, she knew he couldn't be a giant, but looking up at him from deep in the cushions of the couch, she appreciated his size, all broad shoulders and deep chest, trim hips, and long legs. He cut his chestnut hair close on the sides but kept it long enough on top to show off some natural waves her fingers itched to slide through. Though she took in all of him in a flash, his eyes arrested her attention, aquamarine depths so intense she was powerless to look away from them. Idly, she thought if he stretched his sculpted mouth into a real smile, his classically handsome face would transform into something approaching art.

Of course, Ceri riveted the men's attention. Alyssa didn't begrudge her friend her beauty, especially since Ceri didn't flaunt it. It was a part of her she accepted—like breathing. At this moment, however, she tried to harness a jealousy for her friend she'd never experienced before. She should probably acknowledge she and

Rowan had met, but after the awkward experience in his office yesterday, she couldn't find anything to say.

It didn't matter. As usual, Ceri commandeered the conversation, which was one of the reasons Alyssa loved her. Ceri mastered social situations. Alyssa was—quiet. Or bookish, studious, boring as her former boyfriend Bill Forbes had described her. But that was a long time ago, and Rowan was definitely not Bill. Rowan radiated hot, which had Alyssa thinking thoughts she, of all people, didn't think—certainly not about a stranger she only met yesterday.

She gave herself a mental shake and tuned in to the conversation.

"See the guy and his mom at the end of the bar? The bet is that she orders an expensive drink on his tab. I think since she's his mom, she's going to be worried about his finances and will order something conservative, but my friend here thinks she'll order something he's going to have to spend money on."

"What makes you think that?" Rowan asked Alyssa.

She cleared her throat. "She has a carefully maintained salon haircut, and she's wearing tight jeans under her designer jacket. Her boots, though practical, are expensive. She's been making men pay for her for a long time, and her son won't be an exception."

"That's a rather cynical observation of your gender," Seamus said, tipping back his beer.

"Not really. I've spent a lot of time watching people." She paused to watch the couple in question. "There it is. Tall, blue, two citruses, and an umbrella. And he's telling the bartender to put it on his tab. The next round is on you, Ceri." She grinned over the rim of her wine glass before taking a sip.

Seamus turned to Ceri. "If you'll let us stay awhile, I'll cover your bet."

"That's an offer I won't refuse," Ceri said, her eyes sparkling.

Alyssa shot her friend a look, but Ceri shrugged and returned her attention to Seamus.

"We didn't catch your names," he said.

"I'm Ceri Ross, and this is Alyssa Macaulay."

Seamus and Rowan exchanged a look before Seamus said, "Fate must have led us to this bar tonight to meet two beautiful women of Scottish descent. Are you Scots by ancestry or by marriage?"

"I'm no genealogist, but I think my family heritage is Scots. Seamus sounds Irish though," Ceri said.

"Oh, both countries claim Seamus. I'm such a lovable guy that everyone wants a piece of me," he deadpanned.

Rowan rolled his eyes and sipped his beer.

"With a name like Macaulay, you must be Scots, woman," Seamus said, addressing Alyssa. His eye might be on Ceri, but he apparently wanted to include Alyssa too.

Despite the fact he'd called her "woman"—she strangely didn't feel annoyed with him. Something in his voice had her smiling in spite of herself. "My grandmother kept our family tree, and she wanted me to be proud of my Scots heritage, so yes, in answer to your question, I'm most definitely Scots." She laughed. "That's an absurd pickup line, by the way, but it works as an icebreaker."

"I always thought your Scottish heritage was why you chose to pursue Celtic mythology for your thesis," Ceri said, her eyes asking the question.

"I chose Celtic mythology because the stories intrigued me when I was working on my English degree. It had nothing to do with Gram Afton or my heritage or anything."

It took a beat for Alyssa to notice that at Ceri's question, both men had gone unnaturally still as if her answer would unlock the secrets of the universe. Because so many people knew so little about the Celts beyond the professional basketball team that used the French pronunciation with an *s* rather than the British pronunciation with a *k*, she was used to having to defend her choice. It irritated her that Ceri was clueless. She didn't want to talk about her thesis with these men, no matter how hot they were or how Scots their names. In her experience, academics didn't resonate with hands-on types like Seamus and Rowan.

"I believe I owe a round of drinks. What are you having? Better yet, how 'bout you come with me, Ceri?" Seamus said, interrupting the sudden tension at their table.

With Ceri and Seamus safely out of earshot, Rowan turned to Alyssa. "Any particular reason we're pretending we've never met?"

"If we said we'd met, we'd have to explain the circumstances. It's Friday night, and discussing my security issues would be a downer, especially when our mutual friends seem to be hitting it off so well." She hid her nervousness with a sip of wine. "It's never good to talk shop after five o'clock. Isn't there a rule about that or something?"

"If you say so, but you seemed pretty worried yesterday. I had the impression you wanted help right away—or maybe sooner. Something happen since then?"

"No, but I haven't told my friend about the prowler, and I don't want to worry her, so can we leave it alone for now?"

Rowan crossed his arms over his chest. "You didn't say anything about a prowler to me either. New snow fell last night. Were there fresh tracks around your house?"

Their friends' return to the table with another round of drinks interrupted their conversation. Ceri laughed at something Seamus said, and neither seemed to notice the two of them studiously not talking. After a few minutes, Alyssa said, "Please excuse me. I need a little time in the ladies' room."

"Me too. Be right back, gentlemen. Hold down the fort, would you?"

"What is it with women going to the restroom in pairs?" Seamus asked playfully.

"To talk about you. Why else?" Ceri grinned before she followed Alyssa.

When they reached the powder room, Ceri said, "Alyssa, those two are hot and so nice. Seamus is seriously cute in a linebacker kind of way, and Rowan is in to you. You have to learn to let go of your prejudices and trust in the innate goodness of human nature."

A tremor of hope thrilled through her before she tamped it down. "Your imagination is in overdrive, Ceri, love. Make sure I have your car keys when you make your decision about which one is going to get lucky tonight. I don't want to be stranded."

As the men enjoyed their beers, Seamus teased Rowan. "The hot silver-eyed elf is into you, man."

"Uh-huh," Rowan snorted before downing a gulp of his beer.

"Seriously. She can't keep her eyes off you."

"How would you know? Your eyes haven't strayed from Ceri from the moment you spotted her across the room."

"She is definitely one beautiful woman." Seamus waggled his brows and Rowan couldn't help but laugh at him.

Turning his attention to the books and papers strewn over the table between them, he said, "I wonder what Alyssa is learning in her research on Celtic mythology." He leafed half-heartedly through the research notes when his eyes caught sight of an intricate hand-embroidered bookmark. He didn't question why he needed to touch it, but the second his fingertips skimmed the threads, his entire body buzzed with energy.

"You're not even going to try tonight, are you? You still have three months until Morgan cranks up the pressure. Besides, once you find your talisman, no more hook-ups for you. You'll be well and truly on the shelf, old man, and how much fun will that be for me, having to take care of so many women on my own?" He sighed dramatically. "You know how generous I am." He winked.

Rowan gave him a long-suffering eye roll.

After taking a swig of his beer, Seamus continued. "Though you're shielding your thoughts, you've hardly taken your eyes off

Alyssa since we met them, so why not admit your attraction and get on with it?"

"All right. Let's invite them out to dinner. Think of some suggestions."

When the women returned to the table, talk turned to Ceri and her real estate business before Seamus started cracking jokes and telling outrageous stories about their clients' wild and weird security requests. By the time he got around to suggesting dinner, Alyssa had even smiled a couple of times. Rowan sensed this was no small feat.

"I know a great little Italian place within walking distance. It'll be Rowan's treat." Seamus winked at Alyssa and smiled at Ceri.

Judging from the look on her face, Alyssa was about to decline when Ceri pre-empted her. "We'd love to join you for dinner."

With an audible sigh, Alyssa gathered her research into an oversized bag and shrugged into her red wool coat, looking as though she'd rather be anywhere else. He was going to have to work on her. Good thing Rowan enjoyed a challenge.

Seamus and Ceri led the way out of the bar. As Rowan silently ushered Alyssa ahead of him, he admired the sexy way she walked. He held the door for her and casually placed his hand at the base of her spine as she exited the bar into the freezing early March evening.

CHAPTER FOUR

EAMUS HUSTLED THEM along the street to the restaurant. As they walked, Ceri said, "These fat snowflakes are piling up. I bet the temperature's fallen at least ten degrees since we walked into the bar. Brrr!"

"You need to keep your eyes peeled for snow snakes and swirling snow devils on the loose. They try to trap unwary pedestrians on their way to dinner," Seamus teased while pretending to be tripped by some unseen icy creature.

They were all laughing when they reached "the little Italian place"—actually a bar and grill advertising gourmet pizza.

Both women cracked up when they saw they were dining at a popular pizza bar employing live bands on the weekend. "Hey, you can't beat a place that provides dinner and dancing. We can enjoy the entire evening together without having to relocate," Seamus said.

"Did you see how these two maneuvered us into a double date that we can easily exit if it doesn't work out? If that isn't decent, then I don't know what is," Ceri whispered as they stepped through the door of the bar.

Alyssa nodded.

A low divider separated a modest dance

floor and dais for the band from the bar-restaurant on the opposite side of it. Bar stools arranged around tall tables allowed restaurant patrons to watch the action on the dance floor from the restaurant. Muted light reflected in the mirror running the length of the dark oak bar, giving the room an intimate glow. Several patrons conversed at the bar while they waited for the band to begin playing. Waitresses and waiters in crisp long-sleeved white shirts tucked into tight black jeans scurried between tables, working hard to keep the clientele happy under the watchful eye of the host who seated the group at a table overlooking the dance floor.

Inwardly, Alyssa sighed. Being short, she had to use the bottom rung of her chair as a step up into it. Maybe if she wore heeled boots instead of practical winter footgear, she'd be statuesque enough for a barstool.

They ordered a large house specialty pizza—feta and artichokes overlaying grilled chicken—and a pitcher of beer. When the pizza arrived, Ceri was holding court, regaling the men with funny stories from Alyssa's and her undergrad days. She loved her best friend for trying to shine some of the spotlight on her, but she had no illusions about who was the star on this little stage. Normally, she enjoyed watching Ceri work, but Rowan intrigued her, and her secret jealousy of his attention to Ceri horrified her.

When the band started playing, Seamus wasted no time asking Ceri to dance. Alyssa sat back sipping her beer and wondering what to say to the amazingly hot man running in second place for Ceri's affections for the night.

Rowan took care of that for her. "Tell me about your studies. You're working on a master's degree?"

"Um, yeah. My gran used to tell me stories of heroes and monsters, and then I read those same kinds of stories when I studied English for my bachelor's. It seemed a natural progression to study the Celts for my master's."

"When all your stuff was scattered over the table in the other bar, I noticed you had an unusual bookmark. Would you mind letting me look at it again?"

"You want to look at my bookmark?" Alyssa asked. *What the hell?*

"Yeah."

The open expression on his face warred with the command in his voice. Alyssa responded to his voice. Wordlessly, she reached into her bag and retrieved the cloth marking the place in her research. Rowan took it from her, running his fingers over its intricate design of Celtic birds flowing into never-ending, intertwining knots. "Interesting design on this. Where did you get it?"

"I made it. Add embroidery to my list of boring hobbies."

"Did you design it or follow a pattern?" he asked, the look on his face one of intense interest.

"You know something about embroidery?" she asked incredulously.

"My mom's into it." He looked at her. "You didn't answer my question."

"I designed it. The story of Rhiannon and her undeserved penance always makes me sad. No wonder she's the patron goddess of birds." She glanced at her design. "They're forever free, soaring untamed beyond the pettiness of the world, so I created a bird design based on some old photos of Welsh Celtic art that I ran across—wait for it—in a book."

His aquamarine gaze seemed to try to see into her. She didn't know what in their conversation caused his reaction, but she had an odd notion it had to do with her bookmark design. Holding out her hand, she silently asked for its return, and wordlessly, he handed it to her. When their fingers touched in the exchange, an electric charge raced up her arm like it had when they'd shook hands in his office. Her breath caught. Staring at him a little wide-eyed, she wondered what had happened. The look in his eyes said he felt something too.

She returned the bookmark to her bag before reaching for the pitcher of beer and a refill she didn't need. Apparently, she'd had so much to drink already she'd imagined some sort of connection with Rowan Sheridan.

The moment passed almost as quickly as it came as Ceri and Seamus took a breather from the dance floor. Rowan composed his features while she hid hers behind a sip of beer.

"The band is rockin' tonight," Ceri said, catching her breath. "I had no idea this place brought in such great music on the weekends. Good call, Seamus."

"I do what I can." He shrugged, his grin smug. "Maybe you two should try dancing. It might help you be less tense."

Rowan shot him a look.

"What have you been talking about while we tore up the dance floor?" Ceri asked.

"Books," they replied simultaneously then stared at each other.

"Dark beer is great with pizza, but it does nothing to quench my thirst after dancing. I need something lighter. How 'bout you Ceri?" Seamus asked.

"I could take a break from beer."

Seamus nodded and headed over to the bar.

"This would be a seriously progressive place if the bartender *gave* him a pitcher of water. Bet it costs the same as pop," Alyssa said.

Rowan quirked a brow. "What is it with you and bets?"

"It's the excitement of the win, of course." She batted her eyes at him.

"She only bets on sure things. Not much excitement there." Ceri's expression matched her sardonic tone as she patted her face with a napkin.

"Hmmm. The lady with the drink order in the other bar was a sure thing?" Rowan asked.

"Alyssa got lucky on that one," Ceri groused while Alyssa grinned.

The three of them exchanged looks as Seamus returned to their table carrying a pitcher of water in one hand while precariously balancing four glasses in the other.

"How much for the water, Seamus?" Alyssa asked.

"The same as for pop, why?"

"Win." She tipped her beer glass toward Rowan and Ceri before finishing it.

"Your turn to hold down the fort," Rowan said to Seamus before turning to her. "Let's dance."

His invitation surprised her so much she didn't have time to react before he took her by the hand and urged her off her barstool. He didn't let go until they reached the dance floor where the band segued from a hard rock tune to a slow ballad. When he pulled her into his arms, a frisson of electricity flowed through her again.

"Hey, relax. We're only dancing. In public, no less."

She let out a silent breath and willed herself to lighten up. She couldn't figure out why she, rather than Ceri, was on the dance floor, but maybe she should enjoy the attention for a few minutes. When Rowan urged her closer to him, she allowed it, the heat from his big hand in the small of her back warming her all over. In the deep recesses of her mind, she thought she should be afraid of this huge man, but she wasn't. In fact, she wished she could be closer to him, and she tightened her arms around him enough to touch him from her chest to her knees. Behind the safety of her sweater and vest, her nipples hardened at the contact with his body. The fresh scent of the outdoors still clung to him, and she breathed him in deeply, his smell far more intoxicating than the alcohol she'd imbibed over the evening.

It seemed the song had barely started before the lead singer announced the title of the next number, a cover of a popular tune tearing up rock radio. Rowan moved Alyssa in front of him to exit the dance floor. She hoped her disappointment at one dance didn't show on her face as she led the way back to their table, but as she stepped off the dance floor, she felt a sensation like a kiss on her bare shoulder. When she looked over at her shoulder, it appeared as it should—covered in her turtleneck and suede vest. She glanced inquiringly at Rowan who stared back at her expectantly.

That was odd. I could have sworn he kissed my shoulder, but that would never happen. A guy like Rowan wants Ceri, not someone like me. "Not so much."

"Did you say something?" Alyssa asked.

"No."

"Oh. I thought you did. My mistake."

They returned to their table in a silence that had Alyssa wondering what she'd done this time to turn off an interesting man.

As she was about to hoist herself back up into her seat, she noticed an especially charged look pass between Rowan and Seamus. If she didn't know better, she could almost swear they were communicating telepathically. Another charged look passed between Rowan and Ceri.

Watching the other three exchange knowing glances left Alyssa feeling like a fifth wheel. Then Rowan stopped her seating herself by taking her coat off of the back of her barstool and holding it out to her to put on.

"I dance that badly, huh?" she asked, trying to make light of the obvious fact that he at least had had enough of their evening.

"You're quite a good dancer after you relax. But all the same, it's time for me to take you home," he said. His words were casual, but the tone of his voice left no room for argument.

Speechless, Alyssa turned to Ceri for help. Ceri smiled at her and gave her a discreet thumbs up. Something was going on that she couldn't follow. "Ceri, I thought I was driving your car tonight."

"Since Rowan is driving you home, I'll need it to drive Seamus. I hope you don't mind."

Surprise flashed across Seamus's face for a second before he covered it with a grin directed first at Rowan then at Ceri. Alyssa couldn't follow any of it.

"Am I missing something here?"

"It'll be fine, Alyssa. I'll catch up with you tomorrow."

Alyssa stared incredulously at her friend. They'd met these guys a couple of hours ago, and though they'd been gentlemen and were seriously attractive, she had no intention of engaging in a one-night stand and couldn't see Ceri going there either. Rowan's sudden interest in her made her uneasy as well, yet it seemed like she had no choice but to accept his offer of a ride home since everything had somehow already been arranged.

CHAPTER FIVE

OWAN GUIDED HER out of the bar and into what was shaping up to be a terrific storm. The fat flakes falling when they'd walked to the pizzeria hours ago seemed an ominous harbinger of a deep and swift accumulation. Perhaps he drove something that wouldn't make the canyon road to her cabin, and she'd have an excuse for calling her neighbor who drove a four-wheel-drive pick-up.

They walked wordlessly back to the first bar where they'd met, outside of which Rowan had parked his big, black, four-wheel-drive SUV. So much for that plan. She stretched to climb up on the running boards after he opened the door for her. As she watched him walk around the cab of the truck, she thought what at first seemed like an adrenaline rush of fear might, in fact, have been excitement. For the life of her, she couldn't figure that out.

After he settled himself in the cab and started the engine, she broke the silence. "Thanks for the ride, but I have to warn you, I don't do one-night-stands."

He cocked a brow and said nothing, so she tried another tack.

"I live way out of town up the canyon toward the ski hill."

"Is that supposed to discourage me?"

"It does a lot of people."

He didn't dignify her comment with a response. Instead, he changed the subject. "What prompted your fascination in the Celts?"

"Your fascination with my interests seems a little weird. I haven't met many people outside my study group and Ceri who even know who the Celts are. Most people mispronounce the name and think I'm writing a thesis on a professional basketball team."

"My mom is into Celtic mythology, so I know a bit about them. You haven't answered my question." His tone made her think her answer was vitally important to him, adding to the weirdness of their conversation.

"My grandmother used to tell me stories of heroes and gods when I was small. Later, I ran into Celtic mythology during my undergraduate studies in English literature." Watching Rowan's big, capable hands steer his SUV over the unplowed road distracted her. When he flicked a questioning glance her way, she continued. "Reading the mythology led me to study Celtic culture, and the more I learned, the more I wanted to know, so it seemed natural to pursue it for my master's degree."

The strength of his profile interested her almost as much as his hands. When she stopped speaking, he eyed her for a moment, and she quickly turned her face to the windshield.

"Since that same process probably happens to most graduate students, my studies of the Celts is not all that different from anyone else's pursuit of, say, advanced cell biology or business administration."

"Don't get defensive. I think your master's thesis is admirable. Do you intend to go into teaching or research or what?"

"Before I started working on my thesis, I thought I might want to write. Now I may need to explore my options, teaching being one of them. You'll want to slow down since my turn is coming up."

Rowan expertly applied the brakes, slowing without sliding on the slick road, and made a right-hand turn onto the spur road leading to her house.

"You've changed your mind about writing?"

"The thesis is coming at the speed of a glacier, so I'm not sure if I'm cut out to be a writer." She watched the falling snow out the passenger window and wondered why she was sharing her deepest fears with a stranger. And why sharing them with him felt natural.

"How long have you been working on it?"

"All last semester and the beginning of this one. Ceri thinks I need a break. Maybe she's right." She changed the subject. "So how did you get into the security business?"

"It's been the family business for a long time. I don't know anything else. Plus, I like knowing I'm helping other people remain safe."

"You graduated high school and went right to work?"

"No. I went to college on the West Coast, earned my degree in business, and drifted for a while." He looked away from the road and gave her a tiny grin. "I wanted to see if there was anything else out there that grabbed my attention." Returning his eyes to the road, he added, "Last fall, my dad asked me to open a store here and manage it for him, so I did."

Through the swirling snow, Alyssa saw they were close to the turnoff to her house. She guided Rowan down the road, but instead of using her circular drive in the front of the house to drop her off, he parked on the tarmac in front of her small garage. Sliding a sidelong glance at him, she watched him as he appeared lost in thought.

"Thanks for the dinner and the ride. It was all … unexpected. Good night." When she reached for the door handle, he stayed her with a light touch on her arm.

"That's it? 'Thanks' and off you go?"

"I warned you before you put your truck in gear. I may be quiet, but I'm always direct. If you misunderstood, I'm sorry, but I don't invite men I just met into my home. When you come out on

Monday, maybe you should bring your secretary along." She reached for the door again, and again he detained her.

"With all the snow we plowed through to drive up your road, that running board is probably slick. Let me help you." He didn't give her a chance to respond before he stepped out of the truck and came around to her side of it to open her door. His politeness, though disarming, didn't deter her from her goal of going inside her home alone.

"Thanks again," she said as she alighted from the truck. "I can manage from here. Good night."

Stepping around him, she hurried to the front door of her home. The deep snow muffled the sound of Rowan walking in step behind her. She gasped when he stepped beside her as she rummaged in her bag for her keys. Bristling, she said, "I'm not going to invite you in no matter how polite or patient you appear to be."

"Sure you are because you're curious about why I kissed you as we left the dance floor and why I decided it was time to leave immediately afterward," he responded, a smirk ghosting over his lips.

"You really did kiss me? I didn't imagine that?" Alyssa asked, flustered. How could she have felt him kiss her through two layers of heavy clothing? Letting him into her home went against everything she'd been taught about personal safety, yet she wanted to know the answers to those questions. Plus, he was a bona fide security expert. She'd called some of his clients after she'd returned home after their meeting.

"This is probably going to be a long and complicated conversation, so maybe we should go inside." He nodded at the door.

Clearly, this man was used to having his way. Against her better judgment, she shoved her key in the lock and opened the door.

After clicking on a table lamp near the door, she stepped over to the coat closet to hang up her coat and put away the rest of her gear. That's when a shape rose up from behind the couch. Alyssa hid a grin as Rowan stepped back and her enormous white dog materialized in the lamplight. He let out a yip like a puppy before moving between Rowan and his mistress, waiting expectantly for her command.

"Rowan, meet Shadow. He's sort of like you: big and insistent. You won the battle you waged to get into my house by using some underhanded tactics, but Shadow will ensure that I win the war for what happens in here."

"You may be in the market for a home security system, but I think your friend here is a dandy one exactly as he is. Shadow? For a white dog?"

She laughed and bent down to bury her face in Shadow's long fur, greeting him the way she always did. Straightening, she smiled at Rowan yet kept a reassuring hand on her pet. "When he was a puppy, he followed me everywhere. I had to close the bathroom door to take a shower without him. From the moment we met, he's been my shadow. Midnight would have been ironic. Shadow is accurate."

"Is he trained to take out my neck if I make a sudden move like removing my jacket and boots?"

"Only if I ask him to, which I'm seriously considering at the moment."

A grin tugged at his mouth, and Alyssa forgot to breathe at the sparkle she saw in his intense aqua-marine eyes.

After reprimanding herself, she asked, "You don't think I'm serious?"

"If you were going to sic your big dog on me, you'd have done it already. I'm thinking I can ditch my jacket and boots safely for now."

"Fine," she huffed. "Shadow, go lay down. I'll have your dinner to you in a jiff." She walked into the great room off the front foyer and flicked on a couple of lamps on her way to the kitchen. From the corner of her eye, she saw Rowan hang his coat in the closet next to hers before he locked the door and followed her farther into her house.

∽

While Alyssa tended to her beast of a dog, Rowan looked around her great room. To his left, built in floor-to-ceiling shelves filled almost entirely with hard-cover books took up the wall. A few knick-knacks and framed photos rested artfully among the books.

River rock mortared half-way up the opposite wall reflected warmth from the house's main heat source—a black pot-bellied wood-stove. A door next to it led to a laundry room, and on the other side of the door, the kitchen began with pine cabinets along the wall. Beneath a deep window sat the sink. Additional cabinets framed the window before ending beside the refrigerator. An island separated the kitchen from the living room. On the other side of the fridge, a hallway probably led to bedrooms and a bathroom.

Stepping over to the island, he glanced up at the high kitchen ceiling, which held two skylights. The coziness of the living room part of the great room gave way to the airiness of the kitchen in a seamless and pleasing fashion. As he looked back toward the great room, the tree of life and Rhiannon tapestries hanging on either side of the bay window next to the door drew his attention.

On his way to inspecting the tapestry, three small, but stunning, glass sculptures, one on the coffee table in front of the love seat and one each on the end tables bracketing the love seat arrested his attention. One was of the warrior goddess Epona riding her horse and leading another horse. Another depicted a Scottish warrior in full battle gear like something out of *Braveheart*. The last was a three-dimensional trinity knot.

For a moment, he forgot to breathe as he recognized everything that had happened during the evening led him to the place he'd been seeking for nearly seven years. No question Alyssa was his talisman, but she was a prickly little thing who'd doubtless be hard to convince. Especially considering she didn't appear to know she was a talisman, let alone his. Her thoughts were a piece of cake to listen in on, so either she didn't have her shield up, had a weak shield, or hadn't created a shield at all. Then there was the problem of her responding to his sign with a question rather than recognition.

Maneuvering his way into her house by dangling an explanation for a circumstance she should have been anticipating, even actively seeking, troubled him. Not the least because they needed to build an unbreakable bond between them, something a trained talisman would know. He wondered how she was going to respond when he explained everything, and she discovered he had no intention of leaving her house until they'd spent considerable time in bed together. And maybe not even then.

∽

Alyssa talked to Shadow before she let him outside to relieve himself while Rowan wandered around in her great room. When her dog finally reappeared at the back door, the snow clinging to his fur made him look like a walking snow drift. She laughed as he shook off the snow before he settled in to devour his dinner.

When she stepped back into the great room, Rowan was studying the goddess sculpture her grandmother had left to her. While he studied it, she studied him, finding his interest in the art to be as attractive as his arresting aquamarine eyes, strong jaw, and dark beard stubble. Could it be he actually shared her enthusiasm for Celtic mythology and culture rather than wanting to use her interests to work his way into her bed?

Finished with his dinner, Shadow nudged past her through the open doorway and half trotted over to Rowan. He butted his head playfully against Rowan's hand, and instead of flinching or startling, Rowan turned to the dog and grabbed his fur over either shoulder and roughed him around, each taking the other's measure and finding a mutual friend. Alyssa stared, shocked. Shadow never took to strangers like this. Perhaps Ceri was right about Rowan and Seamus being decent guys. Wasn't there an old saying about babies and dogs being able to recognize good people when they meet them?

Catching her eye, Rowan grinned. "I think I've acquired an ally. What do you think?" he asked with an arm draped over her Great Pyrenees.

"I think I need to help my dog develop more discriminating taste. Shadow, maybe you'd like to show Rowan where we keep the wood for the stove while I make something warm to drink. Hot chocolate okay with you, or do you want something with more kick?"

"Hot chocolate is fine." He looked down at the big white dog who returned his stare with something akin to adoration. "Since Shadow seems a bit taciturn, maybe you could direct me to the wood?"

"Go through the laundry room and out the back door. It's stacked on the porch. Shadow probably needs a few private moments after his supper, so he can stay out for a while."

On cue, Shadow raced into the laundry room and whined at the back door. Rowan laughed at the big goof as he headed to the back porch and the cord of stacked wood.

Alyssa made hot chocolate the old-fashioned way by adding cocoa mix to milk she warmed in a pot on the stove. As she stirred the hot chocolate to keep it from scorching, she tried to understand her feelings. For some strange reason, she enjoyed having Rowan in her home.

Somehow, he looked right in her space. Bill had never looked— or felt—right in her home. He knew it too, which was probably why he insisted they spend so much time at his place. That and Shadow growled at Bill and watched him like he would eat him if Alyssa would only give the command. She smiled at that particular memory. Maybe she should have let Shadow enjoy Bill as a chew toy at least once—like the day he walked out on her.

Rowan brought in an armload of wood and set it in the metal cradle on the hearth. Covertly, she watched him stack wood over the glowing coals inside the stove. The whole domestic situation— him lighting the fire, her cooking up something for them in the kitchen—seemed natural.

As soon as the idea struck her, she immediately feared the direction of her thoughts. She'd only known this man for a few hours, and already she was building castles in the air? Plainly, she needed to grab hold of herself. The romantic aspect of the mythology she'd been studying lately must have clouded her thinking. She gave herself a mental shake that manifested itself in rather loud thumps as she set two heavy stoneware mugs on the island.

At the sound, Rowan glanced up from his brightly burning fire. "Was it something I said?" he teased.

She scowled at him before turning her attention to the whine at the back door. He closed the woodstove before letting Shadow back into the house.

"Are you in for the night old man, or do we do this again in a bit?" he asked as Shadow shook snow all over the rug on the laundry room floor. "The wind is picking up. You're getting some pretty deep drifts around your house."

"Maybe that will deter whoever's been coming around here at night," she replied, anger and hope warring with fear in her voice.

Returning to the great room, Rowan sat down on one of the high-backed stools at the island and accepted the mug of steaming chocolate she pushed toward him. He took a sip and closed his eyes. "This is a pleasure I haven't enjoyed since I was a boy," he said with a smile. "Real hot chocolate made with real milk slow cooked on the stove." He savored another sip. "Now about that prowler—"

Alyssa didn't want to talk about the prowler. In fact, she was sorry she'd brought it up since the topic detracted from what she truly wanted to know. "Why did you kiss me as we left the dance floor? I'm wearing two rather heavy layers of clothing, yet it felt like skin on skin. How is that for odd? You said you'd explain if I let you into my house tonight."

Instead of answering right away, he stood up, grabbed his mug, and made himself at home in the leather chair in the living room. When she didn't immediately follow him, he cocked a brow expectantly at her. Huffing out a breath, she seated herself at the far end of the loveseat.

"In your studies of the Celts, have you run into any stories of talismans?"

"You mean like omens and lucky charms? Sure. Those come up all the time," she replied. "What about them?"

"Have you ever read about *warriors* and their talismans?"

"I'm not entirely sure what you're asking."

"For a warrior to be complete, he needs three things: his name, his weapon, and his woman—his talisman. Have you ever seen that in your research?"

"Of course. Most of the greatest heroes of mythology are described as having those things. For example, King Arthur wielded Excalibur and was married to his great love Guenevere," Alyssa said over the rim of her mug before taking a sip of rich chocolate.

"Exactly, except Guenevere wasn't Arthur's talisman, and he knew it when he married her. She was Lancelot's, which was a contributing factor to the downfall of Camelot."

She scooted to the edge of her seat. "What are you saying? That Arthur deliberately took Guenevere away from Lancelot? Have you actually read the stories?"

"I've read the stories both in English and in French, as a matter of fact." Rowan placed his mug on the coffee table. "And no, I'm not saying Arthur deliberately targeted Lancelot. What I'm saying is when Arthur married Guenevere, he knew she belonged to another warrior, not to him. He didn't know at the time who that warrior was, but he didn't care. He thought he could thwart the system, beat the gods." He ran a hand through his hair and took a breath. "In the end, Morgan saw to it he paid dearly for his arrogance, as did all those he loved: Lancelot and Guenevere, Merlin, Gawain, all of them. A warrior needs a talisman, but she must be *his* talisman."

"Who is Morgan?"

"The Morrigan, the most fearsome of the trinity of war goddesses of the Celtic pantheon."

"I've never read where the Morrigan targeted King Arthur. Why do you call her Morgan?"

"Because that's what she prefers to be called these days." He placed his hands on his thighs and leaned toward her. "Sooo, talismans. The tales the old bards told left out the talismans with a couple of exceptions, Guenevere being one. Some other stories alluded to the nature of the relationship between warriors and their talismans, like Aideen, the wife of Oscar, Finn MacCool's grandson, who died of a broken heart when Oscar died in battle. Then there's Aude the Fair, who, when Charlemagne lied to her that her beloved Roland was dead, immediately fell dead at Charlemagne's feet."

Alyssa nodded. She knew those stories too.

He continued. "The stories of these special talismans survived because their connections to their warriors were even stronger than the gods, but beyond Celtic scholars and the occasional bard at a Renaissance faire, the stories have almost disappeared from modern consciousness." He picked up his mug and sipped his chocolate as he awaited her response.

"Apparently, I have more research to do. However, this has been a very enlightening conversation." She considered his words. "You may have rescued me from the doldrums of my thesis, and I didn't even have to leave my house." With a smile, she toasted him with her mug and wondered at the startled look he gave her.

CHAPTER SIX

"YOU STILL HAVEN'T explained about the kiss."

"It's simple, Alyssa. I'm your warrior and you're my talisman. I've been searching for you for nearly seven years, and tonight I finally found you."

"But we've never met before. How could you be looking for me?" She stared at him, perplexed. "What do you mean you're a warrior and I'm a talisman?"

"Have you made other book marks like the one you showed me in the bar?"

"What does that have to do with kisses and warriors and talismans and everything?"

"If you have any others, I'll show you."

She turned to open the cabinet in the end table where she kept her embroidery materials. While she occupied herself searching her embroidery basket for some finished bookmarks, Rowan moved onto the love seat beside her. When she turned back with the bookmarks in her hand, she gasped at finding him so close to her. Giving her a gentle smile, he opened his palm, and wordlessly, she handed the bookmarks to him. While he took his time studying them, she tried to figure out what he saw in them. One was a series of Celtic knots, the other a Celtic cross. The knots were embroidered in green thread, the cross in aquamarine on white linen.

Alyssa had made the green one for Ceri and planned to give it to her friend on her next birthday. She hadn't had any plans for the second one when she'd made it, but she remembered feeling both inspired and compelled to embroider the design when she saw the thread in a craft store before Christmas. While Rowan studied the second one, she tensed when she saw she'd chosen thread the exact color of his eyes.

"This is amazing workmanship. You're a gifted fabric artist. May I have this?" he asked.

Staggered by their conversation, the coincidence of the color, and Rowan's unexpected knowledge and request, she mutely nodded assent. As she tried to assimilate what was happening between them, she didn't immediately pick up that as he pocketed the strip of cloth, he moved even closer to her.

Sliding his arm across the back of the love seat, he leaned toward her to answer her question. "Each warrior is given a sign to use to find his talisman. My sign was to kiss a woman's right shoulder while she was fully clothed. Only my talisman would feel the kiss on her bare skin. I've kissed a lot of women over the past six and a half years, and tonight, I finally found the woman who felt it."

"But Ceri held your interest all night. You could hardly take your eyes off her, not that I blame you," Alyssa hastily added. "I couldn't figure out at all why you danced with me and not with her when you had the chance. Couldn't she be your talisman?"

"Ceri is someone's talisman, but she isn't mine."

"Ceri is a talisman? What?"

He jacked a brow. "She is, but I'm not King Arthur taking another warrior's talisman. While your friend is attractive, I figured out early in the evening she wasn't for me." His eyes danced. "Seamus, on the other hand, is like Gawain—only too happy to enjoy as many women as possible. But he won't try to poach another warrior's talisman."

"Are you saying Seamus is also looking for a certain woman?"

"He's a warrior, yes. Eventually, he'll need to find his talisman, but since he's only twenty-five, he doesn't feel any urgency." Intensity radiated from him as he changed the subject. "Do you know you have the most amazing eyes? They shimmer when you're animated or when you're defensive like you were about your hobbies. And when you're annoyed like you were with me earlier tonight," he added with a smirk. "They're especially gorgeous when you're passionate about something like a moment ago when we were discussing Celtic mythology."

He inched closer to her, his thigh brushing hers. "Even though I found your friend attractive, your eyes grabbed my attention when we met and again at the bar." He ran a finger over the design of the bookmark she still held. "Then I saw the bookmark and knew before you told me that you'd made it. While Seamus enjoyed your friend, I had a chance to study you, and you intrigued the hell out of me, especially your gorgeous eyes that show so much emotion. They lured me in."

Long seconds passed as he held her in his eyes before she blinked and looked away from the intensity she saw there.

"To be honest, I haven't been energetically seeking my talisman for some time. With the clock running out, I'd all but given up on finding her." He touched a finger playfully to her nose. "Then I met this prickly little pixie—twice—and I knew I couldn't give up hope."

He smiled at the face she made at his description. "When we walked off the dance floor, your reaction told me you felt the kiss, and I nearly shouted for joy. If I had, it would have been embarrassing and dangerous for us. Instead, I hustled you out of the bar and brought you home." He glanced at the bay window and back at her. "You know, we'd be frozen popsicles on your front porch if you'd made me explain all this outside."

Somewhere during his explanation, he'd slipped his arm around her, and they were touching along their sides from shoulder to knee. Alyssa's heart pounded in her chest at Rowan's nearness, and she couldn't draw a full breath. While she sat there not daring to move, like a rabbit under a bush as the hawk flies overhead, he used his free hand to smooth her hair behind her ear, giving his mouth access. When he traced the shell of her ear with his tongue, she shivered, the caress arrowing straight to her core.

His lips brushed her ear as he whispered, "I can explain our unique connection better in your bedroom."

His suggestion ripped Alyssa from the web of desire Rowan wove with his nearness and his expert caresses. Jerking away from him, she hissed, "I knew it. This whole story was about getting me into bed." She punctuated her words with a finger to his chest. "It doesn't matter how hot you are"—poke—"or how much you seem to know about things I'm interested in"—poke—"or what you do for a living. I don't sleep with a guy on the first date and certainly not with someone I. Just. Met." Poke. Poke. Poke.

Rowan grinned at her outrage. "Alyssa, you've been in control since we walked in the door. Tell me, is your heart pounding because you're angry with me or because I've aroused you? Be honest—with yourself at least."

Her retort died on her lips. In the privacy of her mind, she had to admit his one small caress had nearly undone her. Never had she reacted to a man as she had to Rowan Sheridan.

Instead of telling him off as she'd intended, she found herself explaining her previous relationship with Bill Forbes and the way he'd treated her.

"You're saying this Bill asshole thought you were cold in bed, so he dumped you the day after you buried your grandmother? Lady, you're vibrating with passion, and all we've done is sit tight on the couch. Honestly, I can't wait to see what kissing you is like." Instead of shutting down his libido like she thought her sad history would, somehow, she'd turned him on.

The desire in his eyes fascinated and terrified her. No man had ever lit her up with only a touch. She needed distance. Perspective. A minute.

When she tried to rise, he whispered, "Please, Pixie-girl, not yet," and put his free hand on her hip as he trailed kisses along her jaw from her ear to her mouth. "A warrior's talisman is also his mate, something your family should have told you long before we met."

"What are you—"

She forgot to breathe as he outlined her mouth with his tongue before fitting his lips to hers. The contact exploded every nerve ending in her body, leaving her incoherent about everything except this man's touch. For reasons beyond her comprehension, she needed to feel his kiss, to feel his tongue stroking and caressing hers. She fused her lips to his, inviting—begging—him to kiss her deeply, their mouths coming together like long-lost halves of one whole.

Wrapping her arms around his neck, she clung to his strength, his heat. He tasted of hot chocolate and outside and some manly spice all his own. His hot kiss left her writhing in his arms, seeking even more contact with his hard body. He groaned and smoothed his hand down her leg to the hem of her skirt, slipped beneath it, and unerringly smoothed up her thigh to her pulsing sex. His long fingers teased her clit with increasing pressure over her tights and panties as they both deepened the kiss. At his touch, her clothes became too warm, his heavy flannel shirt too much of a barrier between her hands and his skin. She unbuttoned it as she tried simultaneously to pump her hips in rhythm with his practiced caresses.

He broke the kiss and pulled away from her enough to whisper, "See, so much passion, but only for me because I'm your warrior." She thought he tried to tell her something important, but his hand still pleasured her through the barrier of panties and tights, and she couldn't comprehend or even care about his meaning. Burying her face in his chest, she inhaled his scent, cold outdoors, musk, and man, his smell oddly familiar. She kissed his chest wherever she bared his skin, and he groaned and removed his hand from its pleasurable pursuits at the apex of her thighs. Stilling her protests with a soft kiss, he stood, lifting her high in his arms as though she weighed nothing at all.

He carried her down the hall and somehow knew to choose the room at the end. After he set her down on her bed, he kneeled on the floor between her legs. Wrapping his arms around her waist, he kissed her again, feather brushes of his lips on hers followed by gentle pressure. He unzipped her skirt and slipped his hands beneath her sweater and pushed her clothes—sweater, vest, and bra—up over her head, dropping the whole works in a heap beside him on the floor. Her nipples pebbled under his intense scrutiny before he trailed his eyes lower to the soft little swell of her belly. He kissed her there first, surprising her.

Again, he wrapped his arms around her waist and kissed her mouth hard as his calloused hands raised goosebumps over her back. Her body tingled in anticipation of his next touch. He nipped and licked a trail of kisses from her mouth, along her jaw, and down her neck before he concentrated his attention on her bared breasts. Her breath caught as he closed his mouth around one nipple, the scrape of his tongue and teeth nearly causing her to come instantly. Tightening her thighs around him, she plunged her hands into the soft waves of his hair and held him to her as he sucked her. The woman he called from her had never existed before, but at the moment, she didn't care. She had no idea who this man was or how he managed to entice her to break all her rules, but it didn't matter. She needed to feel him skin-on-skin *right now*.

She reached down his back, grabbed two hands full of his shirt, and tugged it out of his jeans. He smiled at her and stood to shuck his clothes. Easing back on the bed, her eyes never leaving his, she slid off skirt, tights, and panties in one go. When she sat forward to push her clothes the rest of the way down, he placed his hands over hers and finished the job himself.

His naked body overwhelmed her. Never had she seen such male perfection. From his broad shoulders to his thick sculpted chest and chiseled abs, he radiated beauty. His long powerful legs belonged to a man in his prime. The huge and gorgeous erection between his legs enticed her, and she tentatively reached for him before pulling her hand away. Self-conscious about her imperfections, she tried to cover herself with her arms, but he smiled at her and took both her hands in one of his big ones, raised them over her head, and slowly eased her back onto the bed.

"Don't ever hide yourself from me, Alyssa. I've never seen anything as beautiful as you are right now," Rowan said as he joined her on the bed.

For a few minutes, they absorbed each other, pressed together shoulders to toes. Her breasts felt delicious flattened against his hard chest, and his cock throbbed hotly at the apex of her thighs. When he loosened his hold on her hands, she wrapped her arms around his broad shoulders. Her entire body sparked, sending little shots of electricity into the already charged air around them.

He shifted, sliding his knee between her legs, silently commanding her to open for him, and she did, drawing her knees up on either side of him. Reaching between them, he positioned himself to enter her, taking his time. She sensed him straining to hold back as he slid into her one inch at a time, slowly stretching her, letting her adjust to him little by little before he thrust into her fully.

When at last he sheathed himself inside her, he kissed her on the sensitive spot behind her ear. "Are you all right?" he asked quietly.

The question nearly undid her. She kissed him, a soft touch she leaned into before sliding her tongue between his lips to tangle with his. Simultaneously, she moved her hips against him, wordlessly asking him to finish what he'd started.

She didn't have to ask twice.

He took his time, an easy loving of long slow strokes, their bodies finding a rhythm she thought might slowly drive her insane. With every stroke, Rowan reached deeply inside her, making her want to give and receive pleasure, so much pleasure she wondered if she would die of it.

"Rowan! Oh! This is so … so good. I can't …"

"I know, Pixie-girl. So incredibly good," he groaned into her shoulder.

Steadily, he increased the rhythm, and she came undone as he drove into her hard and deep while her inner muscles convulsed around him.

"It's never been like this for me before. I feel like I'm floating." Alyssa panted. She noticed how hard he still was inside her, and her face clouded over.

"No, Alyssa. Don't go there. I'm letting you rest for a minute."

"What do you mean?"

In answer, he shifted up onto his knees and positioned her feet on his shoulders, changing the angle as he hit a spot inside her no one had ever touched before. She cried out as she started coming again almost immediately. He smiled at her and kept pumping as she screamed her pleasure. As he thrust into her hard, she gripped the tops of his thighs and tried to hang on, but when he came with her name on his lips, she was soaring to a place she'd never been before.

When at last their breathing evened out, Rowan thought, *so this is what it means to mate with one's talisman. This is why sexually voracious warriors suddenly settle down when they meet their fated women. How could any man go back to earth after visiting heaven?*

He remained buried inside Alyssa for several minutes, trying to absorb what had happened between them. When he tried to roll away from her, she tightened her arms and legs around him, holding him to her. Finally, he rolled all the way over, settling her on top of him without breaking their intimate connection. Slowly, she stopped pulsing around him, at last rolling off him to lie quietly at his side, his arm protectively wrapped around her.

"What just happened?" she asked.

"I sealed us together for eternity."

"That's a bit melodramatic, I think. But I had no idea that kind of sex even existed."

"That was only our first time together. Wait till we've practiced more."

"I'm not sure I'll survive the *practice*, but I'm game to try," she said, smiling before a yawn caught her, and she dropped into sleep. Rowan kissed her hair and savored the feel of her body wrapped around him. Whether or not she was ready to know it, Alyssa Macaulay was the gods' perfect choice for him.

CHAPTER SEVEN

HEN ALYSSA AWOKE the next morning, she reveled in the delicious sensation of feeling warm and safe... until she realized Rowan was spooning her. Her eyes widened, her breath caught, and she tensed all over. Carefully, she slipped out of his arms and out of bed and padded into the adjoining bathroom. As she washed her face and brushed her teeth, she tried to puzzle out what such an amazingly gorgeous man was doing with her. She still had no answers when she exited the bathroom in her favorite terrycloth robe and found him awake, his aquamarine eyes staring at her with a force that both frightened and excited her. Somehow, he'd made her want nothing more than to be with him. Somehow, he'd made her break every one of her safety rules, and she had to get herself—and the situation—back under control.

"Why are you still here? I thought it was politic with a one-night stand for the guy to sneak out sometime before dawn, maybe leave a little note about how he enjoyed the evening and a faint promise of getting together again. But it's broad daylight, and you're still in my bed," she said, crossing her arms over her chest.

"Whatever gave you the notion that last night was the

beginning—and the end—of our relationship? Lose the robe and come back to bed," Rowan growled.

He seemed angry with her, and she couldn't understand why. "You know, I broke every rule I ever had for myself. No sex with strangers, no sex on a first date, no man in my house until several weeks into a relationship. I broke them all with you last night. What was I thinking?" The last bit she directed to herself.

"Whether or not you want to admit it, we're not strangers even though we met formally for the first time the day before yesterday. There *is* a relationship here, and neither one of us is going anywhere. So again, lose the robe and come back to bed," he commanded.

She hesitated. When he saw her in the harsh light of day, he'd likely reject her. Bill Forbes had found all sorts of issues with her body. Now Rowan wanted to see what he really had. The idea was terrifying. He was probably remembering the woman from last night. And darkness hid all imperfections.

He cocked a brow and blew out a rather impatient-sounding breath. Taking her cue with ill grace, she jerked the sash loose, slowly placed her hand on the lapels, and opened the robe enough to let it drop to the floor. For a few seconds, she stood motionless, trying to stop the blush starting mid-chest before it raced up her neck to heat her face. His eyes roamed her features before roving down the length of her to her feet and back. "Turn around—slowly," he demanded, then almost as an afterthought, "please."

"Are you going to look inside my mouth next and determine my soundness from the condition of my teeth?" she asked, raising a brow. She felt like a prize horse—or maybe she should have thought draft horse—that he was considering buying.

When she faced him again, he looked steadily into her eyes as he slowly pulled aside the covers to reveal his enormous erection. "You are so beautiful. Now come back to bed," he whispered.

A flash of desire overwhelmed her at the sight of his ready body and the husky timbre of his voice. She slipped into bed beside him, needing to touch him. Her fingertips toured his shoulder, traced the well-defined muscles of his arm, slid back up to his chest and down the washboard of his abs before hesitating at his cock. It amazed her something so large fit so perfectly inside her. Tentatively, she feathered her fingers along his shaft before wrapping her hand around him to stroke his length.

"See. All passion and excitement. God, I'm a lucky man."

Alyssa looked up to see Rowan grinning at her before he took her mouth in a soul-searing kiss as he rolled on top of her. Turning the tables, he explored her, his fingers plucking at a ripe nipple, his palms gliding along the curve of her waist and over her hip before he tangled his fingers in the curls guarding her sex. She shifted her hips while she wrapped her arms around his shoulders to hold herself steady as he kissed her senseless and slid one long finger inside her.

Tearing his mouth from hers, he panted. "Alyssa, Jesus, you're so ready for me. And I can't wait either."

She opened for him eagerly, and this time he didn't go slow. They were both too desperate for his smooth deep plunge into her hot, wet channel. Whimpers sounded from the back of her throat as she met his thrust with her hips, pulling him as far inside her as she could before she lost herself in the power of their lovemaking.

Several rounds later when they were spent, their hearts hammering in their chests, Rowan tried to roll off Alyssa. Though he worked out daily, training for the attacks he could never anticipate but always knew were coming, his quivering arms proved he couldn't hold himself up any longer. When he tried to pull away, she protested. "Rowan, please don't go. I like you inside me like this," and she tightened herself around him—arms, legs, inner muscles.

"I hate to admit this, but my arms need a break. But don't you let go." He chuckled and rolled her over on top of him without breaking their connection. Sighing contentedly on top of his chest, she relaxed into sleep with him still inside her.

Stroking his hands along her back and over the sweet globes of her ass, he stared up at her ceiling and noticed the swirls of deep blue paint over the lighter blue background. As he squinted in the faint light in the room, he made out intricate Celtic eternity knot designs painted directly over her bed. Smiling at yet another sign he'd found his perfect mate, he closed his eyes and drifted to sleep.

An hour later, they awoke to the sounds of their growling bellies. Laughing, he suggested brunch, and they headed into the shower where they discovered another hunger needing to be assuaged immediately.

"We can do this standing up?" Alyssa asked dubiously as she eyed his engorged cock.

"Oh yeah, Pixie-girl. Let me show you," he said with a smile as he slid his hand down the back of her thigh and pulled her leg up over his hip, anchoring her there. He cupped her ass with his hands and pushed himself into her. Jesus, he'd never felt anything as heavenly as Alyssa's body grasping his as he began to move inside her.

The shower-head behind him sprayed warm water over them, the water compounding their sexy experience as it slid over their bodies as they came together yet again. Knowing it wasn't ethical, Rowan still sneaked a listen into Alyssa's thoughts.

This is what people do on honeymoons flitted through her mind.

Rowan heard her and grinned in agreement before he kissed her deeply, taking her cries of ecstasy inside him.

CHAPTER EIGHT

SHADOW STARED BALEFULLY at Alyssa when she and Rowan finally entered the kitchen for brunch. Automatically, Rowan called to the dog as he went out to the porch to collect firewood. As she gathered eggs and vegetables from the fridge for omelets, she tried to ignore the sense of dread hovering at the edge of her consciousness. Whatever was happening between Rowan and her was happening at the speed of light, so when it inevitably crashed around her, she feared it would crash with a spectacular explosion.

After what he showed her both last night and this morning, she knew she was in way over her head. Added to the unbelievable physical pleasure was the strange coincidence of her latest bookmark creation: the thread's color matched Rowan's eyes, and the pattern replicated the Celtic cross necklace he wore and apparently never removed—he left it on after they got naked and even when they showered. Plus, there were currents of understanding between them. It seemed they could almost read each other's thoughts, which both disturbed and calmed her. Though she'd known this man less than two days, she was as comfortable with him as if they were an old married couple.

Proof manifested in the cozy domesticity of Rowan taking care of her dog and the fire while she routinely cooked breakfast, an easy division of tasks without consultation. She didn't know if the man even liked omelets, yet it hadn't occurred to her to ask before she began cracking eggs into a bowl. No doubt, she was setting herself up for a big fall, and she needed to get a grip fast.

When he finished rebuilding the fire, he stepped out into the laundry room to feed Shadow. As her dog ate his breakfast, she heard Rowan quietly quizzing Shadow about his mistress, solidifying his relationship with her pet. She couldn't decide how she felt about that growing relationship either.

Rowan returned to the kitchen with Shadow padding behind him. Staring distractedly out the window, she relaxed when Rowan slipped his arms around her waist and nosed her hair away from her neck to kiss her. He tightened his hold and kept single-mindedly to his purpose until she covered his hands with hers.

"It put down a ton of snow last night. Some of the drifts around the house must be two feet deep," she observed.

"Mmm, yeah. Shadow had to jump through them to reach the back of the yard. He didn't seem to mind though." Rowan inhaled deeply. "What's for breakfast? It smells delicious. So do you." He gave her an open-mouthed kiss on her neck for emphasis, and she shivered with pleasure.

"Vegetable omelets and wheat toast. I didn't have any breakfast meat. Sorry."

She held her breath for the criticism of her lack of kitchen staples, something she came to expect from Bill. Instead, Rowan turned to Shadow and said, "Bummer for you, buddy. You get dry dog food while I enjoy a gourmet feast. I think she likes me better." He grinned at her and stepped around the island to seat himself for brunch.

They ate in companionable silence after which he stunned her again by drying the dishes as she washed them. There were no companionable silences with Bill, and domestic duties like doing dishes were beneath him. In every way, Rowan was so different from what she expected.

"How 'bout we go back to town for supplies? I could use a change of underwear and socks," he suggested.

"You want me to ride into town with you? Why?"

"Because I'm enjoying being with you, and I thought you could help me pick up something exotic you'd like me to make you for dinner."

Alyssa heard the concern in his voice and wondered why he was pushing so hard to stay with her. Yet the idea of him leaving left the pit of her stomach hollow.

"You do dishes and cook? You rebuild the fire without being asked and are kind to animals? You must be out of a fairytale," she teased.

"More like a Celtic myth," he said with a grin.

"Oh no, I've never read where the great heroes dried their own dishes or went home for clean underwear the next morning."

Rowan gave her an unreadable look before he snapped the towel playfully at her backside. "Put on your coat and boots, Pixie-girl. I'll take care of the fire and Shadow."

For some reason she didn't want to examine too carefully, she didn't want to be away from him. If he wanted her to go to town with him, she'd go. Besides, she might discover more about him if she saw where and how he lived.

Grabbing her boots out of the closet, she pulled them on over her skinny jeans. She'd opted for a knobby knit sweater the color of heather, one of her few items of clothing she owned that wasn't some shade of black. When she reached for her coat, she noticed Rowan had hung his next to hers in the closet as though he knew the outcome of the evening when he walked in the door last night. Perhaps, she should have been worried or offended, but she wasn't.

When he came up behind her and reached around her for his jacket, she jumped. "How does a big man like you do that?" she squeaked.

"Do what?" A mischievous smirk played over his face.

"Move so quietly. You're like a cat, all stealthy and quick. I heard you bring Shadow into the house only a second ago."

"You're very observant except when you're lost in thought. It's easy to sneak up on you when you're thinking."

⋘

They locked up the house and walked over to Rowan's truck nearly buried under the night's accumulation of snow. Alyssa walked into her garage and emerged with a broom to help him clear the snow from his SUV. He took his time negotiating the road out of her place, more because he was memorizing the terrain than because he needed to be cautious in the snow. The road hadn't been plowed, but there were no other vehicle tracks on it, which puzzled him. How did the person sneaking around Alyssa's house last night arrive there without leaving tracks on the road?

"It just occurred to me you needed a ride last night. How did you get into town yesterday?"

"My neighbor and I carpool, and yesterday was his turn to drive. Since I was meeting Ceri after my study group, I told him not to worry about taking me home."

"You have a vehicle that's serviceable in these conditions?"

Alyssa pulled a face at him. "I've lived in that house since I was eighteen, and the county never gets around to plowing the road until we've pretty well packed it down ourselves." She grinned. "My SUV isn't as beefy as yours, but I don't have any trouble navigating this road. Sometimes, I even like to challenge it by busting through the drifts that build up on the side."

Rowan gave her a look that no doubt told her how implausible he found her remark, and she laughed.

"I realize I'm a bit tightly wound, but every now and again I like to do something most people would consider a little crazy. Driving fast cars or spinning my SUV through snowdrifts is fun."

"I'll try to keep that in mind before I make a foolish request like asking you to drive my truck," he said dryly.

The canyon road was freshly plowed, but the snow coming down indicated their trip to town would need to be as quick as possible. If anything, the weather was progressively worsening. He drove directly to the apartment he shared with Seamus and invited Alyssa inside.

"Make yourself at home while I gather up some underwear and a clean shirt or two. I think there's OJ in the fridge if you're thirsty," he called as he headed to his bedroom down the hall.

The Spartan interior of Rowan and Seamus's apartment confused Alyssa. The place looked more like a crash pad than a home. A sinking feeling pulled at her gut. Maybe these guys kept the apartment as a last resort when they couldn't pick up women to take them home. The living room had two mismatched chairs that had seen a lot of seat time. Probably they came from a second-hand shop. On a TV tray between them rested the remote for the big-screen TV, gaming system, and the state-of-the-art stereo taking up the opposite wall of the room. No other furniture or photos or paintings suggested anyone lived there at all.

She shivered at the emptiness of the kitchen. In the fridge, she found the orange juice, a carton of eggs, a loaf of bread, an open bag of ready-made salad, half a brick of cheddar cheese, and a twelve-pack of beer. Apparently, the two of them didn't eat in much.

She wandered down the hall and peeked into what must have been Seamus's bedroom where she saw a queen bed and a three-drawer bureau. Again, the amazingly clean room didn't feel lived in at all. Her imagination told her she'd find relatively the same décor in Rowan's room. Interrupting her thoughts, the man reappeared in the hall, carrying a stuffed duffel bag that looked like it might contain all his clothes and a backpack loaded with who-knew-what.

"I thought you said you were stopping by for a change of

underwear, but it looks like you're thinking about moving in," Alyssa said. She tried to cover the hint of nerves quivering in her voice with a half-hearted laugh.

Rowan shrugged. "I threw in a couple sweaters. With the way this storm is shaping up, I might need them. It never hurts to be over-prepared."

Something in his tone made her uneasy, but she didn't have time to think about it as he hustled her out the door and back to his SUV.

"Next stop, groceries. That omelet you made today was the best I've had in a long time, so we definitely need more eggs, spinach, and tomatoes along with one or two additional items for dinner." His patter almost kept her attention away from the loaded duffel bag and back pack he stowed in the rear of his SUV.

At the grocery store, Rowan loaded a shopping cart as if the two of them might be stranded at her place for a month, which with the way the storm was building, could be close to the truth. Then he picked up two bottles of the white wine she'd been drinking when they met at the Under-Cover Lounge and a case of imported beer.

"You have some plans for throwing a party with those supplies you're buying?"

"Maybe."

Instead of elaborating, he pushed the cart to the checkout, giving her no choice but to follow him.

After paying for the groceries and leaving the store, he made one more stop at his office, emerging with a large box and another backpack. "I thought since I was already at your place, I could install your system."

Alyssa lifted a brow, and Rowan talked faster. "I know you have an aversion to mixing business with pleasure, but with the way it's snowing, I might need something to do when you're resting." He waggled his eyebrows at her, making her laugh.

How odd to be getting what she'd come to him for nearly as quickly as she'd desired it. Yet unease niggled at her. Did he know something she didn't? His urgency for her safety seemed even greater than her own despite his attempt at levity.

The poor visibility caused by the storm resulted in the ride back to her place taking more time than the ride to town. Rowan's need to stay focused on the road and avoid obstacles meant no conversation. The radio warned the ski hill was closed due to the dangerous conditions of the canyon road, and a winter storm warning urged people to stay in their homes.

When they turned onto the spur road leading back to Alyssa's home, the snow had obliterated their tracks in the two hours since they'd driven to town. Instead of being energized by the fresh powder snow as she usually was, Alyssa feared the drive. Riding with a competent driver in a much bigger vehicle than she regularly drove, she still experienced an urgency to be back in her house immediately, or maybe two hours ago. She sensed something evil stalking her. The tension rolling off Rowan only increased her fear.

CHAPTER NINE

HILE ALYSSA LET Shadow outside and put away the groceries, Rowan busied himself with moving into her home. Discovering the bottom drawer of her dresser empty, he filled it with his underwear and T-shirts. He pushed her clothes away from one side of her closet and hung up his shirts and jeans. His hiking boots were already in their proper place on the rug in the foyer, and he put his tennis shoes on the floor of Alyssa's closet.

Grabbing his backpack, he left the master bedroom to check out the second bedroom in Alyssa's house, which she'd converted into a kind of home gym-music room. A treadmill, a small rack of free weights, and an exercise mat took up one side of it. Mounted on the wall behind the equipment were floor-to-ceiling mirrors for monitoring form as she lifted. On the opposite wall, a picture window looked out on her back yard and the mountains beyond. In front of the window, she had positioned a baby grand piano, obviously so she could take full advantage of the natural light as she played. The odd combination revealed how she relaxed and how she worked off tension. He smiled. Her methods mirrored his own: lifting and playing music to blow off steam.

Across the hall, he discovered a tiny

bedroom she'd converted into an office. Above a futon hung a tapestry depicting Brighid, Rhiannon, and Scathach, the three most important Celtic goddesses from Ireland, Wales, and Scotland, representing human potential, fertility, and war, the three great motivators of human beings. The wall directly in front of him supported a window austerely covered with ivory blinds, and to his right sat an antique roll top desk with a black leather office chair tucked neatly beneath it.

Every room in Alyssa's house demonstrated her powerful connection to the warrior community—even if she had no idea about it.

Rowan found the wireless modem for her internet on a low table between the desk and the window. Pulling his computer out of his backpack, he powered up and prepared to log on to email to check his messages. When he couldn't make a connection, he checked the modem to see if it was functional, and finding it was, he retried his connection. A huge gust of wind screamed down the canyon, angrily swirling snow outside the window, and he knew the problem.

To confirm, he took his cell out of his pocket and checked for service. When he didn't have any, he turned off the device and tossed it into his backpack. He'd test Alyssa's landline, but he already knew what he'd find. Taranis, the god of thunder, had sent the storm to cut off normal human communication. Rowan had a bad feeling the mountains would impede his telepathy with his parents, brothers, and Seamus as well.

Obviously, the gods were aware he'd located his talisman, and they'd waste no time testing his and Alyssa's connection, trying to break it before it solidified. His father had warned him this would happen and had given him advice about how to deal with it. So far, Alyssa showed intelligence and strength but a terrible lack of confidence and trust, which, coupled with her deficient knowledge and training as a talisman, was going to be his Achilles heel if he didn't take steps to remedy it fast. The truth was probably a good place to start.

❧

When he returned to the great room, he discovered Alyssa in the kitchen making sandwiches from the deli meat, lettuce, tomatoes, and wheat bread he'd bought. The rich aroma of coffee filled the air and his stomach rumbled loudly. Though it hadn't been long since his last meal, he'd burned quite a few calories during the night and early morning, so brunch had been nothing more than a snack.

He noted immediately she was in another mood—amazing how quickly he was learning to read her—so he decided to preempt it. "That's a beautiful instrument you've hidden away in the spare bedroom. Why don't you keep it out here?"

"The dry heat from the woodstove is bad for it." She shrugged. "Besides, a piano bench isn't all that comfortable a seat for reading a book. If the piano were out here, the rest of the furniture would have to be in the bedroom."

"If you don't mind my asking, how does a grad student afford this sweet little house and a baby grand piano?"

She waggled her brows. "I have secret ties to the mafia. It's why I was thinking about that home security system."

"You're a feisty little thing, aren't you?" He smirked. "Fortunately for you, I happen to know some guys who are home security whizzes. I'll see if they can help you out."

She knit her brows. "You drum up business by picking up women in bars and sleeping with them?"

"Now you're being insulting." He leaned against the counter and crossed his arms over his chest. "To be honest, between Shadow and me, you have all the security you need."

She stopped assembling sandwiches and faced him. "That sounds suspiciously like you've decided to move in or something. You're so attractive, you make me forget to think, but thinking was the one skill Gram insisted I perfect." She blew out a breath. "We've known each other for forty-eight hours, and you're talking like we have an endless future together. It makes me nervous."

"I'm nervous too because I want us to have that future, but if we don't learn some things about each other and work out some details, our future is going to be decidedly short. Where are the plates?"

Frowning at his abrupt change in subject, she nodded toward a cupboard by the sink, and he pulled out two plates and coffee mugs.

As he set the dinnerware on the island, he continued. "Some very powerful deities are flexing their muscles right now, and I have a feeling before the weekend is over, they're going to let us know what they think of the two of us finding each other."

"Are we back to that warrior and talisman line you used to get me to open my door to you?"

"That wasn't a line, and yes we are back to that. Something I can explain to you better on a full stomach." He stared at the plate of sandwiches. Wordlessly, she set the sandwiches on the island, shook some chips into a bowl, and poured coffee before seating herself.

Somehow, he needed to make her believe he wasn't using her—and he wasn't leaving her.

"I wasn't completely honest with you last night."

Her face paled, and he hurried to reassure her. "My interest in the Celts isn't casual or slight. Though I do have a business degree, I could have easily acquired a master's in Celtic culture and mythology since my parents made my brothers and me study it more than we studied anything we learned in school." He arranged his food on his plate. "My mom started telling us the myths and legends while we were still in the womb. Celtic lore is as much a part of me as my hair color or the size of my feet."

He took a big bite of his sandwich, chewed, swallowed, and continued. "When I met you, your interest in the Celts intrigued me. The Celtic designs you create suggest your deep connection to our culture, whether or not you're aware of it."

A raven brow arched above her eye, but she remained silent.

"As you've probably discovered in your studies, the Celts connect with the spirit world through art, and without a doubt, your needlework shows your connection."

Alyssa smiled at the compliment. Rowan smiled back. "Your art gave me hope because when Seamus and I walked into that bar last night, I had all but given up on finding my talisman. Which would have meant a short, bleak life either of trying to outrun the supernatural forces of evil or joining them."

He swallowed down some coffee and waited.

"This all sounds like something out of the myths or a fantasy novel. What are you trying to say?"

"There is a race of warriors descended from the great Celtic heroes. I'm a member of that race. So are you." He paused to let that sink in.

"Uh-huh. Pull my other leg."

Ignoring her skepticism, he said, "The female descendants tend to be talismans, women with special abilities who can protect warriors in various ways. Some talismans are seers, some are bards whose wisdom protects warriors with stories of those who have gone before. Some are prophets who can predict the future in ways that help the warriors know what to do to combat the forces of evil before they confront them." He smoothed her frown with his finger. "Some are dreamers who can warn their warriors how to avoid danger in real time." Returning his attention to finishing his meal, he added, "There are also male and female druids among us."

She rose and started clearing their lunch. "Are the warriors and talismans part of some reenactment group like you see at a Renaissance Faire or something?"

He joined her, rinsing dishes and filling the dishwasher. "No, Alyssa. We're actively engaged in the battle against evil waged since the dawn of time," he patiently explained.

"What sort of evil do you confront?"

"These days it's gangs, random acts of violence, drug runners, war." He refilled his mug and walked over to the leather chair in the living room.

"But you're a home security specialist, or at least that's what all your literature says. You have an office and everything." Her breathless delivery revealed her panic.

"The job pays the bills and serves as a cover so I can leave at a moment's notice when I need to. It's also a real-time deterrent for bad guys who want to cause violence to innocent civilians." He blew on his coffee, sipped, and added, "In one way or another, my family has been involved in the security business for centuries."

Joining him in the great room, she curled up on the love seat. "Are you an undercover special ops or part of the police force or something?"

"No. Warriors fight rogue warriors Morgan disguises as drug dealers, gang leaders, warlords, gun runners—you get the picture." He settled himself more comfortably in the chair. "The special ops forces, drug agents, peacekeepers, police—they're the civilians who sometimes accidentally discover rogue warriors or who come in to clean up the mess when warriors have finished off the rogues and left behind their civilian counterparts."

She tilted her head. "Are you implying there's a supernatural war going on at the same time as human conflict, one that actually involves humans?"

"That's exactly what's going on."

"And this supernatural battle is being waged with human foot soldiers too?"

"Yes."

"Please don't take this the wrong way, but I think you might be delusional." For a beat, she stared at him over the rim of her cup before sipping her coffee.

Rowan grinned. "Remember how surprised you were at my speed and stealth earlier this afternoon?"

"You are quick for a man your size."

She squeaked when she realized he stood immediately behind her. "How did you do that? You were sitting over there in the chair a second ago, and now you're standing behind me?"

"Warriors can bend time and space, and when we do, we can move through it at will. I left our conversation midway through it and visualized myself behind you. By the time you finished your sentence, I was standing here."

He casually walked around the love seat and resituated himself in the chair after utterly rending her understanding of physics.

Alyssa stared wide-eyed at him. "You're not a real human? You're more like a god?"

That explains the sex. Can't imagine what he sees in me.

Rowan shook his head as he heard Alyssa's unguarded thoughts. It wasn't time yet to tell her about all of his abilities. "I'm not a god, but I have certain capabilities that make me more than human. Time and space manipulation and strength and skill in battle for example. Unlike a god, I can die; unlike regular humans, we know them as *civilians*, I can avoid death in violent situations like battle when my opponent is a civilian. When I'm battling another warrior, the playing field is more level."

"If warriors are descended from ancient Celtic heroes, why are there rogue warriors? How does that happen?"

Rowan appreciated the ease with which Alyssa moved from disbelief to attempts at understanding. The quality of her questions also impressed him. *She's going to be an incredible force when properly trained.*

"Long ago, Morgan—you know her as the Morrigan—only battled warriors for warriors. She stole men to assuage her blood-lust. Her sister Maeve took a fancy to one of my ancestors, Findlay Sheridan, and when he wouldn't leave his wife for the goddess, she enlisted her sister goddess to exact revenge. Morgan instigated a battle, distracted Findlay and his sons, and took Findlay's wife Ailsa across the river of blood into the mists."

Alyssa visibly started at the mention of Ailsa, a reaction he wondered about, but he continued the tale.

"Ailsa had seen the battle and all the blood in a dream and begged Findlay not to fight, but he wouldn't listen. He hated the Morrigan and determined to defeat her. Instead, he lost his wife—his talisman—and in that moment, he lost his will to live."

She sat forward, her eyes sad. "How terrible."

He nodded. "However, Morgan wasn't finished with him. She wanted more blood and insisted Maeve give her something in return for the revenge on Findlay. Between them, they designed a system requiring a warrior to find his talisman by midnight of his twenty-eighth birthday or be relegated to becoming a champion for Morgan or a fugitive who couldn't call for help from his family or friends. They tricked our father god the Dagda into allowing this outrage, and the first victim was Findlay's son Graeme, who was three days shy of his twenty-eighth birthday at the time of the battle."

Alyssa cocked her head, her facial expression telling Rowan how hard she worked to follow him.

"It wasn't enough time to find his talisman, and he died on the run within a month of the battle because he wouldn't join Morgan nor would he warm Maeve's bed and die a coward. Findlay and his younger sons stood at the ford of the river of death and watched as Morgan led Graeme into the mists."

Rowan rolled his mug between his palms. "Not long after that, Findlay died a broken man. It appeared Morgan had won, but Findlay and Ailsa's twin sons, Riordan and Owen, survived both the battle and the new rules to the game. They found their talismans and started a line of warriors who have battled Morgan and Maeve to this day."

Alyssa studied him. "And you're a part of that line?"

"Yes."

"The rogue warriors are those who didn't find their talismans in time?"

"Some, yes. There are others who have voluntarily joined Morgan and Maeve on the promise of power and wealth."

"That's horrible."

He shrugged. "Even some warriors are corruptible."

"Several times you've referred to me as your talisman. If I am your talisman, what is the ability I have that helps you? I can't do anything special," she said, her lovely mouth turning down.

"I noticed right away you're intensely observant. It makes me wonder if you're a prophet or a dreamer. Both of those types of talismans possess incredible skills of observation. They see things their warrior misses or see things in time to warn him."

"How does a talisman go about discovering what ability she has?"

"It's a process. Unfortunately for us, we don't have much time to discover what your ability is."

She set her empty mug on the coffee table and crossed her arms. "Why not?"

"The storm we're experiencing isn't a normal storm."

She laughed hollowly. "That's obvious. I can't remember such blizzard-like conditions, especially in March. But what does the storm have to do with talismans and warriors in general and us in particular? I bet not even you can control the weather, no matter how much space and time you 'visualize'," she said, using air quotes.

"Put away your cynicism, Alyssa. This storm is absolutely about us. Taranis, the god of thunder and storms, is Morgan's staunch ally. He sought to stop our meeting and then our mating. Too bad he chose snow. It keeps us snuggled in together." He smiled at the blush climbing her cheeks.

"Please, don't insult me. The weather has absolutely nothing to do with people. We're arrogant enough to think we can control it by seeding clouds or flying planes into the eyes of hurricanes, and though those things might make us feel like we're mastering the world, it's an illusion. We're at the mercy of the elements."

"Taranis might let up a little as a reward for your understanding.

But that doesn't change the fact he's directing a storm in an attempt to prevent the mating of a warrior and his talisman, especially a Sheridan who Morgan thought she had because I'm less than three months from my twenty-eighth birthday. Until yesterday evening, I was afraid she was going to acquire her prize." He leaned forward and ran his palm over her knee. "Then I spent time with you and realized I'm saved. Taranis must have caught on at the same time because that's when the storm really kicked in."

"Rowan, the weather is not about people of any kind, warriors or civilians," she said as though explaining a difficult concept to a child.

"Is that so? Explain to me the vagaries of a tornado touching down on top of one house, destroying it while leaving the neighboring house intact right down to the flowers standing in the front yard."

"That's—"

He talked over her. "Or the unexpected tsunami that kills thousands in Indonesia on a bright sunny day while the expected one in Hawaii doesn't even raise waves the tourists would ride."

"But—"

"How 'bout the ninety-mile-an-hour wind in Wyoming that bends a few trees and annoys the locals relocated to Florida where it's a class two hurricane wreaking havoc and causing millions of dollars in damage?"

"Yes, but—"

He stood and paced in front of the woodstove. "Science can explain patterns, barometric pressure, the physics of an earthquake, but not the constant vagaries of earth and sky. Deep in the Celtic soul, the collective unconscious of all Celtic peoples, we know the old gods are still at work healing and destroying as they will whether we admit it or not. You, a Celtic scholar, should know that."

"I—"

He ran his hands through his hair and faced her. "There's also the matter of the tracks I found this morning in the snow around your house. Those tracks were deep and fresh, yet they only ring your house. They appear and disappear into each other. There were no tracks leading up to or away from your house, and there were no tracks on the road."

"But our tracks on the road were obliterated after only two hours this afternoon."

"You're right, but the tracks I saw were fresh, and we left the house not long after I discovered them, so if the entity making those tracks were human, there should have been tracks leading to and away from the house." Rowan stared at her meaningfully. "There aren't any."

"You're saying Taranis walks around on the ground then disappears into thin air or something?"

"I'm saying that the same as in ancient times, the gods can and often do take on human form when it suits them. Maeve especially likes to appear human because it makes it easier for her to appease her voracious sexual appetite with civilians and rogue warriors alike." He sat back in his chair. "Taranis has apparently taken an interest in you, and that's why the tracks are limited to the area immediately around your house. What I don't understand is why he hasn't attempted to enter your house."

"Whoever has been prowling around my house has tried several times to enter it, but I keep the windows and doors securely locked, and Shadow emits a formidable bark when he's guarding me." At the mention of his name, Shadow, lying on the rug between the coffee table and book shelves, cocked his ears. "Each time I've heard the noises outside, he's gone directly to the window or door being disturbed and warned off the intruder. A god wouldn't be afraid of a dog, even a Great Pyrenees, and mere window and door locks couldn't keep out a supernatural being," she pointed out.

"You said Shadow chose you. Tell me about that."

Alyssa looked puzzled but said, "When I was eighteen, I inherited control of the trust fund Gram set up after my parents died. I decided to stay close to Gram and go to college here, but I wanted my own place, so I took the money and bought this house."

She glanced around the room, a small smile tugging at her lips.

"Though Gram supported my decision to live on my own, she thought it would be a good idea if I had a dog for companionship and protection." She gazed fondly at her pet. "Gram insisted the dog be white and large, so she found a Great Pyrenees breeder and took me to meet him. Shadow tumbled over himself to reach me the minute I walked into the yard to check out the puppies." Stretching out her leg, she ran her foot over her dog's fur. "He was so adorable with his fluffy baby fur and oversized paws. I couldn't resist him, and Gram seemed especially pleased. He came home with me that day and has been my protector ever since."

As Alyssa told him Shadow's story, Rowan stilled. "Will you tell me about your grandmother?"

"What do you want to know?" she asked, warily.

Everything.

"Was she your paternal or maternal grandmother?"

"Maternal. She lived down the street from my parents and me when I was tiny when we lived in Colorado. After my parents died, she moved us up here and raised me. She was the wisest, kindest woman I will ever know." The drop in Alyssa's voice as she described her grandmother spoke volumes about her pain at her grandmother's death.

"If it's not too intrusive, can you tell me about when she died?" he asked gently, trying to rein in his intense need to know.

"Thinking about her death will always be painful. She was the most important person in the world to me." Alyssa stared into the middle distance for several minutes. Right when he thought he'd have to do without some vital information, she continued.

"She died of a heart attack on the summer solstice last year. Sudden and unexpected, but I discovered when I went through some of her papers about a month after her funeral that she was a lot older than I thought. What seemed a surprise at the time wouldn't have been if I'd had more information."

Rowan processed the information. *Alyssa's grandmother died on the summer solstice exactly one year from my fatal day. She must have been a druid who understood how to erect barriers against the gods, which explains the white dog and Taranis's inability to attack Alyssa once she's inside her home. It also explains how Alyssa has remained hidden and undisturbed by the gods.*

"Thank you. That helps a lot. I have one more personal question. How old are you, and when is your birthday?"

"That's two personal questions," she replied with a smile.

"They're related."

"And you'll tell me why all this is so important?"

"Deal."

"I was twenty-four on October thirty-first. Halloween, All Hallows Eve, *Samhain*, the day all the worlds are open to each other. The one day of the year that always ended in a fight with Gram that I always lost." A pout turned down her lips at her memories. "I wanted to trick or treat with the other kids so much, but Gram absolutely forbade it. She said the spirits from the other worlds would be watching for me, and I had to remain hidden."

"She was right."

Alyssa stared at him wide-eyed. "When I was nineteen, I went out for the first time on Halloween since I was no longer living with Gram. The evening started out fun but turned into a nightmare."

He cocked a brow and waited.

"My friends and I attended a party at a fraternity where everyone was wasted. Some guy who wandered into the party tried to drag me out to his car. I screamed, and some of the frat guys came to my rescue. I later found out no one had ever seen him before."

He flexed his fists but remained silent.

"It caused a huge scene, and I wanted to go home immediately, but Ceri wouldn't let me. She said the guy would probably follow us to where we couldn't be rescued, so we spent most of the night at the frat house. After that, I've never gone out on my birthday."

"My birthday is the summer solstice, one of the three most important days of the Celtic calendar. Your birthday is Samhain, the first day of the year in the Celtic calendar. When was your grandmother's birthday?"

"February first. *Imbolc*. Her patron saint was Brighid, and she always wore a Saint Brighid's cross." Pointing down the hall, she said, "She made the Saint Brighid's cross tapestry in the hallway. In fact, she made all the tapestries hanging in here and some I have in storage. I trade them around from season to season except for that one. It comforts me too much to store it away."

"Did your grandmother like your old boyfriend?"

"You ask the most random and personal questions. You said you'd tell me why my birth date was important," Alyssa countered.

"Answer me. It's important," he said.

At her wide-eyed stare, he added, "Please."

"As a matter of fact, she didn't. It was the only other thing we fought about. Guess she was right about him too." She set her coffee mug on the table beside her and crossed her arms over her chest.

"Your grandmother left you clues about yourself and your destiny, but until you met your warrior, she wouldn't tell you everything. Have you gone through all her papers?"

"No. She had a box of journals I've been saving until I finish my master's degree."

"I think you're going to need to look at those journals before this storm is over."

Narrowing her eyes, she said, "You say you're a security expert, you say you're a supernatural warrior, so why would you have any interest in some obscure old woman's journals?"

"I realize trust is an issue for you, but you're going to have to learn to trust me, and you don't have much time to do that," he replied leaning forward.

"In case no one has ever enlightened you, one can't demand

another's trust. He must earn it." Abruptly, she stood and took her coffee cup to the sink to wash it.

Rowan sighed. "Yeah, I know. I also have a clue about what's in store for us if we aren't a united pair when Morgan finds proof I'm no longer available as a potential champion, and Maeve discovers I won't ever be her lover."

CHAPTER TEN

HE ENTIRE CONVERSATION disturbed Alyssa on so many levels. She needed time to figure it out, so she headed down the hall to change into her workout gear for a run on her treadmill. Upon opening her closet, she came across Rowan's clothes hung neatly beside hers. On the floor, she saw his tennis shoes. She'd been joking when she said it looked like he was moving in. Apparently, he'd taken that as an invitation. She didn't know what to do, what to feel—fury, fear, anticipation. Squaring her shoulders, she marched up the hall to have it out with him.

Finding him in the kitchen staring out at the storm through the window above the sink, she didn't stop to consider her words. "What the hell are your clothes doing in my closet?"

"They're not all in your closet. Some are in the bottom drawer of your dresser," he replied calmly.

"What were you doing going through the drawers of my dresser? Where do you get off moving into my home without even asking if I wanted you here? We just met. We don't know enough about each other to know if we even like each other let alone if we want to live together."

We like each other fine.

"Did you say something?" she asked.

Rowan arched a brow. "I already told you. We've known each other a long time even though we met formally two days ago. We belong together, which I thought I made clear both last night and this morning." He winked at her.

She opened her mouth and couldn't think what to say. Images of the two of them together flooded her brain, adding to her confusion. Turning on her heel, she marched back down the hallway to her bedroom and slammed the door.

She tore off her clothes and wrenched on her sweats before she stomped into her home gym. After locking the door behind her, she stepped onto her treadmill and didn't bother to warm up before she started running, trying to work her way through everything that had happened to her in the last forty-eight hours.

Thirty minutes of hard exercise later, she still hadn't sorted out her feelings or her understanding of what Rowan had shared with her. What she did know was she was a basket case who couldn't face the man attempting to turn her world inside out. He was so handsome, so compelling. Plus, all the Celtic coincidences and his incredible speed both drew and frightened her. Gram had mentioned something about Alyssa meeting her destiny in the next year, and he would be a warrior, but she thought Gram meant something big would come from her thesis. Gram Afton couldn't have meant a flesh-and-blood man who battled evil regularly, could she?

When exercise didn't help her sort herself, she sat down at her piano and attempted to play out her frustration. The smooth keys responded instantly to her fingers even though she pounded more than played them. Somehow her world had tilted on its axis and was no longer under her control. She could ask Rowan to leave, but if all he said were true, living without him could be a huge, perhaps fatal mistake. Letting him stay would mean she believed everything he told her about the gods, warriors, and talismans. All of what he said was fantastically absurd, wasn't it?

༺

As Rowan stepped through the back door with a load of wood in his arms, he heard faint sounds of a piano. When he investigated, he discovered Alyssa had locked the door to her recreation room.

The locked door irritated him, but he stayed outside it for half an hour listening to her play classical music with skill and passion. When he first put his ear to the door, she was angry, hitting the keys rather than playing them with finesse. The effect vibrated awareness in his chest. He knew that anger, that frustration, that lack of control. His talisman's emotions ran deep and intense. As she continued to play, she seemed to calm down, though the choice of music with so many discords left no doubt she remained upset. When she played an especially drawn out decrescendo, he noted a different sound: she was crying. Deciding she'd had enough time to work things out on her own, he visualized himself into the room.

Her tension told him she sensed him before he reached her, but she didn't stop playing. Tears streamed unchecked down her face. Her blotched cheeks tugged at his heart. Tenderly, wordlessly, he gathered her up, carried her out to the love seat, and sat down with her on his lap. He held her close with one arm while he smoothed away tears with the thumb of his other hand.

"Are you going to tell me about it?" he asked gently.

Alyssa sniffed and visibly tried to calm herself. "I don't know what to do with anything that's happened since Thursday afternoon. It feels like my life has been taken entirely out of my hands. I have no idea who you are, and I've let you into my home, into my bed" *into my heart*—

When he heard that thought, he had to work at reining in his joy at her words.

"I'm not at all myself. The me I know would have walked out of that bar alone last night and called Ceri this morning for details of her evening. This afternoon I would have books scattered from one side of this room to the other as I happily rattled around in my research for my thesis." She dashed the heels of her hands against her eyes. "Instead, I'm a hot mess sitting on the lap of the most handsome man I've ever met, I think I hear you say things that you couldn't possibly be saying, and I'm waiting for the other shoe to drop."

"What other shoe?"

"The one where you say, 'All that talk about warriors and talismans and fighting supernatural forces in parallel time was an elaborate line, and now I need to move on. It was fun while it lasted. See ya around.'"

"Why do you think I'm going anywhere? Wasn't the earlier argument about my nerve putting my socks in your spare dresser drawer? And what do you mean by you hear me say things?" He held his breath and waited.

"That's exactly it. I don't know what your intentions are, or who you are, or how we ended up here together." She closed her eyes. "Forget that last part. I can't imagine what I was thinking when I said that."

He opted to answer the easy questions.

"I'm Rowan Sheridan, and I manage a branch of a home security company for my family. I'm twenty-seven years old, single—until now"—he looked at her meaningfully—"and I find your house much more homey and comfortable than my apartment. Also, I like sharing a bed with a woman as passionate as you are, and while you can't understand it yet, we need each other. How's that for who I am, my intentions, and how we ended up together?" he said, ticking off each item on his fingers.

"Only marginally more enlightening."

He took a chance. "All right then, you're in my heart too."

"*What?*"

"Like I said, we need each other." He distracted her from further conversation, his lips and tongue teasing and tasting the sensitive place behind her ear and enjoying her shiver at his touch.

"Rowan, we need to talk." He could tell she was trying to be firm, but her words came out in a breathy sigh.

"You're right, we do," he replied. "Later."

He kissed her along the pulse beating at her neck while he slid his hand beneath her sweater to explore the smooth skin of her belly. Little tremors danced under his fingertips as she anticipated where he would touch her next. As he worked his slow way up her torso to cup her breast, she turned in his lap and succeeded in filling his hand with her soft flesh. He grinned against her skin and palmed the fullness of her breast before he pleasured her nipple with the pad of his thumb through the lace of her bra.

As he kissed his way up her neck and along her jaw to her mouth, she turned away from him and pushed his hand down and away from her body as she attempted to stand.

"Whoa! What's the problem, Pixie-girl?" Confusion made his voice raw. She'd responded fully to his touch one minute and the next tried to escape him like he'd caught fire.

"Every time you say we're going to talk, you find some way to avoid it. A meal, taking care of Shadow, sex. Rowan, we need to talk."

He sighed and pushed his fingers through his hair.

"I admit I haven't had a lot of experience with men. But even someone with way more experience than I've had would find the speed of whatever is going on between us a bit much."

"You wouldn't if you'd been raised properly in our community." He rolled his shoulders and stared at the ceiling then looked back at her. "Where are your grandmother's papers? I have an idea there's something in them that will help you understand what I'm going to tell you. And I will tell you everything, I promise."

CHAPTER ELEVEN

LYSSA DISAPPEARED INTO her study, emerging a few minutes later carrying a large box. Rowan cleared a space on the coffee table, and she set the box down in front of him. Reverently, she pulled out notebook after notebook and set them on the table, her grandmother's journals, presumably. Though Rowan desperately wanted to confirm his suspicions, he waited with tight patience for an invitation to read with her.

Once she unloaded the box, she set it aside and stared at the notebooks for several minutes. He counted sixteen fat volumes, each hand bound, and one of enormous size that had lined the bottom of the box.

Quietly, she said, "Gram said the smaller volumes contain family history and lore, but I've never seen the large one before. Guess we should start with it." She picked it up, covering her lap with it.

The emotions displayed on her face precluded him from reading her mind. "Alyssa, you're going to have to take a chance and trust me," he said. "On Thursday, you were willing to trust me enough to let me into your home to secure it. Last night and this morning you trusted me with your body, and I didn't break that trust. Today you need to trust me enough to share something that likely concerns both of us."

Instead of replying, she reluctantly opened the book and slid half of it over onto his lap. A note was paper-clipped to the opening page:

Alyssa, if you are reading this, then I have crossed over into the mists to meet your grandfather and your parents. It is my deepest hope that you are not reading this alone. If you are reading this before your warrior has found you, stop. Continuing to read this book alone will undo all the spells I placed on you and your home to keep you safe.

If your warrior has found you, start reading from the end. You'll understand when you get there.

I love you so much.

Gram.

"Gram knew about warriors and talismans. She knew I was a talisman. S-She knew the day when you found me would come."

Alyssa looked away from the note and into his eyes. "I don't understand any of this. How can I be part of something I didn't even know existed before last night?" she whispered.

Gently, he picked up the book and placed it back on the table so he could take Alyssa into his arms. He held her close to his chest as she soaked the front of his shirt with a flood of silent tears.

"You know, I was with Bill for nearly a year, and though he often hurt me emotionally, he never saw me cry. It seems today, that's all you've seen me do." She sniffed as she tried to bring herself under control. "Sorry."

He thumbed away her tears. "Don't be. I think your subconscious is telling you to trust me."

The way she glanced between him and the notebooks told him

she was trying to make sense of the evidence of her identity. Knowing the importance of her believing who she was, he waited her out.

"The rational part of me wants to believe this to be myths and fantasies." She blinked up at him, and he cocked a brow.

Sucking in a deep breath, she said, "I wonder if Gram was a talisman. I never knew my grandfather. He died before I was born, and she never talked about him even when I asked. She said the time was never right. Morgan took him, didn't she?"

"Probably. But if she did, then your grandmother was unprotected and always in danger, yet you haven't mentioned any men in your family besides your dad."

"There were never any men in our lives. We lived quietly in a tiny house in the old part of town. It had an enormous backyard where Gram cultivated flowers and herbs she was forever drying and using in teas, lotions, soaps, meals... Everything I ever put in or on my body had some herb or flower from her garden in it."

Rowan nodded but didn't interrupt.

"She tried to teach me the various uses for the plants she raised, but I wasn't all that interested." She peeked at him from beneath her brows, her expression sheepish. "I'd rather read a book and daydream while I lounged in the hammock in the backyard. I helped her with picking and drying, but I basically followed her directions. I think she wanted me to experiment on my own, but I never did."

"Sounds like your grandmother was a druid. She didn't need a warrior for protection because she could protect the two of you with potions and the enchantments she wove. I bet she chanted in Gaelic often." He smiled at her wide-eyed surprise at his knowing that about her grandmother. "I bet your grandfather was a druid as well because a warrior would need a talisman, so he probably wouldn't marry a druid."

"If Gram was a druid, why didn't she tell me about myself when she suspected I was a talisman? Why set up protections without ever telling me?"

"Without knowing the particulars of your parents' deaths, I'd guess it had something to do with them. She had to protect you, and if you knew what you were without the protection of your warrior father, you were better off ignorant. It explains why she wouldn't let you out on your birthday. The gods are especially busy on Samhain, and even her best protections would be too weak to keep you from their notice if you went outside your home then."

"Will you do something for me, please?"

"Yes," he replied without hesitation.

"When I turn away, kiss my shoulder again. I'm going to distract myself."

He slanted her a disbelieving look but gave in. She stood and walked over to her bookshelves. As she perused her collection, she caught her breath and turned to him.

"Now are you convinced you're my talisman?"

She nodded mutely before wrapping her arms around him, holding him tightly.

"You're right. I have trouble with trust, but I promise I'll work on it," she said into his chest before pulling away and returning to the loveseat and the notebooks. "It's good I had my thesis to distract me from opening this box sooner. The scholar in me would have been hard-pressed to ignore Gram's warning once I'd read it, especially since I would have had no idea how long I would have to wait to get at these papers."

"You ready to begin?"

She nodded. "Be patient. I may need to stop a lot depending on what's here."

"Duly noted."

Alyssa placed the massive book across their laps again. Looking into Rowan's eyes, she gave him a wan smile before she turned the pages all at once to the back. In neat handwriting, they discovered her maternal family tree with her name listed on the most recent branch.

She wrinkled her brow. "Why couldn't I see this by myself?"

"Maybe because of this." He pointed at the tiny letters in parentheses under her name—talisman. He sucked in a breath when he saw her full name—Alyssa Ailsa Macaulay. He placed his finger beside Alyssa's mother's name—Aileen Ailsa Sinclair Macaulay and her grandmother's name—Afton Ailsa Stuart Sinclair. All the women on the most recent page of the family tree were named Ailsa.

Rowan turned to her, his voice tight. "When I was telling you about my family's history and I mentioned Ailsa, you reacted. Though I noticed, I was too involved in the story and didn't stop to ask, but you knew this about your mom and your grandmother, didn't you?"

"I thought it a coincidence." Her tone was defensive. "Ailsa was a common Scots name at one time, and I figured people in my family liked it."

Rowan scrubbed a hand over his face.

"Wait a minute. You can't be mad at me. After all, I've only just learned I'm a talisman, whatever that really means." She stared at him, but he returned his concentration to Gram's book.

Wordlessly, he turned back several pages. "All the women in your family bear the middle name Ailsa," he noted.

The hairs on the back of his neck stood up as the implications of what he'd learned invaded his consciousness.

He turned back to her immediate family to discover notes that enlightened and alarmed him. Beneath Alyssa's mother's name, Afton had written "talisman," beneath her father's name was "warrior" along with their birth and death dates. Her mother had been thirty and her father thirty-four when they died. Written beneath her grandmother's name were "druid" and her birth date. It would be up to Alyssa to supply her death date. The alarming notation, however, appeared beneath her grandfather's name where her grandmother had written "warrior." His dates indicated he died when he was thirty, only six months after the birth of his daughter.

Why would a warrior marry a druid? Rowan wondered. Unless they were convinced she could protect him, and it appeared she did for a time at least. The deaths of her husband, daughter, and son-in-law obviously motivated Afton to do everything she could to protect Alyssa, but even a druid capable of amazing feats couldn't win the final confrontation with death. Rowan had to salute her though. She'd done an unbelievable job of protecting Alyssa even from beyond the grave. He wished he could have met the woman. As it was, his admiration for her ran deep and strong. Without her wisdom and her protections, Alyssa might have been lost to him before he ever had the chance to find her.

"Your grandmother must have placed protections around your home, protections Taranis couldn't penetrate on the several occasions he's attempted," Rowan said. "Her insistence on you having a white dog tipped me off about your grandmother, but she obviously went further and did more to protect you in this house."

Perhaps my telepathy might even work in spite of the barriers Taranis erected with the storm. The weather blocked regular civilian communication, but Afton's spells might have preserved the way warriors and talismans communicated with each other when necessary. For now, he needed to follow Alyssa's bloodline to its source. What he thought he'd find there both excited and terrified him.

He flipped the pages of the notebook back to the beginning of the bloodline. His heart pounded in his ears as he read what he both dreaded and anticipated—he and Alyssa descended from the same warrior bloodline. She came down through Riordan, he through Owen. If Morgan had had any idea who his talisman was, she would have moved the heavens and hell to keep them from meeting.

They both stared at the page for long minutes before looking up at each other.

"I made you a promise to tell you everything, and this page shows why that's necessary. When Morgan discovers our connection, she'll be even more furious—and determined to kill us—than she would have been following her disappointment at discovering she couldn't keep me from finding my talisman."

"My grandmother made heroic efforts to keep me safe until we met, but now I think we both may be in more danger than if we'd never met." Fear tremored through Alyssa's voice.

Ignoring that comment, he brushed a kiss over her temple. "You'll need training once we discover what your special ability is. However, you already have one important ability I can help you control."

"I can't imagine what that might be." A dubious expression clouded her beautiful face.

"All warriors and talismans practice telepathy. You've heard me in your mind at least twice, and I have to admit I've helped myself to your thoughts a couple of times since we met."

Her face flashed scarlet.

He laughed. "I was careful not to snoop at inappropriate times, but I have to agree that last night and this morning did feel like what I've always imagined a honeymoon should feel like."

At this revelation of her private thoughts, Alyssa colored vermillion. *I wish the floor would open and swallow me whole.*

"No, you don't. If you disappeared, I'd be lost. Especially later when we resume the honeymoon," he gently corrected her as he traced her hairline with the pad of his finger.

"That's not fair!" she squeaked. "You can help yourself to my thoughts, and I can't stop you. If you truly want me to trust you, you'll stop doing that this instant."

"Since I do want you—need you—to trust me, I'll teach you how to shield your mind from others hearing your thoughts, and I'll teach you how to hear my thoughts on purpose."

Her eyes saucered.

"I know you've heard them because you've responded aloud to what I was thinking." He traced the silk of her cheek before tucking a strand of inky hair behind her ear.

"We'll often need to communicate telepathically when we're confronted with rogue warriors and civilians in the thrall of evil or civilians who can't understand who and what we are. What humans can't understand, they fear. What humans fear, they try to eradicate, so it's best sometimes not to include them in the conversation," he said.

"Were you and Seamus having telepathic conversations last night?"

"What makes you think we were?"

"There were a couple of times when you shared some intense looks, and then the oral conversation changed directions, like when we came back from the dance floor."

"Your powers of observation make me think you're either a prophet or a dreamer." Cupping her cheek, he rubbed the pad of his thumb along her jaw. "In any case, yes, we were having some private conversations," he admitted. "The last one was when I was doing a happy dance in my head because I'd found you, but I couldn't reveal it in public."

"Why?"

"Because civilians—and you, it turns out—would have thought I was absolutely crazy, and two, because until we're fully bonded, Morgan can tear us apart."

He talked over Alyssa's gasp. "Plus, she would have had the added information about who is my talisman, so you probably wouldn't have lived through the ride back here." He stared deep into her eyes to drive home his point.

Ducking her head, she worried the pages of the notebook. "Um, are talismans and warriors always lovers?"

He smiled at her shyness and what she likely wanted to know. "It's called bonding. Most warriors and talismans build such a close connection that they stay together for the rest of their lives." He slid his arm around her and drew patterns on her shoulder with his finger. "Some pairs don't bond, and though they always protect each other, their emotions lie elsewhere. In those rare cases, the warriors and talismans aren't as strong individually or together. If Morgan can't stop the meeting of a warrior and his talisman, she often tries to impede their relationship."

"I see," Alyssa said, but her tone indicated she wasn't sure she did see. *In one short night Rowan has shown me parts of me I had no idea existed, and he seems pleased with me, but is it enough?*

"I do need to train you on telepathy, but for right now, I think I'll put paid to your worries about yourself as a lover."

He laughed at her shocked stare and gathered her onto his lap as she tried to pull away from him.

"Let's see. Where were we when you were demanding answers to some very complex questions. Hmm, I think my hand was here"—he slid his hand beneath her sweater and unerringly found her breast—"and my mouth was here," he kissed her jaw—"on the way to here." He stopped talking as he took her mouth and slicked his tongue across the seam of her lips, silently asking her to open for him.

When Rowan kissed her, Alyssa seemed to lose control of herself. *How does he do that? More than anything, he makes me want to be naked with him.*

He smiled against her mouth before palming his hand along her thigh to her knee and pulling her around to straddle him. Reaching for the hem of her sweater, he pulled it over her head and enjoyed the view of her full breasts covered in hot pink lace. The previous night when he'd been looking for space for his underwear, he'd discovered the lady who wore outerwear designed to blend in hid a wild streak underneath. Seeing her in her skimpy lace bra turned him on. *"You wear some seriously sexy underwear, Pixie-girl. I like the surprise—and the view."*

Her eyes widened. "Oh!" She smiled and reached for the buttons on his shirt, stopping often to kiss his exposed skin until she couldn't bend any farther. Then she unbuttoned the front of his jeans and pulled his shirt out of them.

Grinning saucily at him, she reached inside his loosened jeans to stroke his thick shaft. He hissed in a breath as he enjoyed her explorations until she had him hard as stone. Holding both of her hands in one of his, he went to work on the fastenings of her jeans. "You'll need to stand up for a minute to pull those off, Pixie-girl." Desire rasped his voice.

Obediently, she stood and slowly slid her jeans over her hips, down her legs, and onto the floor. As she stepped out of them, he slid his jeans and boxers down his lap, revealing exactly how much he wanted her. "*Come back to me Alyssa,*" he commanded. She smiled and straddled him, but she didn't sheathe him inside her as he so desperately wanted her to.

He cupped her bottom and tried to pull her toward him, but she shook her head and took his face in her hands then bent down to kiss him, her tongue sliding over his, their breaths mingling. As she kissed him, she rubbed her slit the length of his cock, driving him wild with the wet slickness she wouldn't quite let him have. Slipping her hand between them, she grasped him and kissed the tip of his erection with her nether lips. He groaned and tried to control the urge to surge up into her, understanding he needed to let her set the pace this time. Though he'd known many women in his life, he'd never known desire like this. It took all of his will to let her have her way.

At last she guided him to her, sliding down his length and taking him inside her completely, tightening around him before she started to move. As he smoothed his hands up and down her back, he rained kisses on her neck, face, and mouth as she pleasured them both with her slow deliberate rhythm. When he needed more from her, he took her breasts in his hands and licked and teased her nipples through the thin barrier of lace, and she rode him faster. When she couldn't continue the pace they both needed, he grabbed her hips, holding her in place while he drove deep. She screamed his name, and two strokes later, he joined her in the most intense climax he'd ever experienced.

Spent, Alyssa rested her forehead against Rowan's bare chest, her arms draped around his shoulders while he smoothed his hands up and down the satin skin of her back. Her pulsing aftershocks continued their pleasure. The late afternoon light faded as the wind and snow howled and swirled in the twilight settling over her home, but neither noticed the storm growing fiercer around them.

A low whine emanating from the laundry room interrupted their idyllic moment. Alyssa sat up and smiled at Rowan. "I think someone feels left out."

"Must be about time to start dinner. I did promise you something exotic," Rowan said with a grin.

She slipped off his lap and stepped into her panties and jeans before reaching for her sweater. He held it away from her, making her lean down to him to grab it. Smiling, he cupped her breast and winked at her.

"You are incorrigible," she said with a laugh.

"No, but I am insatiable where you're concerned, so I'll need a little incentive to get off the couch and make dinner." He waggled his brows at her.

She kissed him long and hard before pulling away and grabbing her sweater while lightly jumping beyond his reach. She laughed at his growl of consternation before pulling her sweater over her head as she walked to the laundry room to take care of Shadow.

Rowan hitched up his boxers and jeans and walked over to the kitchen to cook dinner. He prepared a marinade and set the chicken in it before filling a pot with water to boil on the stove for the pasta. Though she still didn't trust him as he needed her to, he thought they were making progress.

Lost in visions of his beautiful talisman and the passion they'd shared, he didn't notice how long she'd been outside with Shadow. The house rattled with a gust of wind, and an ominous sensation shivered over him. He turned off the burner before racing to the front door to grab his boots and coat. At the back door, he noticed the porch light was off, so he turned it on and headed out into the storm.

⁓

Alyssa couldn't believe she'd become lost in her own backyard. She thought she'd barely stepped past the edge of the porch, but in the darkness and swirling snow, she couldn't orient herself. The porch light should have been directly behind her. She could have sworn she'd flipped it on when she'd left the house. "Shadow!" she called, but her voice died on the wind. *Really, I should have grabbed a coat.* At least her feet weren't frozen yet owing to her slipping on her old hiking boots before she went outside.

She tried to concentrate on small miracles rather than on tomorrow's headline: "Woman Freezes in Her Own Backyard" or something equally stupid. Why she felt compelled to follow her big dog into the storm she had no idea. He could stay out all night in this weather with no ill effects other than hurt feelings.

A vision of Rowan flashed in her head. He probably thought her an idiot for being out here if he even noticed she hadn't returned to the house. A gust of wind swirled snow around her, and she thought she heard someone moaning near her. "Is someone there? Rowan?" she called, but all she heard was a distant eerie wailing that shivered through her for reasons that had nothing to do with the cold.

Wrapping her arms around herself, she stood still and tried to determine what to do. If she stayed still long enough, she'd become a human snowdrift with the snow falling so thickly. Forcing her eyes to adjust to the darkness, she turned in a slow circle, attempting to locate any shape or semblance of light she could use to orient herself. After what she thought had been a full turn, she still couldn't find any landmark she could use for help. Remembering all the stories about people lost in storms, she considered staying right where she was, but since her yard was fenced, she had a better than even chance of regaining her house if she could find the fence line. That idea sent her off in a random direction she hoped would take her closer to her house rather than toward the back fence half an acre away from it.

Rowan stepped onto the porch and surveyed the situation. "Alyssa! Shadow!" he yelled into the gathering darkness. If the wind didn't outright muffle his voice, it definitely distorted it and carried it away. He looked around for some rope or string, anything he could use to tie off to the door before he set off in search of them. The snow piled up in front of the porch, but the porch itself remained relatively free of snow due to the overhang of the roof. Near the woodpile, he found a coil of rope and tied it off to the corner post holding up the roof of the porch before securing the other end to his wrist.

He walked off the porch, calling to Alyssa both aloud and telepathically. After several minutes, she responded.

"Rowan!"

"Where are you?"

"At the fence line of the yard."

"Which part of the yard?"

"I don't know."

"Look for a glow of light. Hold onto the fence and walk toward it."

"Shadow isn't with me. I don't know where he is."

Even though they were communicating telepathically, he could still hear her panic.

"Alyssa, he knows better how to survive out here than we do. Head for the glow of the porch light."

Rowan heard Shadow growl somewhere behind him, and he knew what was happening. Visualizing the porch, he hurled himself through time and space, landing hard on the wood decking when he saw Shadow appear near the edge of it. The dog growled at someone or something he'd cornered against the house. Blocking out the panic he could feel rolling off Alyssa, he concentrated on summoning his claymore to his hand. The familiar weight of his sword comforted him instantly, and he turned his thoughts to his talisman.

"Keep moving toward the light. Shadow is with me on the porch. Everything will be fine."

"Rowan, there's danger near you."

"I know."

Shadow lunged at the intruder as he tried to jump onto the porch. Rowan recognized the prowler as a civilian who apparently had arrived with some divine help. Brandishing his sword, he confronted the warmly dressed man.

"What are you doing sneaking around our house?" he demanded.

"*Our* house?" the man sneered. "Since when did you move in? Alyssa lives alone because no sane man would have her." The man's eyes nearly bugged out when he saw what Rowan held in his hands.

"You like all that medieval nonsense too? Is that the attraction? Don't worry, she'll make you crazy with all that Celtic hero bullshit the same way she does everyone else. Where is she, by the way?" the man asked a little too casually.

"You still haven't answered my question," Rowan said, his tone steely.

"Oh, I'm an old friend of Alyssa's. I was in the neighborhood and thought I'd look her up, see if she's gotten more interesting since the last time I saw her."

"You happened to be in the neighborhood? In a blizzard?" Rowan asked incredulously. "Try again."

Alyssa appeared at the corner of the porch. Shivering and covered in snow, she resembled a Yeti. She stopped and stared at Rowan as he held the man at bay. Then she recovered herself.

"Hello Bill. What an unpleasant surprise. What are you doing sneaking around my house?"

"Hmm, must be some trouble in paradise. The medieval knight here thinks it's his house too." The man's tone taunted.

"Answer the question. It's the third time you've been asked it," Rowan growled.

"Oh, I came by as a favor to a beautiful woman named Morgan. She wanted me to check on Alyssa, make sure she was all right in this storm," Bill said off-handedly, but he watched Rowan and Alyssa closely.

"Don't react. Let me handle this, Alyssa."

Alyssa said nothing, her face a bland mask.

"So you're Bill Forbes." He stared down his sword at the man. "Tell Morgan that Alyssa is fine," Rowan said, drawing out the last word. "Now crawl back into whatever hole you crawled out of and don't ever come back here. Alyssa tells me Shadow has wanted to eat you since he first met you. You come around again, and we'll encourage his desire for a new chew toy. Understand, little man?"

"She's not worth it you know. She doesn't have what it takes to please a man." Bill snickered.

"She can please a *man* just fine. Sniveling messenger boys who sneak around people's houses have no idea what to do with a real woman when they have her." He touched the point of his sword to the man's chest. "Projecting your inadequacies on her is even lower than spying on her. Now get the hell out of here before I lose my temper and take something from you that you don't know how to use anyway."

Forbes apparently didn't notice Rowan had moved until he looked down at the tip of Rowan's blade against his balls. Even in the low glow of the porch light, Rowan could see red anger and fear riding Forbes's cheeks. The man took a slow step backwards and landed in a heap on the ground below the porch. Shadow barked and lunged for him before Alyssa could call him off. Forbes curled in a tight ball until she reached her dog and took him by the collar, wisely keeping Shadow between herself and Forbes.

Forbes staggered to his feet and took off running around the side of the house. Rowan followed him, calling to Alyssa over his shoulder, "Take Shadow inside and lock the doors."

Rounding the corner of the house, Rowan stopped still when he spied a figure waiting on the side of the road. The snow had cleared enough for him to focus on Morgan who turned her face to him, her eyes glowing blood red. Forbes was the scout and a rather inadequate one at that. There would be others and soon. He and Alyssa didn't have much time.

CHAPTER TWELVE

S MORGAN AWAITED her minion outside Alyssa Macaulay's home, she had time to think. So, she'd been right about that rather mousy Celtic scholar. For decades, Morgan had been trying to find ways to determine talismans from civilians. Watching the old families made it easy, mostly, but the descendants of the heroes were becoming increasingly adept at hiding their children's special skills until it became too late for her to do something about them. Afton Sinclair had thwarted her most thoroughly. Clearly, Ailsa Sheridan's blood ran deep in Afton even though she'd been a druid rather than a talisman. Morgan shuddered at the fleeting thought of Afton's power had she been a talisman before shrugging off the notion in disgust. No matter what their skills, in the end, the descendants of the heroes were still mostly human and therefore in her power.

However, the fact this particular talisman had been paired with a Sheridan, and not just any Sheridan, but Rowan Sheridan, the heir to the training room and one of Scathach's particular warrior projects, disturbed her deeply. When she and Maeve had made their pact and tricked their all-father the Dagda all those centuries ago, they'd inadvertently left a loophole the heroes could exploit. Under the right circumstances, the heroes could end the time limit the goddesses had artificially imposed on warriors, the one that allowed her to take Graeme Sheridan so soon after taking Ailsa all those centuries ago. If the Sheridans succeeded in reversing the time limit for warriors to find their talismans, they could stop her from taking talismans altogether. After wading in the comingled blood of warriors and talismans for so many centuries, Morgan couldn't even contemplate the loss.

Probably, Rowan had already mated with Alyssa, but they were not yet wed. She consoled herself—she still had time to impede this pairing, though she would have to work quickly.

The sight of Bill Forbes leaping through the deep snow as though the hounds of hell chased him pulled her from her thoughts. Rowan Sheridan tailed her lackey, his claymore at the ready. Rowan nearly reached his quarry when he stopped short. Too late, she remembered the ethereal glow she used as a beacon to return her goshawk to her after he completed his mission, and her unlikely chance to ensnare her prey vanished in the instant Rowan's eyes locked with hers. He nodded to her before disappearing back into the swirling snow.

Winded, Forbes stopped short of his mistress, standing beside the car she'd parked on the side of the road.

"He has a sword! She's guarded by a giant with a sword! What the hell is *that*?"

"That, my dear man, is a delusional creature. Apparently, your former girlfriend is not the only crazy person on the planet." She smiled at him.

"You've shown me you're a supernatural being, and you promised to give me some of your power if I came up here with you and reported what I saw," Forbes began.

"I never break a promise," Morgan purred. "Besides the man with the sword, what else did you see?"

"The storm attacked my ex-girlfriend. The snow swirled and eddied around her while falling gently elsewhere. Her house is locked up tight like always, and she has supplies—wood and stuff. I didn't get a chance to sneak inside before that wild man and her beast of a dog discovered me." Forbes gave her a greasy smile, panting after his reward.

"You've done—well. Come, let's see about just compensation for your service."

As Forbes climbed into the car, a smile playing about his mouth, no doubt he missed the black shadow that passed over her eyes. She'd promised him to Maeve if he indeed led them to a Sheridan talisman, and he had. As a reward for his efforts, he'd die of orgasmic shock in Maeve's bed, something Morgan thought this one rather deserved.

As he watched Morgan race her car up the road, not for the first time Rowan wished the laws of physics applied to goddesses. Maybe her reckless behavior would lead to her wrapping her car around a tree, thereby eliminating at least one threat to his family and him.

As he walked back to the porch, he coiled up the rope he'd used to tether himself in the face of Taranis's rage and knocked on the door. Shadow's happy yip announced his return, and Alyssa greeted him at the back door.

They clung together for several minutes, reassuring each other they were fine. Then Alyssa started shivering uncontrollably. He recognized the signs. Her extended time in the elements with nothing on but her sweater and jeans coupled with her fear and that not-so-pleasant encounter with her old boyfriend appeared at last to have caught up with her.

He kicked off his boots and tossed off his jacket before picking her up and carrying her through the house to her bathroom. While the tub filled, he stripped off her cold, wet clothing before divesting himself of his own clothes. Carefully, he picked her up and lowered her into the warm water before filling the tub to overflowing when he climbed in behind her. Holding her close to his chest, he gently scooped water up over her arms and shoulders to slide in warming rivulets down her shivering body. When the water cooled, he reached around her, let some out and added more hot water to their bath.

It seemed an age before she relaxed and her shivering subsided. He stepped from the tub and dried himself before helping her up and drying her, wrapping the towel around her before heading into the bedroom in search of her robe. Though he didn't find her terrycloth robe at all sexy, it and a pair of wool socks would certainly keep her warm. When he had her warmly redressed, he carried her out to the living room, nearly tripping over Shadow who hovered outside the bedroom door, and set her down in the chair near the woodstove.

"Hey Shadow, you take your guard dog role seriously," Rowan said. "Good thing too. Forbes might have made it inside without you." The dog snuffled at his out-stretched hand. "Morgan can't directly breach Afton's defenses, but a civilian can." The dog seemed to understand every word. "Now help your mistress warm up. You owe her that much for abandoning her when you were trying to protect her." Rowan ruffled the fur on Shadow's head.

During the time he'd spent warming her in the bathtub, they hadn't spoken. Rowan carefully kept his mind blank in case Morgan had somehow breached Afton's defenses, but he kept himself open to Alyssa's thoughts. She appeared to be numb, her thoughts swirling with no coherent direction, which probably was good, at least for now.

Returning to the bedroom, he dressed in fresh clothes before returning to the kitchen to make coffee. His plan included warming Alyssa from the inside out, and they were going to need the caffeine for the training session he needed to put her through after dinner. Morgan's appearance increased his urgency to prepare Alyssa. Good thing she was so intelligent; she'd catch on easily to opening her mind. Their conversation during the storm showed him that. Shielding, a much harder skill to master, would be a problem, he worried. Then there was still the question of her ability. He had no good ideas for how to discover it, but maybe they'd find something in the journals Alyssa's grandmother left behind for her.

When he handed the cup of steaming hot brew to her, he nudged Shadow out of the way to sit on the floor in front of her. "We need to talk."

"We're no longer safe here, are we?" she asked, her eyes wide with fright.

"I think we're safe in this house, but the goddesses know where we are now, and they know we're together. I made sure of that with the message I gave Forbes, but I didn't need to bother. Morgan was out front waiting for him when I chased him around the house. She used civilian transportation—" At Alyssa's confused frown, he smiled. "A car. Which makes me think she needed Forbes to cross your grandmother's enchantments. Civilians don't have the same limitations from druid enchantments the gods have. I wonder how she found Forbes though."

A cry of distress escaped her, alerting him to how his words had affected her. "How can you be so matter-of-act about this? I know you're used to fighting the gods, but this is all new to me." Unshed tears roughened her voice. "When I was stranded outside, I could swear I heard laughter as snow devils spun me around, leaving me lost in my own backyard. How is that possible?"

He pulled her from her chair and seated himself in it, tugging her down onto his lap. For several minutes, he cradled her before he spoke.

"Alyssa, you did everything right out there. You opened your mind to me and followed my lead. You didn't give away your feelings to Forbes when he baited you, and you warned me of danger I couldn't see." He tightened his arms around her. "At first, I thought the danger was Forbes, but after I rounded the corner of the house, I knew you'd sensed Morgan. You kept your mind blank and didn't let her in, nor did you panic and give Taranis any satisfaction either."

He pushed a silky strand of hair behind her ear. "You may have done these things out of instinct, but what you showed me is you are absolutely the best talisman for me, and we're going to keep each other safe when we take on the gods."

"Did you honestly mean all those things you said about me to Bill?" she asked, her voice wobbly.

Rowan smiled. "Oh yeah. You're undeniably too much woman for that moron. He could never deserve you in a thousand lifetimes." He sobered. "But I'm wondering. When did he take an interest in you?"

"I met him at a sports bar. A few days later, he showed up in the library right after I declared Celtic studies for my master's. He showed interest and gained my trust. He was handsome in a rugged sort of way, and I hadn't dated all that much. Being best friends with a knockout like Ceri Ross makes it hard to get noticed." Alyssa rolled her eyes. Rowan frowned, but she continued. "Anyway, he seemed intelligent and charismatic, and before long we were dating. The rest you already know. Why?"

"Morgan used Forbes to find you. I wonder if she's got other jerks out there trying to discover talismans before they meet their warriors. It would be easy for her to follow the bloodlines of important warrior families to try to discover the special traits of the women."

"Sort of like putting a bug in an office or something?"

"Exactly, but these are human bugs—good term for an insect like Forbes—and their job apparently goes beyond simple eavesdropping. He systematically set out to steal your self-confidence to render you less trusting, less powerful." He rubbed his palm up and down her arm. "Since Morgan and Maeve are not allowed to be privy to the pairings of warriors and talismans, they're trying to circumvent the system. They think to change the rules again." His thoughts thundered through his head as he contemplated the goddesses' evil.

"Is there anything we can do?"

"I'm not sure, but for now, we need to concentrate on your

training, beginning tonight. How 'bout you get dressed while I finish making dinner? We're going to need sustenance for the night we're facing." Softening his words, he stood and let her slide down his body before gifting her with a smacking kiss. Then he gave her a gentle shove in the direction of her bedroom.

"What's that delicious smell?" she asked as she re-entered the great room, clad in a clean pair of jeans and a warm sweater.

Presenting the dish with a flourish, he said, "Spinach ravioli Alfredo and marinated chicken. It's the house specialty."

"Let me get this straight—you rescue damsels in distress, you're kind to animals, you clean up after yourself, and you cook? You're absolutely out of a fairytale."

With a huge grin, he made a big deal out of seating her before he seated himself. "I'm going to bask in your praise for a minute or two"—he drummed his fingers on the table—"before I confess you're eating the one dish I know how to cook that doesn't involve scrambled or fried eggs."

She laughed as she cut a bite of chicken and swirled it through the sauce. "You can cook this anytime you want." She made moaning sounds around a mouthful of ravioli.

He smiled and sneaked a piece of chicken to Shadow who waited on the floor behind them.

"You mentioned training. What is training, and how soon will I need to be ready for whatever is coming?"

"We need to cover several skills," he answered. "Unfortunately, it's going to be a crash course since Morgan knows about us. How 'bout we finish dessert before we go into all of that. It's something I slaved over."

Her arched brow mocked his declaration as she watched him slice off and plate a generous portion of tiramisu. "I'd admire your hard work and tenacity sneaking this into the cart when I wasn't looking, but I found it when I unloaded the shopping bags. Good job though, well done," she said sardonically.

He slid her a look. "It's all in the technique. My brothers and I sneaked all sorts of things past our mom when she took us shopping. That's probably why she stopped taking us when I was around ten. About that time, my brothers started getting really good." Pride curved the corners of his mouth.

"Tell me more about your family."

"I'm the oldest of three sons. My brothers, Riley and Riordan, are twins and three years younger than me. We're all warriors, like our dad." Rowan enjoyed a bite of tiramisu, swallowed, and continued. "My mom is a talisman. Riley found his talisman, Lynnette, last year." He stared significantly at her before dropping his bomb. "All the men in my family bear the middle name of Findlay."

"Oh" Her eyes widened. "Oh. Wow."

"Yeah, I think there's something to that too. Like my dad, I escaped Morgan with only months to spare before she would have had a shot at me, which probably adds to her frustration."

"Sooo, I guess we'd better start the training then."

He carried the dessert dishes to the sink and began washing up. Wordlessly, she joined him, drying and putting away their plates. He hoped she sensed the easy domesticity of their relationship like he did, like they'd been helping each other this way for years rather than days. It would go a long way toward bonding them and besting Morgan in battle.

Rowan topped off their coffees and led Alyssa back to the loveseat and the notebooks. "We need to discover your special ability, and I think the best place to look is in these journals. Perhaps your grandmother divined it or prophesied it, or it's the same one your mother or great-grandmother had. Which journal do you want to read first?"

"Honestly, reading these scares me."

"I know, Pixie-girl." He squeezed her knee. "But it's imperative we find out what your skill is in time to train with it before Morgan unleashes whatever unholy plan she's hatching," he said gently.

She sighed. "I'll start with the most recent one, the one involving my grandpa and my parents."

He took one look at the trepidation and sadness written large on her face and grabbed that particular notebook. "Maybe I should read that one first. I can tell you if the information we need is in it."

"At some point, I'm going to have to know what happened, and if I'm on a short clock, I don't want to die ignorant."

"If you're sure." Reluctantly, he returned the journal to her. "You can always change your mind if it's too much."

"Thank you."

She held the journal tenderly for several minutes while he occupied himself with the journal chronicling her great-grandparents' generation. While he debated with himself, he pretended to read. Was it better to open his mind to hers to discover what happened to her family at the same time she did? At last, he decided if he wanted to gain her trust, he'd have to let her do this unpleasant task in her own way. Either she'd tell him what he needed to know, or he could read the journal later.

With a deep breath, Alyssa opened the notebook and began reading. The first half contained recipes for healing balms and salves, recipes for medicinal drinks and meals, and recipes for enchantments. Scanning over the enchantments, she read how Gram had developed special ways to guard her from the detection of the gods. As the tears streamed down her face, Rowan comforted her with a squeeze on her thigh.

"She loved me so much. It says here she created enchantments to shield me from dreaming and from discovery by rogue warriors," Alyssa choked out over the lump in her throat.

While Alyssa gathered herself, he read over her shoulder. "Your grandmother's love for you transcended time and the gods. Probably, her love more than anything else has kept you safe so far."

Recomposing herself, she continued to read. "The notebook talks about my parents too. Apparently, they found each other right after their twenty-first birthdays while they were students at the same college. My father wasn't in a big hurry to find his talisman because he enjoyed the challenge of taking on Morgan without the help of his other half. He also liked girls," Alyssa said with a chuckle.

"Sounds like Seamus." Rowan rolled his eyes.

A tiny grin tugged at her lips. "It says my dad's sign was to trace a Saint Brighid's cross on his talisman's shoulder. His talisman would feel it like a brand through her clothing." Looking up from the journal, she added, "Brighid is the patroness of druids, but I guess you already knew that." She gave him a sheepish look. "When Gram found out what his sign was, she was completely taken with him and did all she could to help Rory, my dad, and Aileen, my mom, in their battles with Morgan."

Turning a page, she read for a minute, then continued. "Evidently, my parents were seated together at a party, and Dad was teasing Mom. Somewhere during the course of the evening, he slid his arm around her and began idly tracing the Saint Brighid's cross. Gram says he wasn't even all that conscious of what he was doing, but Mom flinched and tried to move away from him. He recognized her for who and what she was and whisked her out of the party." She bumped Rowan's shoulder with her own. "Sounds like someone else I know hustling me out of a bar."

He grinned unapologetically at her.

"It took them six months to marry because his family was engaged in a war Morgan was waging in Africa. They were married for five years before I came along. They settled in Colorado where Dad didn't have far to visualize himself in order to intervene in gang wars going on regularly in the Denver-Metro area. Gram protected their home with enchantments and often came to visit, especially after I was born."

As she read through the next part, she tensed at where the story went. When she turned sorrow-filled eyes at him, Rowan took the notebook from her suddenly nerveless fingers.

She stared sightlessly at Gram's neat handwriting while Rowan read aloud. "'When Alyssa was four, Morgan received some warning or vision causing her to threaten Alyssa. Rory was furious that Morgan, who had changed the rules to take a talisman so long ago would now attempt to take a child, one who hadn't proven the existence of any skill marking her as anything more than a civilian.'" He stopped reading to explain. "Sometimes even in bloodline families, children are born who don't have any special abilities or roles in the warriors' world. Anyway, your grandmother says, 'Morgan laughed and said a child born to so powerful a combination as Rory and Aileen Macaulay would absolutely be a threat to her eventually.'"

Rowan stopped and cupped Alyssa's face with his free hand. "I think Morgan is right about that."

He brushed a light kiss over her mouth before he continued to read. "'It was a feint to draw out and separate Aileen and Rory, and it worked. She set her minions on Aileen when she returned from stowing Alyssa safely with me, and Aileen wasn't ready. Rory lost control when he found the battered body of his wife and died taking a blow in an unguarded moment against Morgan's newest champion, Rory's younger brother Evan who had shown weakness when he didn't find his talisman in time.'"

Tuning in to Alyssa's distress, Rowan stopped again. "Do you want to read a different notebook?" he asked as he thumbed away the tears flowing over her cheeks.

"No. Like I s-said. It's better to know." She rested her head on his shoulder and closed her eyes. "Keep." She cleared her throat. "Keep going."

"'The local newspapers and the official police report said the Macaulays died during a home invasion, but warriors knew the truth, and the truth killed Rory and Evan's parents who couldn't reconcile the loss of one son at the hands of the other. Morgan led a parade of Macaulays across the ford into the mists in a short time, but Alyssa was safe.'"

He put down the journal and gathered Alyssa into his arms, holding her quietly while she mourned her family. The treachery Morgan employed to satisfy her bloodlust was almost more than either could fathom as they read the senseless slaughter of her entire family in her grandmother's neat, matter-of-fact script.

"At least now I understand why she was so overprotective of me," Alyssa said through her tears.

"She'll always have a special place in my heart for that," Rowan said as he stroked her hair. "I wish I could take some of your pain for you, Pixie-girl."

She gifted him with a wan smile.

After a while, they resumed reading.

"Though there are no ominous patterns, there also are no hints about what your ability is. In fact, there seems to be an equal number of talismans as druids in your family tree, second and third children tending to be druids." He stopped reading for a minute. "There's something I remember about the first Ailsa though. She had both druid and talisman skills. Maybe that's why there are so few talismans in your ancestry."

"I need a break. Shadow, do you need to go outside?" Alyssa asked her big dog lazing in front of the woodstove. She let him out the back door but didn't accompany him outside.

As she returned to the great room, she stopped in her tracks. "Do you think Gram's enchantments have weakened somehow? Maybe that's why Taranis was almost successful in catching me earlier."

"Not having been around many druids, I don't know the extent or limitations of their powers against the gods. Usually, I go to a druid when I've sustained an injury, but I do know druids who can enchant an area well enough to keep out the gods. Still, Seamus and I sleep lightly with our swords nearby."

Tilting his head, he asked, "As you read the recipes and

enchantments in the journal, did you feel differently? Did you notice anything as you read? If your skill tends toward druidism, I don't know what that means for either of us."

Alyssa stretched and walked over to lean against the island. "I thought they were interesting, and from a scholarly perspective, I might want to try a few. But I don't have some burning desire to create an enchantment. Honestly, I sort of lost focus in that section and discovered I'd read a bit into the narrative about my parents before I realized I was no longer reading recipes," she said. "Since you grew up knowing who and what you are in a family of warriors and talismans, don't you have some idea of how to discover my ability?"

"My parents say the discovery of the talisman's skill is part of the bonding process that goes on between a warrior and a talisman. Since talismans have different abilities to complement their warriors' skills, there isn't a specific way to determine which one you have." He set the notebooks on the table and joined her at the island.

"How much time do you think we have before it's critical we know what I can do?"

"Probably until tomorrow or the next day. Whenever Taranis blows himself out." His answer did nothing to comfort either of them.

A low whine at the back door alerted them Shadow wanted inside, and Rowan let him back into the house. The big dog sauntered into the great room with remnants of snow clinging to his legs as he sought attention from his mistress. He seemed to sense her distress and lay on the floor at her feet, watching her from beneath his furry eyebrows.

Rowan went into the kitchen to make a fresh pot of coffee, and Alyssa followed him with her eyes. His power and easy grace were an aphrodisiac all their own. Coupled with the solicitous way he took care of her, he was almost irresistible. The one lucky part of all her discoveries this weekend, she thought, was her connection to this alluring man.

Chapter Thirteen

"WHERE DO YOU keep your beans?" Rowan asked, pointing to the nearly empty coffee canister on the kitchen counter. Alyssa indicated a tall cupboard to the right of the sink. When he reached up to grab the bag of fresh beans for the grinder, his shirt rode up enough to expose his lower back, revealing angry red wounds.

She raced around the island to him, pulling up his shirt to inspect the damage.

"We were naked together all night, this morning in the shower, and this afternoon in the bath. How did I not notice these? What happened that you have these vicious wounds?"

"I made sure you didn't see them. You weren't ready for the answers to your questions."

"And now?"

"I was wounded in a gang fight in East Los Angeles on Thursday afternoon. It was the 'service call' Isla asked me to take when you were in my office." He sucked in a breath.

"You visualized the scene and landed there to fight," she said as though she'd grown up participating in their community instead of only recently discovering it.

"Yes." He let out his breath.

Alyssa fisted her hands on her hips. "What caused those wounds? I thought gang-bangers preferred big caliber guns to big knives."

"They do, and they were using them. The rogue warriors Morgan sent to instigate them prefer claymores and broad swords the same way Scathach's warriors do."

Her eyes saucered. "I saw the battle in a dream as I napped in my office. Please turn around and lift your shirt again."

Rowan stared at her before doing as she requested. Cautiously, she touched one of his wounds. She cried out as she watched the battle, saw the two warriors slicing at Rowan's unprotected back as an enormous warrior kept his attention forward. She could see the blood flowing and sense him weakening. Then like a telescoping whoosh through time and space, she was back in her kitchen in the present, trying not to think about what she witnessed—again. It was one thing to have the nightmares when she was sleeping. It was something else entirely to experience them while wide awake.

"Rowan, I have some healing salve in the bathroom. Let me grab it and put it on you. No doubt it'll heal you completely."

He frowned at her over his shoulder.

"When I was a little girl, I was such a tomboy, always scraping or puncturing some part of my anatomy." She huffed out half a laugh. "Gram would cover my cuts and bruises with her special salve, and in a day or two, I'd have flawless skin again. That's one recipe I remember and continue to make," she babbled.

Apparently, Rowan had other ideas. "Alyssa, just now you saw the battle that scarred me, didn't you?"

She closed her eyes and sucked in a breath. "Yes."

"Did you see it in a vision or a dream?"

"In a dream, I thought. Since Gram died last summer, I've been dreaming about battles with warriors wearing leather jackets and jeans as they wield giant swords. Thursday's dream was especially vivid. I remember feeling so afraid. I awoke in my office with tears on my face because I was desperately trying to save the warrior with the odds against him, and I wasn't sure if I returned him to his home."

"What do you mean, you weren't sure if you returned him to his home?" he asked, tension vibrating off him.

"He killed the warrior who kept him occupied while the others wounded him, but he'd lost so much blood. I'd wanted to put him in a hospital, but he wouldn't let me, so I tried to put him in his own bed to rest and recuperate as best he could." She stopped and locked eyes with him. "That was you, wasn't it? Did you wake up at home?"

"Lying in my bed with no memory of having visualized myself back to my apartment. I recall hearing a faint voice begging me to go to a hospital, which I ignored. Warriors who show up in civilian hospitals are generally asked questions they can't answer, so we try to find a druid to heal us when we're wounded."

Alyssa hugged herself. "Oh."

Rowan reached for her and pulled her close. "Honestly, I was in such despair of finding my talisman, I didn't let Seamus call the healer for me. If you count the scars, you'll notice there are six, two for each month until my twenty-eighth birthday." He rubbed his face against her hair. "Morgan was gloating, thinking she had me. I wanted the scars to remind me not to give up."

She looked up at him. "But you don't have to keep them. Let me help you."

Smiling, he said, "You're right. Go ahead and get that salve."

As she retrieved the salve from the spare bathroom, she heard Rowan grinding beans for a fresh pot of coffee.

When she returned, she marveled as his face lit up in a silly grin. "We have something to celebrate. We know your ability."

"We do?"

"You're a dreamer." He caught her up and spun her around. "As a dreamer, you have the power to control some aspects of the battles I must fight. You probably saved me from dying by sending me back to my apartment after the latest one."

As he set her on her feet, Alyssa's mouth turned down. "But I can't control my dreams. They simply come. Usually, I try to avoid them if I can."

"As part of your training, we'll work on you having visions rather than dreams. That way you'll have more control over your emotions and reactions and still be able to help me."

"Rowan, I don't think I want to watch you battle now that I know who you are and what's happening. The dreams haunted me for days after I had them, and I thought they were only reactions to my reading. Now that I know you were fighting for your life every time—"*I'll be too emotionally involved to be helpful to you.*

"You underestimate yourself. When Taranis turned you around in your backyard, your first instinct was to rescue your dog, but when you realized Morgan was nearby and threatening me, you sensed her before I did and warned me." He cupped her face in his big hands. "You didn't fall apart or try to hide from the situation, and you put others before yourself. That kind of selflessness and concentrated loyalty kept us both safe, and you did all that without any training at all."

She nearly lost herself in his beautiful aquamarine eyes before he broke the spell. Turning from her, he walked over to grab their mugs from the living room and set them on the counter.

"It won't be easy being my talisman. I tend to visualize myself into the middle of the action, so I often need to start fighting before I know important details about the situation. You're going to have to warn me fast and often, see all the things I miss in the first few seconds I engage in battle. If I'd landed better the other night, I might have been able to avoid these wounds." He pointed to his back. "Or at least some of them."

Grabbing a carton of milk from the fridge, he said, "Morgan knows my weakness, one I've been trying to fix, and she likes to exploit it. Likely, she'll try to trap you, so you can't see what I miss and communicate it to me—she'll try to prevent you from helping me sort out the situation to my advantage. That's where most of your training will come." He set milk and sugar on the island.

Still dubious, Alyssa sighed audibly.

"When you apply that salve to my back, I want you to massage it in. It's going to hurt like hell no doubt, but by pushing into my wounds, you'll see everything that was going on during the time I received them."

Slowly, she shook her head.

Placing his hands on her shoulders, he continued. "Concentrate on telling me everything you see. Since you know the outcome of the battle, you don't have to worry about what's happening or what's going to happen." He pushed a strand of her hair behind her ear. "I'm standing right here in front of you, safe and sound, so be clinically observant. Will you try that?"

She huffed out a breath. "You're asking a lot, but I'll try."

Rowan turned and splayed his hands on the counter top, took a deep breath, and visibly relaxed in anticipation of her ministrations. She pushed his shirt up onto his shoulders and stared for a minute at the angry red welts on his otherwise beautiful muscular back. As he looked over his shoulder, she shuddered at what had caused them. He cocked a brow at her, and she rolled her shoulders.

Taking a deep breath, she dipped her fingertips into the salve before gingerly smoothing it over one of the wounds. Immediately, she saw the battle, heard the screams of those who were wounded or dying, the shouts of those who were fighting, and faint, eerie laughter. "It's in the past," she reminded herself softly as she applied more pressure and massaged in the salve. As she rubbed her fingers into Rowan's scars, she could feel his determination and courage. Sensing his confidence reassured her, and she began to speak:

"The warrior is stepping away from you deliberately, baiting you to follow him to a more enclosed area where you can't wield your sword as well. It's a strategic move because he has a building at his back. He knows your allies can't surprise him. It also exposes your back to his allies. You're not aware there are two other warriors with him until one of them lands the first blow that slices through your jacket.

"The warrior laughs at the effectiveness of his ploy, but you don't waver from your purpose. Another warrior, who looks an awful lot like you, sees you're outnumbered and tries to come to your aid, but a gangbanger delays him with a well-placed gunshot, which he has to parry. The second rogue slices through your jacket twice. He wields a broadsword, and he's lightning fast.

"You turn away from the champion to strike a blow at this warrior who laughs and strikes you a third time before dancing away to engage the warrior who looks like you. When you turn back to the champion, the warrior who struck you first sees an opportunity to strike again, and he takes it.

"By now, you're losing a lot of blood. You're aware of it, but you're determined to win. With a series of quick feints and strikes, you confuse the champion. He must move away from the wall or risk being skewered to it. When he moves, you feint for a high downward blow, which is where his ally takes advantage of you and strikes you a third time. That was the sixth wound."

Without realizing she'd done so, she'd worked up a sweat as she massaged salve into five scars while her focus remained on describing the battle.

Rowan hissed in a breath as she pressed especially hard against his back, but otherwise didn't react to her ministrations or her words, letting her finish her description.

"You stagger back to the ground. This is when the champion thinks he's won. He comes at you recklessly, and rather than rising to meet him, you lie still yet remain alert. As he lifts his sword for the killing blow, you pull up your claymore, allowing him to run himself through before he can complete his devastating mission." Alyssa paused to recover from the gruesome sight.

"His second ally, the one who struck the last blow, moves toward you, but the warrior who had taken on the third rogue comes in quickly and engages him. Seeing this, you relax and allow yourself to feel your wounds to gauge their seriousness." She feathered her fingers over his wounds. "This is when you hear me calling out to you to let me help you. The other warrior takes care of the rogues, and you stagger to stand and retrieve your sword. You're arguing with me about going to a hospital while one of your allies, an enormous warrior with a California tan, tells you and your ally that he'll deal with the local police concerning the civilian gang in the battle.

"You're about to faint from loss of blood when the warrior who looks like you rushes to your aid right as I tell you to go back to your apartment where I leave you and hope you don't die of blood loss."

Alyssa blew out a breath. She'd thought only a few minutes had passed while she engaged in her task, but now that she'd finished massaging in the salve and describing the fight, she was spent, like she'd participated in battle herself.

She capped the salve and leaned heavily against the counter beside Rowan. As she looked up at him, he appeared equally tired, but an intense light shone in his eyes, engendering fascination and trepidation inside her.

"I'm sorry. After I began the description, I became so engrossed in what I was seeing I stopped paying attention to what I was doing. I hope I wasn't too rough with you."

He shook his head. "You didn't hurt me. Made me a bit uncomfortable a couple times." Grinning at her, he said, "It really pissed you off that the zombie champion's allies were cheap-shotting me, didn't it?" He rearranged his shirt over his back.

She frowned. "What makes you say that?"

"When you were describing that part, you pushed especially hard into my scars."

"Oh, sorry!"

"It's fine. In fact, you gave me more information."

"I did?"

"I know where your loyalty lies. Glad you're on my team," he said with a wink. He handed her a mug of coffee and walked over to the loveseat.

"Who's the warrior who looks like you?" she asked as she joined him.

"My younger brother Riordan. We call him Rio. He told me he was in the neighborhood when he heard me fighting. Lately, he's often been 'in the neighborhood'"—he air-quoted—"when Morgan starts something with me," Rowan growled, and Alyssa sat forward on the seat. "He and Riley are fraternal twins, but Rio and I have always shared a special bond. We sense each other more than other warriors, but he's been annoyingly concerned about me this last year."

"Do you think he knows you found me yet? And what will that mean to your relationship?" Alyssa bit her lip. "I'd never want to interfere with your family."

Rowan smiled. "Rio's been even more concerned about me finding my talisman than I have, I think. If he's sensed we're together, he's probably doing a happy dance."

"But I'm not a warrior. I can't draw a rogue away from you."

"The same way I heard you, so can other warriors if you let them. Even though you're not wielding a sword, you can draw a warrior away from me by what you say to him, kind of like the sirens in Greek mythology."

Alyssa set her mug on the table and leaned toward him. "How do I learn to do this?"

"Your first step was seeing the battle purely as an activity to describe, like one of the myths you like to read. You did that so well you forgot yourself in real time. In fact, you had no idea we were training."

She grabbed his arm, nearly causing him to spill his coffee as he lifted the mug to his lips. "We were training?"

"We were. It's that observant nature—"

"Uh-huh."

He laughed and continued like she hadn't interrupted him. "That will make you an asset to me. It's also a liability if you're unaware of what's going on around you."

"What do you mean?"

"Well, if you're so busy giving me all your attention that you lose awareness of your own surroundings, Morgan can strike you. Since she's demonstrated she'll take a talisman, it's crucial you learn to control your observational skill."

"What are you talking about?" Having never seen the goddess, she couldn't imagine what Rowan meant.

"Your namesake, Alyssa." He gave her a look. "The first talisman Morgan took was Ailsa, remember? Ailsa was Morgan's big coup. She'd like nothing more than to replicate that feat with another Sheridan talisman, so you're going to have to learn how to pay attention to me while not forgetting to take care of yourself." He wrapped his big hand around her smaller one and squeezed.

"How can I do that? I've always been more concerned about those I care about than myself. You can't ask me to change my nature."

Sliding his hand along the couch behind her, he leaned into her and nuzzled her cheek.

Alyssa softened under his touch.

"I don't want you to change. The fact you're selfless is what kept Forbes from fulfilling whatever nasty task Morgan set him on this evening. But you were vulnerable. Your grandmother's enchantments probably kept Morgan and Taranis at bay long enough for you to return to me." Idly, he traced his fingers across her shoulder. "However, I may need you to have a vision when you're away from your home, and those enchantments won't protect you if you're not paying attention to yourself."

"How can I be observant for both of us simultaneously?" Her agitation vibrated through her, and Rowan shifted closer, his big body comforting her.

"It's going to take a few applications of that salve to heal my scars. Each time you touch me, you'll observe the battle where I sustained them. While you're watching that battle the next time, you'll also need to pay attention to the room in which we're working. I'll set some surprises for you and see how you react." With his hands on her upper her arms, he pulled back and looked into her eyes. "Your training as my talisman will only involve that battle for now. Once you've mastered skills such as putting aside emotion for observation and being attuned to both our surroundings, we'll move on to other battles you've seen and work with them."

"This training is going to be intense."

The task he set scared the hell out of her. If Morgan struck tomorrow, she knew she'd never be ready.

CHAPTER FOURTEEN

BY THE TIME the sky started lightening into day, Rowan and Alyssa were exhausted. Even Shadow, who watched the training with interest at first, had retreated to the laundry room hours ago. When Alyssa mentioned she thought it would take years to master the tasks he'd set for her, he assured her that when she observed battles, she'd made no mistakes. She'd seen and interpreted everything perfectly for that moment. But she worried so much about him she often forgot to watch herself. If he'd been Morgan, he'd have taken her several times during the night.

They still needed to train for shielding her thoughts. Rowan knew she must perfect the skill quickly, and he hadn't even started teaching her the basics. However, they both required rest, so he followed her to the bedroom where they undressed in silence and fell into bed. Alyssa fell asleep almost before her head touched the pillow, but Rowan took time to arrange her against him, cuddling her close before he too fell into a dreamless sleep.

Early in the afternoon, he awoke in a rush as he heard Seamus talking to him. He blinked and stared at the Celtic knots swirling on the ceiling above him, momentarily disoriented. Alyssa's warm body wrapped around him reminded him they lay together in her soft bed. He'd thought he heard Seamus on the other side of the bedroom door in their apartment before he recognized his thoughts.

"Hey, old man. Where are you? Rio's been feeling you battle all night, but we can't figure out where you are. He's frantic."

"I'm with Alyssa. I'm safe. We were training all night. We fell into bed sometime early this morning, and neither of us has moved."

"Jesus. When you said she was the one, I was too worried to be happy for you. Hey, why are you open to me and not to family?"

"Because you're in closer proximity, I would guess. I wouldn't have been open to you if I weren't whipped. I'm trying not to let Morgan in. She knows who Alyssa is, and worse, she knows where we are. Alyssa's place is enchanted, so Morgan can't breach it—yet."

"I'll get directions from Ceri and be there as soon as I can. Don't be in bed when I get there."

Rowan wanted to convince Seamus he didn't need any help, but Seamus had shielded his thoughts. He could have sworn he heard Seamus laughing though.

"Shit." He'd had other plans for Alyssa, plans that included spending most of the afternoon in bed. Bonding sexually with one's talisman was as important as training her and a helluva lot more fun. *It'd serve Seamus right to wait on the porch with Shadow growling at him from the other side of the front door while I wake Alyssa properly.* Yet he knew enough about her already to know she wouldn't be pleased to have Seamus catch the two of them in bed.

Uncertain about how much convincing Seamus would need for Ceri to give him directions to Alyssa's house or about the condition of the main road, Rowan couldn't judge how much time they had. But he hoped he had enough to love Alyssa in the shower at least. He rolled out of bed, padded into her surprisingly large master bathroom, and turned on the tap to heat the water.

∽

Alyssa surfaced slowly from the pleasant dream of Rowan kissing her everywhere to discover she wasn't dreaming. Her nipples were damp and hard, and that lovely sensation between her legs was his busy mouth as he slid his tongue up and down her seam before centering his attention on her clit, licking and sucking it into a hard nub of sensation. When she tried to sit up, he threw a restraining arm across her belly. She squirmed beneath his arm, his ministrations driving her wild.

"Rowan!"

He pressed his lips against her body before sliding a finger inside her. She bucked against him and screamed as she fell over the edge into bliss.

He looked up at her with a cheeky grin. "Good afternoon, Alyssa. Sleep well?" he asked as though she'd just arrived for breakfast, which she sort of had—his breakfast.

"You're unbelievable."

"I'll take that as a compliment. Now you need to roll your sweet ass out of bed before we run out of hot water in the shower," he said as he reached for her.

Still reeling from the incredible way he had awakened her, she obediently took his hand and followed him into the bathroom.

Once they were in the shower, she noticed Rowan was in a state requiring her attention. She gifted him an impish smirk as she grasped his shaft, stroking him with one hand while she placed the other behind his neck to urge him down for a kiss.

When she touched him, he surged up into her hand before reaching behind her legs, grasping her thighs and lifting her, fully opening her to him. She sighed and guided him into her.

"You're so responsive, Alyssa. My perfect mate."

His words washed over her as he pinned her against the shower wall and drove into her.

"Watch us, Pixie-girl. See what I'm telling you," he commanded.

Shyly, Alyssa glanced between them and watched in awe as

Rowan moved his big body inside her. So erotic. So beautiful. The sight of them coming together was almost more than she could bear, yet she couldn't look away.

Rowan started moving faster as she tightened herself around him. The intensity of his desire overwhelmed her, and she clung to him through the storm of their lovemaking.

Afterward, as they stepped out of the shower together, Rowan casually mentioned, "You might want to get a move on since we're probably entertaining guests momentarily."

"*What?* Have the gods somehow breached Gram's enchantments?" In a panic, she dragged a towel over her body.

"Nah, it's Seamus—and probably my brother Rio who's apparently been frantic about me since we started training last night. Good thing we went grocery shopping yesterday since it looks like we're having a family reunion for brunch."

She raced into the bedroom and hurriedly threw on some clothes before towel drying her hair. "How do you know Seamus and your brother will be visiting us? I didn't hear any phones ringing. In fact, I don't think any of them are working in this storm."

"Seamus caught me in an unguarded moment. In fact, he woke me up, he was thinking so loud," Rowan groused. "He said he'd get directions to your place from Ceri, which I take it means she'll be with him too."

"Have you been shielding him?" she asked curiously as she rounded the corner into the kitchen.

"Of course."

"Why?"

"I communicate with him telepathically when I need to, but you'll find that using civilian forms of communication is usually much better. It keeps people from thinking you're crazy," he spun his index finger near his temple, "and it's more difficult for Morgan and her minions to know what we're doing and where we are. When we disturb the cosmos with the energy of our telepathic conversations, she can find us." He opened the fridge and pulled out eggs and bacon, setting them on the counter beside the stove.

"Why take chances like the conversation in the bar the other night then?" Seeing what he did, she pulled pans from the cupboard and placed them on the stove.

As he cracked eggs into a bowl, he explained. "Such short bursts usually aren't enough for her to home in on us unless she's looking for us. After her little escapade Thursday afternoon in LA, she probably satisfied herself I'd be no threat for a while, so she wasn't paying attention to me."

"And now?"

"And now, I imagine we're high on her radar and not in a good way." He whisked eggs while she laid bacon to sizzle in the pan. "Our safety and our power will increase exponentially on my twenty-eighth birthday, so she's going to put the pressure on between now and then. It's good Seamus is coming over. He can help us with your telepathic training and learning how to remain observant for your own safety."

Shadow interrupted their conversation with a bark as he leaped up from his spot behind the loveseat and bounded toward the front door. Alyssa walked over and peered out the window to see two large bundled-up figures standing on her front step, but she held back from answering their insistent knock.

"It's all right, Alyssa. Seamus and Rio would like to come in," Rowan said. "Good to be cautious, though."

She opened the door and invited their guests inside.

"Whoa! Your place didn't look big enough from the outside to house a horse in it," Seamus commented as he gazed at Shadow standing guard beside her.

"Hello, Seamus. Meet Shadow. You must be Rio," Alyssa said, addressing the tall stranger who trailed Seamus into her home. "You don't look as much like Rowan in person. Shadow, these are friends—I think."

"What does she mean by that?" Rio asked Rowan who stood behind her.

"She's been watching our battles for the past six months. She thought we might be twins or dual incarnations of the same person," Rowan said.

Rio narrowed his eyes. "This black-haired elf is your talisman?"

Alyssa bristled. "I don't think size has anything to do with it." Dismissing Rio, she turned to Seamus. "Where is Ceri? Rowan thought you'd bring her too."

"There's no question she wanted to come along," Seamus said, "but I thought I might be able to help Rowan with some of your training, so it'd be safer for her not to be here."

"You were a gentleman with her the other night, weren't you?" Alyssa asked.

"Of course! What do you take me for?" He sounded offended. Then he looked between Rio and Rowan and understood what she asked.

"Rowan told you about how I like the ladies, huh?" His booming laugh filled the room.

"He said you're like Gawain from the King Arthur legends. You like all the girls, and all the girls like you," she said.

"That's mostly true. I even got a smile or two out of you the other night. Against your will, I think," Seamus said with a grin before sobering. "I don't poach talismans. But I'll enjoy a civilian every now and again."

Rowan and Rio burst out laughing. Unperturbed, Seamus continued. "I don't use anyone. Every woman I take to bed has as good a time as I do, and they usually thank me in the morning." That comment even brought a smile to Alyssa's mouth. "When I sense a woman might not be an ordinary civilian, I try my sign, take her home, wish her good night, and return to our not-so-comfortable apartment alone. Which is what happened with Ceri on Friday night."

"How did you convince her not to come along today?" Alyssa asked. "My friend tends to be protective and quite determined."

"I told her Rowan's SUV broke down, and he needed help to get it running again. She'd be bored sitting in my truck while we were outside in the wind and snow trying to start Rowan's ride. You weren't even in the picture."

"Of course, you stayed completely out of Ceri's head and didn't give her any suggestions about how safe Alyssa was or anything like that," Rowan mentioned, his words dripping sarcasm.

"I might have." Seamus shrugged. "But only to keep her occupied while we focus on training Alyssa," he finished in a rush.

Throughout the conversation, Seamus and Rio had been removing cold weather gear and now stood rather awkwardly with their outerwear in their hands. Without a word, Alyssa relieved them of their coats, hanging them neatly in the closet.

"We're making omelets for brunch," Rowan said. "I imagine you'd like to join us."

"Don't mind if we do."

Rowan rolled his eyes at Seamus's teasing grin.

Alyssa watched Rio who was more reticent than their more gregarious friend. There was a definite family resemblance, though Rio stood slightly taller than Rowan, his sable hair darker. Where Rowan's eyes were aquamarine, Rio's were deep blue, like a mountain loch somewhere in Scotland. His was built bigger too, all shoulders, chest, and biceps his sweater had to stretch over to accommodate. The three enormous men seemed to take up all the room in her house.

She went into the kitchen to pour mugs of coffee, offering them to Seamus and Rio who sat on barstools at the island. Alyssa shook her head as she watched them.

It's like we've all been together for years instead for the first time. How did that happen?

After serving the newcomers their coffee, she assisted Rowan with the omelets. He whisked eggs and milk while bacon fried in her largest skillet on the stove. She gave him an incredulous look when she noticed the opened egg cartons beside him—he'd used a dozen plus eggs for the omelets.

How on earth will these men eat so much?

"Yeah, these two can pack away the groceries," Rowan said, reading her unguarded thoughts. "You probably need to chop another onion while you're prepping the veggies."

Smacking her knife against the cutting board, she cried, "Stop doing that!"

Seamus and Rio exchanged a grin and settled in for the fireworks.

"Maybe I would have been more successful fending off your pseudo-Morgan attacks this morning if you'd first taught me how to shield my thoughts," she snapped. "The telepathy part of this whole life-change is the least fun for me at the moment."

"If you'd been able to shield your thoughts these last few days, I would have missed out on knowing some very nice sentiments you harbor for me." Rowan winked at her.

Her face on fire, she tilted her head regally. "That's enough, Rowan."

Seamus and Rio doubled over in laughter.

"It's not nearly enough, Alyssa, but we'll take care of that later—in private."

She wanted to throw something at him, but all she had in her hand was a knife, which was more than the situation called for, even in her agitated state. She ground her teeth on her retort and stomped over to the fridge for another onion. Carefully keeping her mind blank, she shared her emotions in the loud and violent way she chopped the onions into tiny pieces. Maddeningly, the three of them erupted into gales of laughter.

Seamus recovered first. "Alyssa, Rowan is an expert at shielding his thoughts. He can even do it in his sleep—literally. But I'm pretty good too, and I'll be delighted to help you keep him out of your head."

"Can we start the training now before I think something truly inappropriate that all of you hear?"

The men grinned at her good-naturedly, but Alyssa wasn't kidding.

"Let's wait until after we eat. It's always better to train on a full stomach," Seamus replied.

Rio watched their exchange like a spectator at a tennis match. "Alyssa, did you see the fight on Thursday afternoon in real time?"

"I thought it was a daydream, but apparently I did. That's how I knew who you were when you walked through my door. I've actually seen you on several occasions over the past few months."

"Did you help Rowan to safety? I tried to help him, but he disappeared. As Seamus said, Rowan can shield his thoughts even in his sleep, so I didn't know where he went," Rio said, his tone accusatory as he stared first at his brother, then at her.

"She didn't know she was helping me, bro. She thought she was reaching out in a dream. In fact, neither of us realized she'd sent me home until last night when we discovered that she's a dreamer."

"When did you two meet again?" Rio asked. His suspicious tone bewildered her.

"Friday night," Seamus said.

"Not quite." Rowan focused on cooking breakfast. "Alyssa came to me on Thursday afternoon because she wanted a security system out here. I would have come out here that day, but Isla informed me of the battle brewing in L.A., so I left during my consultation with Alyssa. Friday night she didn't want to ruin the evening with shop talk," he rolled his eyes at her, "so when Ceri and you went for drinks, we agreed to pretend we'd just met." Returning his attention to his cooking, he folded omelets in the pan.

The look on Rio's face left her uneasy. This man didn't trust her.

"But you didn't realize she was your talisman until Friday night. I know that for a fact," Seamus insisted.

"True. We had a conversation while Ceri and you were dancing, and it made me think she might be my talisman, so I tried my sign, and here we are." Rowan pulled her close to him. "In every way, Alyssa is exactly what I need."

She glowed in the warmth of his comment and his embrace and tried to ignore Rio's obvious skepticism.

"That still doesn't explain how she was able to intervene in Thursday's battle," Rio said.

The look Rowan and Alyssa exchanged made it clear neither of them had even thought about it.

At last she asked the question on all of their minds. "What does it mean that I could help you before I even knew anything about warriors, talismans, the ongoing war with the gods, telepathy, any of it?"

"I don't know, but I think we'd better find out."

The seriousness of Rowan's response set the tone for the afternoon.

CHAPTER FIFTEEN

FTER THIS NEW revelation, the men were quiet. Without the ability to read minds at will, Alyssa couldn't know what preoccupied them to the point even Seamus wasn't joking for once, which worried her. How would this new revelation affect her growing relationship with Rowan?

She tried not to think these thoughts... tried not to think at all. Yet every time she made her mind blank, the white space only lasted a few seconds before filling with images of fear and failure and worry. She was in so far over her head she was drowning and didn't know how to ask for a lifeline.

Rowan shook his head at her. "Will you excuse us for a few minutes, please?" he said to Rio and Seamus. "Alyssa, come with me." With his hand in the small of her back, he guided her down the hall.

Once inside her office, he closed the door behind them. "You did nothing wrong, so stop worrying that somehow you screwed up when you helped me the other night. I think the fact we were communicating telepathically, and you were tuned into me in battle is because we'd met earlier that day. Something about our relationship is so strong we started bonding before we knew what we are to each other. Though something important is happening here, until we can talk to someone more knowledgeable than any of us, we have to sit tight."

He held her lightly in the circle of his arms as he spoke. She wrapped her arms around his waist and snuggled against his chest. For several minutes they clung together, drawing strength from each other.

"I don't know how you figured out I'm a private person, but I'm grateful. Bill loved public displays of affection, as though I were an object more than a person," she said into Rowan's chest. With a snort, she added, "Nothing in my experience with Bill was normal, even contrasted with your supernatural world." Leaning back, she looked up at him. "No doubt I've fallen down the rabbit hole, but the oddities of Warriorland are much easier to deal with than my last relationship."

"I'm working on earning your trust, Alyssa." He brushed a light kiss on her lips. "You ready to go back out there?"

She nodded.

When they returned to the kitchen, they found Rio and Seamus speculating about what it could mean that she helped Rowan before they knew their true relationship. Over brunch, talk continued about how Morgan would respond to this new talisman and warrior pairing and how all of them would be affected. No one had any doubt Morgan's reaction would be terrifying.

"What about the great warriors of Celtic myth: Finn MacCool, Cuchulan, King Arthur, Lancelot, Tristan? All of them had to take on supernatural enemies, and all of them experienced triumphs and failures," Alyssa said before she slumped halfway onto a barstool. "No real comfort there." Then she blinked. *What about the journals we still haven't read? Maybe they contain some information or an example.*

"What journals?" Seamus and Rio asked simultaneously.

"Hello? Now all three of you can access my thoughts? Rowan, I demand you show me how to shield my mind this minute."

The choking noise told her he tried not laugh, the circumstances demanding more from him.

Recovering, Rowan said, "I think instead, Rio and Seamus need to open their minds, so you can access their thoughts while we divide up your grandmother's notebooks for some after-brunch reading. If we're all working together, we may be able to see patterns that will help us figure out our connection, among other things."

"At the risk of sounding a bit thick, I'll ask again. What notebooks?" Rio asked.

"Won't everyone opening their minds invite Morgan and whoever to my house?" Alyssa asked over Rio.

Rowan addressed Alyssa first. "Your grandmother enchanted this place so well I think we're safe sharing thoughts." Turning to Rio, he explained, "The notebooks are a series of journals Alyssa's grandmother kept. The most revealing part of them so far is her family tree."

While Seamus and Rio took over kitchen duty, Rowan and Alyssa arranged the journals, beginning with her great-grandparents since they'd already read about her parents and grandparents and found nothing to help them navigate their own situation. Rowan left open Alyssa's family tree for Rio's examination.

His quick intake of breath followed by a low whistle let everyone know he'd discovered something important. "You're all named Ailsa all the way back to our common ancestor."

"Yeah, we caught that," Rowan said.

Rio wasn't finished. "Also, the firstborn daughters always marry a man whose name begins with an R."

"Let me see that," Rowan demanded. "When I looked at the family tree before, I focused on Alyssa's middle name and its implications and missed the other pattern. Obviously, the women in Alyssa's family are paired with their mates in a way that leaves nothing to chance." He looked at Alyssa and Rio in turn. "Divine intervention is at work here."

"This situation never gets better, does it?" Alyssa's mouth turned down. "You mentioned once that a talisman without her warrior was in more danger than one with him, but I'm not sure I believe you. Before Friday night, the worst I could expect was a scary dream from which I knew I'd awaken. Now my life is starting to feel like a waking nightmare."

Rowan slipped his arm around her and pulled her closer to him, reassuring her with his nearness that she had his protection.

For the next several hours, each read silently, occasionally sharing a funny anecdote or an exciting battle experience, but no information revealing a precedent or explanation for the powerful connection Rowan and Alyssa shared. As the afternoon wore into evening, the team concluded that Rowan and Alyssa sailed in uncharted waters they'd have to navigate on their own.

Seamus yawned and stretched. "Got anything stronger than coffee around here?"

"Beer and wine in the fridge," Alyssa said.

"Beer is fine. What's for dinner?" he asked.

"You never change, do you?" Rio laughed. "Always needing a good time on a full belly."

"Hey, if you treat life like the party it is, it's a helluva lot of fun. I need to work on showing you now that my old partner here is about to go all house bound," Seamus said, winking at Rowan.

"Fighting Morgan and finding your talisman should be your priorities Seamus, old man. Waiting until the last minute to meet your destiny seems too daring to me," Rio replied.

"I didn't wait until the last minute," Rowan said.

"Damn close enough," Rio retorted.

"Rio, son, lighten up. It wasn't like Rowan wasn't trying," Seamus said.

"Early on, he was as wild as you are now, and he almost paid the ultimate price for that. Do you honestly want to wait until the last minute and take a chance on one of us having to face you in battle or worse?" In an exasperated tone Rio added, "You have a decidedly cavalier approach to the single most important task any warrior has after fighting alongside and for his brothers."

Rowan cut him off, mid-rant. *"I think Shadow needs to step outside for a few minutes. Why don't you accompany him, Rio?"*

Without a word, Rio stood and headed to the laundry room, calling for Shadow as he went. The massive dog silently padded after him.

Alyssa had been watching the men's exchange like a spectator at a tennis match. *There are currents of history and understanding swirling around me, but I can't follow them.*

He raised an eyebrow at her, an indication he'd been listening to her thoughts again.

Leaping to her feet, hands on hips, Alyssa glared at Rowan. "That. Is. Absolutely. It. *Someone* needs to teach me how to shield my thoughts, and that training begins now." When he didn't seem inclined to jump to her demands, she turned to his friend. "Will you help me, Seamus?"

"Happy to. Is there somewhere private we can go?" Though he spoke to Alyssa, he directed his question to Rowan. The man scowled but said nothing.

"We can go into my office. It's in here," Alyssa said as she shot Rowan a dark look before leading the way out of the great room. Sticking out her tongue would have been childish, but the message was clear.

Rowan sat alone debating the wisdom of allowing Seamus to train Alyssa when Rio and Shadow came in from the backyard.

"Have you calmed down?" he asked before Rio closed the door.

"He's not nearly serious enough about his responsibilities, Rowan, and you know it. Why don't you say something?"

"Seamus is one of the best warriors I know. I trust him

completely. I also think a lot of his showmanship and womanizing is just that—for show. He never meets a woman he doesn't test with his sign. Since his sign's so easy, a design he traces on the inside of a woman's wrist as he shakes her hand, he has an opportunity with every woman he meets."

Rowan stood and stretched. "To be honest, I respect Seamus. He's unsuccessfully tested hundreds of women in the last four years, and he still isn't discouraged. Even after he picked up that both Ceri and Alyssa were talismans but not his, he cheerfully entertained us all then went home alone. He plays all the time, but he plays fair." He crossed his arms over his chest and stared down his brother. "He could have poached Ceri the other night, but he didn't. He only sleeps with civilians. And he's right about having fun. You might actually learn some things from him."

"Speaking of Seamus and women, where is he? Where is Alyssa?"

A sheepish expression crossed Rowan's face. "I listened in on Alyssa's thoughts one too many unnecessary times today, and she pitched a fit." He scrubbed a hand through his hair. "When I didn't immediately volunteer to teach her how to shield her thoughts, Seamus jumped right on it. They're in the office training right now."

Rio's eyes widened in surprise. "Why doesn't she know how to shield?"

"Long story. Anyway, I thought if I could listen in on her thoughts, I could learn more about her, stuff I might need to know, but she might not want to share yet. It was cowardly and devious of me, I admit, but I couldn't help it. She doesn't trust easily, so I was damned if I did and damned if I didn't train her." Rowan blew out a breath and headed into the kitchen.

Refreshing his coffee, he said, "Seamus made it easy by taking over her training. I let it happen because that way I won't be tempted to train her to shield everyone but me. As the two of us are well aware, sometimes in families especially, it's better if we can't listen in on everyone's thoughts whenever we want."

Rio grinned. "You were pretty merciless teasing Riley by listening to his thoughts about a particular girl and then sharing them with the family at dinner. Good thing Dad took pity on him and trained him to shield his thoughts, especially from you."

Rowan grinned back at his brother. "Anyway, they're training, so we should probably try to create something edible."

Rio opened the fridge to discover leftover chicken dinner from the night before and chuckled. "I see you've already made your two specialties—chicken ravioli and omelets. Guess it's up to me to figure out the menu for tonight."

As he sorted through the groceries in the fridge, Rio asked, "So, about the other night. I saw Morgan's minions slice you at least two or three times. You were bleeding pretty heavily when I got to you right before Alyssa whisked you to safety. Did you see a healer?"

"In a manner of speaking. Alyssa has some salve her grandmother made. She rubbed it into the scars as we trained last night. See for yourself." Rowan lifted his shirt. The angry red wounds Alyssa massaged with salve the night before had miraculously healed to thin pink scars. "A few more applications of the salve, and my body will be perfect again." He waggled his brows as he lowered his shirt.

"Impressive. Are you sure she's a talisman and not a druid?" Rio pulled some burger from the fridge and looked questioningly at Rowan.

"You saw her today. Her eyes practically glaze over when she reads the recipes for healing." He pulled a pan from the cupboard and set it on the stove. "The salve was something her grandmother prepared and insisted she learn. She says she paid attention to that one because she could see how useful it was when her grandma would smear it on her wounds from climbing trees and wrecking her bike as a kid."

"Huh," Rio nodded. "Spaghetti okay for dinner?"

"You know it." Rowan grabbed a pot and filled it with water

for pasta. "To be honest, that salve burned like hell as she applied it, but she was so involved in the vision of the battle she was oblivious to my discomfort. A druid would have had all sorts of physical empathy for my pain had one been applying the salve."

"Still, how could a talisman have such a healing effect on a warrior? I've never seen that before, even with our parents." Then Rio smirked. "Sooo, how are your nights together?"

"Don't go there, little brother," Rowan warned. "That's private between Alyssa and me. I'll tell you though—I understand why warriors don't stray from their talismans once they meet them." He couldn't help his smile.

"With a couple exceptions." Rio didn't smile.

"We don't know everything that happened there, so let's leave Seamus's sister out of this. I'm sure Siobhan had no intention of coming between Duncan MacManus and Jennifer Carlin. As we know from family experience, not all warriors' relationships are meant to be," Rowan said, his tone making it clear the subject was closed.

In the study, Seamus exacted disciplined and demanding training of Alyssa. Over and over he insisted she visualize the barriers she needed to erect around her thoughts. The work gave her a headache and made her sweat, both of which surprised her. Who knew thinking could be such desperately hard work? However, she basked in her progress. Twice already she'd thwarted Seamus when he'd tried to sneak a listen into her thoughts while he distracted her with jokes and stories.

Peeking at him from beneath her brows, she asked, "How do I listen to someone else's thoughts on purpose?"

"That particular skill isn't as critical as keeping others out of your head. Besides, Rowan is a master at shielding," he advised her.

She frowned. "I thought you were kidding about his skill."

If she were honest with herself, she hoped Rowan might come to trust her enough to let her in sometimes. Then she had to laugh. Since she didn't fully trust any of these men, Rowan included, how ironic she wished for his trust. But what did he think, and how did he truly feel about her? Bill Forbes had been nice in the beginning too.

A couple hours later, Rowan knocked on the door to the study to announce dinner.

"Damn. We've been training so hard, I forgot all about food," Seamus said, wonder in his voice. His stomach made a loud announcement of its own, and they all chuckled.

As she preceded him out of the office, Seamus roughed her hair, his voice gruff. "Well done, little dreamer. I think you're going to do fine."

CHAPTER SIXTEEN

THOUGH EXHAUSTED, ALYSSA glowed in Seamus's praise. Normally, she would have taken bristling offense to a diminutive such as Seamus had given her, but oddly, she was comfortable with him, like the big brother she never had. She'd put up with a lot from Seamus Lochlann, especially when she heard him say, "She's quick, Rowan. You're lucky," as they reentered the kitchen.

They seated themselves at the counter while Rowan and Rio placed spaghetti and sauce in front of them. A tossed salad already waited on the island. The brothers each had a beer, and Seamus joined them. Alyssa settled for ice water, fearing alcohol would impede her newly acquired skills—ones she hoped Rowan would test over dinner.

"What did you two do while Alyssa was learning how to keep us all out of her head?" Seamus asked around a mouthful of spaghetti.

"We read more of the journals," Rowan said. "There are a lot of enchantments, spells and recipes for special herbal concoctions the druids in Alyssa's family have perfected over the years. We probably should contact a druid and see what she makes of them."

"Anyone particular in mind?" Seamus asked casually, but he sat straighter in his chair, his hand gripping his fork as he awaited their answer.

"Your sister might be a good choice," Rowan said.

Seamus visibly relaxed and shoveled in another bite of food.

"You have a sister, Seamus?" Alyssa asked. The idea she might have some female insight into the world she'd been forced to enter excited her.

"Yeah. Siobhan lives nearby. She's quite an accomplished druid, but she fell in love with a warrior. Though his talisman lives near them, it isn't an ideal situation. It bothers some warriors in our society," Seamus said, glaring at Rio. The layers of the playboy named Seamus kept peeling away for Alyssa. He was far more complex than she'd thought when she met him on Friday night.

"Since some history of that same situation exists in Alyssa's family, Siobhan is the best druid to consult about Afton's journals," Rowan said, apparently ignoring the undercurrents of attitude swirling around the conversation.

"What do you mean?" Seamus asked.

Rio apprised him of Alyssa's grandparents' unusual situation.

"Her grandmother was widowed when she was twenty-eight and her husband was thirty?" Seamus asked with more than a little concern. "You do realize those are Siobhan's and Duncan's ages?"

"Well then, we'll have to warn them as well as secure their help with understanding the druidic lore in the journals," Rio said sarcastically, not bothering to hide his attitude about Seamus's sister. Turning to Alyssa, he said, "You're going to need extensive training. What are your commitments? Do you have a job?"

She blinked and looked at Rowan who took a studied interest in his dinner. Obviously, Rio had figured out she and Rowan hadn't talked about much personal stuff yet. How embarrassing.

Clearing her throat, she said, "I attend a study group once a week on Fridays and teach an undergraduate class twice a week on Tuesday and Thursday mornings." She shifted her focus from Rowan. "Whenever this storm lets up enough for phone or internet service, I can make a call to a colleague to substitute in the class. How long are we talking?" No longer hungry, she toyed with her spaghetti.

"A few days," Rowan said. "A week maybe. We need to drive up to Flathead Lake where our parents live. We'll invite Siobhan and Duncan along to help us."

"What are they helping us with, other than discovering why we connected so early?"

Rowan set down his fork and took a pull from his beer before answering. "They might be able to give us some insights into any old tales or prophecies concerning the coming together of the lines descended from Findlay and Ailsa Sheridan. Since your family tends to run to women all named for Ailsa, and our family runs to men, all named for Findlay, a connection must exist."

None of Alyssa's recent training helped her shield her thoughts at this news. Somehow, her destiny with Rowan had been determined centuries ago on a Scottish battlefield when a greedy goddess and her vengeful sister stole a talisman against all the rules of nature and heaven. In a flash of insight, Alyssa saw that she and Rowan were the instruments to right this injustice.

She looked up and squirmed at the intense way all three men stared at her.

"That's quite a vision you just had, little dreamer," Seamus said, his tone grave.

"You saw that?" she squeaked.

"We all saw it," Rio said dryly though his tone didn't jibe with the fierce look on his face.

"Sorry, Seamus. I guess I'm kind of a slow student," she apologized before she hazarded a look at Rowan. His demeanor had taken on an ominousness that frightened yet energized her.

"That sort of vision in a novice, even one who learns as quickly as you do, would be difficult to contain. Besides, it gives us a clue about what's happening here with the two of you and why it has the gods in such an uproar," Seamus said, ruffling Alyssa's hair.

Abruptly, Rowan stood. "I'd ask you two to stay for dessert, but Alyssa and I have quite a lot to discuss before our departure tomorrow. Besides, it's going to take you some time to drive back to town in the dark in this storm."

"I kind of thought we'd spend the night," Seamus said as he finished off his beer. "It wouldn't be wise to send warriors, even with the prowess Rio and I possess, out into this storm at night after we've downed a few beers."

"Really, Rowan, I don't think Seamus and Rio should return to town tonight. One of them can sleep on the loveseat." At Rio's raised eyebrows, she explained, "It pulls out into a double bed. The other one can sleep on the futon in the office. Admittedly, neither bed is much for men your size, but it's better than being caught out in this storm."

Rowan's annoyance at the way Seamus engineered an invitation to stay with them showed boldly on his face. Seamus returned his frown with a smirk that Rio echoed when Alyssa looked at him for approval.

"I'm glad we settled that. Now, what's for dessert?" Seamus asked with a broad grin, and Alyssa had the distinct impression she'd been had.

"I think I'll take Shadow out for a few minutes while you guys rustle up dessert," Rio said. "Care to join me, Seamus?" It was more of a command than an invitation, which Seamus answered by moving toward the back door.

"What was that all about?" Alyssa asked when the two men departed to the backyard with Shadow.

"I was trying to have some private time with you tonight before we end up in the loud and public world that is my parents' home.

Seamus knew it and thought it would be a lark to tease us by staying the night."

"But they can't drive back to town in this weather," Alyssa insisted.

"They can. I hope those beds you're offering are short and lumpy," Rowan grumbled.

"They're definitely short for such big men." It occurred to her she'd compromised her privacy with Rowan. Now what? She couldn't share her bed with him with an audience down the hall. The situation had suddenly become genuinely embarrassing.

The look on Rowan's face told her he knew exactly what she was thinking. She threw up her hands. "Ugh! I'll never figure out how to keep you out of my head, will I?"

"You were shielding your thoughts very well, but you weren't controlling your expressions, so I have an idea about what's going on in your head."

She smiled at him. "You really couldn't hear what I was thinking?"

"Not a word. But I can guess you figured out your generous offer of a bed for the night for those two means the two of us have no privacy for what we both want to do once we go to bed."

Her face heated, but she didn't deny his observation.

The back door banging open announced the return of the other two men and Shadow.

"It's let up considerably out there," Rio said. "Something must be brewing for Taranis to ease up so abruptly. The roads are probably passable if we head out now, so we've decided to show some mercy and leave the two of you alone for the night." He smiled broadly at them, and Alyssa gaped at the first real smile she'd seen on Rio's face. He was devastating when he smiled that way. Some woman was going to be very lucky, she hoped.

Seamus couldn't hide his mirth at the joke that resulted in Alyssa's invitation for them to stay the night. "I had no intention of cramping your style, Rowan. I just wanted to mess with you. Alyssa's vision means a major battle involving all of us if I don't miss my guess, so I wanted some fun while I had the chance."

"Wrap up that tiramisu I saw in the fridge earlier and make sure you're ready to go when we arrive to pick you up in the morning," Rio interrupted.

Rowan laughed and took the entire dessert, less the two pieces he and Alyssa had eaten the previous night, and placed it in his brother's hands. "You need all the sweetening you can get, little brother." He chuckled, then he sobered. "Be careful out there. The let-up in the weather may be a trap. We'll stay alert until you let us know you're safe in town."

Rowan stood on the porch as Rio and Seamus climbed into Seamus's four-wheel drive truck for the ride back to town.

Alyssa cleaned up the last of the dinner dishes. When she'd entered the kitchen earlier and saw the mound of spaghetti they had prepared, she thought there would be leftovers for a day or two. As she scraped plates and loaded the dishwasher, she tried to process that hardly any food remained. How these men could eat so much and stay in such excellent shape she would never understand. If she ate like that, she'd have to wear out her treadmill.

Lost in her thoughts, she didn't hear Rowan come back inside until he appeared behind her, slipping his hands beneath her shirt to warm them on her belly. Alyssa jumped and squealed. "Oh my God, Rowan, your hands are freezing! Where did you come from? Siberia?" She squirmed, trying to elude his icy hands, but he held her against his equally cold shirt and simultaneously teased her and warmed himself.

"What is it with you guys and practical jokes anyway?" She panted, her heart racing like she'd run a marathon.

"When a man doesn't know when or where the next battle will come, he learns to have fun in the quiet moments. Besides, you're too easy," Rowan said as he nibbled on her ear. "We're going to have to work on your awareness, Pixie-girl."

His intentions shifted from warming his hands to exploring her body, and Alyssa went still as his thumbs grazed the undersides of her breasts, bringing her nipples to attention, her belly rippling and quivering as he traced his fingers over her skin. Mesmerized, she held her breath in anticipation of his next move.

"You're so responsive, Pixie-girl. A man could lose himself touching you like this. All afternoon, I've been desperate to get my hands on you," he whispered, rubbing his cheek over her hair.

She relaxed and covered his hands with hers, anchoring herself to him. They stood silently absorbing each other for several minutes before he reluctantly slid his hands from beneath her sweater and let her go. She threw a questioning look over her shoulder, and he smiled ruefully. "I need to stay alert until Seamus and Rio confirm they've safely returned to the apartment, remember? And you need to make a phone call to someone to cover your classes."

Nodding, she pulled out her cell. "Hey, what do you know? I have a dial tone. Guess that means we're back on the grid." Dialing up a colleague with whom she'd traded classes in the past, she made the necessary arrangements. When she hung up, she found Rowan sipping a beer and gazing out at the darkness through the living room window.

"What is it?"

"You need to know the plan and why we're taking you away from this sweet enchanted house of yours."

"You don't seem too happy about it."

"I'm not. I'd rather stay here with you and quietly—and thoroughly—get to know you much better."

The hot expression on his face arrowed a shiver straight to her core.

"But Morgan's appearance last night coupled with the storm Taranis visited on us the past few days tells me that's a luxury we have to miss. Your vision earlier today emphasized that fact."

Taking her hand, he led her over to the loveseat. "My mother is a master storyteller and keeper of the Celtic mythology and family history that gives warriors in my family some advantages in our never-ending battles with the goddesses. If anyone knows what our connection means, it's my mom, so we need to go to her for help."

"Why can't we just give her a call?"

"There are too many ways to intercept the conversation, and we don't want to give the unholy trio—Morgan, Maeve, and Taranis—any advantages."

"Oh." Picking at the hem of her sweater, she asked, "Why don't you visualize us there?"

Like he couldn't stop himself from touching her, Rowan tucked her hair behind her ear. "I can't take you with me when you've never seen the place. You don't have the power to visualize yourself anywhere, and the power for a warrior to visualize his talisman to another place depends on her having seen it so she can help him take her to wherever they're going."

She frowned.

"It's a complicated process, unfortunately, because the problem is that we're vulnerable to attack on the road. Have you ever been to the Flathead?"

"No."

"It's a long drive from here, especially on the roads Taranis left us. It'll take most of the day tomorrow if we're lucky. Longer if we're not." He glanced at the notebooks on the coffee table. "We're taking your grandmother's journals with us and all the embroideries you have in the house, so you might want to gather up that stuff while I jury-rig a security system for while we're away. I don't trust Morgan to leave your house alone if she has someone willing to break in." He gave her a pointed look. "Your old boyfriend comes to mind."

"Why do we need to take the journals?"

"Because we don't want Morgan to know what your family knew so she can circumvent the protections your grandma devised to keep Morgan and other malevolent gods at bay."

"And the embroideries?"

His expression softened. "Your designs have power. I felt it when I looked at the first one at dinner the other night. Your state of mind when you created it gives the owner strength and confidence. I can feel it," he touched his pocket, "which is why the one you gave me is on my person and will stay with me all the time, especially when I have to be away from you." He brushed his knuckles over the skin of her cheek. "That sort of power would be lethal in the wrong hands."

"I was practicing a hobby, a creative outlet for stress. I didn't set out to make what you've described." Alyssa shook her head. "I've never felt any of what you say is in my work."

"I'll bet your grandmother did. Did you give away any of your designs?"

"Only to my closest friends when I was growing up. And to Gram, of course." Pain lanced through her chest. "She boxed them with her jewelry," she whispered over the lump in her throat. Sucking in a deep breath, she collected herself. "It surprised me she thought of those silly little designs as treasures."

"They are treasures, and you have to be careful with them from now on." He slipped his arm around her. "Please tell me you didn't give any to Forbes."

"As a matter of fact, I didn't. I wanted to, but he thought my hobby boring and old-ladyish. Gram encouraged his disinterest. She and I fought about that too." Alyssa stared into the middle distance.

"She was a wise lady, your gram." The wistfulness in his tone warmed Alyssa before he switched gears. "We're going to have a short night as it is, so we better get on it." He gave her thigh a gentle squeeze. "You pack while I secure the house as well as I can for now."

"Do you want me to pack your clothes too?"

"If you wouldn't mind. I won't need much. A couple shirts, some underwear, a pair of jeans. The rest can stay." He cocked a brow.

"That sounds suspiciously like you think this is a permanent arrangement." She didn't know if she did or didn't like his heavy-handed way of barging into her life.

"Let's say the potential is pretty good. Besides, you weren't complaining when I woke you up." A slow, sexy smile spread over his face.

"There's more to a relationship than what goes on between the sheets," Alyssa said with a sniff.

"Or in the shower?"

She squeezed her eyes shut, blinked them open, but didn't back down. "Or in the shower. I haven't decided if you're staying or not."

The teasing ended. "Even with everything you know? We're facing a life or death situation whether or not you want to acknowledge it."

Leaving his question hanging, she stood and headed to her bedroom to pack.

Honestly, she didn't know what to think. Her intense attraction to Rowan wasn't in question. His presence had left her tingly from the moment they met. Everything about him appealed, even his size, which oddly excited rather than intimidated her. Maybe because of how well they fit together, especially in bed. The thought of his prowess between the sheets heated her everywhere. Such a virile man so attentive to her needs turned her on as much as his amazing body and remarkable sexual skill.

Then there was his lively and inquisitive mind. More than once over the past few days she'd been impressed with his intelligence and how much he knew about the Celts and their mythology, subjects dear to her for their aching beauty, generous mirth, and timeless lessons. Plus, he was a successful businessman as well as a man who knew his way around the house.

Her breath hitched at the peril in which she discovered her heart. What if he dumped her when he no longer needed her for whatever danger he anticipated Morgan planned? What if being his talisman was her major attraction and he tired of her when the newness wore off? She had so much to lose yet felt powerless to control anything happening in her life, a situation she didn't appreciate. At. All.

Still, for the next couple of hours, they worked in silence, Alyssa packing, boxing the journals, and gathering up embroideries from every book and drawer where she remembered them. The number of designs she'd created over the years amazed her. While she gathered her things, Rowan rigged an alarm system to a remote he programmed into his phone. If anything disturbed any of the windows or doors in her house, he said he'd be alerted and could message the police immediately.

Sitting on the floor in her office, she contemplated her favorite of her grandmother's tapestries. Since she wasn't thinking about anything in particular beyond the beautiful craftsmanship of Gram's work, she sensed Rowan entering the room. "If Morgan, Maeve, and Taranis are the unholy trio, then this must be the holy one—Brighid, Rhiannon, and Scathach, the three great ladies of the Celtic pantheon after Danu, the mother of all," Alyssa said without looking away from the tapestry.

"You said your grandmother wove all the tapestries in your home, right?"

"Yes, why?"

"We have to pack them away where someone like Forbes wouldn't think to look for them. They have power too—power we don't want in the wrong hands."

Alyssa made a face at him. "Who are the 'wrong hands,' and what could they possibly do with these tapestries?"

"If rogue warriors accessed these and could interpret them correctly, which the goddesses would assure, they could breach some of the protections your grandmother placed on you. We have to guard against that as much as we can."

The gravity of the situation weighed her down. First the journals, then her embroideries, now the tapestries. Without a word, she climbed up onto the futon and removed the tapestry from the wall. She folded it and headed down the hall to her bedroom to store it with some others in the sweater boxes under her bed. Rowan removed the large tree-of-life tapestry hanging in the hallway and carried it reverently to her bedroom.

After stowing the first two tapestries, they silently went about removing the tapestries hanging in the great room, and Alyssa noted unhappily how bare her home looked without Gram's decorations. As they packed away her art, Alyssa vowed to herself she'd learn all she could about enchantments, so she could protect herself, her home, and her loved ones, whoever they turned out to be. On the heels of that thought came another. Ceri.

As they put away the last tapestry, she broached the subject of her best friend. "You mentioned Seamus sensed Ceri might be a talisman. Does that mean she's in danger too?"

"For now, I'd say she's safe. Morgan is fixated on me, has been for the past six months. No doubt she'll have to forego whatever diabolical plans she had, but that will only fuel her revenge. Until I reach my next birthday, she's going to focus on me and try to find a way to win. Since you're my talisman, her attention will be on you too, not on a talisman whose warrior hasn't found her yet."

"Still, I have to call Ceri, tell her I'll be out of town for the next several days. Oh, and what am I going to do with Shadow?"

"Take him with us. As devoted to you as he is, he'll be an asset for whatever is coming."

Alyssa beamed at him. She couldn't imagine leaving Shadow behind for a week, especially when her situation appeared so uncertain.

"It's been a long day, Pixie-girl, and tomorrow is going to be longer. We should get some rest."

He held out his hand to her, and she took it, following him down the hall to her bedroom. Gently taking her in his arms, he folded her to him and whispered, "Whatever happens in the next few days, know that I care about you, and I'll do everything I can to keep you safe."

"I know." She lifted her face up for his kiss, a tender beginning that quickly heated to feverishly tearing off each other's clothes before they tumbled together into bed and a joining that seared both of them with its intensity. Rowan's hands roamed everywhere on Alyssa's body even as he buried himself so deep inside her she didn't know where she ended and he began. She ran her hands over all of him, memorizing his skin and muscle and bone as she met him over and over in their hot dance until she exploded, screaming his name.

Rowan took her two more times during the night, his need for her matched by hers for him, both insatiable. When morning interrupted their sleep, neither wanted to wake up.

CHAPTER SEVENTEEN

LYSSA PROTESTED ROWAN'S repeated calls to awaken while he tamped down his desire to wake her properly. They had more preparations to make before Seamus and Rio arrived, and they'd overslept already. When she refused to cooperate, he jerked the covers off her and pulled them out of reach. Sleepily rubbing her eyes, she sat up, her hair a tousled black cape around her creamy shoulders. He'd never seen anything more beautiful in his life, and he fervently wished the world would go away for a little while so they could enjoy each other again.

"Come on, sleepyhead. You don't want to be caught in bed by my brother and Seamus. You'll never hear the end of it."

His comment catapulted her out of bed. Then she turned and smiled seductively at him.

"Pixie-girl, you're killing me. You'll notice I'm already showered and dressed. For a reason. But if you keep looking at me like that, we're going to be busy when Rio and Seamus arrive, so busy in fact we probably won't hear them until they're on the other side of that door." He nodded toward her bedroom door. "But if that's what you want ..." Rowan began to remove his shirt.

"You're right, that wouldn't be good. I'll

be ready in a jiff," she said as she raced into the bathroom and closed the door on the desire he didn't bother to hide as he adjusted the bulge in the front of his jeans.

After prepping his famous omelets, he returned to the bedroom to find her showered, dressed, and carefully making up the bed.

"What?" she asked when she caught sight of him.

"Making sure you were moving." He grinned at her eye roll before he rounded the bed to the opposite side. "Need some help?"

They finished their task and headed out to the kitchen when Alyssa abruptly stopped mid-way down the hall. Without a word, she returned to the bedroom, emerging a couple minutes later with a tapestry in her hands.

"What are you doing?" Rowan asked.

"Making sure Bill doesn't go looking for something beyond what Morgan instructs him if he breaches your security system. He didn't like spending time here, said the place gave him the creeps, so we were usually at his place in town."

"Another example of his poor taste."

Her smile lit up the room.

He helped her hang a reproduction tapestry of *The Unicorn in the Garden* before following her to the great room where she took some framed photographs of herself and Gram Afton and herself and Shadow and hung them on the walls where the tapestries had been.

"Even as obtuse as Bill is, he'd probably notice the absence of the tapestries. He made several snide comments about them not being real art. Their absence might cause his ego to swell, thinking he influenced me somehow to get rid of them. It might be enough to keep him from looking for them."

"You're quick, Pixie-girl." Rowan said approvingly.

As they cooked and ate breakfast, he told her about his family.

"My mom is a bit of a bard, but she didn't see Dad coming until they met with only a few months to spare before he turned twenty-eight. Morgan was furious at losing a prize she thought she had in the bag." He forked a bite of eggs. "When Mom gave birth to three boys, Morgan actually sent gifts, visions of us in battle together with Dad, the outcome uncertain."

Alyssa widened her eyes over the brim of her coffee mug but didn't interrupt.

"The events strangely resembled the great battle Findlay and his sons Graeme, Owen, and Riordan fought. Instead of frightening my parents, obviously Morgan's intent, the visions resolved them to give us the finest training they could. They sought out Scathach to train us." He slid a second omelet from the platter in front of him and slathered it with salsa.

Alyssa sputtered the swallow of coffee she'd taken. "Are you telling me a goddess trained you to fight? The goddess who trained Cuchulan and the others?" Fanning herself, she said, "Either you're crazy, or I'm in way over my head."

With a grin, he said, "Yes, Alyssa, the great warrior goddess who trained all the best in mythological time also trained my brothers and me. She trained my father as well."

"Who, or should I ask, *what* are you? You look like a man, but I think you must be a god. Or maybe I've spent too much time in my Celtic studies for the last year and a half." She said that last part almost to herself.

Covering her hand, he stared into the beautiful silver of her eyes. "I really am a man. I'm mortal, and I have human needs and desires." He leered at her for emphasis, and she blinked at him. "But I come from an ancient heritage, as do you," he added pointedly, "that allows us to tap into abilities beyond everyday human understanding. You wouldn't have found all this so strange if your parents had lived. They would have taught you who you are and what your role is in our world. Your grandmother, for whatever reason, felt she couldn't tell you your true identity. Probably her life without a warrior's protection made her wary."

"Yeah, we've established I have gaps in my education. What else can you tell me about your family that might help me catch up?" Pushing her plate away, she leaned her elbows on the island and lifted her mug back to her lips. He blinked and dragged his mind back into the conversation.

"My mom, Sian, instructed my brothers and me in all our family history and the histories of the great heroes, those who won and those who lost, so when the time came for us to face Morgan, Maeve, Taranis, and the others, we'd be prepared. It's why I know so much about the Celts."

He pushed a bite of omelet and salsa onto his toast, enjoyed the whole works, then continued. "The only contingency over which neither Mom nor Dad had control was the timing of meeting our talismans. That event is in the hands of the gods. The cosmic joke, of course, is that I used to give my brother Riley a hard time about girls because he was so crazy about them from an early age, and he was the first of us to find his talisman." A 'go figure' expression passed over his face. "He married Lynnette over a year ago."

"Rio was angry at you and Seamus last night when we were talking about talismans. He said you were irresponsible. What did he mean?"

Rowan sighed. "He meant I was rebellious. I taunted Morgan by deliberately not trying my sign on many of the women I met. It was wrong-headed and stupid. When I was about twenty-five, I grew up, stopped chasing skirts for the fun of it, and actively started looking for my talisman. Since it took nearly another three years to find you, Rio was making a point that Seamus shouldn't be tempting fate." He wiped his mouth with his napkin and swallowed a sip of coffee.

"Rio, as you may have noticed, is a bit tightly wound. He could lighten up," he added, chuckling.

"Oh."

Gently tipping up her chin with his index finger, he forced her to look into his eyes. "You look especially sad right now. What are you thinking?"

"You don't already know?" she asked, pinkening in a way that had him tracing her cheeks with his fingers.

"No. You're shielding your thoughts well, but once again, your face is giving you away. You're worried about something, so out with it. We can't keep secrets from each other."

"I'm not sure I'm going to be all that helpful with whatever is coming. A couple of days of training, no matter how intense they've been, doesn't seem nearly enough to make up for a life-time of being clueless, especially with all you need."

"Your Celtic studies prepared you well for knowing who the players are and what they're capable of in this game. And you're an amazingly fast learner. We'll be all right, Pixie-girl. You'll see." He gave her thigh a tiny squeeze.

"There's so much more I need to learn, like how to listen to what others are thinking. Can you listen to—what do you call regular people? Civilians? That ability would be helpful when I see Bill next time. And what about the gods? Is it possible to listen to their thoughts as well?"

"Part of the reason we're going to my parents' place is that it's safer than here for the kind of training you and I need to do. As to your second question, yes, you can listen in on civilians who can't shield you, but you need to be ethical about it. Generally, I don't listen except when I'm in a combat situation. The gods are beyond all of our powers, unfortunately."

From his place behind the couch, Shadow huffed a bark before padding to the front door and waiting expectantly.

Alyssa cleared away the remains of their breakfast while Rowan walked around Shadow to usher in their guests.

"Hey, you're up and dressed. What fun is that?" Seamus teased good-naturedly.

"Sorry to disappoint you, old man, but some things are none of your business," Rowan said with a laugh.

"Did you save any breakfast for us?" Seamus called out to Alyssa.

"I didn't know you were coming for breakfast. Rowan said we were late as it was, but I can make you some," she offered.

"He's messing with you, Alyssa," Rio said. "We ate in town. Seamus wouldn't have lasted the trip out here if we hadn't." An eye roll accompanied his comment as he set his boots by the door and hung his coat in the closet.

"Little dreamer, I could eat whenever the opportunity presents itself," Seamus said.

Alyssa gasped. "Hey, what are you doing in my head?"

"You let down your guard. I noticed the minute you saw us walk through the door," he said. "We'll have to work on that." Having removed his winter gear, he wandered over to sit at the island.

At Seamus and Alyssa's exchange, Rowan thought darkly, *Why did she shield me apparently without thinking this morning and let Seamus into her head the minute he walked through the door?*

Seamus seemed immune to Rowan's dark look, but Rio picked up on it immediately. Rowan glanced at his brother who raised a brow in question.

"So, are you all packed up and ready to go?" Seamus asked, seemingly oblivious to the sudden tension in the room.

"We have a few things to do to secure the house, and we'll be ready. How are the roads?" Rowan asked as he joined Seamus at the island.

"Major arteries are plowed but snow-packed. We'll have to take our time, at least for part of the way. When I checked the weather on the satellite, it looked like Taranis concentrated his efforts in this area. We should drive out of the big snow about an hour out of town," Seamus said.

"I put up a skeleton security system around the windows and doors of the house," Rowan said. "Maybe you two could take a look at it, see if there's another layer we can add." He turned to Alyssa. "You said you carpool with your neighbor, right? Do you trust him?"

"Yes, why?"

"Give him a call before we leave. Ask him to keep an eye on your place while you're gone."

"Yes, sir!" she saluted him.

Rowan gave her his best "whatever" stare and headed down the hall to join Seamus's inspection of the security system.

∽

Since he'd made it clear from the beginning he didn't trust her, being left alone with Rio made Alyssa nervous. In spite of Rowan's intense physical interest in her, her whole situation made her feel like she was hiking uphill on shale, every step a disaster waiting to happen. At least Rio didn't pretend with her. His distrust radiated off him in waves. Maybe because the past three days had overwhelmed her on so many levels, she confronted him head on.

"You don't like me much, do you?"

"I don't know you well enough to decide what I think."

"That's honest, I guess."

He chuffed out a sigh. "I always thought I'd feel it when Rowan found his talisman. When Riley found Lynnette two years ago, I knew it almost as soon as he did. I'm closer to Rowan, so I figured the same thing would happen with him. It didn't."

"You're not sure I'm his talisman?"

"If he says you're his talisman, then you must be. I am curious though." He shoved his hands in his pockets. "What do you think of Seamus?"

"How do you mean?" She sensed her answer was important, but she couldn't understand why. The currents in the relationships between these men swirled around her, and she felt rudderless in the eye of a storm brewing over her.

"Do you find him attractive?"

"He's good-looking, and he makes me laugh. You're devastatingly handsome as well, but honestly, you make me nervous."

"What about Rowan? What do you think of him?"

Though Alyssa tried not to, she couldn't stop the heat she knew showed on her face. Images of Rowan and her last night and into the early hours of the morning jumped into her head, followed closely by images of him helping her in the kitchen and rescuing her from the storm. Of Rowan listening to her impassioned retelling of Celtic stories in front of the woodstove and not passing judgment on her concerning her relationship with Bill. She'd fallen hard for Rowan in far too short a time, but she couldn't admit it, even to gain Rio's trust.

A knock at the door saved her from answering Rio's questions. Since Shadow hadn't alerted her to the newcomer, Alyssa knew whoever had arrived was a friend. Still, she couldn't deny her surprise at seeing Finn Daly on her threshold.

"Finn! Hello. Please come in. What are you doing here? Did we arrange to drive to town together today?"

"No. I saw these big black trucks parked in your driveway and thought I'd see if everything was all right. You have so few visitors. Sorry if I'm out of line." The tone of his voice indicated he wasn't sorry at all, and the look on his face as he sized up Rio across the room said he'd reserve judgment no matter what Alyssa might say.

"Finn, this is Rio Sheridan. Rio, this is my neighbor Finn Daly. We carpool together, especially in the winter. Maybe you should get Rowan," she directed Rio. "He wanted me to contact Finn about my plans for the week, and Finn has now saved me the phone call."

She noticed currents flowing around her again and became impatient with her inability to decipher what exactly was going on with every man with whom she'd come into contact recently. Rio nodded at Finn before going to the back of the house in search of Rowan and Seamus.

"Would you like some coffee, Finn? I brewed a fresh pot."

"That would be fine, little lady. I know it's none of my business, but who are these gentlemen, and what's going on?" he asked as he divested himself of boots, coat, hat, and gloves. Shadow danced in front of him, impatient for his attention as usual. The two were big fans of each other, mainly because Finn never arrived without a Shadow treat, and Shadow never offered to eat Finn.

"The two guys I sent Rio to find have a security firm in town. Someone's been sneaking around my house over the last week, and I hired them to put in a security system. Rio is the brother of one of the security men," she said, grateful to be telling the truth at least as far as this was concerned. She adored Finn and didn't want to lie to him, but he'd think her crazy if she told him everything.

"Why didn't you say something?" he asked, his mouth downturned.

"Finn, you can't watch my house twenty-four-seven, and you know it. I only wanted an extra measure of security. If anyone should be miffed at me, it should be Shadow, but he seems to like these guys. He's usually a good judge of character, so this seems like the right move." She handed a steaming mug of coffee to her old friend.

Finn had been coming around since she was a little girl. For a while, she thought he and Gram might have had something going, but apparently, they were only good friends. Since Gram's death, he'd been especially attentive to her, something she'd found comforting until today. His reaction to Rio and Rio's to him made her nervous.

Interrupting their conversation, Rowan, Rio, and Seamus walked into the great room. "Rowan Sheridan, Seamus Lochlann, this is my neighbor Finn Daly, the man I carpool with. Finn, these are the security experts I hired to put a system into my house." The men shook hands and sized each other up as she introduced them.

A tense moment followed when no one said anything, which Alyssa couldn't understand. Finn was an old man, certainly no threat to these warriors. Rowan and Seamus *were* putting in a security system, so Finn shouldn't perceive them as a threat. She was about to step into the conversational breach when all the men started laughing, and Finn grabbed Rowan in an embrace like long lost friends.

"Do you guys know each other?" she asked, perplexed.

Rowan reached out and pulled her to his side. "Finn is one of us: a warrior. He sensed what we were when he walked in the door, confirmed when we shook hands, so we opened our minds to each other and made a sweet discovery." He grinned with delight.

"Wait. What? Finn, you're a warrior? Why didn't you say something? Why couldn't you have helped me? Did Gram know? Stop. Stupid question. Of course, she knew. You have some splainin' to do." A riot of emotions vibrated through her, and she didn't care who saw it.

Rowan interrupted as Finn opened his mouth. "We actually are putting in a security system, and we're almost finished. Maybe you can start your explanation while we finish up, and we can explain the abbreviated version of the plan for Alyssa's training." He gave her a side hug before he nodded to the other two to follow him back down the hall.

"Out with it, Finn."

"Mind if I sit down?" he asked as he seated himself on her loveseat, Shadow dancing in front of him.

Finn ran a hand over his thinning hair. "Afton found me not long after she moved the two of you up here," he said. "You were a wee thing with so much energy and curiosity. It was hard to contain you. So, we decided not to try. Without a warrior relative living with you, you were in great danger from Morgan. Afton created enchantments and potions to keep you safe while I watched out for you when you were far from home." He slipped a treat from his pocket and tossed it to Shadow who had taken up residence at his feet.

"The only time we couldn't personally keep you safe was when you spent that semester in Scotland, but I had a friend watching out for you. It wasn't a coincidence you found that dandy apartment for so cheap."

She faced him, arms crossed over her chest. "Let me guess. My landlord was a warrior friend of yours."

"Exactly so. It gave Afton and me some measure of peace that we had someone there who could look out for you."

"Why didn't she tell me who I am? Why didn't *you* after she died? I'm in way over my head here, and I have no control over what's going on. Rowan has made all my decisions since he 'discovered' me." She air-quoted. "He's taking me away from my home because I need 'training.' Everyone says I'm not safe anymore. And no one has even once asked me how I feel about this or what I want." Her voice rose on each consecutive sentence.

Finn patted the seat beside him. Blowing out a graceless breath, she slumped down on the loveseat.

"You must feel overwhelmed. If Morgan hadn't attacked your parents the way she did, something I still can't understand, then you would have grown up knowing who and what you are. Learning it in your mid-twenties must be difficult." He gave her a grandfatherly pat on the knee. "But you're going to have to trust these men, especially Rowan. He's your destiny." Finn gazed meaningfully at her.

"Yeah? So he and his family are going to give me a lifetime of training in a week? I passed my exam for grad school with pretty high marks, but I'm not that quick."

"Ah. He's taking you somewhere. Where are you going?"

"We're headed up to my parents' home on Flathead Lake," Rowan said as he entered the room, Seamus and Rio on his heels. "Since my mother is a talisman, she's best person to help me train Alyssa. We don't think we have much time owing to the big storm Taranis unleashed the minute Alyssa and I connected and the fact we saw Morgan on the edge of Alyssa's property Saturday night." He looked at Finn warmly. "Thanks very much for keeping Alyssa safe for me all these years. I don't think I said that earlier."

"You're welcome. It was the least I could do for her and for her sainted grandmother."

"Excuse my asking," Seamus said, "but were you and Alyssa's grandmother …?"

"Not in that way. She lost her warrior to Morgan years before, and Taranis gave my talisman to the White Lady during a storm.

We were too dedicated to the memories of our only loves to strike up more than a warm friendship with each other."

A fond expression crossed his face. "She took care of me the best she could with enchantments and potions, and I watched out for Alyssa and her, staving off occasional attacks by rogue warriors. The attacks stopped about the time Alyssa started dating Bill Forbes." His expression turned sour. "He's not a warrior, but he's somehow involved with Morgan. Afton and I could sense it, but we couldn't figure it out. We tried to discourage Alyssa from becoming involved with him, but he was her fiancé, and she didn't listen to old people like us." Finn smiled, visibly relishing Alyssa's discomfort at having family arguments aired publicly.

"You can stop any time now, Finn. I already told Rowan about my relationship with Bill."

"Good thing. But you're not going to stop an old man from saying 'I told you so' when he's in the right."

Alyssa rolled her eyes at him, a gesture she'd perfected over the years. He tipped back his head and laughed.

"She's quiet and observant around people she doesn't know well, but once you get to know her, you'll find she's a sassy lass. Always liked that about her." Finn and Rowan exchanged a smirk.

"Excuse me. I'm sitting right here." She folded her arms over her chest.

"We'd better get this show on the road, or it'll be past dark-thirty when we reach the Flathead," Seamus interrupted.

"That's it. That is absolutely it. All weekend you men have made all the decisions. I think the only reason you gave me any help in shielding, Seamus, was more to goad Rowan than because you wanted to help me. Which was clear when you listened to my thoughts the minute you walked into the house this morning.

"And you, Rio, have some sort of prejudice against me I can't for the life of me understand. I just met you, yet you're passing judgment."

Standing and pointing at Rowan, she continued. "You've decided to take me away from my home to somewhere I've never been to meet people who are supposedly going to give me training my parents didn't have the chance to do, but maybe Gram and Finn here should have. I'm not even convinced I need it." She paced over to the window, turned on her heel, and stared down the men in the room. "My life was fine before I met all of you except, as it happens, I needed a security system to discourage my old boyfriend from coming around. Now you're all talking like I'm not even here." She glared at each man in turn. Rio glared back, Seamus looked bewildered, Finn tried not to grin, while Rowan remained stoic. That annoyed her most of all.

"How 'bout you all have yourselves a lovely little meeting concerning my future while I make my own plans, and we'll see who's in charge of my life!"

Alyssa stomped down the hall to her room and slammed the door, leaving the men in bemused shock at her outburst. Rowan recovered first. "I had an idea by the way she stood up to me on Friday night that this particular storm was going to break over my head. I'm surprised it took this long."

Rio stated the obvious. "Yeah, well, we're in a bit of a crisis here, whether she knows it or not. You're still vulnerable until she's properly trained, and she's in serious danger the minute she steps foot off this property."

"Maybe we all don't need to go with you to the Flathead. Rio can stay here and watch over Alyssa's house to make sure Forbes doesn't breach our defenses, and I can monitor things from our place in town. Finn can run interference if we need him. Alyssa doesn't realize yet how we all watch out for each other," Seamus said.

"Who's going to have Rowan's back on the long drive north?" Rio asked.

"I think the only way Alyssa is going to understand what's going on here and what's at stake is if she sees it for herself, which means we have to take a risk, one I don't like any more than you do. She doesn't trust easily and finding out her old neighbor was actually her guardian warrior probably didn't help our cause," Rowan said.

"I think you have the right of it, son," Finn added. "Alyssa's always been a skittish little thing. Having all this dumped on her at once, from a room full of warriors no less, was not well advised. I'll see if she'll speak to me." He wandered down the hall to Alyssa's bedroom, but returned alone a minute later.

"The door's locked, and she's talking on the phone. My guess is she is having some girl talk with her friend Ceri," Finn said. "Best to let her have a minute before you barge in with orders again."

"After what you've suffered, you, of all people, know how important this is," Rio growled at Finn.

"He's fiery, this one," Finn remarked to Rowan before turning to Rio. "Yes, son, I do know how important this is. But you keep forgetting she wasn't raised in our community. Until Friday night, she considered herself a civilian without even knowing what that meant or that she saw herself that way." They faced each other in the middle of the kitchen.

"You're asking a great deal from her," Finn continued. "And she's coping the best she can. That you've taken her so far that she understands how our telepathy works, including shielding, that she doesn't flinch at the notion of talismans and warriors, that she's even contemplating her training, shows she's uncommonly quick. Have some patience with her. The rest will come."

"But we know our time is limited, and there's something you don't know old man. Every woman in Alyssa's family tree is named Ailsa," Rio began.

"Actually, I did know that. Alyssa's family descends from Riordan Sheridan's line from ancient times," Finn responded.

"Well, every man in our line is named Findlay as in Findlay

Sheridan. We descend from Owen's line. There is also the interesting coincidence that every woman in Alyssa's family married a man whose name begins with an R. Oh, and Alyssa had a sudden vision last night that this particular warrior-talisman combination was destined to right the wrong Morgan and Maeve inflicted on Findlay and Ailsa Sheridan long ago, and—" Rio was nearly snarling when Finn finished for him.

"The potent combination of Alyssa and Rowan will have the gods in an uproar if they're not pretty upset already."

"Exactly. There's probably an ancient prophecy somewhere, but we don't know it and can't find it in the journals Alyssa's grandmother left her. That's why I need to take Alyssa to my parents, particularly my mom who might be able to piece together what all of this means." Rowan's calm assessment contrasted sharply with Rio's intensity.

"I see. I'll try again to coax her to be reasonable," Finn said. "In light of your facts, I think Afton and I potentially made an enormous mistake, one that needs to be rectified as soon as possible."

CHAPTER EIGHTEEN

INN KNOCKED ON Alyssa's bedroom door and called softly to her. She glared at him but walked up the hallway to the kitchen, discovering the men conversing at the island, mugs of coffee in hand.

She turned her back on them and helped herself to the remaining coffee, taking her time adding milk, stirring her coffee to a nice caramel color before she took a sip. Sucking in a fortifying breath, she faced them.

"So, lass, have you forgiven us yet, or should we each be looking for cover when you throw that mug of hot coffee?" Finn asked, a twinkle in his eye.

"Finn Daly, honestly. When have I ever lost my temper and thrown something?"

Rowan almost choked on his coffee. "I seem to remember overhearing some rather murderous thoughts while you were wielding a knife the other day."

She glared at him, and he grinned cheekily back at her.

Finn interrupted the argument before it could begin. "I'm just sayin' we wouldn't blame you if you were a bit put out with our heavy-handed way of dealing with recent events."

"This house had become too full of testosterone, all right? I felt the need to talk to another woman, so I called Ceri. That's still allowed, isn't it?" she asked acidly.

"You didn't tell her anything about your real situation, did you?" Seamus asked.

"You mean about me being a talisman and you sensing she might be one too? Or the part about how all the men in this house are supernatural crime fighters, or the part where the gods are out to get me?" She batted her eyes and sipped her coffee. "Of course not," she huffed as the men standing and sitting around her island waited her out. "I didn't want her to think I'd finally lost it. She's always been interested in my research and has been sort of my *de facto* student over the years, but even she would think me one sandwich short of a picnic if I described what's been going on here the last few days."

"Or maybe not," Rowan mused, and as usual, she was struck by his ruggedly handsome face, the sight which momentarily hijacked her train of thought.

"I hope she wasn't too put out with me the other night," Seamus said, his tone hopeful.

"Shocked, I think. You two were having such a good time, she thought you'd at least exchange phone numbers. That was probably the first time she ended the night with the man walking away from her rather than the other way around. She's still trying to figure it out," Alyssa said, a tiny grin playing about her lips.

"When you talk to her next time, tell her I'm sorry. You know why I walked away from one of the most beautiful women on the planet," he reminded her.

"Yes, but somehow I think you're going to have to be the one to say thanks but no thanks. This is real life, not junior high, Seamus."

"Why is it that I'm the one who's always being tested? Walking away from gorgeous women is so not in my nature." Seamus sighed dramatically and not altogether jokingly.

"It's your punishment for trying to be with every beautiful woman you meet while you still can, old son." Rowan laughed. Sobering, he addressed Alyssa. "While you were on the phone, we made some decisions."

"Imagine that."

Rowan scowled. "We realize we're asking too much of you, but there's no choice." He left his barstool to stand in front of her where she leaned against the sink. "Would it help if Rio stayed here and watched your place for us while we're away? Seamus and Finn can run interference from here, and all of them can join us if we get into trouble on the road. Would that make you feel better?"

"What would make me feel better is understanding what it is that has all of you in such an uproar."

"Lass, we think Morgan will try to separate you two before you've been properly trained. If she doesn't outright kill you," Finn said.

The gravity of his tone sent a shiver through her.

"The trip north is necessary for your training, but you have none of Afton's protections when you leave this house." His grave expression alarmed her. "We think Morgan might have discovered that on her fact-finding mission with Forbes the other night."

"It's no secret she wants Rowan. Maeve is pretty interested in him too, so the two of them will do everything they can to keep him from completing your training," Rio added.

Rowan rubbed his hands up and down her arms. "Disorienting you in the storm the other night was Taranis's half-hearted attempt at killing you before you know what you are. The reason he didn't succeed was that you didn't question or fight what was happening in your head when we communicated telepathically. While that saved your life, it also gave the gods additional information they can use against us."

Looking deep into Rowan's aquamarine eyes, she asked, "Why don't we invite your parents to come here? Why do we have to take the dangerous risk of leaving my home?"

"My twin, Riley, tried to train his talisman Lynnette in her home under similar circumstances. Her sister is a druid who enchanted her house. Because the training involves reliving past battles, it invited the gods to converge on her place. Riley and Lynnette lost the enchantments and had to relocate. They were lucky they didn't lose their lives," Rio stated coldly.

"Oh." She suddenly felt small and inadequate. The looks on the men's faces told her plainly she couldn't avoid her destiny.

Finn joined Rowan and her in the kitchen. He placed a grand-fatherly arm around her shoulders and hugged her gently to his side. "I see now that Afton and I made mistakes as you were growing up, but Alyssa, lass, you're strong enough and intelligent enough to take on this challenge. There are many now to help you. Don't be afraid."

Alyssa looked at the other three men in turn. Rio stared down his nose at her. Seamus smiled encouragingly at her. Rowan regarded her with a look she couldn't read. At the moment, she wished she could hear his thoughts. Taking a deep breath, she steeled herself. "Well, since we're packed already, we should probably hit the road as Seamus said. But maybe we could consider another option about who goes and who stays. Seamus could stay behind and monitor the equipment you installed in my house. By having a warrior here, coupled with Finn's vigilance, the security system should keep any civilians away while not inviting the gods."

Why Alyssa felt uncomfortable with Rio staying in her home, she couldn't say, but he made her nervous. The alternative, however, wasn't more palatable. Taking another deep breath, she plunged in anyway. "Rio should ride with us to have Rowan's back since I'm clearly not ready for whatever is coming."

"See, I told you she was a smart girl. Afton may not have taught you how to be a talisman, but she did teach you how to think." Finn winked.

"Now that we have that settled, let's load up the SUV and head out. We have at least five hours driving time, which means an hour in the dark if we leave now," Rowan said.

Everyone moved at once. Having made their decision, they completed their preparations for their trip in minutes. Alyssa retrieved her small suitcase and Rowan's duffel bag from her bedroom, setting them by the front door before repacking Gram's notebooks into the box and placing it by the door. A cloth grocery bag holding Shadow's bowls and favorite toys along with a bag of dog food joined the growing pile of belongings. Rio stepped outside to supervise Shadow while Rowan and Seamus walked around the house arming the alarm system. Finn cleaned up the kitchen and unplugged Alyssa's small appliances before he banked the fire and turned down the stove.

When their preparations were complete, Finn shook Rowan's hand and gave Alyssa a hug, a quick kiss on the cheek, and a wink before he left.

"Have a safe trip," Seamus said as he shook Rowan's hand. He smiled one of his devastating smiles at Alyssa before climbing into his big truck and driving away.

Rio retreated into the house to grab Alyssa and Rowan's gear. None of them spoke as they loaded the SUV. Rowan entered the final code arming the security system, Alyssa locked up, and they joined Rio and Shadow in the SUV.

Though tense, the drive out of town was uneventful. Rio sat behind Alyssa and radiated his surly attitude at her back. She could sense his eyes on the back of her head, and involuntarily, her entire body stiffened. When Shadow started whining at his mistress's distress, Rowan apparently had had enough.

"Okay, which of you two is going to tell me what your problem is with the other?"

When neither of them responded, he tried again. "It's clear something is going on between you. If you're having a private conversation, let me remind you it's rude when I'm sitting right here, unless, of course, you've decided to start the training without me, in which case you're not being your usual cautious self, Rio."

"We're not having a conversation beyond Rio trying to bore a hole in my head with his eyes. It would make me feel immeasurably better to know that particular skill is beyond his abilities," Alyssa said at last.

"We're incapable of causing any physical damage telepathically, but now that you mention it, Rio does appear to be trying," Rowan said with a glance into the rearview mirror.

"Fine." Rio slumped into his seat and crossed his arms. "Alyssa knows I don't trust her loyalty to you. The fact that she invited me along rather than let me stay in her house says she doesn't trust me much either."

"It isn't a trust issue, Rio," Alyssa said through clenched teeth. "You said yourself Rowan was vulnerable on this trip without other warriors. Because I know you don't trust me, I thought you'd want to come along to be his second since I'm not ready."

"Yeah, fine."

"I'm not sure what's eating you, little brother, but if Alyssa had jumped right into all we asked of her so far and readily joined this trip, no questions asked, I would have been wary of her and far from comfortable. But I know how hard she's worked at the training I've put her through already, and I saw the sweat on her face after her session with Seamus. She's doing everything she can to be of service to herself and to me. You haven't seen any of that, but you will once we reach home and the training room."

Alyssa would have smiled at Rowan's praise if she hadn't been so afraid of this ride and what was to come at the end of it.

CHAPTER NINETEEN

ROWAN KEPT LOOKING in the rearview mirror, trying to catch his brother's attention. Maybe, he desired a private conversation, Alyssa thought, one Rio apparently wanted to avoid as he stared out the window. She turned the radio to a jazz station to mask the tension as the trio traveled for miles without speaking.

Her budding relationship with Rowan topped the list of fears overwhelming her, especially in light of Rio's obvious dislike of her, the source of which she couldn't fathom. Whatever the gods had up their collective sleeve didn't concern her so much since she had no idea what to expect from that quarter. But letting Rowan down terrified her. She longed for someone to give her concrete answers.

Late in the afternoon, they stopped in a tiny town for an early supper at a restaurant resembling an old log cabin. Leaving Shadow inside the SUV, they crossed a gravel parking lot and stepped into the eatery. Yellow chintz curtains gave the room a cheery atmosphere and screened the sun glaring off the snow. The plain wooden tables and chairs looked utilitarian rather than comfortable, but the place was clean, and several people were patronizing it, which seemed a good recommendation.

The expression of open curiosity on the face of the middle-aged hostess who seated them didn't escape the trio, but they remained quiet as they followed her to a table near the partition with the bar. A couple of older gentlemen engaged in an afternoon game of gin rummy at a nearby table. The hostess handed out menus and rattled off the day's special of chicken fried steak and country gravy before leaving them to their decisions.

Rowan and Rio glanced at the older men seated behind them. They appeared to be engrossed in their card game while they checked out the Sheridans' table.

Leaning over to Alyssa, Rowan whispered, "Did you notice the card players behind us?"

"The old guys? Yes, why?"

"They're spying on us, so we want to have some fun with them. Open your shield so you can join in."

"How can I hear you?" she asked, perplexed.

"Keep your mind open and pay attention to me. You've done it before, remember?"

"But I was scared to death and didn't know what I was doing," she reminded him.

He bumped her shoulder playfully. "Let down your shield and give it a try. As quickly as you picked up the basic skills of shielding, you should be able to start listening with a purpose. I'll keep my hand on your thigh so we're physically connected."

"Maybe it would be better if we held hands. In case you haven't noticed, the three of us are already the topic of conversation at nearly every table in the room," she pointed out.

As Rowan looked around, he smiled in amusement and squeezed her thigh with a wink when she tried to bat him away.

Alyssa's whole body jolted awake the second Rowan touched her thigh. Her toes curled inside her thick boots, her legs tingled, and the apex of her thighs tightened in anticipation of what that touch implied. Batting him away was self-defense, but then he captured her hand in his much larger one and entwined his fingers with hers, and she couldn't fight. Not only would doing so have looked strange to all those people surreptitiously and openly watching them, but she'd have had to abandon the lovely electric sensations zinging around inside her at his touch. She wondered if they zinged him too.

The waitress, looking about sixteen, arrived with their coffee. Casually, she asked where they were from and where they were headed.

A dull red stain bloomed on Rio's face, and Rowan smirked. *"Apparently, the waitress already had the anatomy lesson in her high school biology class, little brother. Or she's been sneaking her older sister's* Playgirls. *Either way, lucky you."*

Alyssa heard Rowan and gasped.

He grinned at her. *"Did you catch what the young lady was thinking?"*

"No, but considering the color of Rio's face and your comments, I can guess."

"Did you have those sorts of naughty thoughts when you were sixteen?" Rowan asked.

"Certainly not! My biology class wasn't nearly that advanced, and Gram would have been scandalized." She swallowed at the realization that her grandmother must have practiced telepathy as well. Gram Afton had intercepted Alyssa's rebellious plans on more than one occasion when Alyssa was sure no one she knew would have shared with Gram.

"Likely so, Alyssa, considering what she was," Rowan said aloud.

"A truly scary thought," she responded.

"It definitely made things difficult when we were growing up until Dad taught us how to shield our thoughts," Rio added.

"Somehow I think that's an unfair advantage for parents." Alyssa grimaced at the thought of what her grandmother knew when she was growing up. It seemed invasive from this distance in time, and she didn't like the feeling.

"Let it go, Alyssa. It's too late to confront her now. Besides, she probably saved you from exposure to some powerful and nasty forces by preempting your more rebellious plans." Rowan gave her hand a gentle squeeze.

"Our eavesdroppers have almost stopped pretending to play cards," he communicated.

For the poor men at the nearby table, Alyssa, Rowan, and Rio's conversation had likely taken a very strange turn. The confusion on their faces and obvious lull in their game were pretty telling.

Alyssa still couldn't hear Rio's thoughts, but by the way he was looking at Rowan and the slow smile spreading across Rowan's face, she knew they were up to something.

"So, about that waitress, how big a tip are you leaving her?" Rowan asked.

Rio's responding scowl gave Alyssa a pretty good idea of what he thought of Rowan's question.

"Couldn't really tell by looking at her or by what she was thinking about what you could do to her." He leaned back and slipped his arm behind the back of Alyssa's chair, giving the table behind them a clear view of Rio's ruddy cheeks.

"Rowan, I can only hear your side of the conversation, but between what I'm hearing and the color of Rio's face, maybe you should let up. No wonder your dad had to rescue your other brother from you."

Even telepathically, Alyssa's tone scolded.

"I kind of like it when you reprimand me, Pixie-girl. Rio told you about how I teased Riley I take it," Rowan said.

"It appears you rather enjoy the role of big brother, always teasing and bossing because you're older and stronger and can get away with it."

"He's been teasing me my whole life, but I can handle him. Don't feel the need to come to my rescue," Rio grumped.

"Sorry. I had no idea you were handling this. I guess I

misunderstood the rosy color of your cheeks." Batting her eyes at him, she gave him her best innocent expression.

"Ouch! Careful, little brother. This lovely little rose has thorns—she's also got your number." Rowan chuckled.

Meanwhile, one of the old gossips at the table behind them stage-whispered, "These boys appear to be several bricks short of a load, but at least they're loaded together and will leave together as well. I imagine their lack of coherent thought is due to all the steroids they must have taken to build those huge bodies."

"I see your point, but that doesn't explain the little lady who seems as loco as they are," his friend whispered *Soto* voice.

Alyssa exchanged an amused look with the Sheridan brothers and tried to hold in her laughter.

The waitress's timely appearance with their meal saved them, and all conversation, telepathic and audio, stopped as they gave in to their hunger. When the waitress asked if they needed anything else, she only had eyes for Rio, which didn't escape Rowan's notice. After she walked away, he said, "You could throw her a bone, flirt with her a little."

Rio scowled at him and dug into the special he'd ordered.

The waitress returned several more times than necessary to refill their coffee or check to see how everything tasted or to find out if they needed anything. Rio politely told her she'd taken great care of them, effectively dismissing her.

"Okay, Rio, her attention is becoming embarrassing, even for Alyssa and me. Maybe you shouldn't smile at her so much," Rowan teased.

Before Rio could respond, two large men walked through the door of the restaurant. Unlike when the Sheridans walked in and people looked at them with polite curiosity before resuming their meals, all conversation stopped with the newcomers' arrival. They looked to be Seamus's size, about six feet and two hundred pounds each, most of it in their shoulders and arms. The one's shoulder-length brown hair hadn't seen shampoo or a comb in a while. He wore a scuffed leather jacket, threadbare blue jeans, and square-toed boots. The part of his neck visible above the collar of his jacket revealed a snake tattoo up one side. Tattoos also covered the knuckles of both his hands.

His companion sported a shaved head and a full black beard. Gaudy white rhinestone studs decorated his ears. His suede jacket had seen better days, shiny at the elbows and upper arms of the sleeves and along the zipper. Jeans, the same style of boots as his companion, and long chains looping from his belt half way down his thigh and back to his rear pocket completed his intimidating look.

Their attire aside, the men's faces were hard. Involuntarily, Alyssa shrank from them as did nearly everyone else in the room except Rio and Rowan. The Sheridan brothers showed no outward sign of acknowledgment, but their tensed bodies told Alyssa they were ready for anything. The waitress had been in the kitchen when the men arrived, and she strode cheerily toward the Sheridans' table with their check. She stopped with the clear intent of one last flirtatious attempt to get Rio's attention when she looked around the room, noting the silence and the reason for it. Alyssa stared in fascination as the waitress's demeanor spun on a dime, her interest in Rio evaporating in the glare of the men at the door.

Almost on autopilot, she said, "I'll be your cashier when you're ready," before she bolted for the kitchen.

The greasy-haired man deliberately walked over to their table and addressed Rio. "You flirtin' with my girl, boy?"

Rio cocked a brow. "Aren't you a little old to be interested in high school girls?"

"She's not going to be in high school much longer if I have any say about it," the man drawled.

"Last I checked, jailbait is determined by age," Rio responded, his disgust evident in his voice.

Judging from the waitress's reaction to the man, she wasn't the least bit interested in him.

"You were flirtin' with her. I don't think much of strangers who think they can come in here and poach the local talent. If you know what's good for you, you and your friends should hit the road."

"They can leave their woman behind. She looks older than jail-bait, and she's a helluva lot prettier than anything else I've seen around here," the bald man added with a leer in Alyssa's direction.

Rowan pressed his thigh against hers. *"No matter what happens, stay here. Please."* Addressing the men, he asked casually, "Do you two make a habit of ruining people's dinners, or is this show only for us?"

The bald man turned to his companion and said, "I think we've been insulted, Mike. We need to teach these boys it's not smart to insult a man right after trying to steal his girlfriend." He took a menacing step toward their table.

"You know, it causes people indigestion when you fight in their dining room. Let's take this outside." Rowan backed his words by standing in front of the bald man. Even having seen Rowan's speed before, Alyssa still gaped in amazement at how fast he moved. The bald man's eyes rounded before narrowing to take Rowan on.

Rio was as quick as his brother and stood behind the greasy-haired man who cowed slightly before puffing out his chest and trying to stand taller. From Alyssa's vantage point, she could see the bullies hadn't accounted for the Sheridans' size or their shocking speed. A fearful undercurrent rolled through the café at the imminent fight. Alyssa's dinner solidified into a lead weight in her stomach.

The rough men turned toward the door, but they exchanged an odd glance. In one sickening second, it occurred to her these men might not be ordinary thugs. They might be rogue warriors, but when she tried to hear Rowan's thoughts, she discovered he'd shielded them. Weirdly, instead of feeling frustrated with him, the fact he'd shielded his thoughts calmed her. She considered it a sign the men were civilians and therefore no real threat. When she heard the first gunshot right after Rowan and Rio cleared the door, she realized she should have known better. Even warriors could die of gunshot wounds.

She jumped out of her chair and joined several of the other patrons who rushed to the windows in front of the café.

"Would you look at that!" one of the gin rummy players exclaimed. "Those big boys have some mighty long knives. They look like swords, for cryin' out loud. Who but a fool brings a knife to a gun fight?"

"Boys who move faster 'n lightning, that's who brings knives to a gun fight," said his friend. "I've never seen anyone who can move as fast as those two."

The commotion in the parking lot lured the waitress out of the kitchen to stand near Alyssa. When she saw that her handsome patron and his friend had come to her defense, she elbowed her way to the front for a better view of the show.

The fight was short and decisive. Rowan disarmed the bald man with one surgically placed blow to the pad of the thumb on his shooting hand, severing the tendon. The gun slid off his hand and clattered to the ground. The thug stared with a stupefied look as his gun dropped before he rushed blindly at Rowan who deftly grabbed his outstretched hand and snapped it and his arm behind his back, immobilizing him.

Rio parried the greasy-haired man's gun shots with his blade, sending the bullets harmlessly out over the road and up over the café. At last the man's gun ran out of bullets, and when he raced to his truck to reload, Rio caught the man's hamstring with his claymore, nicking it without severing it completely yet still bringing the man down.

Once the two thugs were under control, the bartender stepped out of the café to help Rowan and Rio finish subduing them.

As Alyssa returned to their table, the collective sigh of relief of the other patrons signaled Rowan and Rio's success. When she sat down, she sensed an evil presence near her and heard a raspy whisper in her ear: *"Chan ann leis a'chiad bhuille thuiteas a'chraobh."* She recognized the sounds as Gaelic, and though she didn't speak the language, curiously, she understood the words: "It is not with the first stroke that the tree falls." Abruptly, she turned to the voice and saw a beautiful woman standing in the back of the café near the rear exit. Long white hair framed black eyes, high cheekbones and red lips on a classically sculpted face. A form-fitted black velvet dress sheathed her hour-glass figure. Alyssa almost laughed at the woman's resemblance to a live-action version of Cruella de Vil from the *101 Dalmatians* movie. As she tried to figure out how she knew what the woman said to her, the woman's eyes glowed red, and Alyssa instantly recognized who she was—Morgan—the Morrigan, the Washer at the Ford and the Sheridans' mortal enemy.

Instinctively, she called to Rowan, *"Morgan is here!"* She stood up and took a step toward the front door of the diner. Instantaneously, Rowan appeared beside her, grabbing her and pushing her behind him as he glared at Morgan, his sword nearly reaching across the room toward her. "No one died today, so you have no business here," he snarled at her.

"That is a pity. I had so hoped to escort those fine men you fought into the mists. However, you've received my message." Morgan smiled smugly at him.

"What are you talking about?"

"Ask your talisman. She knows."

She nodded to Alyssa before she disappeared out the back of the diner.

Rowan turned to Alyssa and cradled her against his chest. She wrapped her arms around his waist and tried to control the tremors coursing through her after Morgan's appearance.

Rio strolled through the door as composed as if he'd stepped outside for a breath of air and walked over to Rowan and Alyssa. In a low tone, Rowan said, "That out there"—he nodded toward the door—"was a warning from Morgan. While we were cleaning out this town's riffraff, she was in here threatening Alyssa."

Rio's eyes widened. "Did anyone else see her?"

"Everyone's attention riveted on the drama you two created in the parking lot. When I called, Rowan came to me so fast he was holding me before any of the others turned around to see what blew through the door," Alyssa said over her shoulder as she clung to Rowan, fear flooding her. If she lived to be a hundred, she didn't think she'd ever forget the evil red glow of Morgan's eyes as she made her intentions known. At last she understood that everything Rowan and the others had told her was true. They were in a battle with evil, and the stakes were their lives.

CHAPTER TWENTY

THE SHERIFF'S ARRIVAL and the arrests of the men along with the subsequent questioning the three of them had to endure set Rowan, Rio, and Alyssa back an hour on the road. However, the cook was so grateful to have his café returned from the bullies' tyranny that he gave the three their dinner on the house and sent dessert with them in a to-go box. The waitress smiled shyly as she handed the box to Rio and thanked him for standing up for her. He nodded and stiffly thanked her for the dessert before turning on his heel and heading for the safety of the SUV. Rowan and Alyssa exchanged a grin at Rio's obvious discomfort, and Rowan left a generous tip on their table before he and Alyssa followed his brother outside.

Dessert consisted of a giant hot fudge brownie smothered in caramel sauce and chopped pecans that Alyssa held steady on the console between Rowan and her as she fed Rowan bites between those she took. Rio, however, ate the most since his spoon was only serving one mouth, and he didn't need to keep his eyes on the road. Alyssa laughed at him as he gave up all pretense of sharing and took the box from her to finish off the last drizzles of caramel along the bottom and sides.

"I bet you used to lick your dessert dish as a kid, didn't you?" she asked with a smirk.

"Only after he couldn't distract Riley and steal bites of his." Rowan chuckled. "All that sugar should have made you a lot sweeter than you are," he teased as Rio deliberately licked the last smooth ribbon of caramel from his spoon, his eyes dancing as Alyssa turned in her seat to watch the play-by-play between the brothers.

"Big brother, I positively sweat sweetness. Ask that waitress back at the café," he said with a grin.

"You're right. Those cherry red cheeks you were sporting in there begged her to take a bite of them," Alyssa added, all innocence. "That and the leisurely way you raced out of there after she handed you the dessert probably left her wishing she'd eaten you right up when she had the chance."

Rio scowled, and Rowan burst out laughing. "I thought you said you didn't hear the waitress's thoughts, Pixie-girl."

"I didn't have to. I merely sat back and watched the show."

Like flipping a switch, Rowan sobered up. "Morgan came to taunt Alyssa. The whole thing was a set up. What I can't figure out is why she planted those two morons in that out-of-the-way town. She couldn't have known we'd stop there. Hell, we didn't know we were stopping there until we pulled into the parking lot."

"There's something big going on here, something involving the two of you," Rio said as he slipped the dessert box back to Shadow to lick. "I hope Mom has a clue about what."

"She whispered in my ear in Gaelic, something about a tree not falling with the first stroke of the ax. What do you suppose she meant by that?"

"You speak Gaelic?" Rowan took his eyes off the road. "Why didn't you tell me that before?"

She winced at his accusatory tone. "You've turned my life upside down, and then you have the nerve to be angry at me because I haven't had a chance during all the excitement to tell you my life story?" Incredulous, she continued. "For the record, I recognized she was speaking Gaelic because I heard the language often when I spent a semester in Scotland. However, I didn't stay long enough to learn to speak it. I have no idea why I could understand her, but I got the notion she was testing me. When she understood I knew what she was saying, her expression changed." Alyssa shuddered at the memory. "H-her eyes glowed red." The evil the goddess exuded chilled her to her soul.

"Morgan thinks to determine how much training you have and what your powers are. She also wants you to be afraid, maybe afraid enough not to trust me. Your understanding of her language and your immediate call to me when you recognized her showed her that her goals aren't going to be easy to reach. You did well, Alyssa." Rowan reached across the console and smoothed his hand over her hair.

Rio leaned forward. "I wonder if her goal included keeping us from home tonight. If we'd killed one or both of those boys, we'd probably be in jail, and Alyssa would be completely unprotected."

Rowan glanced at Rio in the rearview mirror. "The way the folks in that café reacted and the ease with which the sheriff let us go tells me we would have been pretty safe no matter what happened. Those two boys must have caused a lot of trouble in that town in a short time."

"Morgan isn't concerned with regular civilians anyway," Rowan said. "She likes the bullies and assholes she can manipulate to start things. What happens to bystanders in the course of the action is nothing to her." Rowan nodded to his brother. "But you may be onto something about her delaying tactics."

"Can't she attack us while we're on the road?" Alyssa knotted her hands in her lap. The question had gnawed at her since they'd left her house.

"If she attacks us on the road or tries to take us in any fashion besides battle, she doesn't get the pleasure of leading us across the ford herself. Instead, The White Lady takes us into the mists. That isn't Morgan's goal at all. She dearly loves wading in the blood of fallen warriors. Second to warriors are the minions she recruits for her evil games, civilians such as our two delightful companions at the café." Rio's sarcasm didn't assuage Alyssa's fear. "We deprived her of blood today, so when she does launch a real attack, my guess is it's going to be uglier than usual."

"What my brother is trying to say is that barring a tantrum from Taranis or some civilian pitfall like sliding off the road, we're pretty safe traveling as we are," Rowan said, giving Alyssa's hand a soothing squeeze before he returned his hand to the wheel.

"If we stop again, could we have another nasty surprise waiting for us?"

Shadow huffed at the fear nearly rolling off Alyssa in waves. "Exactly, Shadow," she added.

"It's a possibility. Luckily, we're close enough we shouldn't need to stop again before we arrive at the compound," Rowan said. "Unless Shadow can't wait."

He smiled at her, and Alyssa understood what every male in the SUV was trying to do for her. Marginally, she relaxed into her seat.

They crested the hill above the small town at the foot of Flathead Lake. Piles of snow bracketed the road, so obviously Taranis had paid a recent visit to the area. The trees in the cherry orchards on the eastern edge of the town were silent black skeletons standing guard over the soft drifts of snow at their bases. The vast lake behind the trees appeared blackly ominous against the white relief of the rime of ice framing its shores. The mountains seemed to rise directly from the bottom of the lake to scrape the low sky of gathering clouds as the sun slid between them. Alyssa had never seen anything so wild in her life. The rugged beauty of the place touched her very soul. No wonder Rowan's family lived here.

As they drove up the east side of the lake, she marveled at Rowan's steadiness and apparent lack of concern about the narrow twisting ribbon of road they traveled between the walls of plowed snow. Had she been on her own, she didn't think even as daring a driver as she would have attempted the road. Not with the lake so often near the edge of the pavement and nothing but steep mountainside opposite the water.

At last, Rowan turned onto a spur road that at first seemed to disappear into the mountain, a single-track that hadn't been plowed. He shifted into four-wheel drive and continued on as though they were taking a leisurely drive on a summer afternoon rather than plowing snow up over the hood of his SUV. Alyssa decided he must be feeling his way along the road because he certainly couldn't see it. Then she had a thought.

Rowan chuckled. *"No, Alyssa, x-ray vision isn't among any of our skills, unfortunately. That's one I would have used and abused often in my life so far."*

"Stop doing that!" she shrieked.

"What's the problem, Alyssa? Did you forget to put up your shield?" Rio asked.

Her cheeks burned. "I guess I did. But if you were ethical at all, you wouldn't be checking to see if my shield was up or not." She directed the last bit to Rowan who only laughed again.

"Sweetheart, I'm going to listen to you every chance I get. Not only for the sake of safety, but also for the pure entertainment of it. X-ray vision. What a great idea." He chuckled.

"What about X-ray vision?" Rio asked.

"Nothing. Private joke," Rowan said while Alyssa tried to distract them.

"So how much farther on this deer trail?"

"It's about a mile from the main road back to the compound," Rowan answered. "We'll be there in five minutes or less."

Her nervousness at meeting his parents compounded her embarrassment at the thoughts Rowan had overheard. She'd traveled here for their help, but what if his parents didn't like her or want to help her? Mentally, she shook herself. Whatever they thought of her wouldn't matter since Rowan needed her. They'd help her because it would mean helping their son.

Out of the swirling snow arose a two-story log house with upper and lower decks spanning the entire front. A two-car garage attached to the side of the house, but Rowan bypassed it and drove around to a detached three-car garage in the back. Reaching into the glove box, he activated a door opener and drove into the open stall. In answer to her raised brows, he said, "Mom christened this 'the boys' garage' when they built it after I got my driver's license. As you can see, it can snow up here, and it was easier for us to have our cars out of the weather than to be late for school every day during the winter because we never woke up early enough to scrape the snow off. When each of us left home, we took our openers with us. Mom thought it a good sign we'd come home to visit every now and then."

Rowan parked but didn't close the garage door.

"When she saw this monster coming down the driveway, she probably started doing the happy dance, and if we don't hustle inside ASAP, she's likely to wear herself out." Rio gave his attention to her. "I don't know if he's told you, but Rowan has a penchant for wandering. He hasn't been home much since he graduated college. Mom misses him."

She stared in fascination at Rio's pointed comment to his brother, which Rowan just as pointedly ignored.

Shadow interrupted the tense family drama with a low howl, and she jumped out of the SUV to help him out of the back. When she opened the door, he bounded out of the truck and raced out into the snow, yipping happily. She laughed at him and turned to grab her small suitcase. Instead, she found Rowan standing there with it in his hand and reaching for his duffel bag. Rio came around her other side and grabbed the box containing Gram's notebooks, and it was then Alyssa realized he had no gear.

"Where is your stuff?"

"I didn't bring anything with me when I visualized myself into Rowan's apartment."

"But you're wearing different clothes today than you were yesterday."

"Just the shirt—and my underwear," he said with a leer. "I borrowed them from Seamus since Rowan didn't leave anything in his closet."

That bit of information confirmed without a doubt Rowan had indeed moved in with her. She wanted to talk about it on the spot, and her face warmed in anger as she prepared to let loose.

Rowan must have sensed her coming storm and tried to defuse a potential explosion. "We'd better head inside since it would be best if we introduced Shadow to Mom and Dad rather than letting him do it himself." He nodded at the big dog trotting up the steps to the back porch as if he were at home.

"Our conversation is only postponed, Rowan. Don't think for a minute you've avoided it." She turned on her heel and headed after her dog.

"Wouldn't dream of it," he drawled, his tone indicating this particular conversation would take place a long time into the future—if it took place at all.

"What are you two arguing about?" Rio asked.

"Nothing," Rowan and Alyssa said simultaneously.

CHAPTER TWENTY-ONE

STUNNING WOMAN AWAITED the trio outside her back door.

"I saw your SUV coming up the road and couldn't wait to see you," she exclaimed as she enveloped Rowan in a tight hug. "I felt you battling all night on Saturday, but neither your dad nor I could breach your shield." She cocked a censorious brow. "But now you're here, and you're safe. Welcome home."

Turning to Rio, she continued, "What's your story? I couldn't get through to you either, but since you arrived on my doorstep with your brother, I assume the two of you were together dealing with whatever put Rowan in such peril. Thank you," she added as she gathered him close.

After hugging the men, the woman who was obviously their mom stepped back, her gaze landing on Alyssa and Shadow. Alyssa smiled shyly.

"Boys, who is this stunning creature with you? And I don't mean the white beast standing beside her."

Rowan stepped over to Alyssa and placed a proprietary arm around her, pulling her close to him. "Mom, this is Alyssa Macaulay. Alyssa Ailsa Macaulay, my talisman," he said, emphasizing Alyssa's middle name. "Alyssa, this is my mom, Sian Sheridan."

Her eyes widened. "Welcome to our home, Alyssa." She reached out and pulled Alyssa into a tight hug that Alyssa couldn't help but return. "Who is this big fellow?" she asked, indicating the dog.

"This is Shadow. Rowan insisted he come with us. I hope that's all right," Alyssa said.

Sian Sheridan was definitely not what Alyssa had envisioned as Rowan's mother, but her obvious love for and delight in her sons gave Alyssa reason to hope this woman might accept her. Sian was tall, at least five feet seven or eight, with dark hair and aquamarine eyes like Rowan's. Her willowy figure belied her age and the fact she'd delivered and reared three sons. She looked more like Rowan and Rio's big sister than their mother.

"Of course, your dog is welcome. Tell me, why did you name a white dog Shadow?"

"Because from the time we met he's followed me everywhere, though he's infinitely more useful than my actual shadow," Alyssa said, running her hand over Shadow's thick coat.

Turning to Rowan, Sian said, "We have much to discuss, son, but I think we'll get everyone settled first. What are you carrying in that box, Rio?"

"Journals Alyssa's grandmother kept. She was a druid. Since we didn't get a lot out of them when we read them, we thought between you and Siobhan we might learn some things," Rowan responded.

"Ah. Take them into the living room, Rio, while I get Rowan and Alyssa settled," Sian said.

Alyssa and Rowan removed their winter gear and stowed it neatly on pegs attached to the back of a high-backed bench in the laundry room before following Sian into the adjoining kitchen, a space that astounded Alyssa with its airiness and size. An enormous central island dominated the room. The island housed a stovetop with a stainless-steel exhaust hood hanging directly above it. The stovetop sat on a slightly lower level than the surrounding counter-top. Pine barstools lined up along the countertop side of the island where five people could enjoy a meal together.

To the left of the island were two stacked ovens built into the wall. Next to them was a gleaming stainless-steel sink. The room angled into an L shape where a doublewide refrigerator hummed. On the opposite side of the room, a cozy breakfast nook beneath a bay window overlooked the forest flanking the house. A plank table and two bench seats formed a booth in the nook.

When Alyssa registered she was the only one remaining in the kitchen, she hurried to catch up with Rowan and his mother. She walked into the next room, a formal dining room, but where the first two rooms were homey in a mountain cabin sort of way, this room exuded country elegance. The walls were golden tongue-in-groove pine paneling decorated with several landscapes. She was drawn to one that appeared to be Flathead Lake in summer.

Turning her attention from the painting, she ran a hand along the cherry wood formal dining table long enough to seat ten. She fingered the upholstery of the matching cherry wood chairs, the beige-and-forest-green-striped silk impossible to resist. A runner of the same pattern as the chairs decorated the table, and an arrange-ment of pinecones and dried flowers in a basket completed the space. On one end of the room, a massive sideboard took up a wall while the opposite wall supported a picture window revealing another view of the surrounding forest.

At last Alyssa joined the others in the cavernous living room. A river- rock fireplace two stories high caught her attention. In front of it lounged two deep green leather recliners with a knotty pine end table between them. Two couches, upholstered in a forest scene of stags and trees, formed an L in the center of the room. A polished pine coffee table angled in front of them.

More landscape art hung on the walls. The scenes nagged at Alyssa's subconscious like places she should know. A bay window looked out over the front drive, and another large window flanked the front door, which was a medieval looking affair of wrought iron fixtures and a small barred window positioned high above the handle, which was located in the middle of the door rather than in the traditional place along the edge.

Opposite the fireplace was a hallway. Next to that, a staircase led up to the second story. Polished pine dowels formed the open railing, and when Alyssa looked up, she marveled at an open beam ceiling at the height of the second floor. The stairs led to a loft landing overlooking the living room. Rowan appeared on the landing and leaned over the railing. "Alyssa. Come up here."

At the top of the stairs was a short hallway with three doors. Two of the doors opened to bedrooms, and the third revealed a full bathroom so spacious her bedroom at home would have fit inside it.

"This is Rowan's room whenever he comes home. Considering the circumstances, I think you'll be more comfortable if you share with him," Sian said as she invited Alyssa into the room to her left.

Alyssa couldn't decide what she meant. What circumstances? Did Rowan's mom disapprove of her? He frowned at her and pushed into her mind. *"You're my talisman. Of course, you'll sleep with me. My mother is very well aware of that."*

Her eyes widened, but she kept her mouth shut. She couldn't imagine they would do any of the things they'd done together in the privacy of her house while they visited his parents.

Rowan moving in with her after knowing her for a day and the assumption she would sleep with him in his parents' home without any formal understanding of their relationship went too far for Alyssa. Maybe she had old-fashioned notions about relationships because her grandmother raised her, but Sian's casual acceptance of their situation was disconcerting. Being honest with herself, she worried the whirlwind honeymoon aspect of her experience with Rowan was setting her up for a mighty big heartbreak.

As she tried to order her thoughts, she heard an unfamiliar male voice calling upstairs for Sian. The three of them descended the stairs together and met Rio and his dad in the living room. Alyssa's initial observations of Sian's youth echoed in her husband. Rowan's dad stood shoulder to shoulder with him but had the same midnight blue eyes as Rio. Though a little salt shined in his sable hair, his tanned face and honed body called to mind a man half his age.

"Rio tells me you're Rowan's talisman. You have no idea how relieved we are to meet you. Owen Sheridan." He offered her his hand. "I met Sian at the eleventh hour, and we had fears Rowan faced a similar fate—or worse." Turning to Sian he said, "Rio put the box of journals in the study. It would be good for you to take a look at them while I start dinner." He headed for the kitchen while Sian walked in the opposite direction.

Alyssa raised an inquiring brow to Rowan who smiled. "As you've probably already noticed with your perceptive observations, my mother and I are a lot alike, including our culinary skills—or lack of them. Dad does most of the cooking around here, thank the gods. We should join Mom in the study."

Taking her hand, Rowan led her down the hall to a room off the living room. Upon entering, she decided if she lived in this mansion of a cabin, the only other rooms she would ever visit would be the bathroom and the kitchen, purely out of physical necessity. Otherwise, she'd live in the room the family called the study.

Floor-to-ceiling bookshelves lined three of the four walls, the shelves filled with books two rows deep in places. A box bay window looking out over the front of the house interrupted one wall of books and let in natural light. The Sheridans displayed a large Celtic trinity knot sculpture like the one in Alyssa's home in the bay of the window. Before the window rested two recliners upholstered in brick red suede. Between them, a dark walnut table supported a wrought iron lamp with a cream-colored shade flaring in a scallop design. Intertwining trinity knots edged the scallops of the shade.

A matching couch and coffee table dominated the center of the room. Over the back of the couch lay a blanket woven in the tree of life pattern.

On the only wall space in the room hung a tapestry depicting the three goddesses: maid, mother, and crone—the Celtic triple goddess. Beneath it stood a huge antique oak roll top desk, one of the most beautiful pieces of furniture Alyssa had ever seen. A tan leather swivel chair waited in the open space between the lower drawers.

Rio had placed the box of journals on the coffee table, and while Alyssa admired the room, Sian went immediately to the journals. Rowan sat beside her on the couch and drew out the family tree first then sat back and waited as his mother perused it. Alyssa idly wandered around the room looking at the spines of the books and marveling at the breadth of knowledge available in this space. Some small public libraries in the state were less extensive than the Sheridans' book collection.

Several minutes passed in silence while Sian concentrated on Alyssa's family tree. At some point she reached a decision, rose, and strode to the desk where she opened a drawer and extracted an ancient looking scroll. Coming back to the couch, she unrolled the scroll and placed it beside Alyssa's information. Alyssa stepped behind the couch to peek over Rowan's shoulder at the pages spread on the table. Since she had no idea what Sian knew and could see in the information before her, she jumped when Sian gasped, "Holy Saint Brighid defend us!"

The hairs on the back of Alyssa's neck stood at attention.

Apparently, Rio heard his mother's distress as he raced into the room to discover why she cried out. Without looking away from the pages, Sian commanded, "Rio, get your father. Now." The tone of her voice brooked no argument, and he disappeared to call Owen from the kitchen.

Once everyone assembled, Sian proceeded to explain. "The Sheridan family tree has two branches descending from Findlay and Ailsa's twin sons. Owen's side tends to sons while Riordan's side tends to daughters. When the two branches reunite, the talisman from Riordan's side with the warrior from Owen's side, they can reverse the curse that requires a warrior to find his talisman before his twenty-eighth birthday."

Turning to Rowan and Alyssa, she continued. "The prophecy indicates the time for this union is a thousand years after the Morrigan's curse on Findlay Sheridan. You two are the talisman and warrior pair who will end the curse."

Rowan stood, came around to stand beside Alyssa, and slipped his arm around her. "That explains Taranis's interference and Morgan's little visit to your house."

"It also puts the two of you in incredible danger until your twenty-eighth birthday."

Rowan tightened his arm around Alyssa.

Sian continued, "In order to end the curse, you must still be together then. My guess is Morgan is going to do everything in her power to split you up or to take one or both of you across the ford before the summer solstice. If she can do that, she can continue the curse for another thousand years."

"Then we have to do everything in our power to keep these two safe," Owen said.

"The problem is Rowan is a warrior, and as a warrior, he must fight when he's called. Morgan will do whatever she can to take him in battle, so I think he's the primary target," Sian said.

"I'm not so sure about that, Mom." Rio joined her on the couch.

"Why do you say that?" Though Owen appeared to lean casually against a book shelf, his eyes blazed with blue fire.

"We had a run-in with a couple of civilian jerks when we stopped for a late lunch today. At first, it seemed we were in the right place at the right time to help out some folks who were being terrorized by those morons.

"But while Rowan and I were occupied outside dodging bullets and keeping the ricochets from hitting civilians, Morgan visited Alyssa inside the café. What was it she said again, Alyssa?" Rio asked.

She closed her eyes against a vision of Morgan. "'It is not with the first stroke of the axe that the tree falls.'"

"What do you suppose that means, Mom?" Rio asked.

"I don't know, except you may be on to something." Sian caught Alyssa's eye. "What is your ability, Alyssa?"

"She's a dreamer, Mom. And a damn good one," Rowan answered for her, smiling with pride. "I started her training Saturday night, and she's an incredibly quick learner. By the end of the night, we were both exhausted, but she saw all kinds of ways I could have come out of the battles we practiced with no injuries and no chances for Morgan to strike."

"So that's why your mom felt you battling all night. Liked to drive us crazy since not even I could breach your shield," Owen scolded.

Rowan shrugged. "Alyssa's house is protected by layers of enchantments, so between those and the distance, it wasn't likely you'd be able to reach me."

Sian glared at Owen. "Your star student in the art of shielding."

"As we all know, he surpassed the master long ago." Owen stared down his son. "Your skill is highly frustrating when it isn't plain irritating."

Sian sighed before redirecting her attention to Alyssa. "What other training have you had?"

"Seamus worked with me a little on shielding my thoughts, but I'm still not very good at it yet," Alyssa said ruefully with a meaningful glance at Rowan who covered a grin with a cough into his hand.

"Are you telling me the only talisman training you've had took place over the weekend with Rowan and Seamus?" Sian asked, her eyes rounded in shock.

"Until Friday night, I didn't know what a talisman was. Until this afternoon, I wasn't convinced everything that happened over the weekend hadn't been part of an elaborate plan to have some fun at my expense." She left out the part about it all being a ruse for getting into her pants, but the implication hung in the air like a rank vapor.

Sian tried again. "I can't wrap my head around this. You're how old?"

"Twenty-four."

"Twenty-four and you had no idea who and what you are? How can that be?" Sian squeaked her disbelief at nearly stratospheric levels.

"It's a long story, Mom." Rowan sighed. "But the short version is Alyssa was orphaned when she was too little to understand what Morgan had done to her family. Her grandmother, a druid, married a warrior and was widowed young. She had no protection for Alyssa other than keeping her ignorant and out of sight as much as she could. Eventually, she met a widowed warrior who looked after them, and between her grandmother's enchantments and the warrior's limited protection, they managed to keep Alyssa safe."

"From what Finn Daly told me this weekend—he's the warrior Rowan mentioned—Gram and he thought it best not to tell me about myself as another layer of the protections they erected between Morgan and me. But after this afternoon, I'm pretty sure she knows who and what I am," Alyssa said, finishing Rowan's narrative.

"We need to compress years of training into days or even hours. Is that what you're telling me?" Sian asked. "I don't know what I want to do more, go into hysterics or punch a wall."

Rather than succumbing to either of her impulses, she took the situation in hand. "In the amount of time we have, I'm pretty sure I can't teach you the Celtic stories and traditions that dictate our lives and inform our choices. However, I can teach you how to protect yourself while you're helping Rowan. Owen will work on your shielding and listening skills. I can't imagine either will be strong enough in time for your first test, but we'll each do the best we can to take you as far as possible before Morgan launches her first attack." Sian closed the journal on her lap and started to rise.

With a hand on her shoulder, Rowan stayed her. "Before you despair of her, Mother, there are a few things you should know. Alyssa's grandmother did teach her the old Celtic tales, and Alyssa is currently working on a master's degree in Celtic mythology."

Sian eased back down. "Go on."

"And she has an interesting little hobby. Look around in that box, and you'll find some examples."

Sian reached in, moved some notebooks, and discovered the bookmarks Alyssa had embroidered. Her response mirrored Rowan's when he first touched one. "Did you design these as well as stitch them?" she asked, her focus on the Celtic horses design over which she ran her fingertips.

"Yes."

"Did you use models or were you otherwise inspired?" Sian handed the strip of cloth she'd been examining over to her husband whose eyebrows nearly met his hairline when he saw Alyssa's work.

"Ideas come into my head, and I stitch them in. It's only a hobby." She truly couldn't figure out what was the big deal.

"The big deal, my dear, is these designs have incredible power. Anyone who has one of these in his possession has the protection of the deity you've honored in your design. For example, this one," Owen held up the one of three intertwined horses, "calls on the power of Epona, the horse goddess. And yes, we definitely have work to do with you on the skill of shielding."

"Oh."

All the time Gram had encouraged her hobby, Alyssa had thought it was to keep her out of Gram's hair while she put up the fruits of her gardens. She had no idea her designs were another layer of protection for her and for those to whom she gave her work.

"There's more," Rio said, interrupting his parents' focus on Alyssa's needlework.

"More designs?" Sian asked absently as she perused several of the bookmarks at once.

"There's more about Alyssa," Rio corrected, sounding like he'd just bit into a lemon.

When he didn't continue, Owen prompted. "What else about Alyssa, Rio?"

Cocking a brow at his brother, Rowan took over the story. "She visualized me back to my apartment after my last battle before she'd seen my place or knew what either of us was. In fact, we'd met for the first time that day at my office when she hired me to put in a security system for her." His hand tightened on her hip, urging her closer to him. "Rio battled alongside me and tried to help me since Morgan saw to it I had some reminders of how much time I have left until my birthday. In the middle of his attempt to help me, I disappeared because Alyssa took me away." Rowan gave Alyssa a tiny hug. "For the past nine months, she's been having visions of my battles, visions she thought were dreams."

He turned to his brother. "Rio, I know it's driving you crazy that I have someone else to help me, but you have to deal with it. The alternative is something none of us wants to contemplate."

Rio pursed his lips. "Yeah, yeah, but how can she have so much power when she doesn't have a clue about anything?"

Owen and Sian exchanged a look so charged it riveted everyone in the room.

Owen said with deadly seriousness, "Alyssa, we'll eat something first, but your training will begin immediately after dinner. We'll all need to help, even you Rio. The power in this pairing is so strong Morgan won't be able to wait to attack. Our only hope is that she waits until morning."

CHAPTER TWENTY-TWO

IAN AND OWEN'S beliefs about the implications of Alyssa's pairing with Rowan left her so afraid that she didn't eat much of Owen's dinner, which she later realized had been a mistake. Immediately following the meal, without even cleaning up the kitchen, the Sheridans walked out to the laundry room and dressed in their winter gear. Once properly attired, all the men summoned their claymores. Alyssa watched agog as she witnessed them visualize their weapons into their hands, their swords appearing as if by magic.

Owen commanded Alyssa to walk beside Sian while the warriors silently circled the talismans before heading across the backyard to the training room. Alyssa thought they were going to hike up the mountain when Owen produced a key from his pocket and unlocked a cleverly disguised door opening into a long hallway. Instead of hiking up the mountain, they walked right into the heart of it, Shadow trailing behind them.

Alyssa heard the reverberation of the heavy door latching until the echo died away into the center of the earth. The sound made her feel as though she'd been escorted into a dungeon and locked in. Overhead track lights activated by motion sensors flicked on at intervals as they trekked deeper into the mountain. By the time they reached the training room, she estimated they'd walked a quarter of a mile into the bowels of the mountain.

Having no idea what to expect, the training room, hewn out of solid granite, surprised her. Like the spokes of a wheel, overhead track lights emanated from a central chandelier lighting the room. Various carved-in designs from Celtic legend and art decorated the walls. Alyssa recognized most of them. Unable to stop herself, she stepped closer to the walls to examine the designs, already creating complementary patterns in her head for more embroidery projects. Maybe she'd give them as gifts to the Sheridans for their hospitality—if she survived the training and the battles they insisted were coming.

The tiled marble floor mirrored the wheel of lights on the ceiling. Black paint delineated every other spoke, the intervening spokes painted white, all of them converging at a central medallion inlaid with a Celtic trinity knot pattern. A few high backed wooden chairs that looked like rescues from an ancient Celtic stronghold were arranged at intervals around the room.

Other than the chairs, the space was empty. Having had a few hours of training with both Rowan and Seamus, she already knew most of her work would be in her head with her visions and thoughts. The knowledge didn't comfort her overmuch, especially after Sian's assessment of their situation.

The family started training with Alyssa and Rowan standing in the middle of the room. Rowan bared his back as Alyssa touched the remnants of his wounds from Thursday night's battle. The salve Alyssa had used on them while she and Rowan trained Saturday night had worked wonders healing the angry red gashes without marring his skin. When he'd stripped off his sweater, she gasped at the speed at which he'd healed. Even when Gram chanted over her while applying the salve to her childhood cuts and scrapes, she had never healed as quickly as Rowan had from sword wounds that would have required hundreds of stitches for a civilian.

Alyssa felt exposed touching Rowan so intimately in front of his family. Leaning down to her, he spoke quietly. "This is necessary for them to see how we work together."

Once they started with the first battle, she forgot about the other people in the room as she concentrated on observing every aspect of the scene and alerting Rowan to hidden dangers and sudden changes in the playing field or the rules of the game as Morgan randomly dictated.

Without warning, Sian and Owen changed the game, making the battle real and live. Their tactic caught both Alyssa and Rowan off-guard, but because Rowan had more training, he recovered quickly and started a counter-attack.

"Ignore your feelings and do your job, Alyssa," he reminded her.

Sucking in a deep breath, she did as he asked, not only giving him information he needed, but also anticipating the "rogue warriors'" next moves and alerting him to what could come.

Their practice lasted several hours before Owen called a halt. By then everyone in the room had shed clothing down to T-shirts, jeans, and bare feet on the cold stone floor. Still, they all dripped sweat. She had never experienced such bone-deep exhaustion as when she finally sat down on one of the hard, wooden chairs. If someone had asked her about her perch in her current state, she would have described it as a plushy-soft cushion. In fact, she believed she could curl up quite easily on the seat and fall asleep instantly.

However, Owen had other plans. Dismissing Rio and Sian for the night, he started working with Alyssa on shielding. The training in her sapped condition accelerated her ability to shield her thoughts because she didn't fight Owen as he gave her commands and hints. By morning, she could keep Rowan out of her head at will and often Owen as well.

"Damn, you're quick, Alyssa. I can't remember another student who learned as fast or as well," Owen said.

Rowan cleared his throat.

"Well, maybe one," Owen amended with a smile.

Having trained all night, she was nearly non-functional, barely able to mutter "Thank you" at Owen's praise. Rowan helped her back into her jacket, socks, and boots before lifting her high into his arms and carrying her back to the house. She awoke around noon naked in Rowan's bed with no recollection of having arrived there. His big, warm presence against her back, his forearm draped over her belly, comforted her until she realized they were naked in bed *together* in his parents' house.

She gasped and tried to leap out of the bed, but he tightened his hold on her. "Where do you think you're going in such a hurry?" he rumbled against the soft skin at the nape of her neck.

"I can't sleep with you in your parents' house. It isn't right," she hissed.

"Calm down, Pixie-girl. As we've already established, part of your training involves bonding with your warrior—in every way." He traced a pattern over the sensitive skin on her belly. "My parents of all people are well aware of that fact. Actually, I don't think they'd approve if you left me alone in this bed. They might wonder about your loyalty to me," he patiently explained before kissing her behind her ear.

"Maybe if you'd grown up properly in our society, you'd be less squeamish about what my family considers normal—and appropriate—behavior for a warrior and his talisman. However, I'm not in the mood for talking right now." He kissed her shoulder as he plucked first one nipple then the other with his thumb and forefinger.

When she tried to back away from his roving hand, she pushed right into his erection. With a squeak, she arched away from his body only to fill his hand more fully with her breast.

"If you want to wrestle in bed, just ask. I'm certainly game for that."

She batted at his hand. "Rowan." She sighed with exasperation.

If he didn't already know she'd given in, her taut nipples gave her away. Still, she tried to make him see reason. "Rowan, honestly, this doesn't feel right."

"Let's remedy that," he whispered as he turned her toward him. Once she faced him, he pulled her close and took her mouth in a deep kiss. Palming her back from shoulders to tailbone, his calloused hand elicited delicious goose bumps along her skin. Then he cupped her ass and pulled her even closer to his ready body. She couldn't fight both him and herself. Kissing him back, she slid her tongue over his before she pulled back to nip at his lower lip. As she kissed him, she smoothed her hand along his strong shoulders, down the lovely arch of his spine to his ass. She couldn't fight the intense attraction she felt for him any more than she could understand it.

The heat of her kiss, the intensity of her caress as she pulled him closer to her proclaimed her surrender. She completed it when she lifted her leg to slide her knee along his thigh, silently inviting him to take her.

Rowan grinned before he rolled her under him and pushed up on his hands. All the playfulness left him as he commanded, "Watch us." She lifted her head and watched with him as he entered her, a slow delicious sheathing.

"Rowan! Ohmigod, that is—oh!"

When she dropped her head back on the pillow, he demanded again, "Watch, Alyssa. There's more to see." He pulled nearly all the way out before giving her another long slow thrust. This time she couldn't wait for him and lifted her hips to meet him. He took her completely, burying himself to his balls in her hot wet center.

"See? This is so good because it's so right. Because we were made for each other."

"Yes," she said on a sigh as she stared at their joined bodies.

Rational or not, she was falling in love with him. When he wanted her like this, her body and her heart couldn't say no. *How did that happen? How is it that I have absolutely no control over my responses to this man?*

⚜

Rowan increased his rhythm. *Never in all my experience have I known a pleasure as intense as joining with Alyssa.* Her body, though petite, was strong and perfect for him, her passion as powerful as his own. In every way, they were made for each other. He gathered her into his arms and kissed her mouth the same way his body kissed hers, deeply and fully. She wrapped her arms and legs around him, her inner muscles pulsing around his cock as she came. Grinding his hips against her, he joined her in paradise, an ecstasy beyond description, their lovemaking surpassing the time before when he thought they'd reached the pinnacle of physical joining.

As they came down from the heights of desire, Rowan maintained their intimate connection, cupping her ass and rolling onto his back with Alyssa sprawled across his chest. He traced the contours of her back and tangled his hands in her hair. *This connection feels way bigger than merely a warrior and his talisman.* On the heels of that thought intruded another. *Damn, I've fallen in love with her. What if she doesn't feel the same way?* Rowan worried. *Wish Dad wasn't so good at teaching shielding. I'd give anything to know what she's thinking right now.*

A sharp rap on the door and Rio's muffled voice on the other side of it jolted them out of the after-glow of their love-making.

"Wake up, brother. We have more training to do."

When Alyssa groaned into Rowan's chest before rolling off him to lie on her back and stare at the ceiling, her profile told him the prospect of another session like the one last night and into this morning shattered her. Pushing up on his elbow, he traced a finger along the smooth skin of her cheek. "You're so strong, Alyssa, stronger than you know. You impressed everyone last night. You're up to it today, believe me."

She turned her head on the pillow and looked at him through bleak eyes. "It occurred to me when we arrived yesterday that your family's world revolves around you. If I fail when Morgan strikes, how will I ever face them?"

"In case you didn't notice, Dad and Mom already see you as part of the family. That's why they're working you so hard. You aren't going to fail me, Alyssa, and my family isn't going to abandon you. At some point, you're going to have to learn to trust me. Us."

She drew in a breath and exhaled. "Believe me, I'm trying." Taking his hand, she kissed his palm before rolling out of bed.

He squelched his first instinct to follow her into the bathroom and join her in the shower. He doubted his family would appreciate the delay. Instead, he lay back against the pillows and tried to envision what the day's training would entail. *I hope Dad plans on attacking Alyssa as she helps me. She's so selfless and single-minded, it would be easy for Morgan to take her like she took Ailsa all those years ago. If I lose Alyssa now, it'll be worse than anything else Morgan could ever do to me, worse than never having found her in the first place.*

Interrupting his reverie, Alyssa emerged from the bathroom, a fluffy towel wrapped around her as she dried her hair with another. "Your turn, big guy."

"When this is all over and we can live as normal a life as warriors and talismans are ever allowed to, I think I'll enlarge the shower in your house so I never have to wait my turn." Rowan didn't mean for that to slip out, and he held his breath for the imminent explosion.

Alyssa's mouth dropped open. "Do you seriously mean to move in with me for good?"

Rowan pretended not to hear her as he disappeared into the bathroom, closing the door behind himself. When he emerged from the shower, he found she'd already dressed in layers this time. Smart girl. She informed him brunch was served before she headed downstairs to meet the rest of the family.

⋟

As she neared the kitchen, the clatter of utensils against plates alerted Alyssa to the others busy at their meal. Apparently, she and Rowan had taken too long preparing for the day, so the rest of the family started without them.

Shyly, she entered the kitchen. "Sorry for being late to breakfast."

"You're right on time. Please sit. Eat," Sian said as she handed Alyssa a plate piled with an enormous helping of egg casserole.

Her stomach rumbled audibly, and she ducked her head as she took her place at the island.

"I always have the same reaction to Mom's breakfast casserole, especially after a long training session," Rio said with a wink.

She preempted further conversation by taking a large bite of her meal. The symphony of flavors played over her tongue, momentarily causing her to forget Rio's innuendo. Baked in with the scrambled eggs were chunks of ham, green and red peppers, onions, and potatoes, all neatly held together with melted Gruyère cheese.

"This is the tastiest breakfast I can remember," she said with genuine enthusiasm.

Sian beamed and passed her a bowl of home-canned peaches. Talk turned to Rowan's omelets and how he must have learned to make them from his mother. Alyssa felt her cheeks heat as she realized what knowing about his omelets implied to his parents. Her grandmother raised her to be traditional about relationships, and the speed and intimacy of her relationship with Rowan troubled her.

When Owen entered her thoughts, she discovered she'd let down her shield. *"Don't worry, Alyssa. Even knowing what we were, Sian and I had a rocky start. Your relationship with our son is not immoral, and we don't judge you."*

Her eyes widened, as she looked at Owen who smiled blandly at her and returned to his meal.

"What took you so long, big brother? Alyssa is ready for seconds," Rio teased when Rowan walked into the kitchen.

"I checked in with Seamus and Finn. It's quiet at Alyssa's. No one tried to break into her place after we left. At the office, Isla is feeling some ominous rumblings, however. Whatever Morgan is planning, it appears she'll be launching it soon. We need to be ready." Rowan sat by Alyssa and helped himself to two squares of casserole and a nearly overflowing bowl of peaches.

Sian changed the topic. "Tell me about your dog, Alyssa."

"Oh no! I forgot all about Shadow. Where is he?" she asked with alarm.

"He's on the bed I made up for him in the laundry room. He slept outside your door until I let him out earlier today. Once he heard you stirring, he came downstairs to wait," Sian gently answered her. "Tell me about him."

"When I came into my inheritance from my parents and wanted to move into my own place, Gram and Finn insisted I needed the protection and companionship of a dog. We agreed on a Great Pyrenees, found a breeder, and went to meet the puppies. Shadow chose me right away, and he's been following me around for the past six years."

Owen leaned toward her. "You say you agreed on the choice? Why didn't you pick out something yourself?"

"Gram and Finn insisted on having some say in the matter— something about him being a gift from them. Shadow is a very expensive dog, and they paid for him."

"Do you understand the significance of a woman owning a white dog?" Sian asked.

"There's significance to a woman owning a white dog? Seriously?"

"A woman in possession of a white dog means she's powerful and good. You becoming Shadow's mistress was no random choice. I wish I'd met your grandmother. I think she may have been a prophetess as well as a healer," Sian said.

Alyssa nudged Rowan. "Is that why you insisted on bringing Shadow with us?"

"Partly. And partly because he's so protective of you that any civilian in Morgan's thrall who dares to come around you will meet with a fierce guard who will do anything to protect you."

As though aware of being the topic of conversation, Shadow appeared in the kitchen and walked purposefully to his mistress to lie down behind her chair. The comical look on his face as he peered up at her from beneath his eyebrows broke the tension, and she smiled and reached down to run her hands through his thick fur.

"I think Shadow needs to be part of today's training," Owen announced as he rose to rinse his plate and stow it in the dishwasher.

"Good idea," Sian seconded, joining him in cleaning up. "Isla's premonitions have rarely been wrong, so we're better off with as many layers of protection as possible."

Alyssa's agitation spiked as talk turned to training. The thought of another session as intense as the first one she endured a few short hours before drained her already. Rowan smiled reassuringly at her. *"Remember what I told you. You're stronger than you know."*

She returned a weak smile before helping Sian with the kitchen cleanup.

Rowan joined his brother and father in the den as they revisited Afton's journals. "Alyssa's grandmother had many skills, but we aren't going to be able to unlock them ourselves," he began before Owen interrupted him.

"We need to return to the training room right now. This minute, boys."

Rowan and Rio exchanged a look.

"Because you're a Sheridan, you're a prize, Rowan. But the real prize is Alyssa. Morgan's been focused on her since she was tiny."

Rowan's breakfast turned to stone in his stomach.

He stared at the journals as though they might attack. "Before we start the training today, we should invite Siobhan over to have a look at these." He glanced at his dad. "Perhaps they contain enchantments that can add more layers of protection for Alyssa. Siobhan could read the journals in the training room while Duncan and Jennifer join us to train."

"Good idea, son. The more help we have training the two of you, the better our chances of thwarting Morgan."

CHAPTER TWENTY-THREE

LYSSA BARELY HAD time to pull her boots on before the three men hustled Sian and her out of the house, Shadow bounding happily at their heels. Though Alyssa wondered at the sudden urgency, one look at the men's determined faces told her to save her questions until they reached the safety of the training room. As in the old days, the *Tuatha dè Danaan*, the divine children of the goddess Danu, were safest underground or in the hearts of mountains.

Lights illuminated the training room before the group set off the motion sensors. Alyssa figured out why when she saw a woman awaiting them in the center of the wheel—a woman, but no ordinary female. Her short, spiky red hair combined with the definition of her arm muscles revealed by her leather vest evinced an untouchable aura. Rather than diminish her, her compact body exuded strength and power. The way she carried herself radiated confidence and commanded respect. Whoever this woman was, Alyssa hoped she was on their team.

"Alyssa, may I introduce you to Scathach? Milady, this is Alyssa Macaulay, Rowan's talisman and the key to the prophecy," Owen said.

She didn't know what protocol one followed when being introduced to a goddess. Should she curtsy? Should she kneel? Would
she be struck down for her open curiosity? Scathach remedied the
situation by stepping over to her and taking her hand in a firm
grip. "I'm so glad you've survived the various attempts on your life
to reach this point. I'm rather fond of the Sheridan family—have
been for over a thousand years—so I would rather not see Morgan
or Maeve take any more of them. That would be a waste of the time
and training I've invested in them over the years," Scathach said as
she smiled warmly at Alyssa.

"Ah … it's … ah, a pleasure to meet you," Alyssa stuttered.

"I don't imagine you've met many goddesses, Alyssa," Sian said
with a smile. "We're especially fond of this one and grateful she
likes Sheridan warriors so well. Scathach trained all the men in this
room and every Sheridan since Findlay. Today, she has agreed to
help us train you."

The room hewn from solid stone was chilly, the training yet to
begin, but a bead of sweat slipped down the middle of Alyssa's back.
A goddess would train her? She couldn't imagine it even though
Scathach stood before her in all her intense warrior glory.

Scathach laughed. "Do not worry, Alyssa. Considering your
ancestry, I have no doubt you will be a quick study. Your parents
learned fast."

Alyssa's eyes widened, and before she could harness herself, she
blurted, "You trained my *parents*?"

"I trained your father and your maternal grandfather. When
Morgan attacked them so mercilessly even after your father found
your mother, I wondered why. Though I do not think she knew
exactly from where the prophesied talisman would come, she is
aware of both family trees and was probably hedging her bets," the
goddess said as she circled Alyssa, seeming to size her up.

"Does she know now?" asked Alyssa nervously.

"If she did, we wouldn't have met in such cordial circumstances." The goddess struck a pose. "However, after today, she'll know."

"Oh," Alyssa said in small voice.

Rowan slid his arm around her, pulling her close and whispering, "Don't doubt yourself. You're up to this, and now you have the best trainer of any era to help you."

She tried to relax, but the fear of losing him due to her own inabilities demoralized her. How Rowan had come to mean so much to her in so short a time she'd stopped trying to figure out. She only knew he meant the world to her now. No matter how much training she did, she didn't know what to expect in a real battle, and when she figured it out, it might be too late. What she did know was she would rather sacrifice herself than lose him. She slumped into him as the reality of the challenges ahead hit her like a freight train. Scathach gave her a knowing look. As hard as she tried to shield her thoughts, it didn't take a goddess or some mortal genius to know what she had on her mind.

Her innate caring nature made her initial training with Scathach most difficult. After several hours of practice, Rowan praised her for mastering her face and posture no matter what was happening to her new family, especially to him. In a short time, she had bonded completely with her warrior, giving them a distinct advantage in battle.

The rest of the day she spent helping Rowan in battle scenarios with Rio and Owen playing enemy warriors while Sian and Scathach took turns as Morgan and Maeve trying to distract and even take her when her concentration centered on Rowan. At first, taking her had been easy, but by the end of the training, she'd learned how to divide her attention, keeping most of it on Rowan while giving herself a chance by watching her own backside. Even Scathach's most concerted attacks came up short, much to the goddess's visible satisfaction.

"No doubt it has become clear to you that I want nothing more than to best Morgan in this battle for warriors," Scathach said as the group broke for water and snacks Sian and Owen had supplied. "Morgan has taken far too many good men over the years, and she needs to be checked. I am looking forward to the coming time when I can enjoy the fruits of my labors with promising warriors for longer than the first twenty-seven years of their lives."

Alyssa smiled tentatively at the goddess who almost seemed to grow in stature before her. "However, now is not the time to bask in our success. Alyssa, you still need to learn how to listen to another's thoughts on purpose. Your telepathic communication with Rowan will be critical when you are up against the initial onslaughts of civilians in Morgan's thrall."

"Are you going to train me to listen to another person's thoughts?" Her enthusiasm for this training surpassed her exhaustion from the hours of work preceding it.

"Knowing the Sheridans, I can guess why you are so eagerly embracing yet more training in spite of looking like you are about to pass out." Scathach gifted Alyssa with a genuine smile before shifting to a smirk in Rowan's direction. "All right then. Let's work on the skill of listening to thoughts. Owen?"

Owen pulled Alyssa to the side of the room and began the new training. By the early hours of the second morning, Scathach and the Sheridans determined Alyssa's training had reached as near a state of completeness as possible under the circumstances.

While Alyssa trained with Owen, Sian unobtrusively delivered a double cot, bedding, and food for Rowan and Alyssa. In Alyssa's exhausted state, Scathach decided it unwise to remove her from the safe confines of the mountain chamber. The goddess said that once Alyssa and Rowan exited the training room, Morgan would become aware of everything and probably launch an attack immediately. Before that happened, Alyssa needed time to recover. Though they could train her in a short time, they couldn't build her stamina as quickly. Scathach admitted even a goddess of her considerable power had some limitations in the affairs of men.

Shadow stayed with Alyssa and Rowan in the training room while the others retired to the house.

✎

The echo of the outer door reverberated down the long hall and bounced around the training room. Alyssa hardly seemed to notice as she curled up on the cot.

Rowan dished up dinner. "Come on, Alyssa, eat. Dad slaved all day at the Crock Pot cooking up this stew." He chuckled as he wafted a steaming bowl of food beneath Alyssa's nose.

"I'm so tired. Let's eat later," she mumbled.

Dragging her upright once more, he remained insistent. "After the training session we just endured, you need to eat. Here, have a few bites." He held a spoonful of savory dinner to her mouth.

Obediently, she ate barely enough to satisfy him before she shivered in her sweaty clothes and fell over onto the cot.

Admitting defeat, Rowan tucked her under the covers, grousing to himself about why in all the years they'd had the training room, his parents had never thought to put in a shower.

After neatly stacking their plates and utensils beside the Crock Pot and checking to be sure the space heater wasn't too close to their bed, Rowan turned down the lights and joined Alyssa. Though bone tired himself, he couldn't help but look at this beautiful woman who was his destiny. As he trailed the pad of his finger over the satiny skin of her cheek, he fretted over the dark smudges under her eyes, smudges her long sooty lashes couldn't cover. Smoothing his hand over her head, her silky black hair flowing sensuously through his fingers, he marveled at how much he loved her already—a circumstance he didn't even question.

At last, he slid beneath the blankets and settled Alyssa against him, slipping an arm around her and pillowing her head on his shoulder. Holding her like this reassured him. They *would* survive the coming battle together and come out alive and with a future. He swore it.

⋘

Alyssa was enjoying the loveliest dream. Floating on a cloud, she felt both weightless and heavy. Her limbs seemed to be so light as to be almost unattached while her core felt thick and full with desire. A delicious warmth enveloped her, and she turned toward it only to find a barrier trapping her, impeding her movement. From a great distance, she could hear the resonant rumble of a deep soothing voice telling her to lie still and take it. *Take what?* she wondered before she felt a pleasurable probing between her legs. Trying to shift toward the source of that pleasure, she again found her movement restricted.

Her agitation increasing, she slowly became aware of Rowan's voice. The pleasure she experienced stemmed from his clever hand rubbing and plucking gently between her legs. Giving herself up to him, she awakened slowly as waves of ecstasy washed over her. She came sweetly over his hand, and he kissed her nape before nipping her lightly there, signaling her the easy rousing had ended. She came fully awake and discovered herself naked from her waist down. Rowan was hard and ready against the cleft of her bottom.

"Raise your leg," he growled.

She did as she was told, and he entered her with a long slow thrust. She pushed against him, taking him deeper inside her before she clamped her inner muscles around him. Her already hyper-sensitized sex pulsed around him, pleasuring both of them. When he thrust hard into her, she cried out her climax, and he joined her seconds afterward.

"Wow," was all and everything she could manage as aftershocks rolled through her.

"Yeah, wow," Rowan whispered, amazement coloring his voice. *I don't think I came that fast the first time I had sex, and I've certainly never met a woman who did.* He grinned inwardly. *Our apparent mutual ability to please each other so fast might come in handy in the future.*

"In exactly what circumstances would such a 'skill' come in handy, do you suppose?" Alyssa asked, a rather waspish tone to her voice.

"You heard that?"

"You're lying very near me and thinking rather loudly."

"I wasn't sure how much you were learning the last couple of days and how much we were helping you, but now I think I know. Apparently, you can breach my automatic shield. Only Rio, Seamus, and my dad have ever been able to do that, and only after quite a bit more training than you've had." He turned her toward him. "Either you're some sort of talisman savant ..."

She rolled her eyes.

"—Or our connection is deeper than anyone we know has ever experienced."

Shadow's low growl warned them to expect company shortly. Rolling away from her, Rowan jerked up his jeans beneath the covers before exiting the bed. She struggled to redress herself before jumping quickly off the cot. Desperately, she tried to finger comb the tangles from her hair when Owen walked into the training room carrying the box of notebooks. Following closely behind him, Sian carried another box that smelled like breakfast. Rio, Scathach, and two strangers trailed in behind her.

"Good morning! Sorry to wake you so early, but we ran into some issues concerning these journals your grandma kept and decided it would be safer for everyone if Siobhan read them in here," Owen said as he set the box to one side of the room.

"You two look a little rumpled. Were you still asleep when Shadow alerted you to us?" Rio asked with a smirk.

Alyssa sputtered her embarrassment and looked at Rowan for

help. His response? A nonchalant shrug accompanied by a wink. She wanted to melt into the floor.

Mercifully, Sian rescued her from her embarrassment. "Alyssa, meet Siobhan and Duncan MacManus. Siobhan is Seamus's sister."

"Nice to meet you, Alyssa." Duncan shook her hand.

"We're so glad Rowan found you," Siobhan said, foregoing a handshake for a hug. Alyssa liked her immediately.

"I thought the two of you might be hungry, so I brought some breakfast, or what's left of it," Sian said apologetically as she carried the box over to Rowan.

"Mmm delicious! Full Scots breakfast. Yet one more reason to appreciate your visits, Scathach." He smiled at the goddess as he relieved his mother of the box. "Did anyone think to bring us some fresh clothes by chance? The ones I'm wearing feel a little stiff. I imagine Alyssa is having the same problem."

"Sorry, darling. We didn't think about that after Siobhan put her hands on the notebooks," Sian replied.

Rowan stopped abruptly in the middle of unpacking their breakfast. "What do you mean?"

"I asked Siobhan to take a look at the journals after breakfast. She touched one, stopped, and insisted we bring them out here before she opened them. So here we are," Owen said. "While the two of you eat, the rest of us will plan a strategy for today's training session and let Siobhan take a look at the journals. She's been feeling a storm gathering over the house, so the sooner we get to work, the better."

"What kind of storm are you feeling, Siobhan, other than the obvious one we've been wading through for a week?" Rio asked, a tinge of sarcasm clinging to his voice. From the looks he gave Siobhan, Alyssa had the distinct impression he didn't like her very much. Odd.

"The kind of storm involving angry goddesses," Scathach answered for the druid. "I have been aware of them since I arrived."

"Why didn't you say something?" Rio demanded.

"It is a good thing you are one of the quickest learners I have ever trained, and I like you well, Rio. Such an outburst from a *normal* person I would find highly insulting," Scathach bit out.

"Sorry, Scathach. I just can't stand the thought of Morgan taking my brother," Rio said, his voice softening.

"None of us want to see that happen. However, talking about the coming battle does little to prepare for it. We need to train and train hard. Today is probably our last chance before Morgan tests everyone's skills. You should be more worried about yourself. At least Rowan has his talisman," the warrior trainer reminded him.

"Such as she is," Rio mumbled before catching himself and looking away, a red stain creeping up his neck.

Ignoring Rio's sarcasm, Alyssa turned her attention to Scathach. "What do you mean we only have today? How can you know?"

Scathach crossed her warrior arms over her chest and lifted a sardonic brow.

"You've taught me so much, and I am so grateful, but I really don't see how I can be of any real service to Rowan if Morgan attacks tomorrow," Alyssa said.

"You may not even have until then. She may decide to attack tonight. Maeve is urging her on because she has a thing for Rowan." Scathach's answer did nothing to alleviate Alyssa's fear.

Alyssa faced Rowan, but before he could reassure her, Scathach interrupted. "You were a much better student yesterday. No one needs skills in telepathy to guess what is going on in your head right now. Remember, you must always school your face to keep others from gauging your thoughts. Try again," Scathach commanded. In an instant, Alyssa was back in training, and she hadn't even had breakfast.

CHAPTER TWENTY-FOUR

LYSSA CONTINUED TO train with Owen on telepathy skills. Her fear of the goddess's displeasure jumped into the stratosphere as Scathach suddenly interrupted the training session.

"Silence!" she roared, stopping mid-strike as she trained Rio on an especially tricky maneuver she insisted he master, one he'd been working on for months. He nearly toppled over onto his claymore as the blow he obviously expected never landed. Alyssa gaped at Rio who picked himself up off the cold marble floor. He looked questioningly at Scathach as she strode with purpose to an oblivious Siobhan.

"What are you chanting in here?"

When Siobhan didn't immediately respond, Scathach asked again. Loudly.

"I'm sorry. Were you addressing me, milady?" Siobhan asked, her expression dazed as she glanced up from her reading.

"What are you chanting in here?" Scathach's body glowed red-gold in her anger.

"I didn't realize I was chanting." Siobhan visibly trembled in the face of the goddess's wrath.

Having been on the receiving end of Scathach's displeasure, Alyssa had an inkling of how Siobhan felt.

"Any chanting, but especially a protection chant, must be done outside these walls if you do not wish either to compromise what we do here or entrap us in this chamber. Did your teacher absolutely despair of you ever learning the most basic of his lessons?" Scathach demanded, her red hair sparking in her fury.

Alyssa's heart went out to Siobhan as she watched tears spring to the woman's eyes. Watching a goddess physically strengthen before her eyes terrified Alyssa too, not to mention the red-gold fire in Scathach's eyes seemed ready to explode into Siobhan.

"I-I was so caught up in the reading I didn't know I chanted aloud. Please forgive me. It won't happen again." The pages in Siobhan's hands crinkled in her trembling before the goddess.

"See that it does not. Now, Rio, where were we?" Scathach calmed herself seamlessly, taking the exact position she'd held before Siobhan interrupted her. Rio took slightly more time to recover, which earned him a scowl from his trainer, a clear sign she would be even more merciless than before, and he was already soaked in sweat from the work they'd been doing. Meanwhile, Alyssa saw Siobhan needed several deep breaths to collect herself before tackling the journals again.

"Show's over, Alyssa. Back to work," Owen whispered at her side.

She pulled in a shuddering breath after witnessing the goddess's outburst. The Sheridans insisted Scathach was their patron goddess, their friend. If so, Alyssa didn't look forward to meeting deities who didn't like them.

She glanced over at Rowan and Duncan who had been sparring before Scathach's outburst. Duncan stared at the goddess in impotent silence. His inattention cost him a nick from Rowan's sword.

"Why did you do that?" Alyssa asked her warrior.

Rowan cocked an eyebrow in Alyssa's direction, letting her know he knew what she thought. *"I know what I'm doing. So does Duncan. Watch."*

Rowan's move pulled Duncan back into their training, and the two of them went after each other like they were taking on scores of Morgan's rogues. Instead of reassuring her, Rowan's actions reiterated to Alyssa how far behind and inadequate she was.

Again, Scathach left off training Rio in mid-blow, sending him sprawling across the floor. This time she directed her irritation at Alyssa. "You have zero time for feeling sorry for yourself," she snapped. "We will be at war shortly, and everyone, including you, will have to fight in whatever way necessary." She looked down her drawn sword at Alyssa. "We cannot lose concentration even for a moment for any reason if we expect to win. Our enemies have every intention of taking several, if not all of you, across the ford and into the mists. You do not wish to be the cause of their success, I presume?"

Alyssa lost her breath at Scathach's attack. Her eyes stung with unshed tears. Sucking in air, she straightened her shoulders and looked Scathach in the eye. "I will not be the cause of the Morrigan's success, milady. Please forgive my lapse in concentration."

The atmosphere in the training room remained electrified in the silence following Scathach's reprimand and Alyssa's apology. Scathach let everyone feel that charge before she broke the silence with a deep throaty laugh. She returned to her pupil who stared resentfully at his two least favorite females, both of whom had landed him on the cold, hard floor in the last few minutes. "Come, Rio, try that move again. You have almost perfected it." Rio sent another glare at Alyssa, and Scathach struck. "Focus your concentration, lad. Your future sister-in-law is fully capable of taking care of herself."

❧

The training lasted all morning and into the early afternoon. While the warriors and talismans were working with Scathach and each other, Siobhan continued reading Afton's journals. During a water break, Alyssa noticed Siobhan taking notes and wondered at what she learned. She had to admit to some jealousy of Siobhan doing the very thing she would have liked to have been doing if her circumstances had been different.

Apparently, something caught the druid's attention as she stood up with her notebook and headed down the passageway to the outside door. From where she stood near the supplies, Alyssa could hear Siobhan talking to her dog.

"Come on, Shadow, let me pass, you overgrown rug." Shadow's rejoinder consisted of a whine. "Seriously, friend, I need to go outside to work on these spells."

Shadow's whine morphed into a low growl.

"Okaaay, this is serious, isn't it? What do you know about what lurks outside that door?" Siobhan asked.

Rather than challenging Alyssa's furry bodyguard, Siobhan returned to the training room.

"I hate to interrupt when you're all hot and sweaty," Siobhan began, "but I had this idea I'd go outside to attempt a couple spells I have in mind." She glanced at Scathach. "Only I find that a rather large hairy fellow in front of the door has other ideas. Anyone care to speculate on why Shadow thinks I shouldn't leave the mountain?" she asked everyone in the room.

"They have arrived," Scathach said matter-of-factly. "I am surprised it took them this long to find us, especially considering Taranis followed Rowan, Rio, and Alyssa here. Perhaps they knew all along where their quarry holed up and were busy making plans. Not like them normally, making plans that is," Scathach speculated. "At any rate, the time has come to test how much you've retained of my years of training you—and how quick Alyssa really is."

"It was short-sighted of us to come out here without provisions and a change of clothes, especially after what Siobhan and Sian were feeling in the house this morning," commented Owen as he wiped the perspiration rolling down his face.

"You can towel off with the hand towels in the bathroom," Sian suggested.

Shadow barked loudly.

"I don't think so. It seems Shadow is doing his best to hold the door, but he's no match for what's beyond it," Rowan said. He grabbed Alyssa's hand and gave it a quick squeeze before joining his brother, father, Duncan, and Scathach as they headed for the hallway leading to the exit. "Stay inside, Alyssa, but stand in the hallway. That way we can still communicate, but you'll be safe."

Sian and Siobhan apparently already knew this as they followed their men down the passage.

From the end of the hallway, Alyssa watched as Shadow moved away from the door when Scathach reached it. As his name indicated, he padded silently past the warriors, stopping to sit in front of Alyssa. Rowan looked back before he reached the door and gave Alyssa a reassuring smile. "Keep her inside, my friend," he said to Shadow, an idea the big dog had apparently arrived at all on his own as he plopped down, effectively barring her from moving any closer to the door.

Before Alyssa had any chance to proclaim her indignation at such a show of male domination, she gasped at the waves of fury radiating through the open door as the warriors stepped out to greet the enemy. She had no time to consider her feelings since she could focus only on Rowan engaged in battle with a huge body-builder type whose vacant eyes made it clear if he had ever had any humanity, it had long ago deserted him.

Instinctively, Alyssa tried to rush out to help Rowan, but Shadow stood his ground, growling to remind her of her role as eyes and guide, not warrior. Remembering herself, she closed her eyes to observe the entire scene. Rio engaged two rather wiry and quick assailants who looked to be little more than boys of sixteen though they knew their way around their semi-automatic weapons. Clearly, the two were civilians who had no idea what they were up against.

Meanwhile, Owen took on another enormous body-builder type. Duncan dispatched two young men without beards before turning his attention to the rogue who appeared to be their leader, a sinister looking man with black eyes and inordinately red lips drawn back in a sneer as he lunged at Duncan.

While Rowan's full concentration centered on fighting the giant, one of the boys taking on Rio suddenly deserted the fight and headed for Rowan, aiming his gun at the backs of Rowan's knees. *"Rowan! Behind you!"* Alyssa called out to him, and he spun in a deadly graceful pirouette to slice the boy's abdomen, spilling his guts into a steaming pile at his feet, his face a mask of surprise as he sank into the snow. While the boy died, Rowan seemingly didn't miss a stroke against his more experienced opponent.

Somewhere inside herself, Alyssa worried she might be sick before a calmness overtook her. *"Rowan, the rogue's weakness is his right side. He has an enormous raw scar there, which is why he keeps it away from you. Force him to show his right side. A blow there will defeat him."*

Based on what she'd learned so far, Alyssa knew the other talismans communicated with their warriors as she communicated with Rowan. With all the warriors and talismans so engaged in the battle, they didn't recognize where the real danger lay. Morgan's soldiers steadily drew the warriors away from the doorway leading to the training room, and it was too late before Alyssa, or any of the others, sensed it. When the fighting reached a clearing in the forest beside the Sheridan compound, Morgan struck. The first the women knew of it was when Shadow interrupted their concentration with his incessant barking. Sian recovered the quickest. "Owen, Morgan's here! She's breached the enchantments outside the door. Come quickly!" she cried out, loud enough for all to hear.

"It won't be quick enough, my dear." Morgan's voice was an unwelcome chill. "As each of you are aware, your men are quite busy at the moment. While you were so intent on helping them, you missed the merry chase Maeve set Scathach, so she won't be back to meddle in my affairs until I have what I want."

Shadow growled and lunged at the goddess, who silenced him with a blow she delivered with a flick of her hand.

"Shadow! Nooo!" Alyssa cried and ran to her pet.

"Come, Alyssa, it's time to cross the ford." Morgan's eyes gleamed red as she grabbed Alyssa and pulled her toward the door.

"You can't kill me outright. You need a warrior to strike the blow. I may be years behind in the reality that has become my world, but I know the rules," Alyssa stated with a bravado she didn't feel as she gulped back tears of fear.

"Don't worry, my dear. I have that all arranged," Morgan replied, a nasty grin spreading over her features as she stepped out the door, dragging Alyssa behind her.

Outside, the frigid air froze Alyssa's sweat to her skin instantly. With her teeth chattering, she stumbled involuntarily behind Morgan until they reached the woods on the opposite side of the compound from where the warriors battled Morgan's enchanted zombie soldiers. In a tiny clearing stood a rogue warrior who seemed almost non-threatening until he pulled his enormous hands from the pockets of his baggy low-rider jeans. She surmised he meant to strangle her, a slow, intimate death she didn't fancy, and her struggles against Morgan's hold intensified tenfold.

"Do not try to deny your fate, Alyssa. This is precisely the way I killed your mother while I otherwise occupied your father. She struggled too, which gave my soldier and me much pleasure while it only made her death more painful for her." Morgan's voice in Alyssa's ear sounded like a hissing snake.

Her little bombshell produced the desired effect. As Alyssa tried to process her parents' fate, she stopped resisting long enough for Morgan to hand her over to the rogue warrior who licked his lips in anticipation of his job as executioner. Alyssa's eyes widened as she watched him reach for her neck. Then she blinked as the rogue shot backward against a tree with enough force his neck snapped back, his head banging against the tree trunk, his eyes rolling up as he dropped into unconsciousness.

The action left Alyssa and the goddess momentarily nonplussed. Alyssa recovered first and sprinted for the opposite side of the compound. As she reached the edge of the woods where Rowan and the others continued their fight, Morgan met her.

"Apparently, your grandmother perfected her skills as a druid in the years following your mother's trip across the ford. 'Tis no matter. You will come with me and bait the trap I will set for your warrior and his family. They will come for you, no matter what instructions you send, and when they do, I will be waiting to escort them all across the ford, wading thigh deep in Sheridan blood," Morgan said, her voice an evil purr as she ran her tongue over her teeth.

Holding tightly to a frantically struggling Alyssa, Morgan unceremoniously and painfully jerked her through time and space. The last sound she heard was Shadow barking and Sian and Siobhan calling desperately for the Sheridan warriors to come to her aide. Then all she heard was the mournful screaming of the wind, a sound she thought might pierce her eardrums. *So that is how the cry of the banshee sounds,* she thought before her world went black.

Rowan easily dispatched the rogue he'd been battling when the man's concentration faltered at the return of Scathach to the fight. Nearby, he heard his brother address their patroness.

"Thanks for joining us, but I think we've got this." Rio grinned as he perfectly executed the move he'd been working on with Scathach, his opponent falling lifelessly to the ground.

"Now is not the time to gloat, Rio. Maeve suddenly discovered she had somewhere else to go, and Morgan is conspicuously absent."

Rowan sensed something was very wrong.

"These rogues were a distraction, much like one I remember

from long ago," Scathach said as she casually dispatched a six-and-a-half-foot tall muscle-bound giant of a man who had turned his attention away from Owen for a second. When the other rogues realized who had materialized into their midst, they faded away into the trees like smoke. Only then did the warriors finally hear Sian and Siobhan shouting.

Racing back to the entrance to the training room, Rowan's heart leapt into his throat. Something had gone terribly wrong even though it appeared they'd won the battle.

All the hairs on his neck stood at attention when he heard Shadow's high-pitched keening from where he stood in the clearing on the other side of the garage. His chest constricted. So caught up was he in the battle, he hadn't sensed some danger Alyssa faced. When had he lost contact with her? He knew he must have, but the last thing he could remember was her warning about the boy about to cheap-shot him while the giant kept him otherwise occupied.

"Morgan was here. She took Alyssa." Sian panted, fear and horror written across her face as she joined him in the clearing opposite of where the warriors had fought their battle.

Siobhan ran up beside them. "She attempted to kill Alyssa with a rogue, but something happened. I felt a disturbance like a powerful electrical shock bounce through the atmosphere before I heard Alyssa calling for help."

Rowan spun around to find the rogue in question still unconscious at the base of a tree.

His father's hand landed on his shoulder as he came to stand beside Rowan. "That's Tory Ferrell," Owen said. "I trained with him before I met Sian. Even back in the day, he demonstrated an unnatural interest is blood-letting for the hell of it. I'm surprised he's still alive."

"Not anymore. Morgan has used this one long enough," Scathach said as she appeared behind them. Stepping between her warriors, she stood above the unconscious rogue, staring at him contemptuously before she woke him with a slap against his face from the side of her sword. He boiled up off the ground, his sword suddenly appearing in his hand, his body crouched in a fighting stance.

"Who wants the first go at him?" Scathach asked.

"Your talisman has some amazing power, but she's no match for my mistress," Ferrell sneered. Rowan took a step toward the rogue, but Owen's arm shot out in front of him, barring his progress.

Owen sauntered toward his old training partner who stared at him out of soulless eyes.

Ferrell leered evilly. "Like old times, eh Owen?" he asked, inviting the fight. The battle lasted a short minute since rogues didn't benefit from the on-going training Scathach provided warriors.

For Rowan Sheridan, Tory Ferrell didn't suffer nearly enough for the pain settling over him. A life without Alyssa in it was one he couldn't even contemplate.

His family rallied around him. "We'll get her back, son. Morgan is not going to win this time."

Rowan sucked in a breath and tried to take heart in the conviction he heard in his father's voice.

CHAPTER TWENTY-FIVE

LYSSA AWOKE COLD and sore on the floor of a Spartan room she didn't recognize. Walls of undressed gray stone met a marble floor. A tiny lamp on a bedside table emitted feeble light. She thought the single bed looked like something out of a medieval castle. Its heavy wooden frame supported a web of rope on which lay a thin mattress covered with a sheet and threadbare blanket. She half crawled, half walked to the bed and tested it, finding it serviceable—just. From her seat on the bed, she held the lamp aloft to send more light into the room and discovered a heavy wooden door separated her from the rest of the world, wherever she was. The lack of sensory stimulation in the room caused a momentary panic before the strange calm she'd felt at the Sheridan compound settled over her again.

She remembered everything and knew quite well Morgan had imprisoned her in this awful place. She also sensed a benign power had her back. Perhaps her grandmother's love extended far beyond the grave? The thought gave her comfort.

"Ah, you're awake finally," Morgan greeted her as she materialized in the middle of the room.

At Alyssa's wide-eyed stare, Morgan

laughed viciously. "I visualized myself into this room rather than risk your quickness by opening the door the conventional way. Pity your training ended before you could learn the skill."

"What is this place?"

"You are in my American fortress, a penthouse apartment over-looking Central Park. You, of course, don't need the view." Morgan's voice dripped scorn.

Alyssa marshaled her courage. "This room is more like something out of a medieval castle than modern-day New York City."

"Are you questioning me?" the war goddess demanded, her eyes blazing fire.

Alyssa instantly saw where one of Morgan's weaknesses lay, which could be an advantage—or a huge liability if she weren't careful.

"Not at all, milady. It's only that one doesn't find this style of masonry in the city these days."

Morgan's eyes returned to banked coals. "I had this room specially built." She ran her hand over the stone as she walked along one wall. "My sister Maeve convinced some stone masons that this sort of room would be cutting edge. She is so wonderfully persuasive with strong virile men, especially the very malleable mortal types." She stopped in front of Alyssa. "What do you think? Is the retro design cutting edge?"

She refused to show the goddess any fear or weakness. "Depends on its use. As a dungeon, it appears quite serviceable, but I don't think too many people would find it a comfortable venue for entertaining."

"You are wrong. I think you will find this room marvelously entertaining. Even if you don't, I know I certainly will." Morgan smiled, sending chills racing down Alyssa's freezing back. "In the meanwhile, I think it would be best to give you some sustenance since you've been in here the better part of a day. In fact, it's quite dark outside. Your rescue party has made no move to come for you yet—so I suppose I will need to feed you something. Your meal will arrive through there." She waved a hand in the direction of the heavy wooden door. "Enjoy your stay."

Morgan disappeared into thin air, leaving behind the grating sound of her gravelly voice.

A few minutes later a hand bearing a decanter of wine appeared through a metal porthole near the bottom of the door, a feature Alyssa had missed on her initial inspection of the room. Had she not been ready, the drink would have been nothing more than a dark stain among shards of glass on the marble floor. Before she could set the decanter down, the hand thrust through again with a plate of biscuits. She grabbed the plate and squatted quickly to deposit both items safely on the floor, which barely gave her enough time to free her hands to grab the empty tumbler and the decanter of water as they were thrust through and dropped almost before she touched them. Quickly setting them down, she waited for what came next, but she only heard a disgruntled "harrumph" before someone shuffled away from the door.

Sitting back on the floor, she surveyed her meal, which looked more like something out of *The Count of Monte Cristo* than dinner. However, she was famished, so she grabbed the wine decanter and poured a healthy portion into the tumbler before snagging an exceedingly hard biscuit. When she tapped the other two on the plate, she found them equally hard. Remembering how most medieval people took their biscuits—a sop of bread in wine—she followed suit, dipping her biscuit in the wine to let it soften. Her initial confusion about a tumbler rather than a goblet for the wine cleared as she realized even though Morgan functioned in the modern world, she remained a product of a long-ago time.

She was so hungry she didn't stop to think about what she was doing until she swallowed the first taste of biscuit. As she chewed, she noticed an odd flavor, something sickly sweet in an otherwise dry red wine. Poison. Yet Morgan's intention couldn't be to kill her. Upon smelling the wine, she detected a faint scent reminiscent of the belladonna Gram had grown in her garden. Gram had insisted Alyssa smell the flowers and taste one berry from the plant, so she would always know it and avoid it if she ever encountered it outside Gram's supervision. Forgetting Gram's admonitions at so critical a moment in her life left her nauseous.

Setting aside the biscuits and wine, she smelled the water in the decanter before gingerly taking a sip. Finding it cool and comfortingly tasteless, she drank all of it in the hopes of diluting whatever poisons she'd ingested. In a few minutes, however, a strange lightness overtook her, and she decided she should experience whatever was coming lying down. Stumbling across the floor to the bed, she fell on top of the mattress as the room started to spin.

Alyssa fought off sleep, but in the end, she succumbed to a weird semi-conscious state in which visions assaulted her mind. Rowan stood over her bed smiling down at her as he removed his shirt, revealing his powerful chest and defined abdomen. He laughed and bent low to kiss her, but as she reached for him, he disappeared only to reappear across the room, his laughter echoing around her. Next, she heard a woman sighing her pleasure. Someone else was with Rowan, someone tall, lithe, blonde, and sexually aggressive in a way Alyssa knew she could never be. Rowan encouraged the blonde's attentions to his cock, and Alyssa knew she was going to be sick.

Desperately, she tried to escape the pornographic nightmare in which she found herself, but as she fled one scene, another confronted her: Rowan's face buried in the voluptuous bosom of an auburn-haired beauty with a throaty laugh. Rowan with a flexible gymnast who gave him pleasure by contorting herself around him in ways that made Alyssa's body hurt, even in her semi-conscious state. In every scene, the women taunted Alyssa with her personal inadequacies. Watching Rowan with the women showed her how little she meant to him, how little she pleased him, how fleeting their romance.

Alyssa writhed on the bed in suffocating pain. She thought

she saw Morgan and another goddess standing over her, laughing together, their voices echoing from a long distance.

The other woman, Maeve, the auburn-haired beauty pleasuring Rowan a few minutes earlier, stood at the foot of Alyssa's bed. "Maybe if we're lucky, the Sheridans will divide up to discover where you took this one, making the coming battle even more winnable. I've enchanted this warehouse so well it should make engaging in battle with them even more delicious."

"No!" Alyssa tried to cry out, but blackness like quicksand sucked away her thoughts.

❧

What the evil sisters couldn't guess was Rowan and Alyssa's singular, profound, and immediate connection—something no one had ever seen before. Rowan felt Alyssa's pain like a sharp stab to the heart. He doubled over and struggled to catch his breath, a feat compounded by the fear he sensed Alyssa experiencing and his own fear of what was happening to her. Scathach had been explaining to the clan her coordinated plan of attack on each of the goddesses' American strongholds when Rowan reacted to the tortures Alyssa experienced.

Sian and Owen immediately flanked their son in a vain attempt to help him. Siobhan reached into her pocket for her bag of druidic herbs while Rio and Duncan put their hands to their swords. Scathach stopped in mid-sentence and waited patiently.

Gasping out the words, Rowan finally managed to say, "Alyssa's losing hope. Whatever Maeve is doing to her, it's working. But one good thing I know—Alyssa's in Los Angeles, not New York. I can feel her near the place from where she rescued me after we met but before I realized who—and what—she is."

The others waited while Rowan gathered himself. When he could breathe more steadily, he said, "Rio, you know the place. We were fighting some rogues there when I managed to acquire my nice set of scars."

"Yeah, I remember. A seedy gang-banger area in South Central L.A. You think Maeve is holed up somewhere near there?"

"Makes sense. It's a bunch of old warehouses a couple of local gangs claim as their turf. Most of the recent disturbances we've been called to stop have happened in that area, and we know how much Maeve has always desired to have a Sheridan in her control." Rowan righted himself. "Scarring me was Morgan's idea, reminding me my time was running out."

"This is the first I've heard about scars," Siobhan said. "If you'll let me take a look, I think I can alleviate them."

"Don't worry about it. Alyssa is taking care of them. She'll finish when we get her back." His insistence on Alyssa healing him wasn't lost on anyone.

Siobhan raised her brows. "An accomplished druid raised her," he said, exasperation in his tone. "She picked up a few things about healing along the way."

"There's more to this talisman than any of us know. Alyssa is a powerful weapon. We have to get her back before Morgan realizes what she truly has," Owen said.

"Agreed. You are sure they are in L.A., Rowan?" Scathach asked. "Yes."

"Then we will put all our firepower into attacking Maeve's stronghold. Sian and Siobhan, you will accompany us. Our warriors may need immediate healing, Siobhan, and Owen is always more powerful when you are near him, Sian. Duncan make sure your talisman is with you. Rowan, call to Seamus. We need him. Rio, contact Riley and Lynnette to protect our interests here." As she gave her commands, Scathach stared at each warrior in turn.

"Riley's not going to like being on the sidelines during a major battle," Rio reminded his teacher.

"He knows his place. We can't have every Sheridan convened in one area in case something goes terribly wrong. You will convey that to him," Scathach said.

"Of course, milady."

Scathach looked askance at him. "Sometimes I have trouble deciding if you are serious or mocking me. You could be my star champion if you ever harness your attitude and drop that chip off your shoulder. Perhaps your talisman can help you with some of those problems—if I can keep you alive long enough to find her. Clearly, I am far too indulgent of you, Rio Sheridan."

Rowan noticed Rio had the good sense to look chastised.

Turning to Rowan, Scathach asked, "What more do you sense from Alyssa?"

"Nothing," he said, not even bothering to keep his worry out of his voice. "Don't you find it strange I felt anything at all?"

"If Alyssa and you are indeed the fulfillment of the prophecy, it would be stranger if you did not feel anything. You sensing her tells me that what we have suspected since you found her is true. Which is why Morgan tried to kill her rather than you," Scathach replied.

Still smarting from her earlier set-down, Siobhan continued, "Morgan didn't—or couldn't—kill Alyssa. There's a powerful druid involved or something supernatural beyond the ken of the gods—no offense, milady."

"I agree with you, which is the other reason I want you along when we battle Morgan and Maeve. You took notes as you read Afton Sinclair's journals."

Siobhan nodded, absently patting the notebook she'd slid inside her jacket.

"We will leave the journals in Riley's safekeeping, but you should bring along your notes. They may prove valuable."

"What is our plan of attack, milady?" Rowan asked, vibrating with impatience and worry.

"Not to allow Maeve to take you or your brother to her bed and not to allow Morgan to escort any of you across the ford," Scathach replied as though she were speaking to an imbecile.

Owen stepped between his sons and their goddess. "You'll go ahead to determine what awaits us at Maeve's stronghold?"

"Precisely. I will convey that information to you and where I want each of you to visualize yourselves and what I want you to do once you arrive." Scathach pointedly ignored Rowan and Rio.

"Thank you, milady. We'll await your instructions." Owen directed his words at his sons, his glare brooking no argument. Rio glared back at Owen while Rowan tried to connect his mind to Alyssa to ascertain for himself where Morgan hid her.

Scathach left behind a foreboding red-gold shimmer in the air in the spot where she'd stood before she visualized herself away from the Sheridans, effectively making it clear she expected her orders to be obeyed.

Owen placed a restraining hand on his oldest son. "You know if you try to follow Scathach without your talisman's guidance, you're going to end up in a nasty spot. It's one of your talents, son. Wait. The prize is certainly worth your patience this once, don't you think?"

"I can't forget the pain I sensed Alyssa feeling, Dad. Whatever tortures Maeve has devised, they're stealing Alyssa's belief in herself, something we were beginning to build. I can't stand the thought of her being in so much pain." His anguish for his woman resonated in his hoarse voice and the tears shining in his eyes.

Sian flanked Rowan as Owen continued. "We know, son. Morgan tried similar tortures with your mother, so I wasted no time marrying her. Marriage adds a layer of protection for each of us, which is why talismans and warriors usually fall in love. It's pretty clear you and Alyssa have already taken care of the falling-in-love part."

At Rio's derisive snort, Rowan stared at his brother who glowered at Siobhan. Duncan scowled at Rio and slipped his arm around Siobhan's waist, hugging her close to him. "Rio, it doesn't work out for all of us. Siobhan didn't steal me from my talisman. Jennifer and

I are very fond of each other, but there was never any spark—for either of us. Marriage, even for warriors and talismans, must first be based on love. Siobhan did everything she could to avoid me, but in the end, I was too insistent." He pulled her even closer. "For self-preservation, she had to give in." With a cocky grin, Duncan directed the last part at Siobhan before he kissed her cheek.

"Afton's journals show me her druidic abilities kept her entire family safe for a very long time. Perhaps you would be easier for all of us to live with if you spent a little time reading the parts of the notebooks explaining that," Sian suggested to Rio.

"Yeah, I'll keep that in mind," Rio sneered.

"You're not helping here, buddy," Duncan said.

"Whatever. I believe my job is to entrust those journals to my twin. Excuse me while I make a phone call."

CHAPTER TWENTY-SIX

NDLESS VISIONS. EACH woman with whom Rowan shared himself more beautiful, more sexually adventurous and talented than the last. All concentrated Alyssa's inadequacies ever more deeply. Not knowing if the visions revealed his past, his present, or his future intensified her already low self-esteem, sending her into a despair so excruciating she wanted to die. Rowan didn't love her. Though she might be his talisman, she would never be his woman. Because she'd fallen so deeply in love with him, if she couldn't be his woman, she didn't want to be at all.

When she thought the visions couldn't become any worse, she saw him with the most incredible woman she'd ever encountered. The woman's auburn hair cascaded around her perfect body in curls and waves like a living thing. Her violet eyes held endless summer in their depths as she laughed in tinkling merriment while she led Rowan through a series of encounters that overpowered and enflamed him while she insisted on more, ever more from him. Alyssa could see Rowan's exhaustion, yet he couldn't seem to stop himself from pleasuring this incredibly beautiful woman over and over again with no rest.

As the thought occurred to Alyssa, the

woman turned her face fully toward Alyssa, who screamed in agony as the woman's eyes changed from violet to ebony fire.

~

Morgan watched as Maeve could no longer restrain her triumph when she revealed herself to Alyssa. She hid a smile as Maeve growled in frustration.

"What is it, sister?"

"I do not know. At the moment I delivered a scene to cause Alyssa the height of agony—watching Rowan die in the throes of carnal congress with me—she disappeared into some place inside herself that I cannot access."

Noticing Alyssa's inert form on the old bed Morgan had provided, she gasped and shot a blood-red glare at her sister.

"What have you done?" she screamed.

"I'm not sure. One moment I showed her some delicious footage from Rowan's past, and perhaps something of my own fantasies, which *nearly*," Maeve emphasized the word, "stole her will to live. She cried out and thrashed on the sheets like one possessed."

"Your intention, of course," Morgan interrupted, though she'd rather have wrapped her hands around her sister goddess's perfect throat.

"Of course. Right when things were becoming most interesting, she disappeared somewhere inside herself. She's not dead, I'm quite sure. Merely indisposed for the moment. I haven't stolen your prize," Maeve sniped.

"She is not likely to draw in the warriors we seek if she is already dead. I want Rowan to watch me as I reach my goal and take her." Morgan paced around the room. "Like his long-ago ancestor, Rowan has thwarted me long enough. I want to relish the look on his face when he sees me escort his talisman across the ford." She stopped and ran a bony hand down her taut belly. "It will be an even more orgasmic experience than taking Ailsa from Findlay." She allowed her evil to reverberate through the room.

A ripple in the cosmos interrupted the goddesses, alerting them to a powerful being visualizing herself near them. They exchanged a look, acknowledging they both sensed the disturbance before stating simultaneously, "Scathach."

Maeve sniffed. "I am supremely tired of that pompous little warrior trainer interfering in my activities and delights."

"If she weren't immortal, it would truly be a pleasure to escort her across the ford."

"We may not be able to do much *about* her, but we can do plenty *to* her by stealing the warriors on whom she has spent so much effort," Maeve purred.

"It will add tremendously to my pleasure to watch her face as I take her warriors and their talismans while she can do nothing." Morgan laughed delightedly. "Since you have rendered the bait basically useless for now, we may as well watch our champions battle Scathach and her warriors. We wouldn't want to miss the initial skirmishes." Morgan's eyes glowed red at the prospect of the upcoming battle and her chances of escorting several fighters across the ford.

Maeve cast one last longing look at Alyssa on the mattress before the goddesses returned to her solarium to watch the show.

In Maeve's solarium, each goddess held a cup of ambrosia as they watched their warriors and street fighters battle among themselves. With gang warfare in Los Angeles so easy to incite, the goddesses sometimes prompted battles purely for entertainment. There seemed an endless supply of boys and men who wanted to control their turf against rival gangs that almost sprouted like weeds from the cracks of the dilapidated sidewalks. Of course, in their frail human hubris, they failed to understand they controlled nothing, not even their own responses to threats. Maeve and Morgan ran the show, and tonight's battle would certainly be a spectacle.

Sconces strategically placed high up on the wall behind them bathed the room in a golden glow as the goddesses directed their attention outside the floor-to-ceiling window in front of them. The exterior of the building resembled every other metal warehouse along the road. No one would ever guess the opulent interior.

As she reclined on a plush leather couch, Morgan appeared relaxed and calm. "This delicious ambrosia might be scant fortification if Scathach tries to engage me in battle." She sipped and focused her attention on the preliminary skirmishes. "I'd hoped to face the Sheridans without the distraction of other immortals, but I should have anticipated Scathach's interference. It would be convenient if she would show herself."

For some minutes, the goddesses sat in silence as they watched the gangs battle.

Suddenly, Maeve scooted to the edge of her red velvet chair. "I've seen that warrior before," she said, focusing Morgan's attention on a linebacker of a warrior who entered the fray. "I don't know who he is, but he is positively delicious. I noticed his superior physique, his speed and power when we lured Rowan Sheridan here. My plans for him surpass any scenario I've entertained for Rowan Sheridan, even the one I showed his talisman earlier." Maeve leered, clearly relishing the thought.

"Maeve, darling, *do* try to control yourself. The party is only beginning."

Scathach appeared beside the warrior, and both goddesses sat on the edges of their seats in rapt attention.

Morgan, however, recognized the warrior immediately and slammed her drink down on an oak table in fury. "Seamus Lochlann! He is almost as good as a talisman for Rowan Sheridan. Scathach is not playing fair."

"I would prefer if you refrain from taking this particular warrior across the ford today, sister, if you don't mind." Maeve licked her lips. "I have some rather deliciously salacious plans for him first." Her eyes gleamed, and she appeared to salivate as she watched Seamus Lochlann with undisguised interest.

"That will depend on Scathach and the Sheridans. If he impedes my plans for Rowan Sheridan, then I will quite readily escort him across the ford today," Morgan snarled.

"Really, sister, sometimes you are so selfish about taking your pleasure," Maeve pouted. Then she straightened as she watched the powerful warrior disappear.

"What is this? What is this?" Morgan shouted. "Scathach sends him off? What does she do here? What trickery does she plan?"

Morgan could wait no longer in the security of Maeve's solarium. With her long black velvet gown and elegant cloak of black velvet lined with blood-red satin swirling around her, Morgan swept to the door.

Maeve stopped her before she could exit. "Sister, the Sheridans have yet to arrive. We have not seen any indication of Scathach's battle plan other than this apparent sending off of that delectable warrior, Seamus Lochlann." She sat back and sipped from her goblet. "Have some patience, enjoy another glass of ambrosia, wait to see how events unfold. We are close enough to interfere and enact our plan without being premature and tipping our hand."

Morgan paused before returning to the couch, the oak table separating her from her sister. "Fine. I'll wait. But I do not like it. Scathach gathers warriors to her. She does not send them away. I take it you did not penetrate their shields and overhear their conversation?"

"No, though I did try." Maeve stated the obvious. "You had no success either."

"Her warriors gain power to withstand the onslaught of the gods' attempts to penetrate their thoughts. Scathach oversteps herself. She may find giving them such power before they find their talismans is a fatal mistake since we can use it too with the warriors we turn." Morgan picked up her glass again. "Seamus might be easy since he has tried so diligently and unsuccessfully to find his talisman over the past four years," she speculated with glee. Her confidence restored, she settled in to view the event. With a wave of her hand, she escalated the intensity of the battle, a blatant attempt to draw in more warriors to fight the score of rogues she simultaneously unleashed on the gangs.

◈

Scathach communicated with Rowan and her other warriors who still awaited her at the Sheridan compound.

"It is time. I have not located the exact room in which they hold Alyssa, but I've narrowed it to two. We will need Duncan, Rio, and Owen along with some others I have summoned to join the fight playing before Morgan and Maeve as a distraction. Duncan, bring your talisman Jennifer along physically as she will need to help Rio the best she can while Sian helps Rowan and Owen.

"Siobhan, you will chant protection spells from a secure location I have chosen. As much as you will want to protect Duncan first, you must promise to chant for Rowan and Seamus before your husband. Duncan's talisman will do her job for him, and you must trust that no matter what you think you see in the battle. Is that understood?"

"Yes, milady," Siobhan replied, but her voice trembled even in her thoughts. Rowan saw her fear in the look she gave Duncan who squeezed her hand and smiled reassuringly at her.

"Under no circumstances are Riley or Lynnette to leave the compound. Guarding the training room and those journals is paramount to our success. No matter what happens to anyone in this battle, you must do your job," Scathach demanded.

"Yes, milady," they replied in unison though the pout in Riley's tone indicated his displeasure at being left out of the fight.

Sian said, "We're sorry you were the last to know about Rowan finding his talisman, but you'll have to wait to be angry and hurt until after we return everyone home safely."

"Sian's right, Riles," Lynnette added, her tone mollifying as she reached for her husband's hand.

As Rowan watched Riley and Lynnette, he hoped he and his family weren't too late to give Alyssa and him a chance to grow a similar relationship.

He returned his attention to Scathach who continued to instruct the team.

"Rowan and Seamus will accompany me inside the compound. We will enter from a weak spot I have discovered on the side of it. Rowan, you must concentrate on your visualization. If you land in the middle of the battle, we could lose everything," Scathach said.

Rowan's impatience to regain Alyssa and perhaps deal a blow to Morgan ebbed in the wake of the icy fear he felt for his talisman. Cold emptiness had replaced the pain she'd radiated earlier. He couldn't formulate the idea she could be dead because that would mean he'd lost her—and himself—but the intense passions he knew her to possess seemed to have dissipated into nothing. He couldn't feel Alyssa, couldn't hear her, couldn't contact her. She seemed to shimmer beyond his reach, nothing more than a dream.

Never in his life had fear gripped him so completely, but oddly, his fear honed his senses. He could see Scathach and the side of the compound clearly, a necessity for the success of their mission.

"Sian, you will stay at the edge of the mist where you can see both Rowan and Owen," Scathach began.

An old warrior interrupted her by visualizing himself into the midst of the Sheridans.

"I'll protect your compound too," Finn Daly said to Rowan and Rio. *"Sorry for the interruption, milady, but I sensed Alyssa is in distress, and after I disposed of her old boyfriend when he came sneaking around her house, I thought I could be of service here."*

"Welcome, Finn," Scathach said.

Rowan addressed Finn. "You're sure Alyssa's house is safe?"

"Right now, Morgan has her prize. She has no reason to send anyone to Alyssa's house to steal the treasures there. Besides, those treasures will be of little use if we don't rescue Alyssa," Finn replied gently.

"How do you know each other?" Owen asked, an edge in his voice.

"*Would it be all right if everyone trusted each other* and me *this once and acted as I have commanded?*" Scathach growled in irritation at the stubborn Sheridan arrogance and the delay their debate caused.

Chastised, Owen and Rowan replied together, *"Of course, milady."*

"*Duncan, Rio, and Owen will engage the warriors and civilians currently battling in front of Maeve's stronghold. We will give them a few minutes to assure Morgan and Maeve's undivided attention before Seamus and Rowan visualize themselves at my side.*

"*Once you arrive, Seamus and Rowan, you will await my instruction outside the unguarded door. I will visualize myself inside and see what I can see. We may have limited contact, but you will have patience and await my signal before entering the compound. Is that perfectly clear?*" the goddess asked.

"Absolutely, milady," Owen answered for all of them.

Scathach could barely contain her battle lust. "*I have had woefully small opportunity to best those two witches, but the tables are about to turn.*"

❧

"I don't like this. I can't see or feel Scathach anywhere near this battle. The diversion I used at the Sheridan compound did not damage any warriors. The fighters I used were civilians and zombies except for the champion who could not finish the job with our captive. There should be Sheridans everywhere out there taking on my rogues. Without them, my rogues will turn on the civilians I invited along, and that will create problems for future attacks. This little exercise is not going to plan at all," Morgan fumed as she paced before the expansive window overlooking the street in front of Maeve's stronghold.

Maeve's lair resembled an old warehouse from the outside, all corrugated sheet metal in various states of peeling paint and rust. On a different day, Morgan might have appreciated its aesthetics. Protective film cleverly concealed the windows, which from the street looked like uninterrupted metal. The huge delivery doors slid apart only enough to allow Maeve to access her garage and her purple convertible Mustang when she used mortal transportation. The exterior of the building hid a luxury palace of black marble, chrome, and mirrors fit for a goddess.

"Morgan, would you sit down? Your incessant pacing is wearing a path in my Persian carpet," Maeve said before an especially delicious warrior caught her attention. "Oh look, sister, someone new has arrived, and not a moment too soon." Her feral smile reminded Morgan of a cat twitching its tail. "I hear civilian police sirens."

Morgan stopped in her tracks as she caught sight of Duncan MacManus then Rio and Owen Sheridan as they joined the battle, her smile evil incarnate, her eyes red-hot embers in her pale face. "These poor civilians. They have no idea what is going on in their world let alone beyond the mists separating it from ours. The police will look for hours for the battle they can hear but cannot see," she mused as she sat on the edge of a deep cushioned chair to enjoy the fight.

"Your fighters seem especially intent on taking out Owen. Is that your plan?"

"It is always my plan. He has thwarted me for over thirty years, and now his sons do as well. Tell me, do you see any other Sheridans in the fray?" Morgan casually inquired, but the avidity with which she scanned the battlefield contrasted her outward nonchalance.

"The only Sheridan who interests me right now is Rio. He is

positively luscious. I can almost come from watching him move to dodge or to ricochet civilian bullets and your big rogue's prowess with his claymore. Look how his muscles ripple and play across his shoulders, how his powerful legs withstand the onslaught of your giant. Oh, how I will enjoy wearing him to a fine mist in bed." Nearly drooling, Maeve appeared to be working herself into a lustful frenzy.

"He is magnificent," Morgan agreed. "But his father is my real prize since I will not renege on our agreement. I wonder where Owen's talisman is and if I will have a two-for-one today or if I will relish the wailing in the Sheridan house when Sian feels the blow that will send her lover across the ford with me."

Nearby, Scathach summoned Rowan and Seamus to her. Her relief at Rowan's improved visualizing ability showed on her face, and he laughed at her when he appeared at her side.

"Even a little credit, milady?" he asked in a cocky tone.

"As usual, you have no idea how lucky you Sheridans are that I like you so well. Many warriors have paid severe penances for far less cheek than you display," Scathach growled before ruining it with a smile. Turning to Seamus, she said, "Seamus, this is where and when I needed you. Thank you for following orders this time."

Seamus had the good grace to look sufficiently chastised after having appeared at the wrong time in the middle of the fight earlier.

Scathach disappeared from view.

Seamus placed a restraining hand on his friend's arm when Rowan readied himself to follow their goddess. "Patience, old man. None of this works if you go all Captain America on us and stop following Scathach's orders. Give her a few minutes. You know those other two can't do anything to her."

Rowan shook off his hand. "I'm not concerned about Scathach." *Come* on, *Alyssa, respond to me. Come back from wherever you've gone.*

"Maybe don't try so hard to get her to respond to you. Talk to her, tell her, I don't know, something positive, something she wants to hear," Seamus suggested.

"What?"

"Talk to Alyssa like people talk to coma patients about mundane everyday things she can connect to."

"How did you ...? Oh. Wow. I need to get a grip. I thought I was all shielded up, but apparently I was wrong." Rowan scrubbed his hands over his head.

"Yeah, you were thinking a bit loud. Might want to back off this close to the nasty ladies. I'm sure they'd enjoy nothing more than knowing whatever tortures they inflict on Alyssa do double duty torturing you as well," Seamus said.

"I only want to reach her, reassure her I didn't abandon her, let her know help is on the way." Rowan paced in a tight circle. Waiting for Scathach's signal seemed an eternity of torturous scenarios, each more terrible than the last. He wasn't sure how long he could last when he felt a ripple in the air. Seamus must have felt it too because he also summoned his claymore. The two dropped into their battle stances, backs to each other, senses charged.

CHAPTER TWENTY-SEVEN

UT OF THE mist rose a warrior, but he didn't look like any warrior Rowan had seen before. Rather, he looked like something out of the Dark Ages, clad in a kilt and boots laced to his knees and nothing else. Long braids framed his face while the rest of his hair hung loosely over his shoulders. His massive torso, protected with a heavy leather shield, was dyed blue. Though his thick Scots burr was nearly unintelligible to the pair facing him, there was no mistaking his intent.

"Morgan must be short a few warriors if she's reaching this far into the past to find one to take us on," Seamus said in his usual cocky tone.

Before Rowan could respond, the zombie warrior engaged, swinging his long claymore at Rowan while fending off Seamus with the metal targe protruding menacingly from his shield.

Rowan kept the zombie warrior's attention with a deep slice across his side when he focused on Seamus for a split second, but the blow didn't even slow the zombie down. Bellowing something in Gaelic, the zombie shifted his focus fully to Rowan. The shock of the zombie's incredible strength reverberated along the length of Rowan's claymore, up his arms, and into his shoulders as their swords met in a clanging blow that clattered his teeth. He backed away under the onslaught of the massive warrior's relentless thrusts, parrying and looking for an opening to regain an advantage.

Their focus on each other, they forgot Seamus who took the opportunity to come at the zombie from the side, thrusting his sword deep into the zombie's torso. For a moment, the zombie looked surprised before his eyes rolled back into his head, and he dropped to the ground like a giant redwood.

"Thanks, bro. He was more than a handful for me." Rowan panted.

Catching his breath, Seamus said, "Don't mention it. You know, he looks exactly like the last warrior I always pictured your ancestor fought before the curse."

"Something was bugging me about why he was dressed like that and talking in old Scots. Morgan is sending a message. She knows about the prophecy, and worse, she knows about Alyssa's and my part in it. We've got to get inside and take Alyssa before Morgan escorts her across the ford, and all of our chances are lost forever."

As if she knew Rowan was about to visualize himself inside Maeve's stronghold, Scathach shimmered into sight beside him.

"You are so much like your father at this age—not very good at taking orders, Rowan," she scolded. "How did you suppose you were going to visualize yourself inside when you have no idea what is in there?"

"Do you see this?" Rowan pointed at the fallen warrior. "Morgan is sending a message, and if we don't heed it, we lose Alyssa and any hope of future warriors having a chance against Morgan!"

Scathach replied with painful patience. "Yes, Rowan, I am well aware of what is at stake here." She planted her fists on her hips as she stared him down. "That is why we will do things my way. I have located the room in which Maeve is keeping Alyssa. I will describe the doorway outside it so you do not blunder into it and find yourself trapped." She paused, and Rowan nodded. "I believe it to be enchanted against escape via visualization. Move Alyssa outside the room before you try to visualize yourself outside the compound. Do not visualize yourselves to any safe place before you are outside the stronghold since that will make it easier for Morgan and Maeve to follow you. Is that understood?"

"To the letter, milady," Rowan responded.

"Seamus, you will go with him and watch his back. There are ancient warriors inside similar to this fellow"—she indicated the fallen zombie warrior at their feet—"so this is not going to be an easy extraction. I will be with you as well, but Alyssa's rescue depends on Rowan."

"Understood, milady," Seamus said.

"Now open your shields. You need to hear my instructions to the others."

"*Siobhan, chant protection spells for Rowan and your brother. Focus on making them as invisible to our enemies as possible,*" Scathach commanded.

"*Yes, milady.*" Siobhan's response sounded muffled and far away.

"*I know you're not a talisman, sis, but you're the closest thing we have. Be strong and trust us—and yourself. You can do this. Concentrate on your job,*" Seamus said.

"*I know. The gods chose to make me a healer rather than a talisman. I'm doing my best to fight my instincts, believe me. Now stand still for a minute.*" She began chanting:

May the sea protect you,
May the ox of the seven battles protect you,
May the wind protect you,
May the wild boar of valor protect you,
May the hawk protect you,
May the battle lance protect you,
May the sky enclose you and keep you safe.

Rowan exchanged a look with Seamus as warmth infused him at Siobhan's words. Then it was time for their stealthy assault on

Maeve's stronghold. They grasped each other's elbow in the age-old gesture of comrades-in-arms, gripped their claymores, and visualized the hallway outside the door to Alyssa's prison.

An intense fear roiled through Alyssa, but not her own. Struggling to swim up into consciousness, she couldn't quite pull herself out of her self-imposed cocoon. Entrapped in a soft cloud of nothingness, the harder she tried to escape it, the deeper she sank into it. Somewhere in her mind, she knew the mental haze in which she floated protected her from some great evil she couldn't quite remember.

A familiar voice called to her, and all the pain to which Maeve had subjected her slammed into her subconscious, cruelly jerking her out her safe place into a conscious reality she didn't want to face.

"Alyssa, wherever you've gone, wherever you are, please come back. I need you with me now," Rowan said. *"Be strong. We're coming for you."*

He needed her. As his talisman, she was necessary to him, but how could she live with only part of him? The pain of Maeve's visions threatened to engulf her again, and she couldn't breathe when she sensed Rowan somewhere near her. Somehow, he'd found her.

Before she could process that Rowan had come for her, she saw him in a corridor in a medieval stronghold. But something wasn't right. The torches in the wall sconces glowed like electric lights. What sort of medieval castle had electric light? He stood before a thick wooden door with a high-tech locking mechanism where the handle should be. Seamus squatted in front of the door studying the device locking it. Were they working a security job? Her visions didn't make sense.

Suddenly, an ancient warrior dressed in a kilt and lace-up boots bore down on the pair. *"Rowan, behind you!"* Alyssa instinctively called out. She didn't know if she was dreaming or if she was in real time or if she was experiencing another of Maeve's tortures, but

Rowan needed her, and a force beyond her control compelled her to aid her warrior no matter what his feelings for her.

She saw his look of surprise before he wheeled around and engaged the warrior as the zombie nearly landed what would have been a fatal blow to the middle of Rowan's back. Seamus sprang up from his squatting position in front of the door, his sword in his hand, but the narrow corridor barely gave Rowan and the zombie he fought enough room to maneuver let alone to allow Seamus to engage the warrior as well. Seamus looked behind himself. No one else came, so he returned to the lock on the door.

While Rowan worked up a sweat battling Morgan's guard, Alyssa saw Seamus focused on the puzzle that was the lock on the door. His concentration seemed to waver as he checked on his friend every few seconds. Then he removed tools from a pouch attached to his belt.

Rowan grunted, drawing Alyssa's attention back to him. *"Rowan, he has an old injury to his left knee. Forcing him to that side will weaken him."*

Rowan shifted his attack in response to Alyssa's observation. As she watched him, she knew he heard her even though he didn't respond. Still, she maintained her concentration on the battle. The rage of the zombie warrior flared off of him like a solar storm. The area around the battle glowed an unearthly red, and Alyssa feared any minute the warrior would change into the Washer of the Ford herself. Not knowing if that was possible only added to her fear.

The fight seemed to last for hours, Rowan forcing the zombie down the corridor before the zombie would draw on some reserve and drive Rowan back toward Seamus. Their swords sheared off each other and clanged against the walls, an unholy racket in the confined space. Alyssa fretted about others hearing the battle and joining it, but it seemed only one guard was on duty. After Rowan fought the zombie to the end of the corridor where he could maneuver enough to deal a fatal blow, Alyssa breathed. At that moment, she saw the door to her prison opening, and she thought she was awake.

"Seamus? Are you real?" Alyssa whispered. "What are you doing here?"

"Helping Rowan rescue you. Come here quickly," Seamus said, one hand on the door, the other extended to Alyssa.

Alyssa rose from the bed, but she was so weak she immediately collapsed in a heap on the floor. Seamus nearly let go of the door to grab her before Rowan raced past him to reach her.

"Thanks for the help, Pixie-girl. You did well," Rowan said as he knelt to help her up off the floor.

~

Rowan pulled back and looked into silver-gray eyes filled with pain.

"What is it? Are you hurt?" Rowan asked. *What has Maeve done to my woman?*

"I ... I feel drained. I'm sorry to be such a burden." Her thready voice terrified him.

Without another thought, he gathered her up into his arms and strode with her to the door.

"What is it, Rowan?" Though Seamus asked the question telepathically, Rowan heard the concern in his voice all the same.

"I don't know what Maeve's done to her, but Alyssa's in bad shape," Rowan replied, shielding his thoughts from his talisman.

In the corridor, they saw three more of Morgan's ancient warriors cautiously moving toward them.

"We need to get her out of here," Seamus said.

"I know, but we didn't teach her how to visualize herself elsewhere, and she's too weak for me to help her do it now."

"We'll have to sandwich her between us and be very careful to visualize exactly the same place at the same time," Seamus suggested.

"If that doesn't work, we're outside, and she's in here on her own against three bloodthirsty zombie warriors controlled by one of the nastiest goddesses in Danu's realm. We can't risk it." Rowan's voice cracked with emotion.

"All right, old buddy, we'll fight our way out. Sure wish I knew which way was out though."

A series of shimmering colors appeared in the hallway, each a shade of red from purple to blood as three goddesses, Morgan, Maeve, and Scathach, appeared in the crowded corridor.

"I see you found our guest. Tell me, Alyssa, how does it feel to be nothing more than a helpless child in my man's arms?" Maeve taunted.

Alyssa flinched and went limp.

So that's the witch goddess's game, Rowan thought before he opened his mind to his talisman.

"Alyssa, she lied. Open your eyes and look at me," Rowan commanded.

"It's no use, my lover. Alyssa knows what she saw." Maeve's voice dripped with sexual innuendo.

In desperation, Rowan knelt on the floor with Alyssa in his lap, freeing his hands enough to hold her head while he kissed her. There was no subtlety in his touch as he ground his mouth against hers, willing her back to him with his kiss. When she tried to gasp in air, he plunged his tongue inside her mouth and insisted she respond to him. All the while he kept chanting to her telepathically. *"Only you Alyssa. From the first touch, only you. It will always only be you."*

She let out a tiny sigh and raised her hand to his head, holding him against her mouth as she kissed him back.

A shriek of rage burst from Morgan, and her warriors waiting at the end of the corridor came barreling down the hallway to engage in battle. "Go after the woman! Kill the woman!" Morgan screamed.

Nuzzling the silk of her cheek with the rough stubble of his, Rowan whispered, "Whatever happens, don't let go of me, Alyssa. Do not let go."

Though she clung to him as he stood, she slipped down his body to stand on her own once they were upright. "Are you sure you can stand, Pixie-girl?" he asked, worry warring with fear for her in his voice.

Her eyes burned silver fire as she looked into his. "I can do anything except fight enormous sword-wielding warriors. That's your job, and I suggest you shut up and do it."

She was back. His talisman was back. He grinned at her and turned to engage the first warrior. As they fought, Rowan saw the deep wound in the warrior's side, the one Seamus had given him in the fight outside the compound. This warrior died outside, yet here he was up and fighting again. *What the hell?*

It was difficult to move in the narrow hall, and triply so with 115 pounds of weight clinging to him, but his adrenaline pumped in overtime as he fought not only for himself, but especially for Alyssa.

He forced the warrior to his left side, causing him to turn and expose the already gaping wound. Seamus shouted something that distracted the warrior momentarily, and Rowan struck, killing the warrior—again.

Seamus pushed past Rowan, hopped over the downed zombie, and took on the second queued up behind his companion. Rowan looked up to see the second zombie also sported a fatal gash in his side.

Alyssa called out to Seamus, "His left leg is injured. Force him to that side."

Rowan scowled as he realized her hint worked much better when she telegraphed it silently. Now the warrior knew the strategy and countered it by redoubling his strokes and forcing Seamus back toward the downed warrior. From the corner of his eye, he caught Morgan watching, licking her lips in anticipation of Seamus faltering when he became stranded between the living and the dead.

Maeve bristled at her sister. "How hard would it be to let me enjoy even one incredible warrior before you take him across the ford?"

Rowan held onto Alyssa with his free hand as he readied himself to come to Seamus's aid. Then he heard Scathach summon his family, and relief washed over him.

"Owen, I need you inside the compound now. Visualize yourself at the end of the corridor I described to you earlier. You will find a warrior there ready to take on Seamus and Rowan. Dispatch him. He is only a decoy. The real threat is already engaged.

"Duncan and Rio, you must clean up the mess and leave a tidy group for the civilian police to find. Then go to the women. Make sure they are protected when the real battle we came to fight reaches its peak."

Being a goddess meant Morgan could wage and enjoy several battles simultaneously. She'd called her mists to shield the civilian world from the battle she wanted to watch this night. However, once the actual fighting moved inside Maeve's stronghold, the mists were no longer necessary, and they lifted like the anomalous fog they were, which made Sian Sheridan and Siobhan MacManus vulnerable.

While one part of her fumed at the turn of events inside Maeve's stronghold, another part avidly watched as Sian and Siobhan sought shelter in what they believed to be a deserted warehouse near the battle. Morgan smirked as too late they discovered how poorly they'd chosen. The building served as Morgan's warriors' staging grounds, and the biggest, most imposing warrior in her arsenal lurked inside the double doors of the warehouse.

The two women turned to slip back out the side door through which they entered when he stood in front of them blocking their way. Siobhan gasped, and Sian pulled the druid behind her. Though she was a talisman and not a warrior, Sian did know some things about battle, much to Morgan's chagrin.

The warrior, clad in nothing but an old-fashioned kilt, leggings, and leather boots stood menacingly before them. He said nothing as he pulled his enormous claymore from the scabbard on his back and swung it over his head with deadly intent. He affected a battle

stance, slicing the air in front of him. Sian flinched at the disturbance of the air as the warrior intimidated them with his sword.

"He's some sort of enchanted being, one of Morgan's zombie
champions. We're in a whole bunch of trouble here, Siobhan,"
Sian said.

Morgan laughed inside as she watched Sian glancing everywhere
for some means of escape.

Siobhan began feverishly whispering incantations while Sian
closed her eyes.

Morgan knew Sian called telepathically to her family. Morgan
especially hoped Sian's desperation focused on Owen who had
entered the fray outside the cell where she and Maeve had held Alyssa.

With a wave of her hand, Morgan escalated both battles, testing
the warriors to their limits—she hoped.

CHAPTER TWENTY-EIGHT

OWAN'S HAND TIGHTENED painfully on her back, but Alyssa said nothing.

"Open your mind, Alyssa. The whole family is communicating telepathically, and you need to hear it."

When Alyssa followed his instruction, she heard Owen's desperate plea. *"Milady, Morgan splits us up—Rio and Sian outside, Rowan, Alyssa, and me inside with you, and zombie warriors everywhere. Sian and Siobhan are in trouble outside, but the big prize Morgan seeks is here. We need to unite somehow."*

Apparently, Morgan had out-maneuvered Scathach by engaging the Sheridans in separate deadly battles, which she orchestrated from a position of strength right in the middle of them.

Alyssa watched Scathach's aura glow red-gold before she acknowledged Owen's observation with a nod of her head. Scathach spoke to Seamus and Alyssa. *"You must take Alyssa outside. She can still help Rowan as his talisman, but we need to get her outside the walls of this godforsaken place. You will also be in the right place when the battle spills outside, which it will shortly."*

Alyssa glanced in question at Seamus who, during the course of the fight had maneuvered behind her.

"The physical exit is at the end of this hall and down two flights of stairs. Morgan tricked you into believing it to be the opposite direction by sending warriors from a room on the other end. Go now, and don't ask questions," Scathach commanded.

When Alyssa didn't immediately respond, Seamus prodded, *"You heard her. Let go of Rowan and come with me, Alyssa. We have to trust Scathach."*

In her research, Alyssa had read enough of the perfidy of the gods that she wondered if their situation might be some sort of cosmic plan, a way for the gods to entertain themselves by interfering in the lives of mortals. A vision of how hard Scathach had worked her in the few short days of her training flashed behind her eyes, and she knew this particular goddess was on their side no matter what. Alyssa's job was to be Rowan's talisman. If the goddess said she could do her job better from outside, she would do it. Still, doing her duty tore her heart in two as she let go of the man who in less than a week had become her life. While the clone of a dead warrior distracted Rowan, Alyssa grabbed Seamus's hand and raced down the hall for the stairs leading outside.

♨

Rowan's fatigue at fighting supernatural opponents started to show as the sweat ran down his face, and he worked to collect all his strength before he could deal a blow. The warriors who confronted him didn't tire. The only way to best them was to find their weaknesses and dispatch them as quickly as possible. He'd seen his father appear at the end of the corridor and tried to fight his way to him.

Fear flooded him when he sneaked a glance around himself and didn't see Alyssa where she should have been behind him. Seamus had disappeared too.

"Milady, does Seamus have Alyssa? Is she safe?" Rowan asked as he landed a deathblow to another zombie.

"She is safe for the moment. However, you must finish here quickly

and visualize yourself outside. The real battle is about to begin, and Rio and Duncan are going to need some help with it," Scathach responded.

The hallway took on deathly red glow, something like a funhouse in a Stephen King movie, and Rowan knew Morgan was ratcheting up the pressure.

"Dad!" he cried out as he saw zombie warriors pouring into the hallway on either end of them.

"You two must visualize yourselves outside this compound now. There is no time to lose," Scathach commanded.

Seamus all but dragged Alyssa down the hallway.

"Seamus, I'm sorry." Alyssa panted. "I can't keep up."

He gathered her into his arms and carried her down two flights of stairs to the exit. When he opened the door to freedom, they confronted a sight that drained the blood from his face. Alyssa gasped as Seamus seemed to lose his strength, nearly dropping her on the ground. She looked up to see what had scared him so and sucked in a scream. An enormous warrior held Sian and Siobhan captive while he single-handedly fought Rio and Duncan who appeared to be losing.

"Siobhan, Morgan thinks to take us all with this zombie. Can you devise a spell to protect me while I join the fight?" Seamus asked, his tone desperate. *"Siobhan?"*

Siobhan apparently didn't respond. Alyssa had no idea why she could hear him, but all the same, she could.

From where she stood, Alyssa could see the expression of abject terror on Siobhan's face and knew exactly how the other woman felt.

Seamus interrupted her thoughts. *"Rowan, I don't think your mother can speak to your father. You two need to visualize yourselves outside now. Morgan kept us distracted while she busily went about setting up to take us all."*

Alyssa also tried to warn her warrior, but when she called him to come to her, he didn't reply. It seemed he hadn't heard her.

In that moment, Rowan and Owen visualized themselves outside. Rowan stared at her, a look of painful disbelief marring his handsome features. His eyes roamed her body while she clung to Seamus who physically shielded her from the biggest warrior anyone had ever seen.

Rowan walked toward Seamus and Alyssa in a daze, his expression like a man who had seen the end of the world. When Seamus reached out to him, Rowan shrugged him off and faced Alyssa.

"Our thoughts are shielded here. The goddesses have enchanted this place against us. The only ones we can hear in our thoughts are the immortals. Scathach is on our side, but we must talk out loud to each other and keep talking to each other to keep Morgan and Maeve at bay. I need you to hold on to me, and this time do not let go." Rowan's voice sounded hard.

She couldn't understand why he was angry with her. Didn't he know she left him at the command of the goddess?

There was no time for conversation as the enormous warrior bore down on Rowan. The other Sheridans and their friends fought to distract him, but Alyssa could see they had other problems as zombie warriors poured out of the compound. Morgan and Maeve followed close behind the zombies, apparently to relish the destruction of the Sheridan clan that had defied them for so long.

The battle raged wildly with warriors cursing, swords clanging and shearing off each other, the banshees wailing. Sian called both to Rio and Owen as she watched the battle ebb and flow in front of her. Owen swore in pain, and Rio's protective leather jacket hung off his frame in tatters.

Suddenly, the mist impeding the talismans' telepathic abilities lifted, and Alyssa looked to Siobhan who sported a smug smirk.

"While you all kept busy fighting Morgan's zombie army, I skimmed through the spells and incantations I read in your grandmother's journals to find a way to counter the evil goddesses' two-pronged attack—zombie warriors and involuntary telepathic shields." Siobhan smiled fleetingly at Alyssa from her vantage point near the warehouse.

"Can you reach Rowan?"

"I'll try. Rowan, open your mind to Alyssa," Siobhan said.

Alyssa hoped Rowan had left his nearly impenetrable shield open at least a little.

Apparently not. After the way the zombie reacted inside the stronghold, Alyssa feared saying anything aloud.

Rowan sweat and cursed as he fought the zombie with Alyssa clinging to him. Fleetingly, she wondered if the two of them were Findlay and Ailsa all over again, fighting to balance the odds for warriors and talismans that Morgan unbalanced all those centuries ago.

"Rowan, listen to me," Alyssa tried. *"The only way you can best this warrior is to appear to sacrifice me. When he comes in for the kill, you must strike your blow up underneath him and take out his heart, or whatever is there in its place."*

Alyssa couldn't be sure Rowan had heard her, but she knew she couldn't express her directives out loud. She'd heard Siobhan's entreaty to Rowan and knew somehow Siobhan had freed the exchange of their thoughts. She also knew Rowan could shield anyone except for maybe Scathach, and even then, Alyssa couldn't be sure he hadn't found a way to exclude his goddess from his mind if he chose.

"You can't ask that of me. Please. I just got you back."

Ah, so he had heard her. *"This battle is bigger than we are. We must win it at all costs. I imagine Ailsa said something similar to Findlay before he faced this same warrior long ago."*

Beneath her hands he hesitated for a fraction of a second before he reached behind her and thrust her to his side, leaving her vulnerable to the zombie's attack. Watching the battle rage from behind Rowan's shoulder had been one kind of terrifying but looking up into the vacant eyes of a killing machine focused solely on her nearly made her faint, and she staggered.

The zombie moved so fast when she no longer clung to Rowan. She'd forgotten the supernatural speed at which these warriors fought. However, time seemed to slow down as she eyed the razor-sharp blade bearing down to cleave her in two. The sword glowed with an unearthly light, paralyzing her. Something about that long-ago time when her namesake crossed the ford shimmered into her consciousness, and she felt the keen mourning Ailsa Sheridan experienced as this warrior took her life. Alyssa closed her eyes, held her breath, and steeled herself for the killing blow, the blow that would give Morgan her ultimate prize.

Rowan stepped in front of her and dealt the rogue a death-blow to the zombie's chest. The gaping hole where his heart should have been caved in around Rowan's claymore, suspending time. Alyssa saw life flicker in the zombie's eyes in the form of surprise and then something like relief before he toppled forward to lie inert in the churned dirt at their feet.

Like the morning mist, the other zombie warriors evanesced into the ether at the death of their champion. Alyssa thought her eardrums might explode at the sound of Morgan's anguished cry. A blood-red shimmer hung in the air where the goddess had stood, which unnerved Alyssa almost as much as Morgan's voice.

As Morgan's essence faded, Alyssa saw the other terrible goddess of the unholy trio bent on stealing her life. Maeve seemed to survey the field with a slow speculative glance before she too visualized herself elsewhere, leaving behind a reddish-purple sparkle in the air.

Having never experienced battle before, Alyssa watched the other warriors and talismans for cues. Rowan held himself up on the hilt of his claymore, resting his head on his hand, panting for breath. Siobhan ran to Duncan who gathered her to him in a fierce embrace. Regally, Sian walked to Owen, who wrapped his free hand around her shoulder and hugged her to his side. Rio and Seamus labored to catch their breaths by stretching and walking in circles to calm the adrenaline coursing through their bodies. Alyssa hugged herself and stared fearfully at the inert form of the giant warrior whose job it had been to kill her to maintain Morgan's status quo for another thousand years.

Dispassionately, Scathach interrupted her warrior band. "It is time to return to your home before Morgan and Maeve decide to regroup. I will return to you in a few days."

Seamus spoke up. "Pardon me, milady, but we need to get Alyssa home with us, and she doesn't know how to visualize herself yet."

At Seamus's use of the word home, Rio scowled at him. The fact that Seamus, not Rowan, asked after her was not lost on Alyssa, and she struggled to drag in breath as the despair of the last day nearly suffocated her.

"I will take her to the compound by the lake. See that you are right behind us," Scathach said. Then she walked over to Alyssa and touched her hand.

Alyssa immediately felt herself compress and spin through time and space. She thought maybe she'd fainted when she opened her eyes and found herself swaying on her feet in the middle of the kitchen in Owen and Sian Sheridan's Montana home.

A couple sitting in the breakfast nook glanced up inquiringly. Both appeared dismayed to see Alyssa arrive first and alone. Disoriented, she stood in the middle of the room shaking, the adrenaline of the battle finally leaving her body.

Finn Daly walked in from the direction of the living room.

"There you are, lass." He gathered her in his arms. "I've been repeating incantations Afton taught me. I don't have a clue about the words, but I know the effectiveness of their protective power. I've been chanting ever since you disappeared with Morgan." He pulled back and gave her a long once-over. "All right then, missy?" It was an endearment he'd used with her since childhood whenever she'd had a scrape or dustup.

Involuntarily, she started laughing at the incongruity of Finn's question in light of what she'd experienced. Her laughter bordered on hysteria before she broke into uncontrollable sobs.

Her reaction obviously terrified the couple in the kitchen. Both talked over each other, asking frantic questions.

"Who did we lose? Please tell me it wasn't Rowan or Rio or my father," the man pleaded.

"Where's Sian, and what happened to Duncan and Siobhan? Where is Seamus? What happened in LA?" the woman shrieked.

Alyssa's fear and grief for her doomed relationship with Rowan coupled with the harrowing experience of visualization with a goddess—again. She couldn't cope with their questions. Mutely, she clung even more tightly to her old warrior protector. Finn gently guided her through the kitchen and dining room to the warmth of the living room. He tried to shush the couple's questions over his shoulder before Seamus's arrival rescued him from deflecting their inquisition. Immediately following Seamus, they could hear the others as they arrived in the kitchen. Finn busied himself settling Alyssa on a couch in the living room.

"Where is Alyssa?" Rowan shouted as he shimmered into the kitchen.

Rowan's question hung in the air.

Alyssa buried her face in Finn's chest as he rocked her, fresh tears she couldn't control overwhelming her. For a long time, she cried out all the hurt and fear she'd bottled up over the last days. But an ocean of tears couldn't wash away the pain of knowing she would never be woman enough for the only man she'd ever love.

When at last she raised her head from Finn's shoulder, she noticed Seamus seated on the couch across from them. "Thank you, Seamus, for looking out for me. I know you wanted to second guess Scathach, but you did the right thing," Alyssa whispered.

"You heard that did you, before Morgan shielded all of our thoughts from each other?" Seamus asked.

"I think when you were training me on shielding, you revealed more than you intended. I didn't hear Scathach. I heard you respond to her. I couldn't hear Rowan, and he clearly couldn't hear me because I tried to tell him, but I could hear you. That's weird, isn't it?" Alyssa said.

She looked to Finn, who shrugged. "I've never heard of such a thing, but everything that's happened with you the last few days is beyond my experience."

"Yeah, it is weird," Seamus said before he glanced behind her with a look she couldn't interpret. "I think you're going to have to open some chinks in your armor, buddy, to let your talisman in when she needs to contact you, not only for when you need to contact her."

From the corner of her eye, she spied Rowan, who stopped pacing behind the couch where she sat with Finn.

Alyssa started in Finn's arms at her discovery of Rowan in the room. Her surprise at seeing him must have shown on her tear-stained face.

"Where else would you think I'd be except with you?" Rowan asked, his expression perplexed.

Somewhere in the house, a door slammed and an enormous ball of white fur bounded into the room and headed straight for Alyssa. For a moment, both Seamus and Rowan stood alert, claymores ready, before it became obvious Alyssa's other protector, Shadow, was racing in to greet his mistress. She slid off the couch to sit on the floor and bury her face in his thick fur, drawing strength from his unconditional love for her. "I've missed you too, little guy."

Shadow's hair muffled Alyssa's words, but Rowan and Seamus exclaimed in unison, "Little guy?" before they burst out laughing. Like a dam breaking, all the tension, fear, and adrenaline of the last two days melted away.

CHAPTER TWENTY-NINE

LYSSA SIGHED AS she sensed the rift between Seamus and Rowan to be nothing more than the pent-up emotions from the aftermath of battle. Shortly after Shadow bounded into the house to greet her, she gathered herself enough to face a shower and a change of clothes. Wishful thinking caused her to hope Rowan would offer to share the shower with her. Instead, he and Seamus retold the battle to Finn, who like most old warriors, thirsted for the details of a battle he didn't fight himself.

When Alyssa decided she looked at least somewhat presentable, a pair of black skinny jeans hugging her legs and a silver-gray knit sweater draping gracefully from her shoulders, she silently padded down the stairs. The heavenly smell of spices and meat cooking had her stomach thinking it had been days since she'd eaten. However, the conversation in the kitchen halted her inside the dining room, and she peeked around the door.

Seated at the island in the middle of the room, Rio and his twin were drinking beers and talking—about her.

"It's not all that weird. Her grandmother was a druid who married a warrior. He died when Alyssa's mother was four because he didn't have a talisman. He stopped looking for her when he met Alyssa's grandmother," she heard Rio say.

"Yeah, but Alyssa is a talisman, not a druid, and she clearly knows Rowan is her warrior," Riley stated.

"You didn't see her and Seamus together at her place. Supposedly, he was training her to shield her thoughts, but the sexual tension radiating off them when they came out of her den after their 'training' session"—he air-quoted—"made me want to throw up," Rio sneered.

"We haven't been around them together to judge, but your parents seem to think Rowan and Alyssa are a love match," the woman, who must be Lynnette, interrupted from her seat at the breakfast nook.

"They haven't been around Alyssa and Seamus together. Don't forget, Seamus is the one who was carrying Alyssa out of Maeve's stronghold, not Rowan," Rio said.

Alyssa figured out Rio didn't like her much from the moment they met, but his accusations and the venom in his tone sucker-punched her. It wasn't enough that Rowan preferred other women to her, but it seemed his brother didn't want her to be Rowan's talisman. She and Seamus? How absurd. She almost marched in to set all of them straight but stopped herself as she took a step toward the kitchen. Defending herself would only legitimize Rio's accusation. Instead, she walked back into the living room and called loudly for her dog.

Apparently, Shadow caused quite a stir as he raced through the kitchen at her summons. A light came on in the dining room, and she heard someone setting the table for dinner. Her innate good manners prodded her to help, but her fear of having to answer personal questions kept her securely on the couch absorbing all the love Shadow so freely gave her.

Dinner started out a tense affair with Rio sending seething looks at Seamus and Alyssa until Seamus and Rowan began recounting past battles and wild escapades they'd enjoyed during the three years they'd been roommates.

"Do you remember that time when you accidentally visualized yourself into a party some rogue warriors were hosting?" Seamus asked Rowan with a chuckle.

"Oh yeah. We sure surprised those boys. There were a couple of them literally with their pants down. I should have felt bad about that, but even if a talisman's warrior hasn't found her by the time she turns twenty-eight, there's no excuse for hanging out with rogues," Rowan replied with a grin bordering on a grimace.

"I hadn't heard about that one, bro. Gives a whole new meaning to party crashing," Riley said with a laugh.

"Gave a whole new meaning to party. The looks on their faces were purely comical when they realized we weren't giving them any time to right themselves before Seamus and I started our own kind of party."

"Thinking about all those zombies in skirts dead in the hallway of Maeve's little funhouse feels kind of like a party to me." Seamus waggled his brows before he forked another bite of spicy jambalaya into his mouth.

"Those witches pulled out all the stops for their little soiree, that's for sure," Owen said with a grin. He tore off a hunk of bread from the loaf in front of him, passed it to Lynnette on his left, and added, "Besting them on their turf feels especially sweet, doesn't it boys?"

A chorus of "Hell, yeah!" "No doubt!" "So sweet!" echoed Owen's pronouncement.

The dinner of spicy jambalaya, French bread, and cucumber salad disappeared quickly in spite of the story telling accompanying it. Though Alyssa's thoughts were in turmoil, she was famished, so she ate plenty. Plus, stuffing her face meant she didn't have to join the conversation much.

As the meal ended, she quickly volunteered for clean-up duty.

Siobhan joined her while Sian and Lynnette dished up the frozen key lime pie Sian had tucked away for a special occasion.

"What's the matter, Alyssa?" Siobhan whispered while the two rinsed dishes and loaded the dishwasher.

"I don't want to talk about it, but thank you for caring," Alyssa said quietly.

"I saw the daggers Rio was sending you during dinner. You mustn't let him get to you. Anyone with eyes can see the only man in your life is Rowan."

"Rio isn't the problem, though I can't understand why he wouldn't want his brother to find his talisman," Alyssa said. She rinsed a couple more plates then took a chance. "There's something you can do for me, but it would be out of your way."

"Name it."

"Shadow and I and my grandmother's journals are going to need a ride home. Since I know Duncan and you are going back to your home tomorrow, and you didn't visualize yourselves here like Finn did, maybe you would have room for us?"

"You're not going home with Rowan?" Siobhan blinked.

"I think I've done what I was destined to do for Rowan." Alyssa's mouth turned down. "He doesn't have any feelings for me besides relief for finding and bonding me to him as his talisman. Maeve showed me as much in graphic detail."

"Alyssa, are you sure? You didn't see him when we discovered Morgan had kidnapped you," Siobhan said, her hand falling short as she reached out to comfort Alyssa who flinched.

"Please, Siobhan, don't build castles in the air. I'm a realist. I don't have what it takes to attract and hold a man like Rowan Sheridan, not even with the advantage of being his talisman. You're sweet for trying to soften the blow, but I've already felt it." Alyssa pulled in a breath to stem her emotions. "So, anyway, about that ride?"

If she didn't escape this kitchen and this well-meaning woman, she was going to embarrass herself and Siobhan too with the tears shimmering right below the brittle surface of her self-control.

"I'm sure Duncan will try to talk you out of it, but we have plenty of room, and you're not that far out of our way."

"Thanks. Excuse me, will you?" Alyssa dried her hands and hung the towel on the rack beside the sink. "I don't have room for dessert. I think I'll go to bed."

From across the room, Sian said, "After the last couple days you've had, I'm surprised you're still on your feet. Sleep as long as you like. I'll set aside breakfast for you before the horde descends on it." She walked over and kissed Alyssa on the cheek, reminding her of the way Gram always kissed her when she knew Alyssa had had a particularly trying day. The gesture undid her, and she brushed a tear from her face with the heel of her hand as she turned and hurried away.

Using the back hallway off the kitchen, she skirted the dining room, avoiding the men, especially Rowan who hadn't said anything to her since their return to the Sheridan home. Seeming to sense her sorrow, Shadow followed her to the bedroom she shared with Rowan, which was good. Now when she relocated to the unused room across the hall, Shadow would be with her.

After locking the door behind her, she changed out of her clothes and into the T-shirt she'd packed to wear to bed. Though it probably was bad manners to invite Shadow to sleep with her when they were guests in someone else's home, she did anyway, needing the comfort of his familiar size and smell. Though exhausted, sleep eluded her. The nightmares of the last few days threatened her even when her rational side reminded her that for tonight anyway, she was safe from Maeve and her emotionally eviscerating images. Still, it took a long time for sleep to come.

～⚬～

Rowan noted Alyssa's withdrawal at dinner. Chalking it up to everything she'd been through, he decided to give her some time and space to recover. It never occurred to him she'd want space from him. Several hours after dinner when he headed to bed and discovered she'd moved out, he was stunned. Could Rio be right? Were Seamus and Alyssa somehow involved? When had they had time to do that? After everything he and Alyssa had experienced together, he couldn't believe she'd leave him for another warrior.

Still, he had to know. Stealing himself against a pain he knew he'd never survive, he walked downstairs to the guest room that Seamus preferred beside the study. Walking in on the two of them in the middle of something intimate scared the hell out of him. Yet he sucked in a deep breath and knocked on the door. He heard his buddy humming, the sound growing louder as he neared the door. With his customary lack of modesty, Seamus pulled open the door wearing nothing but a towel wrapped low around his waist.

A toothbrush hung from his mouth as he asked, "Hey buddy. What do you need?"

Rowan cleared his throat. "You haven't seen Alyssa by chance?"

"Come to think of it, not since dinner." Seamus jerked the toothbrush from his mouth. "Something hasn't happened to her, has it?"

"No, but she's not in our room, so I, uh, I'm wandering the house looking for her."

Seamus wrinkled his brow. "Oh-kay. Well, let me know if you don't find her and want some help."

"Thanks."

Jesus, son. Get a grip. You know Seamus of all people would never betray you that way.

Walking back to his room, he glanced over at the closed door to the smallest guest room across from his room. Trying the handle, he discovered the door to be locked and knew where Alyssa had relocated. Why she'd done that, he couldn't imagine, but it was late, and he'd had enough confrontations today to last him a while, so he let it go. In the morning, he determined, they were going to come to an understanding.

⤳

Alyssa awoke early, feeble morning light barely disturbing the darkness of the bedroom. She listened for a few minutes to discern the state of consciousness of the rest of the house and decided something was happening in the kitchen. Before heading downstairs, she padded down the hall to the bathroom, washed her face, brushed her teeth, and returned to the bedroom she'd shared with Shadow.

After donning the same outfit she'd worn the night before, she packed her clothes and toiletries and carried her bag downstairs. In the kitchen, she found Sian humming softly as she prepared a feast of breakfast. Bacon sizzled on the stove while a sausage-and-egg casserole baked in the oven. Sian alternated between buttering toast as it popped up with cutting melon wedges on the counter beside the toaster.

As Alyssa watched, she marveled at Sian's seemingly effortless skill at cooking for a crowd. Hadn't someone said Sian couldn't cook?

"My cooking skills are quite limited. Breakfast is my specialty. The rest I leave to Owen who is a far better cook than I."

Alyssa nearly jumped a foot. She'd been afraid of startling Sian while she wielded that big knife, but the joke was on Alyssa.

"You were thinking rather loudly and unguardedly, dear," Sian said, her voice gentle.

"It's clear I need to practice shielding more. Is there anything I can do to help?"

"You can crack these eggs into a bowl for omelets." Sian handed her two cartons of eggs.

"*All* of them?"

"Everyone fought hard on little fuel. They'll need to catch up. Nothing will go to waste I assure you," Sian said with a laugh.

As Alyssa began cracking eggs into a bowl, Sian said casually, "I understand you're leaving us today."

"Yes. I have study groups to lead and a thesis to finish, so I need to return home. Besides, I think I've addressed the reason for my being here, at least for the time being." Relief flooded her when the sadness she tried so desperately to hide wasn't evident in her voice.

"Tell me about your studies."

"My thesis is about Celtic warriors and warfare, specifically women warriors. Ironic, isn't it? I had no idea when I started this project I'd be studying my ancestors. I see now why my grandmother became giddy with excitement when I told her what I'd be pursuing for my master's degree." She cracked the last egg into the bowl. "Do you have a whisk?"

Sian handed her a whisk from a drawer on the other side of the sink. "After reading through some of your grandmother's journals, I understand her reticence in telling you your identity and your role in our world, but at the risk of offending you, she did you a disservice."

"She did?"

"After you reached the age of twenty-one, she had an obligation to tell you at least who and what you are. After her death, I'm surprised Finn didn't do at least that much." Sian grabbed a carton of milk from the fridge and added some to the eggs as Alyssa whisked them.

Blowing out a breath, Alyssa said, "I've been thinking similar thoughts. But you didn't lose nearly your entire family to Morgan, and Gram and Finn did."

Sian nodded.

"I can see their point of view. Besides, Scathach's boot camp training session caught me up rather quickly I think. When I go home, Finn can continue to help me, which no doubt he's looking forward to."

Sian cocked a brow and opened her mouth to ask the obvious questions when they were interrupted by the simultaneous arrival of Siobhan, Duncan, and Finn.

"Mmmm, something sure smells delicious in here." Finn hauled himself onto a barstool with a grin. "The smell of frying bacon could drag the dead out of bed." He helped himself to a melon wedge from the platter Sian left out on the island for appetizers.

"No doubt Finn. I love the days when I wake up to the smell of bacon sizzling in the kitchen." Duncan slid a sly glance at his wife.

"I like those days too. A shame I don't get many of them." Siobhan gifted her husband with a condescending look before she broke into a grin.

Teasing him, she stepped into his embrace then reached around him for a melon wedge she refused to share. Watching the two of them made Alyssa's heart ache. Busying herself with the eggs, she swallowed down the lump in her throat. Someday this scene would play out again in this same room with Rowan and the woman he'd ultimately find to love while Alyssa lived alone and waited for the times when he needed her to be his guide in battle.

Slowly, the others trickled into the kitchen, also lured out of beds by the heavenly aroma of Sian's cooking. When Owen wandered into the room, Siobhan left Duncan's side to check on Owen's poultice, and seeing the infected wound she'd treated yesterday had nearly healed overnight, she nodded in satisfaction.

Siobhan wordlessly stood in front of Rio when he entered the kitchen. In equal silence, Rio removed his shirt for her inspection. The little nips the zombie warriors had taken from his shoulders and chest were almost healed. Owen's deeper gash would probably take another day.

Turning to Alyssa, Siobhan said, "Thanks to your grandmother, these two are in good shape. I'll leave a second poultice behind for you Owen, but you're good to go, Rio."

"You were injured?" Alyssa asked. How had she missed that?

"Some nicks and scratches. Nothing to worry about," Owen said. "Thank you very much, Siobhan. It might have been Afton

Sinclair's recipe, but it was your skill that healed us." He glanced at his son. "Right Rio?"

"Thanks for your help," Rio mumbled as he pulled his shirt back over his head.

Riley and Lynnette slipped in for breakfast as the others were seating themselves in the dining room. One look at their clasped hands and dreamy expressions revealed to everyone why the two of them were slow to arrive for the meal. Watching them, Alyssa couldn't suppress a stab of grief at what might have been for Rowan and her if only she'd been more of a woman.

Conspicuously absent from the group were Seamus and Rowan. When Finn commented on it, Owen said, "After the stress the two of them endured during the battle, I'd be surprised to see either of them before noon."

That knowledge both dismayed and comforted Alyssa. She wouldn't see Rowan before she left.

After breakfast, she waited at the breakfast nook, nursing a cup of coffee while Duncan and Siobhan packed to return to their home.

When Alyssa headed into the laundry room to don her winter gear, Sian spoke up. "You're leaving without saying good-bye to Rowan? I can wake him," she offered as Duncan loaded Alyssa's bag and the box of journals into his SUV.

"Please don't bother Rowan. I've done my job, and now it's time for everyone to return to normal before Morgan initiates the next big crisis."

Sian tried another tack. "Without Rowan, your safety is suspect."

"For the ride home, Duncan is with me, and his talisman will alert us to any danger, I'm sure. Besides, Morgan can't take me out-side of battle."

Finn interrupted when he danced out of the house and clapped Duncan on the shoulder. "Since I live right up the road from Alyssa, I wouldn't mind a ride home civilian style."

"See Sian. I'll be perfectly safe with two warriors and this big oaf," Alyssa said, pointing at Shadow who lumbered up to the truck. "It was a pleasure to meet you. Thank you for everything."

"I hate to see you leave like this, and I hope I see you again very soon. Take care of yourself, Alyssa," Sian said, her tone sad, the hug she gave Alyssa tight.

CHAPTER THIRTY

OWAN CLAWED AT his throat. Whatever monster Morgan had sent to fight him this time didn't fight fair. Hand-to-hand combat meant the use of a claymore not hands to the throat. At last he grabbed the big paw and tore it away from his neck before wringing it into submission. His breathing labored, he struggled into a sitting position when he awoke to discover the choking entity he held at bay was the sheet on his bed. Somehow, he'd tangled himself up in his bedding. Pouring sweat, he tried to recall the dream that awakened him in such a state. Alyssa was there, on the edge of his reach. He kept calling to her that she would always be the only one, but she continued moving away beyond the mists. Had he lost her?

He broke out in a fresh sweat as he recalled the events of the previous two days. He hadn't lost her. Scathach visualized her home. Finn held her until she stopped crying. Shadow comforted her. Siobhan checked her for external injuries and pronounced her safe. Why then did he feel so afraid?

She'd been subdued at dinner and relocated to the other bedroom afterward.

Why didn't she want anything to do with

him? What had Maeve and Morgan told her? Whatever their lies, she had to know the truth. He'd come for her and saved her, saved them all, hadn't he? She'd been there. She'd seen it.

Then he remembered how he hadn't held her, hadn't touched her, hadn't spoken to her since he carried her out of that dank room where Morgan and Maeve imprisoned her. Quiet, retiring Alyssa. He'd wanted to give her space, let her process the battle in her own way. What had she said to him at her place when he first told her he wanted her? Men like him didn't want women like Alyssa. They wanted women like Ceri. Alyssa's former boyfriend made that abundantly clear while he told her all about how unsatisfactory she was in bed.

Jesus, what an idiot. He should have broken in that door last night and demanded she share his bed, debrief the battle together, reassure each other of their feelings.

Well, he'd take care of that right now.

As he stepped into his boxers, he thought about her sleep-softened features and all that glorious inky black hair framing her beautiful face and the sparkle in those quick-silver eyes as he aroused her. He thought about her full breasts with their half-dollar-sized nipples that puckered so prettily when he looked at her just right. He thought of the lovely indentation of her waist and the enticing flare of her hips and the incredible length of her legs—a sweet surprise considering her short stature. He smiled ruefully to himself. If he wasn't careful, he'd scare her to death with the raging hard-on he'd given himself simply by thinking about her.

When he opened the door and stepped into the hall, he saw the door to the room she'd occupied was open, the bed neatly made up, and no sign Alyssa had ever been there. Panicked, he raced back into his room, threw on his jeans, and pulled a shirt over his head as he descended the stairs two at a time. As he ran through the living room, he sensed an eerie stillness in the house. Five sets of eyes staring at him when he entered the kitchen told him the monster in his dreams was real.

"Good afternoon, son. Rested up after Morgan's latest run at us?" Owen asked a little too cordially.

"*Afternoon?* What time is it?"

"A bit before one. I saved you some breakfast, but I guess for you, it's brunch." Sian smiled wanly at him.

"What's going on? Where are Alyssa and Seamus, Duncan and Siobhan?" Rowan asked.

"Alyssa and Finn headed home several hours ago with Siobhan and Duncan. Alyssa said she had to return to school to lead her study groups and work on her thesis. I think Duncan and Siobhan were tired of Rio's badgering"—Sian glared at her other son—"and Finn wanted to return home the civilian way, he said."

"Where did you say Seamus was?" Rowan asked, a steely edge to his voice.

"I'm right here, old buddy. I've packed my gear into your rig. I would have packed yours too, but I didn't want to risk your attitude by being the one to wake you with the good news," Seamus said as he breezed into the kitchen from the back door.

"The good news?" Rowan asked confused.

"Yeah. That Alyssa went home without you. Thought you'd take it better from someone in the family." Seamus cocked a brow and waited.

Rowan jammed his fingers through his hair. "Why would she do that?" But he had a pretty good idea.

"Couldn't be because you paid so much attention to her after everyone returned yesterday. All of you were bragging to yourselves and each other about how well you'd taken on Morgan, and no one but Finn said anything at all to her before dinner," Lynnette spoke up from nursing her coffee in the breakfast nook. "After dinner, Siobhan tried to talk to her, but she excused herself and went to bed. You didn't even notice when she didn't come back to the table for dessert."

"She was there. She knows what I did for her," Rowan said lamely.

"Well big brother, you weren't here when Scathach unceremoniously dropped her off in this kitchen. She was swaying on her feet and shaking like a leaf, on the verge of hysteria. When Finn walked into the kitchen, she lost it. When you arrived, you should have taken her from Finn and comforted her like a talisman needs comfort after participating directly in a battle, but you didn't," Riley taunted, putting his big brother in his place for once.

Stunned, Rowan sat down hard on the bench of the breakfast nook. Dropping his head into his hands, he experienced the greatest despair of his life. A pain worse than the anguish he suffered when he thought he'd lost Alyssa to Morgan and her ever-flowing river of blood. Though Alyssa still lived on this side of the mists, he didn't have her. She'd passed her first big test with flying colors while he'd royally failed his. He had to go to her, take care of her, make her see she was more than his talisman.

She was his world.

Watching his friend's distress, Seamus suggested, "If you get your gear together in the next fifteen minutes, we can be back to the apartment by midnight or so, depending on the roads."

Rowan regarded his friend through bleak eyes and nodded. Hauling himself to his feet, he felt like a man twice his age.

"Thanks, Seamus. We appreciate how you look out for Rowan," Owen said.

Seamus shrugged. "He's my best friend. He'd do the same for me."

"Listen, son, she's not more than an hour or two ahead of you on the road. You can catch up to her before she unpacks, I expect," Owen said encouragingly.

"I'll pack a meal for the drive," Sian added as she busied herself pulling Tupperware containers from a cabinet.

"Thanks, Sian. If Rowan's not hungry, I know I will be. Especially since I don't think we'll be stopping for much more than gas in the next ten hours or so," Seamus said.

"The two of you don't need to take any unnecessary chances," Sian admonished with a steely glare at her eldest son.

∽

Seamus was wrong. Taranis apparently had heard the news of the Sheridans' success against Maeve and Morgan, so he threw down a terrible storm. He warned Seamus and Rowan with swirling flakes in a half-hearted wind for the first hour after they left the compound and saved the nasty stuff for when they were traveling through the middle of nowhere. After five hours of battling blizzard conditions of wind and heavy snow, they finally reached a small town on the side of the interstate and stopped for gas and to stretch their legs. The radio announced they were in the midst of a fifty-year storm, but Rowan and Seamus knew better. Taranis would conjure up this sort of wickedness on a daily basis if it meant impeding Rowan from reaching his goal. Rowan only hoped Alyssa and her companions, having departed the compound so much earlier, hadn't encountered Taranis's wrath.

"What do you think, buddy? Do we push on, or do we camp out here for the night?" Seamus asked as he pumped gas into Rowan's SUV.

The civilians made the decision for them as the radio announced road closures all around them. Even the frontages and the back roads were closed.

"Jesus, I hate this, Seamus. The longer I'm away from her, the farther away from me she's going. Maybe I could visualize myself into her house," Rowan began. His wildly rampaging emotions were taking their toll on his common sense.

"The kind of storm we're in implies Taranis has no intention of allowing you to visualize yourself anywhere right now. You might aim for Alyssa's place and find yourself somewhere dangerous on the other side of the world before Taranis is finished spinning you around. What we need to do is gas up, so we're ready to go whenever Taranis lets up, then we find somewhere to bunk for the night," Seamus said.

"Yeah, sure. Let's do that," Rowan replied listlessly.

Seamus squeezed his shoulder. "Have you tried to talk to her?"

"All the damn day, but her shield's up, and she's not letting me in. Thanks a lot pal." Rowan tried to say it lightly, but it just came out sad.

"Sorry about that. Truly, I am," Seamus said as Rowan stared skeptically at him. "I think you should keep trying though. She's new to all this, so she's bound to let down her guard sooner rather than later."

Rowan stared out the windshield as they waited their turn to gas up his ride. "Jesus, I hope so. Seamus, she's the most amazing woman I've ever known. She does things to me I never even imagined." Leaning his head back, he stared at the roof of the SUV. "I've only known her a short time, but I can't face a life without her in it. When Morgan had her, I died a thousand deaths, but this is infinitely worse." He stared at his friend. "What if she doesn't want me and this life I thrust on her? What if she shuts herself away from it the way her grandmother did? What will I do then?"

"You're getting way ahead of yourself. Let's find somewhere to hole up for a few hours until the roads reopen then head out again. You can worry about the rest after we get back."

"You sure you're going to be all right here by yourself?" Duncan asked for the hundredth time as he and Siobhan shrugged into their coats at Alyssa's front door.

"I'm perfectly fine here. Before we left, Rowan and Seamus installed a state-of-the-art security system. Plus, I've still got Gram's protections, Shadow, and Finn. I'll be fine," Alyssa said. "Besides, I don't think I'll be Morgan's target again anytime soon. According to the prophecies in both the Sheridan family lore and Gram's note-books, all Rowan and I had to do was defeat Morgan's champion together to give back to the warriors their full chance at finding their talismans before they were forced to turn rogue or go to ground." Alyssa crossed her arms over her chest. "Since we did that, what reason would she have for going after me now?"

"She's a vengeful creature. If anything, I think you're more of a target now than you were before." Siobhan bent down to pull on her boots as she spoke. "Part of the reason for the training room at the Sheridan compound is its double duty as a fall-out shelter when Morgan is trolling for Sian. Morgan enjoys stealing talismans from their warriors and forcing the warriors to watch while she does it." Siobhan stood and faced Alyssa.

"But I imagine that it's more fun to take a talisman who has a relationship with her warrior beyond battle. In some ways, I think I'll be safer than Sian or Lynnette because while Rowan cares for me as his talisman, he isn't going to be involved with me otherwise." She addressed Duncan. "Like Jennifer does with you, I'll live close to him, but since I don't matter to him beyond my official duties, taking me wouldn't be as enjoyable for Morgan as taking Sian from Owen or Lynnette from Riley or Siobhan from you."

"I still don't like this. Is there some incantation in those note-books you can add to the layers Alyssa's grandma put on this place while she lived?" Duncan asked Siobhan.

"There's one I can do in the next few minutes, though it will involve you and Finn taking places on the east and west sides of the house. Alyssa will need to stay inside, so we'll say our goodbyes now. That way we won't break the spell when we leave," Siobhan said.

"That makes me feel better, babe." He kissed his wife on the cheek, a gesture that had Alyssa hugging her arms tighter around herself as she watched.

"You keep in touch with us, alright?" Duncan framed his com-mand as a request.

"Sure, Dad. I'll check in often."

"I mean it. This isn't funny, Alyssa," he ground out.

"I know." She sighed. "I'll check in with you often. Just so you know, Finn and I ride to town together nearly every day during the winter, so if something goes wrong, it won't take much for everyone to know."

Finn looked at Alyssa fondly and pulled her into his embrace like his own granddaughter. Letting her go, he patted Shadow on the head. "You know your job, boy. Take care of our girl."

The dog whined and thumped his tail on the floor. As Finn left the house to take up his post for Siobhan's spell, he said, "I did this several times with Afton over the years, so I know my place and what's expected."

Siobhan hugged Alyssa hard. "I hate to leave you, Alyssa. You're the bravest woman I've ever met, taking on Morgan and Maeve and not only surviving, but giving warriors like my brother hope. Casting a protection spell seems like a feeble thank you after all you've done, but it's the best I have." Sounding like she had a throat full of unshed tears, Siobhan continued. "Be careful. You've become too precious to us to lose. We'll talk again soon."

Alyssa hugged her back hard and spoke around the lump in her own throat, "In such a short time, you've become a good friend. Thank you."

Her companions stepped outside in the gathering twilight, each taking his proper place around her home before Siobhan walked outside and started chanting:

May home and hearth be your fortress,
Brighid, Protectoress of her chosen ones,
Protect your family.
No storm shall overwhelm you;
No waters shall drown you;
No sword shall run you through.
May you not fear the mists!

May you not fear the Washer at the Ford!
May no man wound you.
May the Great Goddess protect you.

As Alyssa stood in her doorway listening to Siobhan's words, she choked back a sob. *Men have been wounding me since I began to date, Rowan the most deeply, and the scars will never heal.* Hurriedly, she waved to Siobhan before closing the door. She sank onto her loveseat and gave way to the wracking sobs she thought she'd cried out on Finn's shoulder the day before. *Was it only yesterday I faced huge otherworldly warriors and angry goddesses bent on my destruction? Was it only yesterday that after seeing me prove I could perform my role to perfection, Rowan walked away from me?*

Intellectually, she understood what had happened as the logical end to their whirlwind courtship. He knew the whole story, where their union would lead, what was at stake for them. Pulling in a shuddery breath, she reminded herself of the necessity of what he did with her, to her, but she had no idea how to gather up the remnants of her heart and put it back together.

Sensing his mistress's distress, Shadow tentatively climbed up on the couch beside her before nudging his way to lie across her lap. Alyssa buried her face in her faithful friend's neck and sobbed her heart out.

"Hey, old son. I think Taranis is taking a break. We should probably hit it while we can." Seamus's loud and hearty observation battered Rowan's senses. They'd been stuck in a beat-up hotel room with threadbare blankets, thin walls, and two viewable channels on TV for the past two days while the local highway department tried to reopen the roads. Rowan noticed a feeble light trying to break free of the clouds and understood daybreak had arrived. The snow finally stopped, and the wind ceased its incessant howling.

He'd slept in his clothes as a way to stay warm, so all he had to do was pull on his boots to be ready to go. As he tightened the laces he asked, "Have you been awake long enough to check the weather report, or are you basing your assumption purely on observation?"

"I called the number for the road department. All roads are open but still treacherous going. We'll have to take it at a crawl, but at least we can get moving. I'll drive," Seamus insisted. "Honestly, buddy, if I have to spend one more day in this tiny room with you pacing and snarling like a caged bear, I might chance the wrath of the local highway patrol and smash through their barriers."

"It's my truck. I'll drive," Rowan growled.

"Not if we want to get there in one piece, old pal. Besides, I took the precaution of commandeering the keys while you tossed around in bed last night." Seamus's grin was all teeth as he dangled Rowan's keys in the air.

"Fine. You drive. Let's get the hell on the road."

Rowan knew it was probably safer for Seamus to drive, but he couldn't help his impatience. He'd been trying desperately to breach Alyssa's shield, but so far, he'd had no success. He'd left his own shield open to her, trying to reach out to her that way, but she hadn't responded. She hadn't even tried to call out to him.

Maybe he was courting disaster by trying to reach her telepathically, but the storm had knocked out cell service. Frantic with worry and being stuck for days in this backwater hadn't improved his mood. What if Morgan had taken her again? What would he do then? Surely, he'd have sensed if Morgan had her though, wouldn't he? What if something more mundane but equally devastating had happened to her? What if she'd been in an accident, or that creep Bill Forbes had come around to bother her and somehow breached their security system? He drove himself crazy with scenarios to explain why he couldn't communicate with her. He had to rely on them because the alternative—that she didn't want to talk to him—held more pain than he thought he was man enough to take.

CHAPTER THIRTY-ONE

FTER A LONG cry, Alyssa spent the first night at home returning the tapestries to their proper places, arranging the sculptures, doing unnecessary cleaning. She couldn't face the night alone in her bed after having last slept in it with Rowan. Finally, she curled up on her couch and slept fitfully with Shadow keeping guard on the floor in front of her.

The next day, she dutifully conducted her study group, picked up some groceries, and stopped at the hardware store to buy a safe in which to keep Gram's journals. While she trusted the security system Rowan and Seamus had installed, an extra layer of protection couldn't hurt. Perhaps her lack of knowledge about the value of the journals had kept them safe so far, but since all that had changed, it made sense to take precautions.

On her way home, she checked in with Finn, not so much because she'd promised Duncan and Siobhan she would, but because she needed help unloading and arranging the heavy safe. His approval at her caution warmed her heart, but the censorious looks she caught a few times upset her.

"Something's bothering you, Finn. Maybe rather than frowning at me when you think I'm not looking, you might say what's on your mind," Alyssa said, not quite hiding the exasperation she felt.

"You left him without telling him goodbye. If my talisman had ever done that to me, I don't know which emotion I would have felt more—anger or hurt." He grunted and let his side of the safe down to the floor in the kitchen.

After setting down her side, she stood. "Finn, you loved your talisman. Of course, you would have been angry and hurt if she'd left you, but it's different for Rowan. He didn't fall in love with me. He succeeded in bonding me to him, we fought well together, I fulfilled my role, and that's it. If there had been anything more, he would have said something, done something while we were at his parents' place, but he didn't." She opened the cupboard door where she planned to hide the safe and turned back to Finn. "Beyond thanking me, he didn't acknowledge me at all. You were there. You saw it."

Though she tried to sound matter-of-fact, her own words broke her heart, and she found herself struggling to keep from falling into Finn's arms and begging him to make it all better.

"He was in shock Alyssa. So were you. The two of you fought an epic battle, the one Findlay Sheridan fought all those years ago. You took on the Morrigan and won. I don't think even now with the distance of a few days that you fully comprehend what that means, especially since you weren't raised in our world," Finn said.

She raised an eyebrow, and he continued. "Rowan, however, does know what your victory means. He succeeded where Findlay did not because he kept his talisman close and listened to her, did as she told him to do." He moved around the safe and gave her a one-armed hug. "You, my dear, were wise and brave, something we all knew you needed to be, something I trusted you to be. Likely, Rowan was trying to come to grips with everything and expected you would know he loves you." He gave her a tiny squeeze.

"How could I know what Rowan is feeling? He has the most formidable shield, one I'm not sure even Scathach can breach unless he allows it. He didn't let me in even once after we arrived at the Sheridans'. We've only known each other a short time, so how could I know what he's feeling if he won't talk to me or let me into his thoughts?" Alyssa paced into the living room and back. "He didn't seek me out for any reason once we were all back together. You were all busy reliving the battle, and I was a shadow in the room."

Finn flinched at her accusation. "You have a point lass. In typical warrior fashion, dating back to the Middle Ages, the Sheridans and their friends recounted the entire battle and spent a great deal of breath bragging and congratulating." He couldn't seem to help a small smile. "Women like Sian, Siobhan, and Lynnette, having grown up in warrior culture, indulged their men in their conversations knowing they would earn their due in other ways. You didn't have the advantage of this knowledge, and Rowan did have an obligation to help you after the battle. However, at the risk of sounding indelicate, didn't you share Rowan's bed when you returned?"

She blushed at such a question coming from her *de facto* grandfather, but she answered him honestly. "By the way Rowan was acting, it seemed like sharing a bed with him would have been presumptuous. I moved my things into the room across the hall. If that had been a problem for him, I'm sure he would have let me know, but he didn't. As you know, he didn't even come down to see us off, so I don't think I've misunderstood anything concerning Rowan's feelings for me." She nodded at the safe, and the two of them heaved it into the space she'd cleared for it.

Swiping her brow with the back of her hand, she continued their conversation. "We won't be living next door to each other like Jennifer does with Duncan and Siobhan, but we live near each other, so I think we're in a position to take care of each other when we need to. Obviously, Rowan is fine with that."

"But you're not." It wasn't a question.

"It doesn't matter what I feel, Finn. What matters is that I do my job for Rowan. Which I will do," she said. "Weirdly enough, I was doing it before we met, before I learned about our community, so I guess now that I do know, I'll be even better at having his back when he goes into battle."

He held up his hand. "Wait a minute. What do you mean? Are you saying you were acting as Rowan's talisman before the two of you met?" His eyebrows nearly melded to his hairline.

Alyssa shrugged. "Apparently. After Gram died, I started having what I thought were these incredibly vivid dreams of men fighting battles. Only they made no sense because these were modern men in modern clothing fighting on modern city streets." She grabbed two mugs from the cupboard and poured each of them a coffee. "They used swords to fight other men, some of whom also used swords and some who used guns. One man in particular kept appearing in my dreams, and I felt compelled to call out warnings to him, which he heeded."

She handed Finn a mug, and they seated themselves at the island.

"The day I met Rowan, I daydreamed him fighting again. I thought it was because I'd just met him and found him especially attractive. He was outnumbered, wounded, and bleeding, so I called to him to return to his bed, and he did."

Finn's brows shot up again, but he didn't interrupt.

"The next day after he brought me home from an impromptu date, I discovered that over the last several months, I'd been watching him and helping him fight battles while I thought I was dreaming scenes related to my research."

"Alyssa, something very deep is going on here, something probably even beyond the gods. When Rowan returns, you must be with him, live with him," Finn insisted.

Her shoulders sagged. "I can't impose myself on him, especially after what Maeve showed me while I *vacationed* with Morgan and her at her stronghold. Rowan needs a lot more woman than I am to keep him satisfied," she said, hugging herself.

"So that's it. I should have known. She's used that trick so often.

One would think a goddess would have more imagination, but then again, it does work well and regularly for her."

Alyssa looked at him quizzically.

"When Rowan returns, promise me you'll see him. When he comes to the door, don't turn him away."

"Fine. Whatever you say."

After everything she'd been through over the last week, what difference would one more nail make in the coffin of her happiness?

"Since you're now aware of who and what you are, I think I can safely continue the training Scathach and the Sheridans began with you. We'll work a couple of days each week on your shield and your communication powers. We'll also work on visualizing. That's a skill you absolutely must master, and sooner rather than later. We'll start tomorrow evening?"

"Sure, Finn."

Alyssa transferred the journals into the safe, and Finn carried the cardboard box to his truck. If anyone was watching, they'd think Alyssa gave the journals to him for safekeeping.

Alyssa bid her old friend good night and returned to the lonely business of researching her thesis. The fire had gone out of her project, but she was too close to the end to walk away. Doggedly, she waded through piles of books and articles, finding long-forgotten stories and obscure characters. All the while, she wondered which tales and people were mythic and which were cleverly disguised warriors and talismans fighting for and against the gods in the never-ending tug-of-war between good and evil. She also wondered if there were bards among modern druids like Gram and Siobhan, poets who even now were recounting the exploits of warriors battling beyond the mists of modern consciousness. Would she be included, disguised as some bystander who happened to make a magical observation that saved the day? The thought made her laugh, though it came out as sort of a choked gurgle as she remembered the only person she wanted to remember her had forgotten her when she sat right in the same room with him.

⤳

After spending the night on her couch again, Alyssa tidied up her research notes and the box of books and articles from which she'd been working before phoning Ceri. Seeing her friend might lift her spirits.

Dressing in a conservative brown tweed jacket over a black turtleneck and slacks, she tied her new blue scarf around her neck and surprised herself at how it enhanced her eyes and deepened the midnight of her hair. Too bad a certain warrior couldn't see her today. Then again, would he even notice a new scarf?

After Finn had gone home the other night, she'd boxed up the clothes Rowan had left behind. The thought of him moving in with her had frightened and disconcerted her when it appeared it was his plan. Now she lamented that scenario wouldn't exist. She tripped over the box of clothes yet again, so she carried it out to the closet in the foyer. At least his stuff would be readily accessible when he came to fetch it.

The weather hadn't improved, so she slid on a pair of dressy snow boots before she slipped into her red coat and topped her hair with her black beret. Petting Shadow and admonishing him to take care of the place, she armed the security system and let herself out of her house.

Twenty minutes later, Ceri sat across from Alyssa at an off-campus coffee shop and marveled at how much she'd changed.

"Spill, girlfriend. What's going on with you and that incredibly handsome home security expert you picked up?" Ceri asked, her green eyes dancing. "I want details, the more intimate the better." They seated themselves at a table in front of the windows.

Alyssa laughed as she hung her coat on the back of her chair. "You have no sense of propriety, have you?"

"Where you're concerned, none whatsoever." Ceri sat forward, her hands cradling her cup in the middle of the table. "He's is so powerful and smooth when he moves. Tell me, what's he like in bed?"

"Personal question, Ceri." Her voice conveyed an unmistakable edge.

"Don't go all prickly on me, Alys."

"All right, already. He's amazing in bed. He even seemed to like me too. But it turns out, I was a means to an end. He needed me to do my job, and now that I've proved I can do it, he won't be around much."

Alyssa tried not to let her mouth turn down as she admitted the last part aloud, though the pain of it made her die a little inside.

"What do you mean a job? Have you been holding out on me about some security expertise you have?" Ceri grinned over her coffee cup.

"It turns out I have several hidden talents and the potential to develop a few more. Interestingly enough, you share some of those talents, Ceri." Alyssa waited.

"What are you talking about? My talent is selling. I chose real estate, but I could sell anything, I think. After that, I can't do much."

"Except be a great friend who is so beautiful you can make even happily married men have inappropriate fantasies." Alyssa smirked.

Ceri rolled her eyes.

Sobering up, she said, "It seems my interest in Celtic mythology has some deep roots in my ancestry. You're the one friend I have with a true interest in my research. You've even helped me a time or two with obscure facts you just somehow seemed to know." Ceri colored under Alyssa's meaningful stare. "I thought it odd the times it happened, you not being a Celtic scholar and all, but it appears there is a 'logical' explanation for that." She quirked a brow. "You and I are talismans." She sipped her latte and gauged her friend's reaction.

"And Seamus and Rowan are warriors."

Alyssa almost choked on her coffee. "They are. When we met them, they were both looking for their talismans." She edged forward in her chair. "As you clearly already know, warriors had to find their talismans before they reached their twenty-eighth birthdays to avoid death or a fate worse than death. After Rowan found me, we accomplished our first and most important test. We returned the birthday caveat back to age forty-two as it was in ancient times."

Ceri stared at her in disbelief.

"That was my job, to help Rowan balance the playing field between warriors and some spiteful goddesses."

Ceri reached across the table and covered Alyssa's hand. "*Aunt Shanley and I have known for years you were a talisman. You and I were the only two of the warrior community in our school. It's why I so desperately wanted to be your friend.*"

Alyssa gasped. "Why didn't you say something?"

"Your gram was keeping you hidden. We couldn't understand why, and she wouldn't say, but part of her strategy included keeping you ignorant of who and what you are. My aunt strongly disagreed with her, but it wasn't Aunt Shanley's call to make." Ceri squeezed Alyssa's hands. "I can't tell you how many times I wanted to communicate with you telepathically, especially when we were around the mean girls in school, but I couldn't without breaking your grandmother's trust, which I couldn't do and remain your friend."

"Why didn't you say anything after she died?" Alyssa didn't try to hide her hurt.

Her friend gazed at her sympathetically. "Finn said we should wait and see if your warrior found you. If he didn't find you before my warrior found me, then we would tell you when I met my warrior. You would have had all of our protection then."

"That night at the pizzeria, you were communicating with Seamus telepathically, weren't you? That's how I ended up catching a ride home with Rowan while you took Seamus home."

"I felt bad about that, but your warrior had found you, and I had to stay out of the way and let nature take its course. Now will you please explain to me what you mean by Rowan will only be coming around when he needs you? By the way you're acting, your feelings for him run deep, which is what's supposed to happen between a talisman and her warrior."

Alyssa looked around at the full tables in the coffee shop. "Can we finish this conversation in a more private setting? I feel conspicuous telling you about what happened with all these people nearby."

"Sure. Let's pop over to my place since it's a lot closer than yours."

"Now don't get your panties in a wad," Ceri started as she let herself and Alyssa into her condo. "We all were doing as Gram insisted. Would you have believed me if one day I happened to mention you're a special type of person who has no counterpart in the general population? Quite frankly, you had a terrible time believing Rowan until Morgan showed herself to you."

Alyssa gasped. "How did you know all that?"

"You're not keeping your shield up. Maybe it's because you're new to all this or maybe it's because I'm your best friend no matter what, so I know you well with or without the aid of telepathy," Ceri replied matter-of-factly as she tossed her keys onto a table by the door and headed into her kitchen.

"I'm not sure if knowing my background would or wouldn't have helped me with what happened over the past few days." Alyssa sighed as she removed her coat and boots. Ceri was right. How could she blame her best friend for Gram's decision? How could she blame Gram for trying so desperately to protect her?

"So, what happened?" Ceri uncorked a bottle of merlot and poured generous portions into two wine glasses.

Returning to her spacious and ultra-modern living room, she handed Alyssa a glass before seating herself with her feet tucked beneath her on her eggplant-colored couch.

Alyssa paced around the room for a few minutes sipping her

wine and gathering her thoughts before she sat on the love seat at right angles to her friend.

"It seems Rowan and I are descended from the same family patriarch through the bloodlines of his twin sons. Apparently, there was a prophecy stating that when the bloodlines linked up in the form of a warrior and his talisman, we'd have to face the Morrigan's test and do better than our common ancestor had done if we wanted to defeat her and thwart her from taking more young warriors than the fates decreed were her due."

"Did you do that?" Ceri's expression was avid fascination.

Alyssa recounted the short version. "We faced an ancient zombie champion and defeated him. Morgan watched and raged but could do nothing about it. Afterward, Scathach returned me to Rowan's family home where most of the other warriors involved in the battle returned. The men congratulated themselves on winning another battle, and a warrior named Duncan and his druid wife Siobhan drove Finn and me home. The end."

"Whoa! You're not getting off that easy." Ceri placed her wine glass on the table. "What was Finn doing there? Why is this Duncan married to a druid instead of to his talisman? Why did you drive home rather than visualize yourselves home?"

Alyssa gaped at her. It was so new and therefore so difficult to remember Ceri knew more about this world than she did. At last, she gathered herself and answered. "Finn showed up when Scathach summoned him to watch over Gram's journals while the rest of us were away taking on Morgan and Maeve. Duncan and Siobhan—"

"Maeve was involved too?" Ceri interrupted.

"Yes. As part of a triple goddess, the two of them work in tandem. Anyway, Duncan met his talisman, a woman named Jennifer Carlin, who takes care of his warrior needs as a talisman should, but they had no romantic connection, no spark. Apparently, that happens with some warrior couples."

Ceri's incredulous stare compelled Alyssa to defend her new

friends. "Duncan and Siobhan met after Duncan had found Jennifer, his talisman. Siobhan resisted Duncan for as long as she could because she too knows that a warrior should be with his talisman, but in the end, he was too persistent. They married with Jennifer's blessing." Alyssa sipped her wine. "In fact, she was Duncan's best woman at their wedding," she added with a smile. "Jennifer lives next door to them, and Siobhan's protection spells cover both of their homes together. It seems to work for them. Siobhan is Seamus's sister by the way."

Ceri gave a slow nod, but otherwise didn't interrupt again.

"Anyway, we drove home because I don't know how to visualize yet—don't worry, Finn has plans to take care of that," she hastily added at Ceri's incredulous stare. "Plus, we had Shadow with us. Does that answer your questions?" She gulped a big swig of wine and focused on the lovely warmth it spread through her body. Until she sat with her friend, she hadn't acknowledged how cold she felt inside.

"My aunt told me something one time about Gram being married to a warrior. Was that true?"

"Yes, why?"

"Maybe that's why you don't find it strange with Duncan and Siobhan, but it's highly irregular for a warrior to marry anyone other than his talisman."

"Maybe I don't find it strange that Gram married a warrior because until a week ago, I didn't know what that meant. You also might recall I never knew my grandfather, but according to Gram's journals, he didn't find his talisman in time, and he loved my grandmother, so they married and had a daughter together." Alyssa stood and paced the room. "Gram's spells kept him safe for five years after his twenty-eighth birthday even when he had no talisman, so she must have done something right."

She wearied of feeling off-balance and out of the loop. The more she thought about it, the more she believed the secret her friend kept from her all these years was far less defensible than Duncan and Siobhan's relationship or that of her grandparents.

Ceri sighed. "Let's not argue. I liked Seamus a lot when I met him, so chances are I'll like his sister when we meet. What I want to know is why you think you and Rowan are like Duncan and his talisman."

Sitting back down, she closed her eyes and collected herself before she looked Ceri in the eye and bared her heart. "Rowan made me want him like I have never wanted anyone, and he was amazing. Then Scathach put me through probably years of training in a few short days, and right as I seemed to be making progress, Morgan struck."

Ceri gasped, but Alyssa plowed on. "She tried to kill me with one of her rogue warriors, but he couldn't do the job. So, she kidnapped me and took me to Maeve's stronghold where the two of them had quite a good time at my expense." Thinking about Maeve's particular tortures nearly undid her, and she finished her wine in one go.

Ceri stood up, went out to her kitchen, and came back with the bottle, refilling Alyssa's glass without comment.

"Anyway, after it was all over and we returned to the Sheridan compound, Rowan ignored me. I took the hint and returned home a couple of days ago with Duncan and Siobhan. Since I've returned home, Rowan hasn't once tried to contact me. Maybe not marrying my warrior is a family tradition."

"Oh, Alys. I'm so sorry—about everything. I can see how much you're hurting. How 'bout if you spend the night with me? We can order in, rent some movies, drink copious amounts of wine... What do you say?"

"As much as I'd prefer not to face my empty house, I do have a rather large and fuzzy roommate who will take offense if I take you up on your offer. Thanks though. Speaking of Shadow, I'd probably better go home to him. I've been out all day." She set down her untouched second glass of wine and uncurled herself from Ceri's comfy love seat.

"I wish you'd stay. There's something bothering me about your return home. Maybe I should spend the night with you."

"Ceri, I'll be fine. Between Gram's old spells, Siobhan's new spells, the security system Rowan and Seamus installed before we left, and Shadow and Finn, I have more protection than one person could possibly ever need." She glanced around Ceri's apartment. "You, on the other hand, could use some." She reached into her bag and extracted the special bookmark she'd been saving for her friend's birthday. "I made this for you. I intended to give it to you for a special occasion, but something Rowan said about my designs made me think you could use it sooner."

"After I saw the ones you made for Gram, I always hoped you'd make one of these for me." Ceri stroked her fingers over the threads. "I'll treasure this, you know I will, but what did Rowan say about it?"

"He said there was some sort of magic in the design and the choice of color. I chose this green because it matches your eyes." She gazed into the middle distance. "Weirdly enough, I picked a unique aquamarine for another design." She returned her focus to Ceri. "Turns out it matched Rowan's eyes, and the design is an exact match to a necklace he always wears. Maybe I'm some sort of hybrid druid-talisman or something." The last bit came out as almost as an afterthought. "We'll talk more later. Thanks for the wine, the pep talk, and the shoulder. I needed all of them." She gave her friend a warm hug.

"Let me know you arrived home safe. I can't seem to shake some bad vibes. Maybe it's the after effects of hearing your story, but don't take any chances, promise?"

"Yes, Mom. I'll be careful." She laughed half-heartedly and headed out the door and back to her own place.

CHAPTER THIRTY-TWO

LYSSA AWOKE TO the not-so-subtle banging of someone at her front door. As she slipped into her bulky terrycloth robe, she noted with some dread that Shadow hadn't barked a warning to the stranger who so rudely and insistently wanted into her house in the middle of the night. When she reached the door, she flipped on the porch light, peered out the small window high in her door, and gasped at the sight of the man standing impatiently on the other side of it.

She remembered to disarm the security system before cautiously opening the door. "It's the middle of the night. Why are you here? What's wrong?" Worry trembled in her voice.

Blowing into his hands, Rowan said, "Can we have this discussion inside please? It's damn cold out here."

"Sure." Trepidation surged through her at the anger pulsing off him and echoing in his voice. She opened the door enough to allow Rowan entrance, which proved difficult with Shadow dancing in delight at the back of her legs.

He stepped across the threshold, shrinking her great room with his size and the intense menace he exuded. Staring her down, he took the door from her, forcing her to take a step back, and closed and locked it behind himself before automatically resetting the security system.

Alyssa couldn't understand why he rearmed her system when he was in the house with her. Whatever threats were out there could surely breach a civilian security system. He was all that stood between her and the supernatural forces threatening both of them with or without the electronic system. He was also the biggest threat to her tenuous hold on her emotions. His actions told her he planned on staying a while. The prospect didn't make her feel any safer.

"Would you kindly explain to me why you left me without so much as a 'see you around?' I rescued your sweet ass, and what do I get? A locked bedroom door in the night and an empty house the next morning. Really, lady, I thought you had better manners," he said through gritted teeth.

Dumbfounded, it took her several seconds to recover.

"Is it common practice in the warrior community to trade sex for acts of heroism? I'm still new to all this, so you'll have to excuse my ignorance." Her words dripped acid.

"Now you're just being nasty. It's common practice whenever anyone does something helpful for you to say thank you. Even civilians do it sometimes," Rowan responded sarcastically as he removed his coat and boots.

"What about that little matter of you completely ignoring me for the entirety of the night we returned? I tried to thank you, but you had your shield so firmly in place I don't think even Scathach could have gotten through to you." She crossed her arms and stared him down. "Not once did you even ask what those two witches put me through while I spent a little time as their *guest*, the bait to trap you and destroy you. You're welcome for the help, by the way." Her anger approximating Rowan's, she turned and stomped back into her great room.

Shadow stood beside his mistress and emitted a low whimper.

Petting him absently, she turned and stared intently at Rowan, her hackles clearly raised.

As Rowan stared back at his furious talisman, she thought she heard him mutter, "Did I have it all wrong?"

She watched with fascination as all the fire seemed to go out of him at once.

He modulated his tone. "Do you mind if I take off my jacket and boots? It seems we have some things to discuss."

"It appears you're already doing that but fine. Whatever." After switching on a lamp, she pushed aside the blanket and pillow she'd been using on the love seat, sat in the opened space, and waited. Shadow parked himself between the chair and the love seat, looking almost comical with his brows moving up and down as he watched Rowan and her.

Rowan opened the closet to hang up his coat, paused, and turned to Alyssa, his voice once again filled with anger. "Why are my clothes in a box? Were you planning to send them to me, or did you have something else in mind?"

"When I saw you last, you weren't talking to me, and you've made no effort to contact me since I returned home three days ago, so I boxed up your clothes. I didn't need anyone to draw me a map about where I stood with you, and I thought you might need your clothes back. However, donating them to charity doesn't sound like a bad idea."

Rowan stalked over to her and stared menacingly down at her. *I don't know if I want to shake you or throw you over my shoulder and carry you off to the bedroom to settle this.*

"*Now* you let down your shield? By the way, neither of your options is very good at the moment," she said, looking up at him defiantly.

He froze. "You heard that?"

"Yes. Do you want to try again?" She lifted a haughty eyebrow.

He stared at her for a few long seconds before finally seating himself on the chair. "It seems we have some misunderstandings." Holding his hands between his knees, he explained, "I wasn't ignoring you at Mom and Dad's. I was trying to give you space. Finn suggested that, and since he was the one you ran to for comfort, I thought it best to listen to him." He sighed. "As for not contacting you, Seamus and I were stranded in hell's own snow storm with absolutely no cell service or internet connection, and you had your shield firmly in place." He raised his brows, clearly demanding an explanation for that.

After a beat, she said, "Finn reached out to me, asked after me when your brother and sister-in-law subjected me to the inquisition before we'd even been formally introduced. Nothing that happened in the training room prepared me for what I went through at Morgan and Maeve's pleasure let alone for the experience of a live battle where the stakes were life and death." She reached for Shadow. "I guess all of you are so used to it that it never occurred to you I might need a little help dealing with it all afterward."

Rowan flinched but didn't interrupt.

She sat back against the cushions and pulled the blanket over herself. "Anyway, you did what warriors do, I guess. You relived every nuance of the battle and did your warrior-bonding thing. I've read plenty of Celtic tales to recognize what I saw in your parents' dining room that night."

She plucked at the blanket. "It didn't help me though. It only reminded me of the terror I felt during the entire ordeal. So instead of ruining your evening, I went to bed."

"Yeah, across the hall behind a locked door. You want to explain what that was all about?"

Alyssa blinked at the hurt she heard in his tone. "You didn't seem interested in me any longer, and I didn't want to impose myself or make erroneous assumptions. If you wanted me in your bed, all you had to do was knock on the door—or visualize yourself through it. I locked it so Rio couldn't make more nasty accusations. Why he thinks something is going on between Seamus and me is beyond my comprehension, but then I don't know very much about warriors, it seems." Though she tried, she couldn't seem to keep a tiny note of sadness out of her voice. Nor could she deny the searing pain of a sudden vision of Rowan with a particularly beautiful blonde who appeared to be satisfying him quite well.

He dropped to his knees in front of her. "Alyssa, anything Maeve showed you is in the distant past. I hadn't slept with anyone for at least a year before I met you. No matter what she showed you, none of those women made me feel the way you make me feel. Please believe me," he begged.

"Alyssa! Listen to me! After having had you, I could never be satisfied with anyone else. You have to believe me. Maeve lied to you. It's what she does. Don't let her win," Rowan desperately pleaded, taking her icy hands in his.

She blinked and looked at him as if seeing him for the first time. "You want me?" she whispered, a fear-filled kind of hope blooming inside her. After spending so much time since the battle believing she'd be another Jennifer Carlin only without the benefit of merely sisterly feelings for her warrior, she could hardly dare hope for what he seemed to be saying.

"Alyssa, even without the built-in advantage of warriors and talismans being destined to want each other, I was attracted to you. I'm lucky you're my talisman, or I easily could have been another King Arthur loving another man's talisman no matter what the cost to the other warrior, the talisman, or me." He rubbed his hands over hers. "You had me when you walked into my office looking to hire a security firm." Incredulous, she raised her eyebrows, and he smiled.

"When we engaged in conversation, I discovered you to be intelligent, funny, interesting—everything I've always desired in a woman. When I came home with you the first time, I admit to being worried about what sex would be like since I knew exactly who you were and what our relationship was going to be." He gave her hands a gentle squeeze before joining her on the love seat. "Then we went to bed, and I discovered that as long as I live, I will never find another woman who makes me as happy in the sack as you do, Pixie-girl." Fingering the collar of her bathrobe, he grinned. "Even this incredibly ugly robe I often have the misfortune of seeing you wear can't dampen my desire for you."

"I don't wear it to be sexy. I wear it to be warm." She sniffed.

"I can think of some ways to warm you that don't require any clothes at all." He wickedly waggled his eyebrows as he gazed at her. "In fact, I think we need to banish any lingering doubt about my feelings for you that Maeve may have managed to plant in your head." He grabbed the sash of her robe, giving it a none-too-gentle tug. "This towel you insist on wearing will work quite nicely as a chamois when I'm washing my truck this spring," he teased.

"You can't do that," she squeaked. "This was a gift from Gram." She tried to wrest the sash from him.

"Clearly, your grandmother had an agenda when she gave it to you. But we took care of that when I moved in. Speaking of which, I'm still living here, in case you were wondering. You can put my clothes back tomorrow." He smirked at her and placed his hands on the lapels of her robe.

"You have a lot of nerve, Rowan Sheridan. Ordering me around in my own home." The fire went out of her as she sensed their relationship had made a major shift.

"*Our* home. And I'll be doing a lot of ordering you around when we're home since you get to give all the orders when we're on the battlefield. It's only fair." He grinned. With a flick of his wrists, he opened her robe.

"What do you think you're doing?"

"Disrobing you, obviously." He tried to be serious as he delivered the pun, but he couldn't maintain the façade with his eyes dancing and a grin tugging at the corner of his mouth.

"You think you can storm into *my* house in the middle of the night, rage at me for a bit, tell me you've moved in, and then drag me off to bed without a by-your-leave? Seriously? You have more nerve than any one man—"

Rowan cut her off mid-rant with a hard kiss before whispering against her mouth, "Yes."

He stood and pulled her off the love seat and tossed her over his shoulder.

"You. Are. Unbelievable!" she sputtered.

"That's what we need to work on. You believing in me," he said as he purposefully strode down the hallway to the bedroom.

The indignity of being carried off to bed like some medieval prize gave Alyssa a vague sense of sisterhood with some of the women about whom she'd read in her research. What she'd never admit was she kind of liked being a prize. Apparently, Rowan did want her as much as he said he did.

When they reached the bedroom, he reached up and supported her back as he dropped her onto her bed. Then he stepped back to remove his clothing. As he pulled his thermal shirt over his head, her cell phone rang on the nightstand beside the bed.

Holding his shirt in his hand, he said, "Who is calling you at three o'clock in the morning?"

"I have no idea." She sat up quickly and grabbed her phone. The caller I.D. revealed Ceri on the other end of the line, and her heart leaped into her throat. "Ceri, what's wrong?" she gasped into her phone.

"You tell me. I woke up to intense pain, and I sensed it was yours. Are you okay?"

"I'm fine. I can't imagine what you were feeling."

Rowan grabbed the phone out of Alyssa's hand. "Hello, Ceri. Rowan here. Alyssa's going to be a whole lot better in a few minutes if you'll leave us be. Good night." He clicked off the phone and put it on airplane mode before setting it back on the table.

"I'm starting to think you're rather heavy-handed. We need to work on that," Alyssa said as she watched him shuck his jeans and boxers in one smooth motion.

"What we need to work on is removing that hideous robe and whatever you're wearing underneath it."

Alyssa felt a momentary panic. The robe was one thing, but the T-shirt underneath it belonged to Rowan. She'd decided to wear it to bed because it smelled like him, which simultaneously tortured and comforted her. What would he think when he saw it?

"Now, Alyssa."

Slowly, she stood and dropped the robe, revealing one of his black T-shirts over a pair of lacy white panties.

"I've never seen anything so sexy in my life. Even when you thought we had no future, you wanted me close to you." He took her in his arms and held her, his hands smoothing up and down her back before he grasped the hem of the shirt.

"As sexy as my shirt looks on you, I like you even better without it." He lifted the shirt off her torso. Leaving her arms entangled in the sleeves, he guided her arms over his head, effectively tying them together as he pulled her into his embrace.

Looking deeply into her eyes, he said, "I love you so much, Alyssa. No matter what happens in our lives, never doubt that."

Backing his words with actions, he took her mouth in a hot kiss that sent her senses reeling, and she hugged his huge, hard body close to her. Needing to touch him everywhere, she melded herself to him from shoulders to knees. He tightened his hold on her as he slipped his tongue inside her mouth, their kiss flashing into a hot fire of need.

Somewhere as Rowan kissed her, Alyssa experienced a tiny pop in her head, like equalizing pressure, followed by a sense of absolute trust and calm. Rowan loved her no matter what. She interweaved her emotions to that thought and kissed her warrior deeply, all of Maeve's torturous pictures fleeing her mind.

Seemingly of its own volition, her leg slid up, hooking over his hips and pulling him closer to her. He broke their kiss and panted. "Love, I haven't finished undressing you." He slipped from her embrace, hooking the elastic of her panties with his thumbs and smoothing his hands down her legs, taking her panties with them.

After settling her back onto the bed, he palmed his hands up and down her legs. She shivered in anticipation of his touch as he leaned forward to kiss the tops of her thighs, burning a path with his mouth to the sensitive spot along her groin. Sighing, she relaxed her legs, opening a little for him. "More, Pixie-girl. Wider. Make room for me," he whispered, his lips feathering her skin.

Her body hummed in anticipation of his next move. He kissed his way to her sex, tasting her, flicking his tongue over her swollen nub before teasing her folds with his fingers until she cried out, her hands fisted in his hair. Giving no quarter, he blew on her, inflaming her further.

As she calmed down from the first storm of his lovemaking, he came down on top of her. "Let me in, Pixie-girl. I want to feel all of you, your passion and your fire, wrapped all around me."

"Yes," she breathed and welcomed him into her body, wrapping her arms around his shoulders, her legs around his hips. As they came together in the oldest, most intimate embrace, they opened their minds simultaneously to each other, their connection complete.

"Jesus, Alyssa, no one could ever feel as good as you do. You drive me completely wild, Pixie-girl."

"Rowan, I never want to be anywhere but in your arms. I love you so much."

Then neither of them was thinking much of anything at all as they gave each other everything.

EPILOGUE

THE WEDDING TOOK place in Alyssa's backyard on the evening of the summer solstice. Ceri stood in as chief wedding planner and shoulder. Her nerves frazzled over her master's thesis and her on-going talisman training, Alyssa would occasionally become fed up with the whole wedding ordeal and determine to ask Rowan if they could elope—an idea so abhorrent to her friend that Ceri nearly had a stroke every time Alyssa mentioned it.

Holding a small jeweler's box, Sian entered Alyssa's bedroom as Ceri helped her to dress. Right as Sian opened it to reveal a golden Celtic cross pendant resting there, Owen sauntered into the room.

"May I, Sian?"

His wife extended the box to him. After he extracted a necklace matching the gold one Rowan always wore, he moved behind Alyssa. Carefully avoiding her tiara and veil, he settled the pendant in the hollow of her throat while she angled her head and held her hair away so he could do up the clasp.

Rejoining his wife, he settled his arm around Sian's shoulders, giving her a loving squeeze.

"We will treasure you always, Alyssa," Owen said.

"Because of you, our son is celebrating this most special day rather than mourning it," Sian added, her eyes misting.

Finn interrupted them. "My, my, missy, if your gram could see you now. Look at you. You make an old man's heart turn over in his chest. Walking you down the aisle will be the proudest moment of my life." He took out his handkerchief and pretended to wipe a bit of dust from his eye. Owen discreetly looked away from him while the women openly beamed.

Walking up the aisle, Alyssa only had eyes for Rowan. When she smiled at him, all the love she felt for him radiated from her face. Like in a fairy tale, she lit up the space beneath the canopy set up in her backyard when she took her place by Rowan's side.

The wedding proceeded in a blur for bride and groom. However, when they had time to talk after their last guests left, both remembered the lingering kiss sealing them together forever in front of their friends and family. Alyssa said she'd never felt so cherished. Rowan said he'd never felt so heroic as when they held each other and turned off the world for the space of that kiss.

When they were alone and spent, they shared other bits that each remembered: the wedding cake that said "Happy Birthday, Rowan," a feeling of peace when the druid included Gram and Alyssa's parents in his wedding prayer, the way Shadow seemed to cover his ears with his paws when the bagpiper launched into a reel at the reception. All of it was so important yet secondary to the moment when they became forever one.

Alyssa snuggled closer into Rowan's embrace and inhaled deeply of his outdoors and musk scent. They'd already taken each other twice, and though they were exhausted from their triumphant day, they each knew they'd have trouble letting the other one sleep through their first night as a married couple. *So this how a honeymoon feels,* Alyssa thought.

"Yes, Pixie-girl, it is. But this honeymoon is going to last for the rest of our lives."

When Rowan listened in on her thoughts this time, Alyssa didn't mind at all.

Thank you for reading *Talisman*.

Turn the page for an excerpt from *Warrior*, Book Two in the Talisman series. Look for it in March 2020.

CHAPTER ONE

Summer Solstice

RIO SHERIDAN TOOK a long pull of his beer and watched the party with thinly veiled disgust.

The woman is shameless. A single talisman in a party full of warriors, and she flirts outrageously. He shifted his gaze to his fellow warrior. *Seamus isn't any better. He must have tried his sign on her, which obviously didn't work, yet he acts like they have plans for later. Maybe they do. After all, his sister thought nothing of stealing another talisman's warrior.* He snorted. *Probably a family trait.*

"Hey, little brother. No one needs to breach your shield to know what you're thinking," Rowan remarked as he joined Rio at the edge of the reception.

Sipping his beer, Rio didn't take his eyes off Seamus Lochlann dancing with Ceri Ross. "I think you should be careful around your new wife's best friend. She doesn't appear to have any scruples about horning in on warriors who aren't hers."

"Ceri? Without her, we wouldn't be enjoying my *very* happy wedding day," Rowan said, his tone warning Rio not spoil it. "She did all the work for this reception so

Alyssa could finish her master's thesis, earn her degree, and still marry me on the day we wanted. I owe her a ton, and I won't have you attacking her based on some half-assed idea she's a flirt."

Rio shrugged.

Rowan arched a brow at his brother and smirked. "Maybe instead of judging her, you should ask her to dance."

Rio ignored Rowan's suggestion. "Speaking of your new wife, Alyssa looks lovely today. You're a lucky man. You found your talisman in time, married her on your birthday no less, and thumbed your nose at the goddesses so determined to keep you apart." Rio sipped his beer. "I wouldn't be too cocky if I were you though. The day isn't over."

Rowan gave him the side-eye. "Between Alyssa's grandmother's protections over this house and Siobhan's reinforcements, I think we're safe for the day." He glanced up at the knotwork design on the outdoor canopy. "Morgan and Maeve are probably in Scotland or Ireland licking their wounds from the sweet little comedown we gave them in L.A. last winter. Still, I'd rather not upset the cosmos by discussing them on my wedding day." He clapped a hand on Rio's shoulder. "Lighten up and join the party. Today's a great day, and Alyssa and I want you to celebrate—please."

"I've been doing a number on the imported beer you're serving. I'm celebrating." Rio laughed hollowly and moved off to join his twin, Riley, and Riley's wife, Lynnette.

Being the last unbonded and unmarried Sheridan compounded his sour mood. That and it didn't matter where he strolled among the wedding guests, he could still hear Ceri's tinkling laugh like happy chimes on the wind.

Standing beside his twin, his attention zeroed in on one stunning Ceri Ross.

She'd twisted her hip-length, honey blond hair into some sort of braids and curls concoction that fell gracefully from the side of her head over her right breast. The light green satin sheath she wore deepened her sparkling green eyes. The dress hugged her long lithe body, outlining every luscious curve, and his hands itched to smooth over the fabric clinging to her exquisite figure.

In a moment he'd later regard as sheer weakness, he downed the last of his beer and strolled over to where Ceri stood in animated conversation with Alyssa's old protector, Finn Daly.

"Afternoon, Finn. You clean up good for an old warrior," Rio said, unapologetically interrupting them.

"You do too. And who are you calling old?" Finn puffed himself up. "I think I had a few moves you didn't know at Scathach's last training session." His lively gray eyes twinkled.

"Thanks for going easy on me. I'd already had quite a day before you showed up," Rio said with a smile.

"It's your story. Tell it any way you want, Rio." Finn winked.

"Will I put you out too much if I steal your companion for a dance?"

"Not at all. I'd much rather see you dancing than scowling by yourself over your beer."

Rio ignored the old man's barb and turned his attention to Ceri. "Shall we?"

He placed his hand on the small of her back, propelled her toward the dance floor, and took her into his arms. His hand engulfed her slender hand as he held it loosely. Resting his other hand behind her, he guided her around the dance floor. Though he kept his touch light, she tensed in his arms.

Leaning in, Rio whispered in her ear, "Relax. It's only a dance. We're not making a commitment here."

His breath fanning her ear had the opposite effect, judging from the way she missed a step. Tightening his hold on her, he pulled her against his chest. Ceri gasped. He willed himself to remain relaxed while every nerve ending came alive with her response and the touch of her lush curves against his body.

She felt even better than he imagined, all toned and sensuous.

Like a siren, she called to him everywhere their bodies touched. Like a siren, she was dangerous, even deadly. But like the ancient mariners, he couldn't resist her. Instead of righting her when she'd stumbled, he'd pulled her closer, relishing her firm round breasts against his chest, her soft hand resting easily in his palm, her lovely toned thighs occasionally brushing his.

"You did a nice job with the wedding. Rowan told me he owes you," he said blandly to break the tense silence.

"Thank you. Alyssa and I have been best friends since we were six, and I knew she didn't have time to plan this. I wanted to keep her from eloping because selfishly, I wanted to be part of her wedding day," Ceri blurted. Her face pinkened, and she looked away from him.

Rio tried to reconcile her gushy answer with the picture of sophistication and poise she radiated to the world. *Huh. I think I make her nervous.*

"Eloping doesn't sound like a half-bad idea, but I think my parents would never have let Rowan hear the end of it if he hadn't included everyone on his big day, especially with today being his birthday and all."

"Did you see I had the caterer include 'Happy Birthday Rowan' on the wedding cake?"

"No, I hadn't noticed. I just grabbed the biggest piece before Seamus could beat me to it."

"Oh." Ceri's face fell. "Well, Alyssa and Rowan seemed to like it."

The disappointment in her voice gave him heartburn. When the song ended, Ceri stepped away from him like he'd scalded her.

"Thanks for the dance. Hope you enjoy the rest of the party." She turned on her heel and headed straight for the back door of Alyssa's house.

That was smooth, dumbass. She all but ran away from you. He scrubbed a hand over his face. *Why do I feel so attracted to such an obvious flirt?* Glancing up, he caught Seamus's eye and scowled. *Who flirts with everyone but me? What does he have that's so appealing to the ladies while I make them nervous? 'Course, Ceri Ross probably should feel nervous if she knew what I've been thinking about her.*

The wedding and reception were held in the former Alyssa Macaulay's backyard, complete with a temporary dance floor set under an awning elaborately painted with Celtic designs. Ceri hustled out of the reception and through the back door of the house. Making a beeline for the bathroom in the hall, she closed and locked the door and sat down hard on the edge of the tub, her emotions roiling.

All day she'd been enjoying compliments on her planning and hard work, but maybe she'd been too preoccupied with her part rather than the reason for the day in the first place. Did Rio think her selfish and full of herself? Her silly response to his blasé comment about the wedding didn't seem to improve his low opinion of her, the one he'd made clear not long after they'd met last winter. *For someone who can usually take care of herself, I wasn't much out there.*

Taking a deep breath, she tried to calm her swirling emotions. She checked her appearance in the mirror and tried to think of mundane items to disguise the distress she saw in her eyes. It was a trick Aunt Shanley made her practice repeatedly as part of her talisman training. "Never let the enemy guess what's going on inside your head," Shanley had admonished her so often it had become her mantra.

When she was ready enough to face the party with at least the façade of her usual cheerful self, she exited the bathroom and returned to the reception. Promptly, she sought out Siobhan MacManus, to talk to. During the rehearsal the evening before, she'd noticed Rio pointedly avoided Siobhan and her husband, Duncan. Perhaps if Ceri spent time talking to them, Rio wouldn't feel obligated to ask her to dance or even to speak with her again before the end of the afternoon.

As she made her way to where Siobhan and Duncan sat near the refreshment table, Seamus intercepted her.

"What happened between you and Rio? You rushed into the house and he went straight to the bar right after the two of you danced," he said as he twirled her over the dance floor.

Ceri looked up at the burly blond giant, deliberately widened her eyes, and teased, "Do you need details about how I realized in the middle of that dance I needed to use the ladies' room? I don't think I've taken a break from the party since I joined you to witness the wedding hours ago."

"So that was it." Seamus's speculative look made her uncomfortable. "Why do I have the distinct impression the two of you weren't getting along?"

Tilting her head, she asked, "Were you spying on us?"

"I just noticed you from the edge of the dance floor, Ceri. I saw you blush and his face stay blank. I've known him long enough to know he's not happy about something when he looks like that."

He dipped her, and she gasped, but his ploy didn't work. "We were talking about the wedding. He isn't one for the finer points of wedding planning and execution, and I may have let my feelings get hurt. Now I'm over it. Satisfied?"

"For the record, you're quite welcome to plan my wedding. I rather like what you did with this one. Maybe that can be your next business venture when you tire of selling real estate." His smile mollified her.

"You're a very nice man, Seamus Lochlann. Too bad I'm not your talisman. You at least appreciate my considerable party-planning skills." She batted her eyes at him.

The day they'd met, Seamus and Ceri had figured out they weren't destined for each other after he tried his sign and discovered that she wasn't his. However, she enjoyed his easy company. Unlike Rio Sheridan. Out of the corner of her eye, she caught him watching them. Silently, he brooded from his place by the bar, and a shiver stole over her.

⤳

"Alyssa, I hate to ask, but may I borrow your car? Shanley drove off without me, and I doubt you need a chaperone on your wedding night," Ceri said with a grin. The stragglers had left the reception, and the caterers had dismantled the tents, loaded up the tables and chairs into their vans, and driven away minutes earlier. Ceri assumed only she, Alyssa, and Rowan were left at Alyssa's house.

Then Rio walked down the hall and entered the kitchen.

"Oh hey. Rio, I didn't realize you were still here. If it's not too much trouble, could you give Ceri a lift back to town? It seems Shanley drove off without her," Alyssa said.

Ceri's heart dropped into her stomach.

"Your *aunt* left you? Don't you mean your date?" Rio scowled.

Confused, Ceri said, "I didn't have a date."

Wrapping his arm around Alyssa, Rowan interrupted. "Listen kids, no fighting on the way to town."

"Alys, about using your car—"

"That's silly, Ceri. Rio is headed to town too." Rowan stared down his brother. "He can be civil enough to give a pretty lady a lift, can't you little brother?"

"Come on, Ceri. I think the lovebirds want some privacy."

It wasn't the first time in the six years since Alyssa had bought her house that Ceri wished ten miles didn't separate it from town.

"Congratulations again you two. I'm so happy you found each other." Ceri hugged Alyssa then Rowan.

She picked up her ivory shawl from where she'd laid it over the back of the love seat in the great room and walked to the front door. Desperately, she filled her head with mundane items like trees, peanut butter sandwiches, and patio furniture to try to calm down and reveal none of her trepidation about the ride into town with the man to whom she was so attracted and who felt nothing except maybe loathing for her.

Once they were in Rio's big black pickup truck, she couldn't keep her mind on anything ordinary, which likely meant her shield wasn't up. So she attempted conversation. "Do you work for your family's business too, like Rowan and Seamus?"

"Yeah."

"Oh." She watched the scenery on the mountain road then tried again. "Do you work out of the local office or one of the other branches?"

After several awkward moments when he didn't answer, she snapped, "I'm not planning to write an exposé. I was trying to make conversation. Usually the polite thing to do is to ask about the other person who politely replies with *something*."

Rio gave her a side-eye before returning his attention to the twisty road. "I usually work with Riley in the western part of the state, but I'll be filling in for Rowan while he takes Alyssa on their honeymoon. Polite enough for you?"

"Gosh that was difficult—and enlightening." She crossed her arms and stared unseeingly out the passenger window.

"How long have you known you were a talisman?"

"That was random."

"The polite thing to do is to ask about the other person who *politely* replies with *something*."

She blinked and wondered about his hostility, but responded anyway. "Since I was tiny, since my parents died," she said quietly.

Seeming to ignore her answer, Rio asked, "How long have you known Alyssa was a talisman?"

"Almost from the moment we met when we were six."

"And in two decades, you didn't tell her? You didn't help her with her training?"

The accusation in his tone stunned her.

"Like your parents did, I imagine, my aunt warned me not to seek out other kids like me and not to give it away if I met or sensed other kids like me. Doing so would put us all in danger, which was enough when I was tiny." She tightened her wrap around herself. "As I grew older and more rebellious, I was determined to talk to Alyssa about it, but her grandmother forbade it, and I knew better than to mess with a druid of Afton's caliber."

"You're saying Alyssa's grandmother deliberately kept her ignorant? *Unbelievable.*"

"Ask Finn. They fought about it often, but Afton wouldn't budge. Having seen her whole family die at the hands of the Morrigan caused her to try to protect Alyssa by keeping her ignorant."

Ceri stared at Rio's knuckles turning white as he gripped the steering wheel. "Her ignorance nearly cost my brother and her their lives. Too bad her grandmother was a healer rather than a prophet. Maybe she would have done things better."

"Who are you to criticize?" Ceri bristled. "Afton did everything she could to help Alyssa be ready when the time came, if it did, without telling her who she really was. Why do you think Alyssa is a Celtic scholar? Why do you think Alyssa's house even now is nearly an impregnable fortress against unruly gods with vicious intents?" She sat back hard against her seat. "You're too quick to judge before you have all the facts, Rio Sheridan." Folding her arms protectively over her chest, she looked resolutely out the passenger window. Conversation didn't seem important any more.

"If someone close to her"—he took his eyes from the road for a minute—"would have helped her, Seamus wouldn't have had to teach Alyssa how to shield her thoughts, and the whole family wouldn't have had to rally at our training room while Scathach gave Alyssa a crash course in talisman training that left no time for visualization, something Rowan's been teaching her over the past few months. And she still hasn't mastered it."

His vibrating anger filled the cab of the truck. Ceri remained quiet. What more did he want her to say?

"Damn it, Alyssa should have been well trained when Rowan met her, and you, as her 'best friend'"—he air-quoted with one hand—"should have insisted on it. Especially after her twenty-first birthday."

They rode the rest of the way to town in silence. When they reached the city limits, Ceri tersely directed Rio to her condo and barely thanked him for the ride as she scrambled out of his truck. Hugging her shawl to herself, she all but ran to her front door.

Before she could slide her key into the lock, she gasped as Rio placed his big hand on her shoulder and turned her toward him.

"I didn't mean to piss you off, Ceri. I just can't understand why Alyssa's grandmother left her so woefully unprepared and you were complicit in that. I also don't understand why I can't stop myself from doing this when I know better."

Answering Ceri's unspoken question, he cupped her face in his hands and kissed her. When their lips met, her senses exploded, and the gentle kiss he promised with a barely-there caress morphed into something dark and intense in half a heartbeat. She opened for him, their tongues dancing like they'd done this together many times rather than once.

When he finally tore his mouth away from hers, she was stunned. Gingerly, she touched her fingertips to her kiss-bruised lips.

"Sorry. I couldn't resist. Goodbye, Ceri," he said, his voice hoarse. Turning on his heel, he strode determinedly to his truck, climbed into it, and backed out of her driveway without even once looking at her while she watched after him long after she could no longer hear the truck's engine humming in the still summer twilight.

ACKNOWLEDGEMENTS

Thank you for reading *Talisman*. Writing a book has been my dream since I was twelve years old, and what you're holding in your hand is my dream-come-true.

The romantic fantasy of a writer sitting in a cold attic slaving away at a keyboard, bottle of gin close at hand, doesn't quite fit my reality. I like hanging out with people too much. Thank you to my writer friends, Angela Forister, Alison Packard, Sue Ellen Turnbull, and Angie Randak, for the plot parties, the writing retreat, the beta reads and comments, and all the laughs and commiserations we've shared on this adventure called writing romance. Thank you seems so little when I owe you ladies so much.

To my life-long best friend Coleene Torgerson, your encouragement and your honest early reads kept me going. Your enthusiasm for every milestone, no matter how pebbly, made me believe in myself. You're truly the sister of my heart, and I am ever blessed to have you in my life.

Bri Brasher, you were my student who became my friend. Your willingness to take time out of your insane university teaching schedule to beta read for me means more than I can ever express. Thank you.

My amazing editor, Nikki Busch, you have made all the difference in my writing. Your patience, suggestions, and reminders have helped me grow, and I am forever grateful to you.

My copy editor, Rhiannon Root, keeps me honest and catches all the little things that never occur to me. Thank you. (Here's your name in print—again. It's such fun how much you love this.)

Maria at Steamy Designs, your cover design for this book rocks! Thank you so much.

Finally, none of this happens without my family. Austin and Trey, when I started this writing odyssey, the two of you learned fast that if the office door was shut and you weren't bleeding, it was best not to interrupt me while the muse was visiting. Thank you. I love you more.

Grady, you've been up for every adventure I've concocted, introduced me to the fun of playing in old cars, and traveled the world with me. You are the warrior of my heart, and I'm so lucky to be married to you. I love you.

To find out more about this series, see what's new, or discover how you can create your own luck, please find me on Instagram @tamstales32, on my website www.tamderudderjackson.com, on WordPress at Try Thirty New Things, or on Facebook at Tam DeRudder Jackson.

About the Author

In her previous career, Tam DeRudder Jackson was an award-winning high school English teacher. These days, she's living her dream of writing novels. When she's not writing, she's reading all the books or carving turns on the ski runs in the mountains near her home in northwest Wyoming or traveling to places on her ever-expanding bucket list. Her two grown sons are the joys of her life, and she likes supporting her husband's old car habit. If you ever see her holding a map, do her a favor and point her in the right direction. Navigation has never been her strong suit.